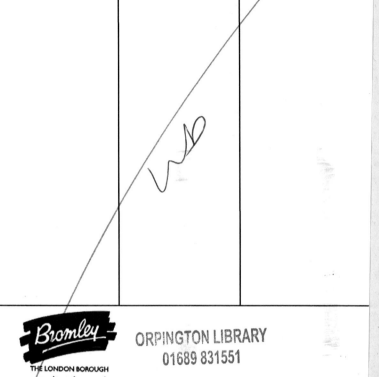

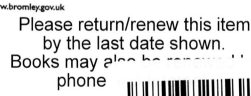

Published by Accent Press Ltd 2018
Octavo House
West Bute Street
Cardiff
CF10 5LJ

www.accentpress.co.uk

ISBN 9781786156075
eISBN 9781786156068

Printed and bound in Great Britain by Clays Ltd,

Elcograf S.p.A

Also by Jodi Taylor

Author's note

A part of this story was inspired by the archaeological discovery of a small house at the very centre of Avebury. This tiny house was attached to a single obelisk and the whole surrounded by a rare, a very rare, stone square. Not a circle – a square.

Everyone else is, of course, having a rational and balanced discussion about this find. I, however, being neither rational nor balanced, have – and without any evidence whatsoever – immediately leaped to the unlikely conclusion that the square was built to keep something in.

As I speculate in this story – reputable archaeologists and historians might want to look away now, please – suppose our prehistoric stones were by no means as benign as we suppose. They're all dormant now, but suppose, suddenly, they weren't. And never had been. What could happen if they suddenly woke up?

Suppose something the size of Avebury suddenly switched itself back on …

Dark light shines on a different world.
A world we could not reach if we travelled ten thousand times ten thousand years. And yet it is less than a hair's breadth away from our own. And sometimes the walls are very thin.

Prologue

My name is Elizabeth Cage and I've never done anyone any harm in my life – at least, not intentionally. But I have what some might call a gift. I call it a curse. Let's call it a talent. I can see things. No, not dead people – although I have seen dead people – I see something else. I see people's colours.

Years ago, when I was a child, before I'd ever heard the word aura, I called it a colour. Everyone has one. A shimmering outline of colour that constantly changes shade and shape as they react to whatever's going on around them. Everyone's is unique. Some are a distinct shape, thick and clearly defined. Some colours are rich and strong and vibrant. Others are pale and insubstantial. Sometimes there's a dirty, dark patch over their head or their heart and that's never good.

Sometimes, friends or family, people who are close, have similar colours. Colours that are related in the spectrum. You may have noticed that there are people for whom you feel an affinity. That's because your colours are similar. Some people repulse you. You feel an urge to keep your distance. You might not know why, but your colour certainly does.

Your colour tells me things about you. Things you might not even know yourself. Things you might not want others to know. Give me ten minutes and I can tell you whether you're happy or sad. I know if you're lying. I know if you're afraid. I know if you're bluffing. You don't have to say a word, but you're telling me just the same.

1

I don't know how Dr Sorensen found out about me but he did. He runs a clinic – ostensibly a rest home for those rich enough to be able to afford his very discreet services, but that's just a front. He works for the government.

I'd never actually heard the phrase 'psychological warfare' until Michael Jones explained it to me, but apparently that's what Sorensen does. He devises ways of misleading, deceiving and intimidating people. And don't fall into the trap of thinking he confines these dubious activities to 'enemies of the state'. According to Jones, he's pretty indiscriminate in his targets. Sometimes our friends can be more dangerous than our enemies. He'll have a go at anyone he's told to. And, from my own experience, he's not above using his resources for his own ends either.

He's an expert on people's behaviour, which is what makes him so dangerous. He can predict how people will behave under certain conditions and how to manipulate them accordingly. He can tailor-make propaganda tools. He can advise on how to mislead, deceive or even intimidate anyone he's instructed to. He seeks out other people's vulnerabilities. And not for good reasons.

I know he has plans for me … As Michael Jones once said, 'My God, Cage, we could sit you down in a room full of world leaders and you could tell us everything we needed to know. Who's lying. Who's afraid. Who isn't …'

Except I didn't want to be sat down in a room full of world leaders. I just wanted to live a quiet life. I didn't ask to see these things. It's not a gift to know what people are thinking. And it's definitely not a gift to see those shadowy figures, half in this world and half out of it … I just wanted to ignore it and move on from my husband's sudden death and I thought I had. I thought I had found a friend. Someone I thought might, one day, become

2

much more than a friend. Michael Jones was big and competent and damaged. His colour should be a rich mixture of reds and glowing golds, but by losing someone he'd lost his own way. He was vulnerable. And that bastard Sorensen had exploited that vulnerability and used him to get to me.

It was Jones himself who told me what he'd done. It was Jones who gave me the opportunity to get away. Jones who told me to run while I still could.

I had no choice. I had to escape this web of Sorensen's making.

So I ran.

Chapter One

I stared out of the big black window. The darkening sky and the lights in the railway carriage meant that, for most of the time, all I could see was myself. I gazed at this other self and my other self gazed back again. My face was a pale blob surrounded by darkness. Actually, that's not a bad metaphor. A small white face surrounded by big black nothingness.

I was in trouble. I was in so much trouble. I'd been running for three days now, although it seemed much longer. I could barely remember a time when I wasn't hurtling through the night on a half-empty train or rattling down strange lanes on a rural bus boarded at random.

My strategy was simple. To keep moving. If I never stopped moving they'd never be able to find me. Whether that was true or not, I didn't know, but I found the thought comforting. Keep moving. Keep moving. Keep moving. The words ran through my head in time with the clack of the train wheels.

I couldn't afford to fall asleep. I had to stay awake and keep checking my fellow passengers. I had to watch for anyone leaping on at the last moment or look out for someone who might be discreetly paying me extra attention. At any moment, I expected to hear the shout, 'That's her,' or feel a heavy hand on my shoulder. Or hear the sudden screech of brakes as a car pulled up and I was bundled inside before I had a chance to call for help.

I'd begun well. I'd run from my house in Rushford, suitcase in hand, down the hill and across the bridge. In a blind panic I might have been, but the sensible part of my brain took me to the bank.

Inventing some family emergency – I don't know why I did that. I kept telling myself I had no need to account for my withdrawals, but it seemed I couldn't help it – I withdrew as much cash as I could without awkward questions being asked.

From there, I pushed my way along the crowded post-Christmas pavements, heart thumping with fear, always looking over my shoulder, desperate to reach the railway station.

Mindful of the ever-present CCTV cameras, I kept my face down and, to the bemusement of the ticket clerk, bought a one-way ticket to Edinburgh and then another to Penzance. I was hasty and frightened and I dropped things and my hands were shaking and I knew he would remember me. Just for good measure, I used my credit card to buy the tickets. I was certain they would be monitoring my bank account.

From there, I trundled my suitcase into the Ladies and turned my coat inside out. It looked odd but that was the least of my worries and now it was silver instead of black, which was the best I could do for the time being.

Leaving the Ladies, I left the station as well, heading for the bus depot next door. I counted three buses down the line and jumped on the fourth. I had no idea where it was going to but that wasn't important. It was the going *from* that was so vital.

I jumped off the bus at the next town and did exactly the same thing again – three buses along, catch the fourth, jump off that one at a randomly selected stop – and do it all again.

I ate sandwiches of varying quality as I went. I slept in snatches, sometimes only for seconds, waking with a jerk at strange noises or sudden braking. Or I huddled, too cold to sleep, on hideously cold metal seats in bus stations. The ones specifically designed to prevent anyone ever being comfortable on them. I had no idea where I was most of the time. I kidded myself this was a good thing. That if I had no idea where I was then neither would anyone else.

And always, I kept moving. I never stopped. After three days, I was exhausted. I smelled. I looked dreadful and felt worse. Three days seemed a very long time and they hadn't caught me yet. Was it possible I had escaped? Had I actually managed to get away? And for how long could I stay away?

It was when I was alighting from my umpteenth bus on its way to somewhere unknown that my legs gave way. I struggled to a nearby bench and sat down heavily. People were looking at me, probably thinking I was drunk or on drugs or both. This had to stop. I hadn't been well when I'd run from Michael Jones and now I was making myself really ill. I'd done headlong panic – now I needed to slow down and think carefully. I'd run from the past. Now I needed to plan for the future.

I emerged from the bus station into a busy but anonymous town. Traffic roared past in several different directions. I stood for a while, getting my bearings, while people streamed around me on the pavement. Everyone seemed to have somewhere to go. Except me. There was a large department store opposite and I trundled shakily across the road to use their facilities. They had a very nice restroom and I washed as much of me as was possible and scrabbled in my suitcase for something else to wear.

I'd only packed for the Christmas holiday – and what a long time ago that seemed now. Almost another life – so I didn't have a great deal of choice, and then I realised I was in a department store. They sold clothes. And toiletries. And I had money. I could hear Michael Jones's exasperation. 'Really Cage, you're not bright, are you?'

I bought another pair of jeans and a couple of t-shirts and warm sweaters. And a beanie. All in greys and blacks. I had gone off colour forever. Colour had been the curse of my life. And I bought a new coat as well. I asked them to cut off all the labels and changed in the toilets.

Examining myself in the mirror, I looked completely different. The beanie covered my hair and a scarf covered my face. I was pleased with the result and this gave me enough confidence to sit in their café and gulp down a hasty bowl of soup and a sandwich. I was huddled in a corner, as out of the way as I could manage, but when someone dropped a plate it frightened me so much I nearly jumped out of my skin, and the urge to move started up again. I stuffed down the rest of the sandwich and headed back to the train station where I bought a ticket for the first town whose name I recognised. I wouldn't go all the way. I'd jump off at a random station and do it all again.

Keep moving. I had to keep moving.

Anyway, here I was, staring at myself in a blank window, wondering what I was doing, where I was going, and what on earth I was going to do when I got there.

Chapter Two

I exited the train station to a downpour. It wasn't just raining – it was hurling it down. Grey rain cascaded from the sky and bounced off the pavements. It gurgled from downspouts and spread across pavements. Cars splashed through oily rainbow puddles. The sky was dark and overcast. This was rain that wasn't going to let go any time soon.

I stood under an awning and looked around me. The street lights were coming on. People hurried past, entangling their umbrellas in their race to get out of the wet. The carpark was rapidly emptying as those travellers lucky enough to have someone to meet them were whisked away to warm homes and warmer welcomes. The last taxi disappeared and I stood alone in the rain.

On the other side of the car park, an engine started with a throaty cough and a single-decker red bus – the only splash of colour in the entire afternoon – opened its door with a hiss. Passengers filed slowly on board.

I didn't even stop to think, splashing across the car park and dragging my by now quite battered suitcase behind me.

The driver looked at me. 'Yes, love?'

His colour was a soft dove grey, tinged with fawn and pink. In a way, he reminded me of my dad.

I cursed myself for an idiot. I hadn't thought to look at the front of the bus. I had no idea where it was going and if I asked he might remember me. For all the wrong reasons.

'How far do you go?' I asked. Same question, but slightly rephrased.

'Greyston,' he said, printing out the ticket before I could say anything else. The decision had been taken out of my hands. It would seem I was going to Greyston. Wherever that was.

The bus was crowded but I was able to get a seat at the back on the right-hand side – and no one could see me from the pavement there. We wove through the traffic and I watched the other passengers disappear one by one. I don't mean that anything sinister happened to them, only that they got off and, after we left the town, no one replaced them. The interior was very warm. The lights were bright and reflected off the drops of rain running down the window.

I kept an anxious eye on my suitcase, parked in the rack near the front. It wasn't much but it was all I had and without it I would be in trouble. No – I was already in trouble. I would be in even worse trouble, although it was hard to see how that could be possible.

The bus bumped and lurched is way down ever narrowing country lanes. The journey seemed endless, which bothered me not one bit. I was warm, I was safe, and there was no sign either of Michael Jones or Dr Sorensen so it could go on forever as far as I was concerned.

It didn't, of course.

Eventually there was just me and a young woman only partly visible behind the most enormous rucksack on her lap. Her colour was a mingled turquoise and blue – rather pretty, I thought.

She turned to me. 'Greyston?'

I nodded. As if by not speaking I wasn't committing myself. As far as I could tell, this was just a friendly enquiry. I made an effort to be polite. 'Are you going to Greyston too?'

She pulled her scarf away from her neck. It was hot on the bus. 'Well, you have to make the effort for the New Year thing, don't you?'

'Mm,' I said, not wanting to say the wrong thing.

'Yes, I always come home for the New Year. We all do.'

I assumed she meant members of her family and said no more.

The rain eased, the sky lifted slightly and I rubbed a patch on the steamed-up window and tried to catch a glimpse of the outside world. I saw a jumble of lights reflected in the wet road and that was about it. The bus slowed and splashed to a halt. The driver called, 'Greyston,' and switched off the engine. Wherever Greyston was, plainly we had arrived.

He busied himself with a clipboard, checking off figures and ticking boxes, and paying no attention to us. My fellow passenger nodded farewell, said, 'See you on New Year's Eve,' collected her gear and disappeared into the night.

I made my way slowly down the bus and hauled my small suitcase from the rack.

The driver looked up. 'I go back in ten minutes, pet.'

'Is there nowhere here to stay?' I asked in sudden alarm, wondering if, like Jane Eyre in her headlong flight, I'd been dumped in the middle of nowhere and would nearly die of exposure and starvation on the high moors.

'I think the pub puts people up and there's a small guest house.' He jerked his pen – presumably in the direction of this guest house. 'On the other side of the green.'

'Thank you,' I said, preparing to step down. Of course I had to get off. I couldn't spend the rest of my life yo-yoing between town and village because that wouldn't be strange at all, would it? Should one of Sorensen's minions come looking for me with even the simplest query, 'You haven't seen a woman, have you?

11

Behaving oddly? You know, a bit strange?' and a positive forest of hands would point in my direction. Besides, I could see by his colour that the driver meant me no harm. He was simply a kindly man making sure I had somewhere to go on a wet night.

I thanked him again and stepped out into the darkness.

There's something very disorienting about arriving in a strange place after dark and I'd criss-crossed England so many times over the last few days that my sense of direction was more tangled than a ball of wool after a couple of kittens had been at it.

There was some sort of village green ahead of me so I skirted it, carrying my suddenly heavy suitcase. It felt strange to be travelling under my own steam, rather than sitting still while the scenery whizzed past of its own accord. And there was the silence too. Everything seemed very quiet. I suddenly missed the throbbing diesel engine of my bus.

I struggled on, trying to keep my shoes dry, pulling up at the only three-storey building around the green. The windows were lit, giving it a welcoming appearance. The sign over the door read, appropriately, 'Travellers' Rest,' and the outer door was open.

I walked up the path, pushed open the inner door, stepped over the threshold, and knew at once that I had made the right decision. This was everything an exhausted traveller could possibly desire.

A real fire crackled in a real fireplace, with three or four armchairs set invitingly around it. A low coffee table carried a selection of today's newspapers, all carefully folded. A number of amateur watercolour landscapes hung around the walls. A tall bookcase was jammed with colourful paperbacks. In the corner, a small reception area had been built. It was empty at that moment, but someone had to be around because a very tempting smell was wafting into the room from behind a door marked 'Kitchen Staff Only'.

Some might have sneered at it but I thought the homely, slightly old-fashioned atmosphere was wonderfully welcoming. The whole place promised clean, lavender-smelling sheets, claw-footed enamel baths and home cooking. All of it exactly what I would have chosen for myself.

I suspected there would be no TV in the bedroom and that while there might be a TV lounge, there was definitely no WiFi. I'm not one of those people who believe the government is watching us through our own electronics – although going on my past experience, I do suspect that one day I'm going to end up wearing a helmet made of tin foil to stop them listening to my thoughts – but at this moment, this lack of contact with the outside world was very reassuring. I was, to use an expression, at the arse end of nowhere and very happy to be so. I couldn't run forever and it was time to rest and take stock. I had to run smart – not far.

I let my suitcase fall with a thud. It was heavier than it had been when I set out to spend Christmas with Michael Jones and just before my life had fallen apart, but for the purposes of providing for the needs of a fugitive, it was pathetically inadequate. As it hit the highly-polished floor, however, the kitchen door opened and a woman came out.

She was extremely tall and slender, wearing a severely cut black dress and jacket that emphasised her dark good looks and highlighted her pale blue eyes. I caught a glimpse of gold jewellery at her wrist and neck. She looked respectable and competent and fitted in perfectly with her surroundings. I felt a great relief. If the place had been awful I'd have been in real trouble, but it wasn't – it was lovely.

13

Her colour, a very striking combination of blue and turquoise with a little purple around the edges, swirled gently towards me.

'Ah, there you are,' she said, as if she'd been waiting for me, and I assumed she had seen the bus come in. 'You'll be wanting a room.'

I nodded. 'Yes, please.'

'Certainly. For how long?'

'I really don't know how long I'll be staying. Not for very long, I think.'

'You'll stay for New Year.'

It wasn't a question but I was too tired to notice. And it was warm in here. And something smelled delicious. And for all I knew I might be staying for New Year. Why not? I'd only been running since the day after Boxing Day and it seemed like forever. Another world ago. A normal world. A normal world that I'd once inhabited.

I hadn't played any major part in this normal world, but I'd been married to a wonderful man. His name was Ted and he hadn't been handsome or dashing or exciting, but he'd been everything to me. We'd lived quietly because that was what we liked. He, because a quiet family life was all he ever wanted, and me, because I could use marriage to hide from the world and pretend to be normal.

To Dr Philip Sorensen, the rather nasty man in charge of the Sorensen clinic, I was some kind of asset to be acquired. He'd kept me in his clinic, against my will, and I'd only escaped with the help of Michael Jones, who, it turned out, had his own agenda.

I'd accepted his invitation to spend Christmas with him because I thought ... well, never mind what I thought. Even now I cringed at what I'd thought. He was acting on instructions from Sorensen. They'd taken advantage of my absence to search my

14

house and plant a number of surveillance devices. In my house. In my lovely little house where I was supposed to be safe.

Every time I thought of it my mind filled with images of angry snow and I had to force myself to calm down, because I'd seen the damage that could do. I'd seen the sinister, swirling snow that could consume us all.

Anyway, that was Sorensen – keen to avail himself of my talent. I, on the other hand, was really rather keen not to be availed of. Hence the flight from my home, my world, everything. And now I was here.

She moved around behind the desk. 'Have you come far?'

Paranoia kicked in again. Why would she want to know that? Her colour curled around her, gentle and welcoming. Soft tendrils reached out towards me, but I told myself this was only the natural curiosity of a proprietor ensuring her latest guest wasn't a homicidal maniac or escaped criminal. Or, in my case, avoiding sinister government agents. The question was simply a polite enquiry and I should pull myself together and answer it.

'Yes,' I said, and then wondered if she would wonder at someone who had obviously been on the road for some time, only to arrive at an obscure village in the middle of nowhere, so I lied. I was doing that a lot these days.

'I missed my train, caught another I thought was going in the right direction – which it was – but it didn't stop at my station so I jumped off at the next stop, tried my luck with a bus and somehow ended up here. And now I seem to have been travelling for ever and I'm very tired.'

She smiled sympathetically and pulled out the register. 'Well, I'm sure we can help with that.' She opened the book and I studied her as she flipped through the pages.

'We have three rooms,' she said.

'Is anyone else staying here?'

'No,' she said. 'We don't normally have guests at this time of year.'

I remembered the backpacker on the bus. 'There was someone who came in on the same bus as me.'

'Oh yes. A dark girl. With an enormous backpack.'

'Yes, that's her.'

'Ah, that will be Joanna. She always makes an effort to be here at this time. We all do.'

For a moment, her colour flickered. Only for a moment and then it was gone. I had imagined it. I put it down to tiredness.

She handed me my key. 'Room Three. It's at the front and you'll have a nice view out over the green.'

'Thank you.'

'I'll bring your case up for you.'

The room was lovely – everything I could possibly want. It was all done out in shades of creamy yellow and pale blue. Like everything else it looked slightly dated but very clean and comfortable. Two long sash windows looked out over the green. She drew the curtains, shutting out the rainy night.

'You won't be able to see them until the morning, but your room looks out over the Three Sisters.'

'Does it?' I said, politely.

She laughed. 'You haven't heard of our main attraction then?'

I shook my head.

'The Three Sisters – our group of standing stones?'

I shook my head again.

'Well, we're not Avebury or the Devil's Arrows, but we're very proud of them anyway. Legend says they were here long before the village was built. Three women lived here, all alone until one day one of them became sick or injured or something, and a passing man tended her. Why he was in this out of the way

16

spot, who he was, or where he was going is unknown, of course.'

She was bustling around the room and turning down the bed.

'Anyway, he stayed. He provided for them and they provided for him. It's been that way ever since.'

She wasn't quite telling the truth but I assumed this would be the tourist version. The nice version. The one that omitted blood, pagan rites and sacrifices.

'They're fine examples of prehistoric menhirs and popular with sightseers. We get quite a lot of visitors in the summer.'

'But not at this time of year, I imagine.'

'Oh no, not at this time of year.' Her colour had brightened as she talked about the stones.

'They must be very good for business.'

'Indeed they are. We look after the stones and they look after us. As it has always been.'

She showed me the small bathroom with towels laid out ready. I might never leave this place. I could have a bath, swill out my underwear, change into nightclothes and sleep. Comfortably. In a bed. I felt sleep tugging at my eyelids. I was nearly dead on my feet.

'You look so tired,' she said kindly. 'Why don't you have a bath and we'll serve your supper in your room. You're our only guest so it won't be a problem. Shall I get Becky to bring it up in say, thirty minutes?'

'That's very kind of you. If it's not too much trouble.'

'We want you to be comfortable.'

I made myself ask politely. 'Who's we?'

'Well,' she said, laying my key on the bedside table, 'there's the three of us. My name is Veronica, Veronica Harlow. Becky, my daughter, you'll meet later, and my mother, Miriam Harlow, who isn't too well at the moment, and is staying in her room.

'I'm sorry to hear that.'

She shrugged. 'She's had a long life. And she's said to me, more than once, that she's ready to go. I often think we know our own time, don't you?'

'I don't know,' I said, uncomfortable. 'I've never thought about it.'

'Young people never do.' Her colour reached out towards me again. I stepped back and went to open my suitcase, hoping she would take the hint, which she did.

I had a bath, luxuriating in the warm water. I would have liked to take longer, but mindful of Becky bringing up my supper, I climbed out very reluctantly and put on my pyjamas and dressing gown. My room was gently lit and warm. This time yesterday I'd been on a train, hurtling towards yet another unknown destination. Tonight, I was warm and safe. I sat in the armchair and curled my legs around me.

I hadn't realised I was so tired. I looked at the jumble of clothes in my suitcase. I'd sort it all out tomorrow. There was plenty of time. I'd stay a few days and gather my resources before … before what? Where was I going to go? I couldn't run forever. I had money but it wouldn't last indefinitely and the second I shoved my card in the cash machine they'd know where I was. I couldn't find somewhere permanent to live without getting a job. And I couldn't get a job without an address. Or an NI number. I know there are people who live off the grid – and very successfully, too – but I wasn't one of them. I wouldn't know where to begin.

All my doubts and fears came rushing back again, threatening to overwhelm me. I pushed them away. I was tired. That was all. There would be a solution somewhere. There always was. All I had to do was find it.

Becky brought up my supper. I disliked her immediately and it was mutual.

I was astonished that someone as physically and mentally dominating as Veronica Harlow should have such a small, spindly and insignificant daughter. Unlike her mother, whose long, thick, black hair was swept up in an elegant bun, Becky's was thin and mousy and hung around her face. Her eyes were so pale as to be unnerving. I looked at her and thought – weak, but resentful with it. Her colour was the same as her mother's, but more muted, and trembling around the edges, with just a hint of modern orange. Did our Becky have a rebellious streak? She certainly wasn't happy about something and for some reason, that resentment seemed to be focused on me. I wondered if perhaps she'd planned a night out and the sudden arrival of an unexpected guest had put paid to that.

The food was excellent. Cream of mushroom soup, lamb chops and lemon tart. There was a slightly old-fashioned feel to the menu and the crockery, but it was all delicious.

I fell asleep ten minutes after finishing my meal. I just had time to leave the tray outside, lock the door, climb into the soft, warm bed and that was it.

I dreamed and it frightened me.

Reality ripped itself apart in a maelstrom of blood and death and suddenly there were two alternatives. In one, I died. Jones died. Sorensen died. Everyone died. Crushed beneath the white silence of the angry snow.

In the other reality, the world did not end. Everyone lived. Everything survived. Everything except for the slow-growing trust I was beginning to feel for Michael Jones. That did not survive. As if from a great height, I saw myself running. As far and as fast as I could. That had been only three … no four days ago and now I didn't know where I was or what to do. I was a swirling snowflake, lost in the storm.

And then I was awake.

The sheets were tangled and the bed was hot. Throwing back the covers, I slipped out of bed and went to the window for some fresh air. I drew back the curtains. The rain had stopped and the night was clear and bright and I was looking at a monochrome landscape. Moonlight painted the frosty grass a sparkling silver. The same moonlight cast three impossibly long black shadows. I craned my neck but couldn't make out the cause. Only the long shadows they threw. The famous Three Sisters, I guessed.

I fumbled with the catch but the window wouldn't open. I left it because I didn't want my rattlings to disturb anyone at this hour. Wandering into the bathroom, I ran myself a glass of water. Then I straightened the bed, climbed in and went back to sleep.

I knew I'd missed breakfast the minute I opened my eyes. Weak winter sun streamed in through the windows because I'd left the curtains open. Yesterday's rain had not returned and today was a new day.

I showered and slowly dressed. I should be sorting out my clothes. I should be planning to move on. There were so many things I should be doing and I was so tired. More tired even than yesterday.

There was no one downstairs. I wondered if Becky was at school but of course, it was still the Christmas holidays. I was losing track of time. The fire was freshly lit and today's papers lay unread, but I wanted some fresh air. I pulled my coat around me and stepped outside.

The first thing I saw was the Three Sisters and they were impressive. I wandered across the grass to see them up close.

This was not a stone circle. These were menhirs, three solitary stones standing in a tight group. The central stone was massive, over twenty feet high, a solid, unbroken slab, black against the blue sky, thick and strong, dominating the group.

The left-hand stone was shorter, thicker and lighter in colour, and it was damaged. A large crack ran down from one corner. The stones were roped off, presumably in case a lump fell off on someone, but I stepped back anyway. It looked as if it could come down at any moment.

The third stone was small and slender. Almost a baby stone.

I stared absently at them, trying to imagine how the world had been when they were young. Because they weren't young now. They were rugged, lichen covered monuments that looked as if they had been here since the dawn of time. They stood before me, sleeping and silent in the chilly sunshine.

And then, suddenly and without warning, they weren't. They had opened their eyes. They were awake and I was the focus of their interest. Their will. I was looking at the stones and the stones were looking right back at me. They reared above me, dark and dangerous, drawing me in. I could feel the attraction. Involuntarily, I took a step backwards. I've been to Stonehenge. I've seen the stones there. Massive and impressive, but lifeless. There had never been anything like this. This deep, intense interest.

It was frightening. I stepped back again, feeling the need to keep a distance between us. This country is riddled with ancient stones everywhere. Some standing in groups, others solitary and alone. All of them silent. Switched off, you might say. Or so I'd thought. I shivered. Suppose a monument the size of Avebury suddenly switched itself back on. What would happen?

21

Thousands – hundreds of thousands of people visit these sites every year. Suppose one day the stones woke up. Woke up and lashed out.

I made myself take another step back and the feelings were gone. They were just three ancient stones standing motionless and mute in the sunshine, as they had done for millennia.

I decided to leave them to it.

The village green was ringed by tiny cottages, each with its own front garden. Immaculate grass verges were edged with staddle stones to keep the cars off. Not that there were any cars in sight anywhere. In fact, the only sign of modernity that I could see was the bus stop outside the pub, which itself was imaginatively named The Three Sisters.

I walked slowly around the green, admiring the cottages and enjoying the sunshine. I walked past the combined village shop and post office, miraculously still open in these days of rural closures. Just the other side of that was the village hall, stone built and neat. The building was set back from the road behind a clipped privet hedge, but the notice board informed me there was a lot on these days. The Mothers and Toddlers group met Monday, Wednesday and Friday mornings. Yoga classes were held on Tuesday mornings, step aerobics on Thursday evenings and watercolour classes on Friday afternoons. I couldn't help reflecting that even the village hall enjoyed a fuller and more active social life than I did.

Oddly, there was no church. I turned slowly and looked all around, but no spire or tower peeked out from behind leafless trees. No church. No War Memorial either, which was also odd. I'd never met a village without a War Memorial.

The pub was thatched. Most buildings in Greyston were, and even those that were tiled had attractively uneven roofs, weathered over the years with moss and lichen. The pub's tiny windows twinkled in the sunshine and a number of wooden tables and chairs were set outside for those who wanted to risk pneumonia for the sake of a cigarette.

Everything in this village was neat and in apple-pie order. It was like the backdrop for an Agatha Christie story set between the wars. Or more recently, one of those midsomer villages where half the population is dead by the end of the second advert break and everyone watching makes a mental note to avoid the southern counties like the plague.

I looked around. There was no denying it was beautiful. In summer, with the gardens full of bright colours and all the horse chestnut trees in leaf, it would be outstanding. I would bet good money they played cricket on the green on Sunday afternoons. It was rural England as it should be but very often isn't. There wasn't even the traditional housing estate of locally unaffordable five-bedroomed, two-bathroomed executive houses to mar the beauty of Greyston. By the looks of things, nothing new had been built here for a good while now.

I stood, hands thrust into my pockets, watching my breath frost in front of me. There was something here that both attracted and repelled me at the same time. There was no litter anywhere. Not a broken window or a peeling front door or a neglected garden. Everything was just perfect. It was the Stepford Village. A nice place to visit but I wouldn't want to live here.

Mindful that I'd missed breakfast, I slipped into the village shop, intending to buy a snack or two to take back to my room.

Another slender woman, about my own age and with long, dark hair that curled to her shoulders, emerged from a door behind the counter. She stared silently for just a moment longer than was comfortable. I was conscious of being appraised.

'Welcome.'

The word was more welcoming than her tone of voice. I was a little taken aback, but said, 'Thank you.'

Her silence was slightly unnerving. For some reason she seemed to expect more from me. I remembered I was British, saying, 'Better weather than yesterday.'

She said shortly, 'It's always fine for the New Year.'

I wondered if they had some kind of open-air New Year's Eve party planned. I said politely, 'That's good.'

The conversation languished and an awkward silence fell.

'My name is Alice Chervil,' she said, as if the name should mean something to me.

I smiled. 'How do you do, Mrs Chervil,' and hoped she wouldn't notice I hadn't introduced myself.

'That's Miss,' she said, shortly, and once again I had the impression I'd said or done the wrong thing. Her colour was more inclined towards turquoise, but here again was the familiar mixture of blue, turquoise and purple, very similar to Becky's, even down to the streak of rebellious orange. Here was another one who wasn't happy about something.

'You're at the Travellers',' she said, again making it a statement, not a question.

I nodded. 'I am.'

'I hope they're making you comfortable,' she said stiffly, while her colour told me she doubted it. 'Let me say that if there's anything you need – anything at all – you can just ask me and I'll arrange everything.'

'Thank you,' I said, slightly mystified as to why she would say such a thing. Did she perhaps have a spare room and was poaching business from the Travellers' Rest? Despite their slight resemblance, I could imagine Alice Chervil and Veronica

24

Harlow having no love for each other. But was it more than professional rivalry?

Whatever lay between them was not my business however, so I changed the subject. 'I'm afraid I was more tired than I thought and missed breakfast this morning.'

She thawed slightly, as if this somehow demonstrated declining standards at the Travellers' Rest. 'Well, I can certainly sell you a bar of chocolate or some crisps, but I'm sure you'd prefer something a little more satisfying. Why not pop next door to the Sisters. My niece works behind the bar and I can assure you they do very nice lunches in there.'

I was surprised. 'Are they open?'

Now she looked surprised. 'They will be in a minute. It's nearly noon.'

'Oh dear. That's embarrassing.'

'Yes. I can't understand why they wouldn't have woken you.'

I felt an absurd desire to defend the Travellers' Rest.

'Well, I've travelled a long way and I expect they thought it best to let me sleep in.'

She leaned over the counter. 'How far?'

I was slightly taken aback again. 'Um … I'm not sure,' and repeated my silly story about missing the train.

'Well, never mind, you're here now,' as if I'd crossed oceans and continents to get here, but her tone was grudging. She disliked me, but there was more to it than that. There was resentment – just like Becky – and, for some reason, jealousy too. I wondered again about business rivalry. This was a very out of the way spot to run two guest houses, and customers must be scarce at this time of year. I suppressed a mad picture of Veronica and Alice waiting at the bus stop every day, trying to entice potential guests into their respective establishments.

Her colour was boiling towards me. There was something a little more than normal village curiosity here. I felt a reluctance to let it touch me, taking a casual step backwards to survey the display of chocolate and saying politely, 'Your village is very beautiful.'

She smiled coldly and once again her colour surged around her in a way I couldn't understand. 'Yes, it is, isn't it?'

I don't know what made me say it. 'You must all work very hard to keep everything looking so lovely.'

Her smile faded. I had the strongest impression she was about to say, 'Why, what have you heard?' when a door behind the counter opened and another woman appeared, an almost complete replica of Alice Chervil but smaller and stouter. I didn't need the by now familiar combination of blues and turquoises to tell me this was probably her sister. A close relative, certainly.

Without even looking at me, she said, 'Is this her, Alice?'

Mrs Chervil's colour snapped defensively around her. 'I don't know what you mean. This is just an ordinary visitor.'

'Oh.' She stared at me in disappointment and I felt strangely … I don't know … unnerved. Just as I had at the stones. 'I thought this was her.'

'Go back inside, Ruthie,' said her sister, sternly. 'We'll have lunch in a minute.'

'Yes,' I said, glad of the excuse to leave. 'I must be going too.'

'They're not open quite yet,' she said. 'Why not wait here a while. In the warm,' and once again her colour bubbled towards me.

I felt a sudden need for some fresh air. 'Actually, I'll take a bar of chocolate,' I pulled one off the shelf at random and handed her the money, 'and have a stroll around the green until the pub opens. Why are the stones roped off?'

'One of them's cracked,' said Ruth, and I didn't much care for the way she said it. 'Cracked' was a word I thought could very well apply to Ruth as well.

'Not safe,' said her sister. 'Don't get too close.'

'Can it be repaired?'

'Oh yes., and they have been over the years. Many times. They're very old you know. They were here long before the first people built the village. They've had all sorts of repairs over the years. After the New Year they'll be as right as rain, you'll see.'

Their combined colours were filling the room.

'I probably won't be here that long,' I said, determined not to be here that long.

Miss Chervil just smiled. 'Enjoy your walk.'

'Thanks,' I said, edging out of the door. Anything to get out of here.

Once outside, I walked as fast as I could to the other end of the green.

And I threw the chocolate in the litter bin.

I shouldn't have gone into the pub. I needed to hoard my money. I needed to make plans for the future. I should have bought a snack and eaten it in my room and caught the afternoon bus out. The one I came in on.

Half of me wanted to do that. I *should* have done that, but the momentum that had propelled me halfway across the country was slowing. I was bone tired. I just wanted to stay in one place for a while and gather my thoughts and where better than this quiet village? Never mind that its beauty alternately attracted and for some reason, repelled me, I had to rest, at least for another day.

I looked around me. I'd start with a good lunch at the pub, then a brisk walk around the other end of the village, and then I'd make my way back to the guest house. I'd sort through my clothing and then read a book in one of those comfortable armchairs in front of the fire. Suddenly, that sounded like an excellent plan. But first, lunch.

Chapter Three

Once, I would have been nervous about going into a pub on my own. My mum wouldn't have liked it. She would occasionally accompany my dad to his working man's club, where she'd sit, primly upright, with a port and lemon in front of her, while my dad threw darts at the other end of the room, but you could see she hadn't liked it.

I, however, had seen some harrowing stuff over the last twelve months and walking into a pub alone wasn't the worst thing that had ever happened to me. I stepped into the porch and pushed open the door.

The traditional English village theme was continued inside the pub. A huge box of umbrellas and wellingtons stood in the hall, just inside the door. There were two log fires crackling away and the usual hunting prints and horse brasses hung on the walls.

A board behind the bar announced that today's specials were battered fish and chips or beef hot pot. I smiled at the barmaid – Mrs – sorry, *Miss* Chervil's niece, presumably – who smiled back at me a little uncertainly. Her colour was a grey blue, shot through with purple and only a very little turquoise flitting around the very edges, but the resemblance was there. I wondered if nearly everyone in this village was related in some way. It was possible, I suppose, the village was very remote. On the other hand, it was well maintained – there was obviously money here ... there must be some outside influences ... I gave it up. None of it was anything to do with me. I ordered an orange juice and the hot pot, taking my drink to a table near the fire.

There weren't very many people around. Two elderly ladies sat at a table in the window, sherry glasses half empty, watching the world go past, and as I watched, another woman came in with some sort of delivery and left it on the bar, calling a cheerful greeting to those in the window. All their colours flowed and blended together. This was obviously a tightly-knit community.

'You're at the Travellers' then?' said the barmaid, bringing me my cutlery wrapped in a paper napkin and a tray of condiments.

I agreed that I was, wondering why she was so nervous of me. Her colour streamed away from me almost in fear. More out of a desire to make conversation than a request for information, I asked if she was busy at this time of year.

She nodded. 'New Year's Eve coming up, of course. There's always a ... big do then and we do the catering.'

I noticed the two elderly ladies had stopped talking. I could practically hear their ears flapping.

'And you have your own guest here,' I said, not even concentrating on what I was saying. It was just conversation. 'Just for the New Year.'

Her response was startling. Her face just ... shut down. Her colour whirled away from me as if I was unclean and then curled itself in close, wrapping protectively around her. I wondered what I'd said.

'The girl who came in on the bus?' I said, trying to put things right.

Relief flooded through her colour. 'Oh. Joanna. Yes, of course. She's gone off to see her family. They don't have the room to put her up so she stays here. It's a big family. And their cottage is very small. She just sleeps here at night.'

She was gabbling. She was scared. I looked around. The two old ladies immediately stopped looking at me and stared out of the window. I didn't care, but it did make up my mind for me. This place was weird even by my standards. I was still too tired to go now, but I could stay tonight and then leave on tomorrow's bus. It probably wasn't a good move – I had nowhere to go and it would be New Year's Eve, the streets would be lively and there wouldn't be a room available anywhere, but I was experiencing a very strong urge to leave this place. As soon as possible.

'Yes,' I said, casually. 'Well, I shall be off in the morning. I'm only here by accident. Missed my train.'

'Oh, but you can't go,' she said involuntarily.

I stiffened. 'Why not?'

She gabbled. Red flashes of anxiety coursed through her colour. I began to feel alarmed.

'I mean, you've only just arrived. Miss Harlow said …'

'No,' I said, interrupting her, my mind suddenly made up. I would leave this very afternoon. Some instinct warned me not to mention that. 'I'm leaving tomorrow. Will my hot pot be very long?'

'I'll just check.' She almost ran behind the bar. I heard a door bang.

The two old ladies were watching me again.

The hot pot arrived, served by the girl from the kitchen, with a warning that it was very hot. I nodded and stared at the steaming dish, still bubbling in places, feeling grateful because it gave me an excellent reason for sitting and doing nothing while I pulled myself together and thought about what to do.

There was no point in panicking and just dashing off into the blue. I should at least finish my lunch before returning to the guest house, packing and quietly leaving on the afternoon bus. Quite a large part of me rebelled at the thought of more travelling, but there was no other alternative to going back on the road again.

Actually, yes, there was. The thought came from nowhere. Home. I could go home. Home to my little house in Rushford. I hated what was happening to me. I'm not adventurous or brave. I've always had a settled home life – as a child and as a wife – and now I found I very badly wanted to go home. I wanted my tiny house at the top of the hill with its lovely wooden floors and its hugely inconvenient staircase. I wanted to look out of the window and see the castle opposite. And the moat. And the swans. I wanted to wave to Colonel and Mrs Barton next door as they sat in their window watching the world go by. I wanted to go home.

I was swept with a sudden wave of homesickness, but if I returned home then Sorensen would be waiting for me, a man I should avoid at all costs.

No, that wasn't right. I wasn't being honest with myself. I stared blindly at my still bubbling hot pot and finally admitted it – it wasn't Sorensen I was running from. It was Michael Jones. The man who had betrayed me. Yes, he'd admitted it. And yes, he'd given me the opportunity to get away, but the pain was still there. I'd liked him. I'd trusted him. And he'd betrayed me to Sorensen.

Only to get his job back, argued the other half of me. He had no choice.

There's always a choice, was the response. He's made his and now you must make yours.

I had a moment of clarity. Nothing had changed. Yes, Sorensen still wanted me, but he always had. There was nothing new there. It was Jones I was running from and the feelings I was beginning to have for him. There was attraction; I only had to close my eyes to see him smiling down at me. And there was fear. Fear of betrayal and cruelty. Because sometimes when I closed my eyes I saw him cold-faced and blank-eyed as he attacked me. It wasn't his fault, but it wasn't mine, either. I just didn't know what to do and that was what I was really running from. If I could deal with the feelings then I'd dealt with the problem.

I had another moment of clarity. It wasn't Jones I had to deal with – it was myself. Deal with myself and I could go home.

I picked up my knife and fork and calmly ate my very delicious hot pot and drank a cup of coffee afterwards. I had only to pack, settle up and catch the bus. I could be home by tomorrow night. The day after at the very latest. I could sleep in my own bed. Yes, my home might be full of government surveillance equipment but I could deal with that. I'd ring Jones and order him to remove it. Or, if he refused, call in a surveillance expert. I'd no idea where I'd get one of those from, but Yelp or Google would help there. I'd get him to do a sweep – or whatever it was called – and have it all removed. I had no idea how, but I'd think of something. There was always something that could be done and that was what I should be doing – not fleeing around the countryside like a hysterical girl just because a man had let me down. If every woman did that then the country's transportation system would have collapsed years ago. I felt so much better with this new decision. Deep down I knew it was the right thing to do.

I left the pub. The time was still only half past one. The bus arrived at four o'clock so I had until then to get myself organised.

There was a rack of tourist leaflets in the porch. I paused, buttoning my coat against the cold and pulled a few out. Here was a list of local attractions and a brief history of the village. There was another from the Woodland Trust, detailing the work it had done in the area. There was a list of walks and things to look out for. On the back was a map.

I turned it over and stared in horror. I'd travelled day and night. I'd leaped from bus to train and back again. I'd set off at random, with no plan and certainly no intended destination. And now, according to this map – and I'm sure the Woodland Trust had no reason to lie – I was less than twenty miles from Rushford.

All that time and effort and I was less than twenty miles from where I'd started.

Chapter Four

I didn't know whether to laugh or cry. Less than twenty miles. That was practically next door. I had no idea I was so close. But at least any lingering doubts about my next move were gone. I could be home in a few hours. I could see my house again. And I was strong there. I would find a solution somehow. Suddenly, I don't know why – Sorensen seemed the least of my problems. The first thing to do was to get out of this place as soon as I could.

That turned out to be easier said than done.

Veronica Harlow was sitting behind the reception desk, entering invoices on her laptop. She looked cold and calm and as immovable as one of the Three Sisters themselves. She looked up enquiringly and pinned a smile to her lips.

'Did you enjoy your lunch?'

I passed over how she knew.

'Yes,' I said shortly, 'it was excellent. May I have my bill please?'

She blinked. 'Why?'

'So that I can catch the afternoon bus.' Which wasn't quite the answer to the question she'd asked.

Silence settled in the room. I could see her colour solidifying around her and knew there was going to be a problem.

She made no move. I glanced pointedly at the clock. 'I'll pick it up after I've done my packing.'

She slid smoothly out from behind the desk, blocking my path upstairs.

I felt a flash of anger, overlaid by fear. I should have stayed away from here and just got on the bus. Blame my parents who brought me up to be honest and settle my debts. Not a problem, however. I'd abandon my belongings. I had my handbag with my purse inside. I could leave everything else. I was determined. Come hell or high water I was going to be on that bus. I turned for the front door.

An old woman blocked my path. This, I guessed, must be Miriam. Veronica's mother. Short, blocky, white haired and with Becky's disturbing pale eyes. I know Veronica had told me she was sick, but she looked as immovable as one of those stones outside to me. Her colour was mostly purple, thin in places, but spiky and aggressive. I heard a movement behind me and didn't have to turn around to guess that Becky was sliding out through the kitchen door. Their colours reached out to each other, each reinforcing and strengthening the other. These were very powerful women.

I stood very still. My first thought was to wonder if Dr Sorensen had got to them somehow and they were to hold me here until he turned up to claim me, but surely that was nonsense. He couldn't possibly know I was here. Could he?

And here came that familiar slide into panic. I had to stop doing that. I fought to stay calm, saying, 'Did Sorensen make you do this?' but I could see by their colours they hadn't a clue what I was talking about. So, if this was nothing to do with him, then what was going on here?

I knew from experience there are worse things in this world than Sorensen and it was dawning on me, rather late in the day, that I had catapulted myself into the middle of one of them. I had wild thoughts of barging Miriam aside and running – just getting out somehow, but I was willing to bet there were more of them out there.

As if reading my mind, Miriam smiled sourly and stepped aside. Through the glass panels in the door I could see three or four women gathered oh so casually at the gate. One of them was the barmaid from the pub, and I think the two elderly women were there as well. I was trapped. I wouldn't get six feet and somehow the thought of any of them laying hands on me was not pleasant.

Unbidden, a thought came into my head. What would Michael Jones do?

Lay out the old hag with a single punch, kick down the front door, fight his way through the massed ranks of his adversaries and escape in a black helicopter was the answer to that one, and not tremendously helpful.

No, he wouldn't. He would say, 'Bide your time, Cage. Your chance will come.' And he would be right. Good to know he was making himself useful even though all this was his fault.

I drew myself up and said calmly, 'Is there some problem?'

'I don't know,' said Veronica. 'Is there?'

My heart began to thump. 'Not that I am aware of.'

'We understood you were to stay, Mrs Page.'

Well, at least she didn't know my real name. I'd blurred my signature in the register. I could have been Cage or Page and she'd gone for Page.

'I've had a message,' I said. 'Family illness. I have to leave.'

Becky giggled. 'No signal here.'

I didn't have a mobile anyway.

Veronica looked at me. 'Why would you lie?'

'Why would you keep me here?'

'You were sent.'

I thought about the seemingly unending stream of trains and buses I'd taken over the last few days. Here, at least, was one statement I could answer truthfully. 'No, I wasn't. My arrival here was entirely random.'

'You were brought here. To us. At this special time.'

The only sound was the crackling fire. A log dropped, making me jump and sending sparks everywhere.

Her mother frowned. 'Becky, see to the fire.'

Becky sighed heavily. Orange rippled through her colour but she complied, poking the fire viciously and almost hurling on another log. The fire crackled and more sparks whirled up the chimney. So, Becky didn't like being told what to do. Becky didn't like being the baby of the outfit. Becky wasn't happy with the hierarchy here. All very interesting, but not helpful to me at this particular moment.

I turned back to Veronica, swallowing down a sick feeling of fear. I was in trouble. I was sure I was in even more trouble than I realised. My instinct was to demand to know why they would keep me here against my will, but I mustn't allow myself to be distracted from the most important thing of all which was to get out of this place as quickly as I could. Even if I had to walk. A year ago, I would have laughed and said this was England. No one could be held anywhere against their will, but I'd been held against mine. I'd been a prisoner in Sorensen's clinic. Michael Jones had got me out. Obviously now, when he could have made himself useful, there was no sign of him.

I made my voice firm. 'In case I haven't made myself clear, I would like to leave now. If you won't prepare my bill then I'll leave without it. If you won't allow me to pack my belongings then I'll abandon them, but leave this place I will.'

She smiled. 'You are very welcome to make the attempt, Mrs Page, but I doubt if they'll let you go.'

'Who won't?'

'The ones who brought you here.'

I controlled my temper with an effort. 'Who brought me here?'

She didn't answer me directly. 'We knew you would come.'

'No, you didn't,' I said, doing my best to throw cold water on all this mystic claptrap. 'Even I didn't know I was coming.'

'Well, not you specifically. We just knew someone would come. Someone always answers the call.'

'I am here by accident. Random chance.'

'There was nothing accidental about it. You were called.'

I became aware that all this discussion was wasting time. I turned to the door again. 'Be that as it may, I have to go.'

'I'm afraid that's just not possible.'

'People are looking for me.'

'No, they're not.'

'Actually, quite a lot of people are looking for me,' I said, suddenly hoping to God they were.

'Well they're not likely to look here.'

'They're very good at getting what they want.' Again, hoping to God they were.

'Are you wanted by the police? Because if so there's no need to worry about that any longer.'

'They will find me.'

'They won't. Really, they won't. You know they won't. You belong here. With us. Now, you've had another tiring day. Why don't you lie down in your room with a nice cup of tea?'

Their interlinked colours were glowing. They were strong. I wasn't going to get out this way. I would go to my room, wait until the bus turned up, climb out of the window, sprint across the green and jump aboard. They could hardly pursue me in broad daylight, could they? And even if they caught me and dragged me back, the bus driver would have something to say about it. Even if only to his mates on his return to the depot. And surely then someone would take some action …

'Becky, make some tea.'

'Why me?'

'Because I'm making Mrs Page comfortable and your gran isn't well. Go on now.'

She sighed in the way only teenagers can and swung back in through the kitchen door.

'After you, Mrs Page.'

I allowed myself to be taken to my room.

She seated herself at the dressing table, but I heaved my suitcase onto the bed and began to pack.

'You're wasting your time, Mrs Page. Please believe me. They won't let you go. Please understand, your life will be so much easier – indeed your life here will be very pleasant indeed – if you can simply accept what is happening.'

'My life is already very pleasant indeed, thank you very much.'

She very pointedly didn't mention my bedraggled appearance yesterday, my obvious exhaustion, or the fact that there was obviously something very wrong with my life.

I ignored her, concentrating on folding sweaters and jeans and carefully placing them into my suitcase. I took my stuff from the bathroom and zipped it into my toilet bag. She was still talking. I checked the wardrobe and under the pillows.

Someone tapped at the door.

She said brightly, 'And here's our tea,' for all the world as if we were about to enjoy a pleasant afternoon in front of the fire.

I said nothing. A plan was forming. Not now. Not while there was two of them. I'd get rid of Veronica somehow. I was betting they'd send whining, sigh-heaving Becky to collect the tea tray. Veronica was bigger and taller than me, but I reckoned I could take Becky easily. And then … So I sat in the armchair and allowed Veronica to pour my tea.

She smiled at me. 'I'm sure you have all sorts of clever plans to escape but they won't let you go, you know.'

I was looking at my tea. It was fine – no dark colours swirled around it – they hadn't tried to drug me, but I didn't mind betting Becky had spat in it. I set it on the small table beside me and said, 'Go on then, tell me. Who won't let me go?'

'Oh, I think you know who has brought you here to us.'

I was too tired and frightened to play silly games.

'Pretend I'm stupid.' Although I couldn't help reflecting that I must be very stupid indeed to have got myself into this situation. Yes, I was tired and disoriented and heartsick, but the signs had all been there and I'd missed or misinterpreted nearly every single one of them.

She sipped her tea. 'You have rested and eaten here. You have partaken of the Stones' bounty. They will not let you go.'

I was grateful for the gathering shadows in the room because half of me wanted to laugh – although that might have been hysteria. They were all obviously mad. The other half was suddenly very afraid indeed.

'We knew you would come.'

'Me?'

'Well, we knew someone would come. Someone always comes.'

I tried to keep my voice calm. 'I told you. I am here by accident.'

'There was nothing accidental about it. You were called.'

Her colour said she was telling the truth. The truth as she saw it, anyway. She genuinely believed the stones had power – and I knew they did because I'd sensed it myself when I got too close to them. I could feel fear begin to build inside me and tried to shut it down and think clearly. Because powerful or not, they were just stones. So forget the stones and any possible weird goings on – my first priority was to escape three slightly batty women. In a village full of more slightly batty women. One of whom was in here with me.

'Why?'

'I told you. You were called.'

'I don't mean why me – I mean why anyone at all.'

She got up and switched on the bedside lamp. 'Miriam is dying.'

'What has that to do with me? I'm not a doctor.'

'Doctors can't help her now. Her time has come.'

I shrugged. 'I'm sorry to hear that but there isn't anything I can do.'

'Oh, but there is. We are three. We are always three. When one moves on, another always turns up to take her place.'

'And you think that's me?'

'I know it's you. The Stones have brought you here – to this place and this time. Exactly where and when you are needed.'

'But …'

'I must go.' She stood up. 'There are arrangements to be made.'

'But …'

She closed the door behind her and turned the key.

I got up, finished my packing, closed and locked my suitcase, turned off the light, and waited for Becky in the dark.

Chapter Five

She took her time but Becky turned up eventually. I heard her footsteps coming along the corridor and then the rattle of her key in the lock. I rose silently to my feet and took a firm grip on my case. It was only a weekend bag but I would be putting some force behind it.

She opened the door into my dark room. The tray was in plain sight on the dressing table. She took a step into the room. I got behind her and swung my case at the back of her head. It nearly whirled me off my feet so I don't know what it did to her – I didn't stop to check.

I ran out onto the landing. Straight into the arms of Miriam. Sick she might have been, but she was still more than a match for me. I'm not a violent person. My parents had loved me a lot and I'd loved them. Ted had been a wonderful husband and I still missed him every day. And then he died too and my life had changed. All I knew of violence was garnered from watching re-runs of Buffy the Vampire Slayer.

I struggled as much as I could. She didn't do anything. She didn't have to. She just held on tight until Becky staggered back out and the two of them manhandled me, kicking and struggling, back into my room again. I was flung face down onto the bed and before I could do anything, the door slammed. And then opened again as someone threw my suitcase back in after me. Somehow, that added insult to injury. I thumped the bed in frustration and then thought – the bus – and ran to the window.

It hadn't opened last night and it wouldn't open now. Neither of them would move. I ran from one to the other but it was useless. I tried everything but nothing worked. I suspected they were nailed shut. I banged on the window. No one heard. And even if they had ... It wasn't just the three women at the Travellers' Rest. I had a feeling I'd be taking on the whole village. There was no way I'd even be allowed to get to the bus stop, let alone board the bus itself.

I stood at the window and watched women and children going home at the end of the day. Groups of chattering women gathered, broke and gathered again before finally turning off into their cottages. Doors closed shutting out the night. Lights began to appear in windows around the green. Except in the village shop where the lights went out. The village prepared for the night. Darkness had fallen. In every sense of the word.

It was at this point I realised I was never going home. Something awful was about to happen here.

My handbag had fallen open, spilling its contents onto the dressing table. Among them were the leaflets I'd picked up from the pub. How I wished I'd just walked away. I could have walked to the next village and picked up a bus there, although a small voice told me I wouldn't have got far. They'd have found me long before that.

One was the Woodland Trust leaflet and the other gave the history of The Three Sisters. I skimmed over the bits Veronica Harlow had already told me but there was an interesting section at the end. It was headed The Year Kings and Their Function in Ancient Societies.

I won't tell the whole story here, but in all its variations it is a simple one. In a matriarchal society, the function of the Year King was key. Every year, a young man, sometimes a chance visitor but sometimes specially chosen, was appointed as Year

King. Nothing was too good for him – he would have the best of food and drink and any woman he desired. His only function, apart from having a rollicking good time for twelve months, was to be sacrificed at the year end. His death – often extremely violent and bloody – would ensure the harvest for the coming year and general good luck and prosperity for all. Failure to die at the appropriate time could spell ruin for a community.

The writer went on to speculate whether the Ceremony of the Year King could possibly be connected to the Three Sisters, happily assuring his readers, however, that the coming of the Christian church had put a stop to all that pagan nonsense.

I read this cheerful little snippet through several times and then crumpled the pamphlet and threw it across the room.

No one came near me for the rest of the night. There was no evening meal.

When I couldn't bear my thoughts any longer, I went to stand at the windows and watched the moon travel across the sky. Then I lay on the bed and thought and thought. And I didn't make the mistake of thinking like Elizabeth Cage either, with her touching but misplaced trust in the authorities to make everything right. I lay in the dark and thought like Michael Jones.

Presumably because of my failed attempt yesterday, Veronica and Becky brought breakfast together. Veronica stood by the door while Becky, resentful and aggrieved, banged the tray down on the dressing table and then, at a nod from her mother, departed, slamming the door behind her.

Veronica remained behind. Michael Jones would tell me to take this opportunity to gather as much information as I could, so I did.

I poured myself a cup of tea because I was thirsty, took a deep breath and said, 'This is the ceremony of the Year King, isn't it?'

Her colour deepened significantly and her voice took on that faintly fanatical tone. 'The Stones demand blood.'

'I bet they do, but what do you get in exchange?'

'There is a covenant which dates back thousands of years. When the first traders visited these shores, they brought the Great Mother cult with them. It's a simple arrangement – we feed the stones and they keep us safe. As they have always done. You've seen for yourself. Our village is perfect. Not for us the hideous developments of the 21st century. No motorway slices this village in half. We haven't suffered the slow decline of village life. Look around you. You've seen this place. Everything is beautiful. No one even gets sick here.'

I took a chance. 'Well, not if they're female.'

She shot me an appraising look. 'You've noticed.'

'There are no men here.'

'Well, there are, of course. There are hundreds and hundreds of men here. You could say they never left.'

It's one thing to have suspicions. It's quite another to have them confirmed. I swallowed hard.

'You give them to the stones.'

She was quite casual about it. There was no shame – no guilt.

'We do, yes. Every year a man is sent and every year we renew the covenant.'

There was no need for me to feign anger or outrage. I could hardly speak. 'That's ... monstrous.'

She remained calm. 'It's only one life.'

'Not to the owner of that life.'

'It's only one life to preserve many.'

I was hot and furious. 'It's still monstrous.'

Her colour deepened to a rich purple. She was genuinely hurt. 'How can you say that? Look around you. This place is beautiful. It's perfect. It's safe for our children to grow up in. There's no crime, no poverty, no ugliness ...'

'No ugliness? You murder an innocent man every year.'

I could see she was becoming impatient at my failure to appreciate her point of view.

'It's only one man, Mrs Page, and not a very important man at that. No one ever misses them. No one ever comes looking for them.'

I was still struggling to ground myself. None of this could be true, surely.

'Men don't just vanish without trace.'

'A certain sort of man does. And it's not as if they make any sort of useful contribution to the world. Really, you could say we're doing society a favour, taking men like that out of circulation.'

This calm, callous disregard for others very nearly took my breath away. I had to struggle to speak through my anger and fear.

'Are you crazy? Do you know what sort of men you could have been bringing back here? Drug addicts, criminals, schizophrenics, violent men, psychopaths ...' I couldn't go on.

She smiled a sudden, sly, secret smile. 'Yes, it's exciting.'

I turned away in revulsion.

'No, you misunderstand. We take in some useless wretch, clean him up, give him the best year of his life and ...'

'And then you *kill* him.'

'His death gives us life. He serves a useful purpose. And it's not as if he was a useful member of society. He's of far more use dead than he ever would have been alive.'

'A man dies just so you can live a nice life?'

'He dies for the Stones!'

'How can you do this? Every year. How can you live with yourselves?'

She shrugged. 'It's always happened and it always will. Our mothers, our grandmothers ... it's in our bones.'

I stared at her hard, handsome, fanatical face. They'd been doing this time out of mind. At what point had it become a normal part of their lives, like a Harvest Festival or May Day?

I hated myself for showing an interest, but I had to ask. 'For how many years has this been going on?'

She shrugged. 'No one really knows. We've always done it.'

'So, you kidnap a man ...'

'A man is *sent* ...'

I scoffed. '*Who* sends him?'

'The Stones, of course.'

'The way the Stones were supposed to have sent me?'

She smiled.

'I'll tell you again – no one sent me. Your stupid stones had nothing to do with it.'

Her smile congealed. 'You are tired and overwrought. I will allow you one mistake. That was it.'

I refused to be overawed. 'The stones didn't *send* me. The stones don't *send* a man. It's not a holy ritual. It's *murder*. Plain and simple. You're murderers. All of you.'

She said patiently, 'You are wrong. Every year at this time a man is sent. A man is always sent. There has never been a year when a man has not arrived at this place. The place of the Stones.'

'And you just *kill him*?'

Her voice dripped exaggerated patience. 'No, of course not. I keep telling you. He is the Year King. He lives a wonderful life. Wine, women, song – all his needs are more than catered for.'

'But not for very long.'

'Long enough. He gets a year. A whole year to sleep with whatever woman he chooses …'

'Whether she wants to or not?'

She shrugged. 'We consider it an honour. He eats, he drinks, he gets whatever he wants. We make him very happy.'

'For a year.'

She shrugged again. 'A year more than he would have had living on the streets in some grimy city. Drunk, diseased, filthy, malnourished.'

'And then?'

'And then he dies.'

I was watching her colour, shining bright, weaving itself around her. There was something almost sexual about it.

I whispered, 'How does he die?'

The words dropped like black stones into the silence.

'In the last minute of the old year, we hang him upside down and cut his throat. The Stones drink the blood and everything is as it should be for another year.'

'And a new king takes his place?'

'On the first day of every year another man arrives.'

'And never leaves again.'

She was becoming impatient. 'Why would he want to? He is a *king.*'

'For a year.'

'As you say – for a year. He sires the next generation and then we give him to the Stones.'

I had a sudden, cold thought. 'What happens to the boy children?'

She shook her head. 'Not what you think. We're not barbarians, you know.'

I could see she genuinely believed that.

'So what does happen to them?'

'Nothing. There are never any boy children. No male child has been born in this village for hundreds of years.'

I could hardly believe what I was hearing but I could see she wasn't lying. Ritual murder, blood-drinking stones possessed of a malignant intelligence – no, not intelligence, malignant *will* was a better description. What sort of a nightmare was I trapped in? I tried to focus.

'And what of me? You're keeping me here against my will and you've told me your secrets. Will you give me to the stones as well?'

'Oh no. No, no, no. Whatever gave you that idea? You're far too valuable. You're really quite unique aren't you? I recognised it as soon as you walked through the door.'

This was not something I wanted to discuss. Especially not with this woman.

'What are you going to do with me, then?'

She hesitated. 'My mother is dying.'

Well, I'd suspected it and now I knew.

'There are always three of us.'

I thrust aside the implications of that statement and thought I saw a way out. 'But I'm not from your family.'

She shrugged. 'That's not necessary.'

'But surely there's someone here ... someone from the village who could take Miriam's place?'

For some reason I thought of Alice Chervil and suddenly a lot of things became clear. Now I knew the reason for her hostility. She'd hoped she would be the third member, with all the prestige that entailed, and Veronica had chosen someone else. Alice had wanted it badly and now, at the very last moment, I'd turned up and they would be three again. I'd read

50

about this. The Three Ages of women. Men are always just men, but women are classified differently.'

I nodded. 'Yes, it's the traditional roles of womanhood, isn't it? The Mother, the Maiden and the Crone.'

She grimaced. 'Not my favourite descriptions. Sad to say, however, my mother is about to move on and I will take her place. Becky is not yet old enough, and so you, Mrs Page, will take mine.'

I seized on the flaw. 'That is not possible. I am not a mother.'

She paused and I knew something bad was coming. 'You soon will be.'

I suddenly grew very cold. Was she saying what I thought she was saying?

'Tonight, the Old King will die.' She paused and said quickly, as if she was in a rush to get the worst over with, 'Tomorrow the New King will arrive and take his place. You will be given to the New King. It will be our gift to him and your … initiation.'

My mouth was suddenly very dry. I remembered her description of the men who arrived here. Drunk. Dirty. Diseased. I mustered everything I had and said flatly, 'No.'

Her colour flared out towards me. 'It will be an honour.'

I leaned away from it. 'No, it won't.'

She shrugged. 'There are many drugs I can use. I do urge you to avail yourself of at least some of them, because this *will* happen. It always happens. An unbroken cycle since time began. If you wish, I can prepare something that will not only overcome your reluctance but make it a very enjoyable experience for you. The choice is yours. But, whether you accept my offer or not, I can assure you, Mrs Page, it will happen.'

'It will not. I refuse to submit.'

She turned away. 'It's not your decision. You belong to the Stones now. As do we all.'

'I'm sure the new Year King will have something to say about it as well.'

She laughed at me. 'Oh really, Mrs Page. How many young men do you think need to be forced to have sex? Believe me, most of them are quite gratifyingly eager to sire the next generation. Many of them take it as a personal challenge.'

'Even when they know they're going to die?'

'Well, we don't tell them that, of course.'

'I'll make sure he knows, trust me.'

She smiled. It wasn't pleasant. 'Trust *me*, Mrs Page, you will be incapable of speech. Both before, during, and after. And once the deed is done, of course, it's too late because ...'

'Yes, I know. He will belong to the stones. So he has no idea of his ultimate fate?'

'Not until just before the very end. We make sure he knows then. Terror increases the heart rate and makes the blood taste sweeter. The Stones are drenched and all is as it should be.'

I couldn't believe what I was hearing. Couldn't believe the nightmare I had strayed into. That this had been going on for centuries and no one had even the slightest suspicion. She had said the stones protected them and I suspected she was right because this place was perfect in every detail. Unless you were a man, of course.

I had to ask. 'And the body? What do you do with the body?'

'There are the woods above us. We return him back to the soil whence he came to ensure a good harvest next year. We have another ceremony for that.'

'But the Year King legend goes back for ...'

'... For thousands of years,' she said. 'Back to the Old Days. To the days of the Mother who gives life to us all. Back to the days when all men feared and served the Mother and women were her handmaidens.'

I had a sudden flash. Rows and rows of men, as still as the trees around them. Waiting …

She was suddenly brisk, standing up and smoothing down her dress. 'So – until this evening then. You'll want to wrap up warm. It's going to be a chilly night.'

'I shan't be going.'

'Don't be silly. Of course you will attend. You won't have a choice. And just a tip – closing your eyes does not help. They do tend to scream a little at the end. And then there's the smell, of course. And then tomorrow night will be *your* big night. You won't be able to wrap up at all for that one, I'm afraid, and it will be a little public. Well, very public, actually. Al fresco, if you like, but there must always be witnesses. Including the Stones themselves, of course.'

I tried to swallow down my fear. 'I tell you I won't do it.'

'You have no choice. It's an important ceremony.'

'It's a *rape*.'

'I told you, I can give you something to make it more pleasant. You're not a virgin, are you?'

'None of your business.'

'Shame. Still, never mind.'

'I'll fight you every inch of the way.'

She shrugged.

'He won't do it. No man would.'

She just laughed and walked out of the room, locking the door behind her.

I suddenly realised I was freezing cold and shaking all over. Sitting at the dressing table I stared at myself in disbelief. How could this be happening? How had I managed to get myself into this? More to the point – how was I going to get myself out of it?

I sat, fists clenched, breathing deeply, struggling to swallow down my panic. The smell of bacon reminded me my breakfast was here. I should eat. I would need all my strength tonight. I lifted the lids and inspected the food. It wasn't drugged. I could tell. I wasn't hungry now, but I might be later on, so I should eat now. The food was tasteless and cold but I ate it anyway.

It was as I was stacking the empty dishes for collection that I had an idea. I wondered if they would trust Becky to take the dishes away again. It seemed very likely. Gran was too old and sick and Veronica would surely have better things to do. It would almost certainly be Becky. Becky who probably disliked me more than ever. Becky, the weak link …

Rummaging in my purse, I found my credit card and stared at it thoughtfully, an idea slowly forming. I wouldn't do anything as unsubtle as leaving it lying around in plain sight. That was far too obvious, so I left it peeping from between the pages of my book – as if I'd used it as a bookmark. The dishes were stacked alongside. She couldn't miss it.

I heard the key in the lock and in she came. I scowled at her and she scowled right back again. Her colour was flat and defensive. She really didn't like me.

I stayed well back from her just in case …

She made no move to take the tray, standing in the middle of the room, fists jammed on her skinny hips, her colour boiling with impotent teenage fury.

'It was supposed to be me. I'm the one who should take my mother's place. I was supposed to the first with the new Year King. It's my right. They promised me. And then *you* turned up. Why did you have to come here?'

I didn't understand what she was talking about at first. And then I did. Veronica Harlow must be desperate to keep Alice Chervil out if she had been contemplating using Becky, who couldn't be more than fourteen, if that. But Becky had looked forward to the enhanced status. This might be a tiny and enclosed community, but she would have been important and now, with only hours to go, it had been snatched from her. No wonder she hated me.

She continued with all the petulance of the child she still was. 'Why did you have to come here? You've spoiled everything. I should be the one to take my mother's place. It should have been me.'

'Then help me get away.'

Her colour boiled around her. For a moment it spiked a clear, bright orange and I honestly thought she might, and then it faded. She'd been passed over and she was angry. Really angry. But not angry enough to disobey her mother. Or the stones. I would have to think again.

I shrugged and sought to pour more fuel on the fire. 'It's not my fault you're not pretty enough for the new Year King. Or strong enough to take your mother's place. You're just a child. Really, you know, these things are best left to adults, don't you think?'

Just in case she wasn't annoyed enough with me already, I gestured towards the dishes and said brusquely, 'I've finished here. Take these away,' To make it easy for her, I took myself off into the bathroom. I sat on the loo, counted slowly to sixty and then went back into the room again.

She'd gone. And so had my credit card.

It was contactless so she wouldn't need to bother with a signature or PIN number. She'd only be able to spend thirty pounds, but that might be a lot of money to a bored young girl living in the back of beyond in a village full of women. A bottle – or two – of wine, some make up, some sweets – she'd find something she wanted and the second she used that card ...

... Because if Michael Jones wasn't monitoring my back account then he wasn't the man I took him for.

I stood in the window, craning my neck to watch Becky pick her way around the green, heading, I hoped, for the village shop and its off-licence shelves.

She disappeared inside and I waited. I was banking on a lot here. Becky's dishonesty. Miss Chervil not checking the card too stringently. She must know Becky would never have a credit card. She must know from whom she would have got it. If she was privy to my future then why wouldn't she turn a blind eye? She would know I'd never need that card again. For the first time in my life I was praying for people to show a little greed and dishonesty. And frankly, if they were sacrificing an innocent man every New Year's Eve then they were unlikely to be that morally fastidious about pinching someone's credit card in the first place. Or so I hoped.

I stared and stared until my eyes watered. The shop was double fronted but both windows were full of display goods. I could see the lights were on inside but very little else. Given tonight's excitement, I was just grateful they hadn't closed early. I closed my eyes and imagined Becky, card in hand, wandering the shelves, choosing this, discarding that, taking her time ...

The door opened and out she trotted, carrier bag in hand. A heavy carrier bag by the way she leaned into it. Her colour boiled around her – a strange mix of swirls and spikes. She was both excited and defiant. Exactly what I would expect from a young girl using a stolen credit card for a few illicit treats.

I drew back behind the curtain although she couldn't possibly see me and watched her as she approached the Travellers' Rest.

Interestingly, she didn't use the front door – was her mother manning the reception desk and watching the stairs? Almost certainly.

No, Becky sloped off down the side of the building, through the back door and from there, presumably, straight to her own room. I didn't care. I'd lost interest in the card. All my thoughts were now on Michael Jones and hoping he hadn't had a belated fit of conscience and decided to let me go. I swallowed hard. Dr Sorensen, I was sure, would never give up, but suppose Jones thought he was doing me a favour by discontinuing the surveillance. Typical. You just can't get the spies these days.

Or – and this was a grim thought – suppose everyone at the monitoring desk or station or whatever they called it had gone home? It was New Year's Eve after all. Suppose that somewhere, a red light was flashing away to an empty room. Tomorrow was New Year's Day and a bank holiday. The little light might still be flashing the day after that, but that would be far too late for me. And for the Year King too.

I sat on the bed and thought about him. Who he was. And where he was. Was he at the Three Sisters? Was that why the barmaid had panicked when I asked if they had guests there? What sort of state would he be in at the moment? Was he mercifully drugged, or drunk, or was he aware of everything going on around him? Veronica had said the king's terror was a necessary part of the ritual. That fear made the blood taste richer. And what about me tomorrow night? Who would the stones find for me? Drunk. Dirty. Diseased. Would they clean him up first? Or would my terrified struggles with a soiled and sullied stranger make the ceremony that much more enjoyable for the watchers?

In a sudden panic, I shot to my feet and tried the door again, but sadly, no one had mysteriously turned the key while I hadn't been paying attention.

I tried the window again as well but it was still unbudgeable and there was no window in the bathroom at all. I was forced to accept there was no way out of this room.

All right. Forget that. How could I prepare myself for whatever was about to happen tonight? I was already wearing jeans and a thick sweater. I pulled my coat out of the wardrobe and tossed it on the bed. If I could find an opportunity for escape – what would I need?

Money. I tipped my handbag on the bed, grabbed my purse, shoved it into an inside coat pocket and zipped it up. Gloves. They went into an outside pocket. What else? I didn't have much else. No torch. No map – except for the one kindly provided by the Woodland Trust. I know they're all for rural traditions but it seemed unlikely they would be involved in whatever was about to happen here.

Oh, and my house keys. How embarrassing to overcome massive odds, struggle all the way home and then be unable to get in.

I was already wearing boots. What about spare underwear? I whipped my last clean pair out of my suitcase and pushed them into a pocket as well. What can I say? My mother always insisted on clean underwear whenever I went out. Her thinking seemed to centre around what they would think at the hospital should I be involved in an accident while wearing less than pristine knickers.

So – money, warm clothes, sensible boots, clean knickers. That was me all set to go.

I sat on the bed and waited.

Chapter Six

I sat alone for so long that I began to think Veronica had changed her mind about forcing me to attend the ceremony – if ceremony was the word I wanted. Or that they had forgotten about me. That seemed unlikely. I knew people were assembling on the green because for the last hour I had been seeing the torchlight flicker across my bedroom walls and heard their murmuring as they tramped past. Someone had a drum, beating out a strange, hypnotic rhythm in the distance. Occasionally cymbals clashed and a high-pitched, female shout would go up and despite all my best efforts to stay calm, my heart would clench with fear. I'd refused dinner because I thought it might be drugged. It wasn't, but I didn't want to throw up when they … when the king died.

Unbelievably, I could smell frying onions. Carefully peering out of the window I thought I could see a burger stand set up on the grass. There was no hope for any of these people. I felt cold dislike settle in my stomach. A young man would die horribly tonight and they would be munching burgers and chips. I made up my mind that whatever was going to happen here tonight, I would do my utmost to prevent it. As if anything I could do would make any difference. There was just me and I was a prisoner – and soon to be unpleasantly inducted into Team Greyston. What could I possibly do? This was an ages old ritual, performed in secret, in a remote location, far from assistance of any kind. No one had the faintest idea of what had been going on here for millennia.

I used to have a touching faith in 'the authorities'. That there was always some reassuring presence – the police, the government, the council –   forces for good, who would sort things out and make everything all right again. Over the last twelve months I'd discovered it was usually 'the authorities' you had to watch out for. But there are degrees of danger. Sorensen was a problem, but he was far away. This threat was immediate and present, but there would be no help tonight. No welcome police car with sirens and flashing lights. The forces gathering here tonight would not be human. What could just one person possibly do? Especially when that one person was only me.

. But – perhaps not just me. Perhaps there would be Michael Jones as well. I wasn't sure what he could do, but I had faith he would do something. Unable to sit still any longer, I crossed to the window again and craned my neck for the headlights of an approaching car. I imagined him pulling up outside the Travellers' Rest, pushing open the front door – I imagine locks meant very little to him – bounding up the stairs, kicking open the door, and rescuing me with one hand and the Year King with the other.

I stood at the window and stared and stared. Nothing happened. No car approached. No one kicked down my bedroom door. No cavalry galloped into town.

I heard the footsteps coming along the landing and briefly considered locking myself in the bathroom. I was certain it wouldn't do the slightest bit of good but perhaps I could delay things a little. For instance, what would happen if the ceremony was an hour late? If the Year King wasn't killed at the exact moment the old year rolled over into the new? Common sense said it probably wouldn't make any difference. They'd been doing this long before clocks were invented and I was sure I'd read that long ago, the new year had been celebrated in March anyway. It was the blood that was important … and the intent … not the time of the ceremony.

I went back to the bed and sat quietly. If I gave them no trouble there was always a chance they might relax sufficiently for me to get away somehow. And people do tend to underestimate me. I know I'm not a Warrior Princess, but on the other hand, I've dealt with some bad stuff in my past. I might not be as helpless as they thought.

But – and this was what was really frightening me – what had Veronica Harlow said? 'I recognised you as soon as you walked in.' The one thought I couldn't deal with was that I was supposed to be here. That this was my destiny. That this was something I couldn't fight because I was supposed to be here. I've said before – I don't know who I am and sometimes I wonder what I am. Tonight, I might be about to find out.

No. Never. Not in a million years. Whatever I was, I wasn't this. Whatever Veronica Harlow and her family were, that was not what I wanted to be. I would keep quiet, do as I was told, seize the first chance offered, and if I died trying – well, I died, and that was the end of it, and what a lot of problems that would solve.

I had hoped they would send Becky, but it was Veronica herself who turned up, elegant in a long, black gown. One of us would be showing disrespect by showing up in scruffy jeans and I was happy to think it would be me. I wasn't going to spend the rest of my life serving a bunch of rocks.

And she was alone. Interesting. Granny was ill so did this mean that Becky was well under the weather having been slurping surreptitious wine all day? Which just left Veronica. Big, strong, dark Veronica.

I took my time, trying to delay events by going to the bathroom. 'Leave the door open,' she said, sharply. I washed my hands, slowly pulled on my coat, fumbled for my gloves and generally did everything I could to put off the moment I had to leave this room, still hoping against hope that Michael Jones would show up, although if he was coming then surely he'd be here by now.

She showed no signs of impatience, waiting silently in the doorway, arms folded, and finally I could spin things out no longer.

We emerged out of the front door and into complete darkness. Even the streetlights were off. Everything was black with darker patches of blackness. I knew there were people out here because I could hear them. A crowd of people can never be completely silent and the sounds were unnerving in the dark.

We left the road and began to crunch our way across the frosty grass. She held my arm tightly. She was very strong.

Somewhere in the dark, off to my left, cymbals clashed. A great shout went up and suddenly there was light. A hundred flaming torches flared into life. Sparks flew skywards and the flames cast jumping shadows on the frost-white grass.

My heart sank. My vague plans for somehow overpowering Veronica and escaping into the darkness dissolved into dust. There were considerably more people here than I had expected. Hundreds of faces appeared in the torchlight. Strange, long faces, thick with chalk-white paste, roughly applied. Their eyes were heavily outlined in black. As if they were looking up at me from deep holes. And given their expressions, some of them might well be.

The few women I had met were obviously the acceptable face of Greyston. These others were the inevitable casualties of a too restricted gene pool. Women who, for one reason or another, were only allowed out on special occasions.

They had formed into two lines facing inwards, making a kind of human processional way, lit by torchlight. They waited in silence. No one moved or spoke. Not even the children. I couldn't believe it – there were babies here.

I was pushed into place at the head of the processional way with my back to the stones, which made me uneasy. I could sense them behind me. Malevolent and expectant. I tried to turn around but Veronica pulled me back. I stood between her and Miriam. Of Becky there was no sign. I didn't know whether she'd been relegated to the crowd or was passed out somewhere. No matter – there were only two of them present at the moment and their power would be diminished accordingly. Or so I told myself.

The night was freezing. I could feel the cold striking up through my boots. Inside my gloves my fingers were numb. The sky was crystal clear and each flickering torch had its own nimbus of light around it. The figures holding them were sharp black and white. I imagined this scene taking place, unchanged, down all the long years of history.

A big wooden X frame had been erected in front of the Three Sisters. It hadn't been there this afternoon so I didn't know when they'd put it up. I had a sudden vision of it being trundled across the green on modern wheels, like a cricket screen, and had to fight back hysterical laughter. Alongside the frame was a cloth-covered table. I could see three large bronze bowls – for the blood offering to the stones, I assumed, and in front of them, a sickle shaped knife, also of bronze. The urge to laugh left me.

And where was the King? I craned my neck. He wasn't here. Had he somehow managed to get away? Had he got wind of his fate and escaped?

No. Here he came. The front door of the Three Sisters pub was flung open, sending a shaft of light across the road. A young girl, dressed all in white, wearing a flower wreath in her hair, skipped out. She was beaming with importance, thoroughly enjoying herself and thumping away on a hand drum. Somewhere in the crowd, a woman jumped up and down in excitement and waved. For all the world as if her daughter was appearing in a school play. Behind the little girl, four women, also in white, escorted a young man, wearing a long golden robe over which he tripped occasionally. Vital though he might be to the prosperity of the village and ensuring future harvests, it was interesting to see no one had bothered to take up his robe. After all, the next Year King might be taller.

His colour was a murky green, shading to a sickly yellow at the edges. It streamed around him, flaring with eagerness and sexual anticipation. He was excited, keyed up and thoroughly enjoying the attention.

They entered the processional avenue, walking slowly between the rows of silent, torch-bearing women.

Veronica pushed me to stand in front of the table and Granny joined us, granting the stones a clear view of their victim.

I opened my mouth to shout a warning and Granny took my other arm in a vice-like grip. A warning.

I ignored her, but as I opened my mouth to shout, around us, the women began to sing. A strange, discordant song in a minor key. A song not of this country. Or even of this age. The rhythm was compelling. An incantation to the Mother, perhaps, imploring her to receive this sacrifice. Their chanting spoke of cruelty and death. Their feet stamped a beat that chilled the blood. My head began to swim and much against my will, my own blood pulsed in response. Was this something in my genes? Something I couldn't control? Did all women have this? A chilling thought on an already icy night.

No. Not me. I would not do this. I would not give in. I shook my head to keep it clear and made myself concentrate. Now that my eyes had adjusted a little, I could see gifts of all kinds placed around the stones. Small dolls, wreaths of dried flowers probably made way back in the summer, cakes, and long, long red ribbons that looked disturbingly like streams of blood.

An unearthly scream of exultation tore the air asunder, but not from any human throat. The stones themselves were giving welcome to their sacrifice. The air around them rippled. My ears hurt and I cried out in pain, twisting my head, desperate to escape that dreadful sound. The young man trod onwards unhearing.

Veronica stared at me complacently. 'Yes, I knew you were the one. There's really no point in you trying to deny it.'

Around us, the women took up the same cry, shouting, screaming, shrieking even. The noise reverberated off the buildings around the green.

Slowly, and to the beat of the drum, the Year King's procession made its way towards the stones. For how many thousands of years had feet trodden this path? How many men had walked to their death? That this could happen now, in this day and age was wrong. Plain wrong. This was a left-over from a bloodier age. Something that should have died out centuries ago and sent scuttling back into the darkness from which it was born. It set my teeth on edge. Like biting into tin foil. A black malevolence had awoken this night. A bargain would be struck and a man would die.

From somewhere, Becky appeared beside me, wiping her mouth. I swallowed down my disappointment. She wasn't as disabled as I'd hoped. Her mother stared at her, coldly disapproving.

I was handed over to two other women, one of whom I think might have been Joanna from the bus, and then the three of them, Granny, Veronica and Becky turned to face the approaching Year King, like some grotesque welcoming committee – all dressed in black and standing with their backs to the black stones. The Mother, the Maiden and the Crone. Relics of a darker age.

Had there once been a time when *all* stones demanded blood? A night when hundreds of men had died, right across the land? I thought of all the standing stones, the monoliths, the rings, the dolmens scattered around this country, right now standing silent and still in the moonlight. At least I hoped they were silent and still. Were they waiting for their turn? Were they patiently waiting for the return of the Old Days?

I looked away, bunching my muscles to run. I wasn't doing this. I wasn't doing any of it. I opened my mouth to shout a warning to the Year King, still happily making his way along the avenue of women and apparently oblivious of the fate in store for him.

I tried. I swear I tried. I shrieked, 'Go back. Run away,' until my throat hurt, but my shriek was only one of hundreds. There was nothing I could do. I tried to make 'Go back' gestures but even I could see he wasn't interpreting them correctly. I stopped shrieking uselessly and tried to think of some other way of warning him but everything, the chanting, the stamping, the smell of the torches, the stones themselves, all of it was clouding my mind. My head was throbbing in time to the beat of the drum. I could see only the stones. Even if I closed my eyes I could only see the stones. They were filling my mind.

I forced myself to look at them. It wasn't my imagination – the stones were throbbing with anticipation. They were alive. They knew what was about to happen. Everyone here knew what was about to happen. Except the Year King himself, smiling and waving as he trod the path to his own death.

The women shrieked, the drums beat and the cymbals clashed. Their combined colours lit up the night. Flashes of blue and purple and turquoise exploded into the sky before dropping back again to merge into one throbbing mass of colour. Colour with a dark heart. I could see ribbons of red running through this sea of movement. Hysteria was in the air. The stones appeared to throb in time to their rhythm. They were alive. Everything was building towards a bloody crescendo.

I shouted again. 'Go back. Get away while you can. They're going to kill you. Run away,' but even I couldn't hear my own voice, let alone this young man still some way off. Joanna and her accessory had me in a grip of iron. There was nothing I could do. I twisted and struggled and shrieked. Anything to get his attention. Why couldn't he realise what was about to happen to him? Why didn't he try to run away?

If anything, he looked … well … jaunty, striding through the avenue of screaming women, waving, smiling, and giving all the appearance of a young man who was thoroughly enjoying himself. I couldn't understand it. And then I had a sudden thought. Did he think he was here for a repeat of last year's … introduction … to the life of a Year King? The ritual sex with a willing partner. Had he given any thought at all to the meaning of the word, 'year'? Whatever he was expecting, it wouldn't be to be upended by a bunch of frenzied women and have his throat cut. I thought of Veronica's remark. That fear made the blood taste sweeter. More palatable to the stones.

Whatever he was thinking, this young man wasn't going to be of any use whatsoever. Not until the moment he realised what was about to happen to him and by then it would be too late. I redoubled my efforts to break free and just for a moment a complacent smile crossed his face. Did he think I was there for him?

The watching women redoubled the noise. There was chanting. And stamping. And screaming. The beat got faster. Some women pulled out their hair. Some scratched their faces, drawing blood, dark against their bone white faces. Hysteria had many in its grip. Their daughters watched, big-eyed and taking it all in. Learning for the future.

The Year King paused some twenty yards away and held out his arms. At once, two women stepped forwards. One of them was Alice Chervil, her colour bubbling dangerously. Hers was not the only one. Many others were going the same way. The signs of people about to lose control. The whole area around the stones was a shimmering sea of turquoise, blue and purple encircling a black heart.

Carefully – which was rather ironic considering what they were going to do to him in two minutes' time – they removed his robe. He was naked underneath and very obviously enjoying himself.

He strutted – there was no other word for it – he strutted towards the stones and a bloody death. But the important thing was that he was free and he was close. If I shouted now then he might be able to hear me. He was young. He looked fit enough, a little soft around the middle perhaps, but he could run. Run for his life, out of the torchlight and into the darkness beyond. This was my last chance to warn him.

As if guessing my intention, Veronica glanced over and nodded. Joanna said, 'We meet again. How are you enjoying it so far?', clapped her hand over my mouth and held me tightly. She'd been big and strong on the bus. She felt even bigger and stronger now. I could smell the wine on her breath.

The three black-clad women stood in front of the stones. The Mother, the Maiden and the Crone. Veronica looked across at me. Her meaning was clear. Tomorrow, I would stand here with them. There would be Veronica in her new role as the Crone, Becky would remain the disgruntled Maiden, and I would be the Mother. Tomorrow night, this would be me and a man, a complete stranger. The new Year King.

Now he was closer. Close enough to see the table. To see what lay on the table. He slowed, puzzled. He stopped and looked around, and at that moment they closed in behind him and the song changed. They were singing him to his death. He gave a great cry of fear and at the same moment five or six women laid hands on him.

He struggled like a madman. More women piled on. They were hurting him.

He screamed and screamed. No one listened. No one cared.

A dozen women subdued him, pinning his arms and lifting him off his feet. He was carried to the stones – who, again, seemed to lean forwards in anticipation.

I wrenched my head free and tried to turn to face Joanna, shouting to make myself heard over all the racket around us. 'You can't do this. This is murder.'

'This is life,' she intoned. Waves of stale wine gusted past me.

The women gathered in a rough semi-circle, pushing forward for a better view. They'd brought the children. Little girls, hair in bunches and wearing My Little Pony backpacks held their mothers' hands and watched intently.

There was a great shouting. They were counting down. Veronica reached for the ceremonial sickle and held it high. There were only seconds left.

It would seem that Michael Jones had let me down again.

Chapter Seven

I have never felt more helpless than I did at that moment. Because this wasn't about me. I wasn't the one at risk here – not yet, anyway – but if I didn't do something soon – now – then this man would die. And then another one on this same night in twelve months' time, and so on and so forth, in an unbroken cycle until the end of time. I had to do something. Anything.

I struggled and kicked out but to no avail. Joanne had tight hold of my wrists. I redoubled my efforts and we struggled together. She was hurting me but that was the least of my problems because I had to do *something*.

The screaming built to a crescendo. A great cacophony of noise bounced off the stones and was sent back, redoubled, as they roared their anticipation of the blood to come. The sound travelled back and forth, back and forth, making my head ring.

And then, without warning, something was different. Women were still screaming but their cries were of alarm, not celebration. I jerked up my head and strained to see. Something was happening. Something unexpected that was not part of the ceremony.

Powerful lights stabbed through the night, white and blinding. Dark shadows fled. The stones themselves seemed to recoil before this onslaught. Above everything I could hear a roaring, rushing sound and for a very quick moment I thought – dragon.

My second thought was slightly more sensible. Helicopter.

My third thought was really rather mundane. Car.

Barely had I come to this conclusion than twin headlights rounded the stones, dazzlingly bright in all this blackness and illuminating a scene of total chaos. Women were running in all directions, bumping into each other, shouting for their children, falling over, even knocking each other over in their efforts to get away. I suspected that, while I'd been thinking dragon and helicopter, they were thinking – paparazzi.

Someone crashed a gear and a familiar voice shouted, 'Look out, Jerry'. There was the nasty crunching sound of a vehicle clipping the left-hand stone. One headlight blinked out. Was it my imagination or did the stone groan? But Granny definitely dropped heavily to the ground.

The car hurtled straight past me, bumping over the rough ground and scattering people right and left. I caught a very quick glimpse of Michael Jones in the passenger seat, shouting instructions, and my treacherous heart soared. He *had* come. Why had I ever doubted he would come? Although how he would find me in all this confusion ... The table had been knocked over and the basins scattered. Torches lay spluttering on the ground. And screaming women were running everywhere.

Joanna pushed me away from her so hard I nearly fell over. She plunged into the milling throng without a backward glance. Everyone was disappearing – rushing home as fast as they could go, to lock the door and pretend they'd been in all night watching the TV. I clenched my fists, all prepared to lay about me should anyone stand in my way and shrieked, 'Jones.'

He couldn't hear me – not over the panic all around us. I caught a glimpse of Veronica forcing her way through the crowd, an ugly expression on her face. I didn't know if she was looking for me – and if she was, whether to save me from this unknown attack or kill me, I had no idea, but I knew it wouldn't be a good idea to stick around to find out. I had to find Michael Jones. Because sooner or later the element of surprise would be gone and it would dawn on someone that there were hundreds of them and only one of him.

I don't know why I worried. His single headlight was splitting the night like a one-eyed dragon and the next moment an amplified voice boomed through the night, the echoes bouncing off stones and buildings alike.

'Be advised – this is an armed task force acting within the limits prescribed by Her Majesty's Government as laid down in the Counter Terrorism and Security Act and the Public Order Act of 1986. You are harbouring a dangerous fugitive. Surrender her at once or suffer the consequences. No further warning will be given.'

The car wheeled about again, scattering those who had wrongly thought it safe to run in that direction. I fought my way to the stones. They were no longer the Three Sisters. Two and a Half Sisters would be more accurate. Jones's headlight hadn't been the only casualty of that glancing blow. The top one third of the left-hand stone lay on the ground, snapped off cleanly along the break I'd seen earlier. I felt a sense of great satisfaction. I deliberately stood on it, ripped off my scarf and waved it over my head and shouting, 'Jones, over here. Over here.'

The car swung around for another pass. A distorted voice dopplered towards me, 'Where are you?'

I shouted back, 'I'm over here,' and tried not to feel the whole evening was descended into some sort of farce. I don't know why it is, but things never seem quite so bad when Jones is around. Although very often they become worse.

Unfortunately, by making myself conspicuous to him, I'd made myself conspicuous to Veronica as well.

The crowd was thinning as people raced away into the anonymous darkness. I could see her crouched over a prone figure on the ground. Granny. When the stone went down, so had Granny.

Slowly, Veronica straightened up, turned and faced me. I felt my heart fail. Her colour was murderous. Thick blue and purple spikes stabbed towards me.

So sudden and vicious was her attack that I had no time to avoid it in any way and for a very brief second, I was encircled by her colour.

I braced myself for pain or nausea or even – if she was channelling the power of the stones – for death, but I felt nothing. For a moment, I was peering out at a blue and purple world and then everything shattered as that brilliant white headlight cut through the night and the shadows flew away.

Along with my eyesight. That sudden flash had robbed me of my night vision. Forgetting I was standing on the fallen stone I took a step backwards, lost my balance and fell heavily.

I lay for a moment, my wits as scattered as everyone else's and then I remembered what was happening. Scrambling to my feet, I pushed my hair out of my eyes and stared around.

Veronica's colour still boiled as she strode towards me across the grass.

I instinctively put out an arm to ward her off and she stopped as abruptly as if she'd run into a wall. I could see the shock in her face at the unexpectedness of it. She shouted to someone and a second later, Becky was at her side. Hatred twisted their faces and made them ugly. Their colours swirled together, reaching out for me. The world darkened around me.

I struggled for breath, at the same time fighting an insane desire to run towards them. My right leg was actually lifting of its own accord when, out of nowhere, a battered SUV screeched to a halt between them and me, leaving long skid marks on the frosty grass. I stared in amazement and Jones leaned out of the window and shouted, 'Don't just stand there Cage. Get in.'

I had my hand on the ice-cold door handle when I remembered the Year King. Where was he in all this panic? Had he managed to get away? Surely he wouldn't be stupid enough to hang around? On the other hand, he *was* naked. I couldn't leave him here. Even supposing we got away, there was nothing to stop them regrouping, picking up the table and carrying on from where they'd left off.

So where was he? He shouldn't be hard to find. He was the only man here. Or had been until a minute ago. Unless he'd been spirited away. I stared wildly around.

Jones hung out of the window again. 'What are you waiting for Cage? Get in and let's get out of here.'

'I'm looking for a naked man.'

'Well, there's no way I'm taking my clothes off – it's brass monkeys out there. Get in.'

'I have to find the naked man.'

'Any particular reason why?'

'They're going to kill him.'

'They'll kill us all if you don't get a move on,' said a voice from the driver's seat. 'Never seen such a bunch of nasty tempered women in all my life. And I've met a few I can tell you.'

'We'll find him,' said Jones. 'Just get in the car first, Cage. I feel so much happier when I know where you are.'

I climbed into the back and clipped on my seat belt. Two heads turned to look at me and I said defensively, 'Well, it's the law, isn't it?'

Jones said, 'Cage, you are an abiding delight to me,' and at the same time I caught the very faint flash of what could have been a white buttock.

The driver said, 'There he is. Over there,' and shoved the car into gear again. We slewed our way across the grass, tearing up great divots of previously pristine village green as we went. It occurred to me that this village was not going to look anywhere near as immaculate as usual when the sun came up.

If the sun comes up, came a treacherous thought. How do you know you're not meddling in some centuries old but vital ritual that will bring about the end of the world if not fulfilled?

I told myself that was Veronica talking.

We bumped and skidded across the grass, swerving around the few women still blindly running, to where a naked man was trying to scuttle off into the night and skidded to a halt beside him.

I unclicked my seat belt and reached across to open the door for him, shouting, 'Get in.'

He recoiled. 'You!'

What did he mean – me?

'Just get in,' shouted Jones. 'There's hundreds of them and only three of us. Get in.'

'She's one of them.'

'No, I'm not,' I said, indignantly. 'I was the one trying to warn you.'

'No, you weren't. You were the one shrieking at me.'

'They were all shrieking at you, mate,' said the driver. 'Either get in or don't but we're leaving. Now.'

He gunned the engine.

The ex-Year King cast one final look over his shoulder at the screaming chaos around the stones, decided no better offer was likely to be forthcoming, and scrambled in.

The driver let in the clutch with a jerk and the naked Year King sprawled all over me.

I squeaked and Michael Jones twisted around to look. 'Everything all right back there?'

'I'm in the middle of some blood-soaked pre-historic ritual, in fear of my life and with a naked man on top of me. Define all right.'

He laughed. 'I've missed you, Cage.'

The ground was much bumpier than it looked and the Year King and I were being thrown around all over the place. Accidentally or otherwise, he kept falling on top of me.

'Will you get off,' I said, trying to push him away for the umpteenth time. He seemed reluctant to move. I suspected that after twelve months of having any woman wherever and whenever he pleased, he might be having some difficulty adjusting to his changed circumstances.

'Stop that this minute and sit up properly,' I said, trying not to sound like a primary school teacher. I'd just saved his life. The lack of gratitude was astounding. And he was very heavy.

The weight lifted suddenly. Jones had him by the scruff of the neck and hurled him back into his seat.

'Thank you,' I said, straightening my clothing and smoothing my hair.

'My pleasure. You ...' he addressed himself to the Year King. 'Sit still and keep your hands – and your other bits to yourself. Old Jerry here's not keen on having your naked arse on his nice upholstery and if you touch this lady again we'll drive you straight back to those weird women and they can pick up where they left off.'

Did he say Jerry? Jerry was the man who had broken into my house. Yes, admittedly it was only to pack up my clothes for me, and he'd helped us escape from Sorensen's clinic, but even so

… Jerry was a criminal. I was all set to become indignant when I remembered how neatly he'd done it. Nothing in my house had been disturbed. My clothes had been beautifully packed. He'd even put tissue paper between the layers. I suspected not many burglars can provide that sort of service.

I said, 'Jerry, is that you?' A stupid question but he knew what I meant.

'It is,' he said, swinging the wheel. 'Pleasure to meet you at last, missis.'

'And you,' I said. 'One day you must show me how to pack so neatly.'

He was pleased by the compliment. His rusty brown colour was coiled neatly around him, but as I watched, the edges glowed slightly, turning a golden colour.

We bumped off the green and onto tarmac.

'Hold on,' said Jerry as we accelerated away.

Houses flashed past in the beam of our one headlight, then there were hedges and tall grass verges, and then we were out into the dark, and to my eyes, very sinister countryside.

'Well,' said Jones, settling himself comfortably. 'I think that went quite well, all things considered. Don't you?'

Chapter Eight

We didn't go far. Three or four miles only, and then Jerry pulled into a layby for us all to sort ourselves out. He switched off the engine and turned out the headlights. Sorry, headlight. Singular.

We sat in the dark for a moment, getting our breath back.

'Right,' said Jones, 'we need to make a few minor modifications to the plan because we hadn't factored in Cage dragging naked men along.'

He paused and turned to me. 'I have to ask, Cage – and I think I speak for Jerry here as well – why?'

'They were going to kill him.'

'No, they weren't,' said the Year King, quite indignantly.

'Yes, they were.'

'No. You've got it all wrong. It's just an old fertility rite. You know, from the old days when everyone believed in that sort of thing. Ensuring a good harvest, keeping the sheep healthy, all that sort of thing. Why would they kill me – I'm their king?'

'Their *Year* King.'

'Yeah ...? So ...?'

'King for *a year*?'

'Yeah, they said that. This was my last night. They said – big party, lots to eat and drink, some girls, you know.' His eyes slid sideways to me.

'Don't even think about it,' I said, shifting away from the naked man on the back seat with me.

'Ah,' said Jones. 'That explains the naked part. Was he expecting to be naked all over you, Cage?'

'I was there in the capacity of observer,' I said, primly.

'You like to watch? Well, that opens up some interesting possibilities.'

'No,' I said, annoyed. 'It's simple. The Year King lasts twelve months. On the last day of the old year, they kill him …' I glared balefully at this year's victim '…and tomorrow a new one takes his place. The whole thing is run by a bunch of madwomen – three of them – the Mother, the Maiden and the Crone. Granny's dying and I was scheduled to be the replacement.'

There was a bit of a silence and then Jones said cautiously, 'As the Crone?'

'No,' I said, even more annoyed. 'The Mother.'

There was another silence and then Jones said, 'Um …'

'That was for tomorrow night,' I said quietly, the narrowness of my escape only now beginning to dawn on me. 'The New King turns up and I'm the … introductory offer. The thinking was that I would then soon be a mother.'

There was a different sort of silence.

'Right,' said Jones, briskly. 'There's a blanket in the boot with which our friend here can cover his fundamentals. Jerry, can you drive him to the hospital? Better get him checked out I suppose.'

I leaned over the front seat. 'But what will he tell them?'

Jones shrugged. 'Whatever he likes.' He turned to the Year King, now shivering in the corner with his legs tightly crossed. Reaction had set in. 'Just a word of warning – telling the truth will involve drug tests, the police, widespread disbelief, and possibly being Sectioned under the Act. I'd go with the whole stag party gone wrong scenario if I were you, but it's your choice. You don't know our names apart from old Jerry here …'

'Less of the old,' said Jerry, opening the door and getting out.

'And that's not his real name and this isn't a real car so that's a bit of a dead end, but it's up to you. This lady is under my personal protection and if you ever see her again you will turn and walk in the other direction as fast as you can. Any attempt to implicate any of us in what happened tonight will result in you being found face down in the River Rush the next morning. We're going to say goodbye soon and …'

The car jolted. We were sitting in a layby without lights and my first thought was that something had driven into the back of us. I was actually looking around for another vehicle when it did it again. And then – then the car moved. Backwards. About a foot or so. But on its own. I grabbed for the door handle, unable to understand what was happening. How could the car move? Jerry was round the back and rummaging in the boot for the blanket. And the engine was off. I looked at Jones who reached out and grasped my wrist. His other hand was under his jacket. Was he armed? I certainly hoped so. Although what good that would do …

The car moved again – jerking backwards for a yard or so and throwing me against the door. I put a hand on the front seat to steady myself and looked wildly around. How could this be? The driver's seat was empty. Jerry was actually outside the car.

He shouted something and slammed the boot shut with such violence that the car rocked.

'Left it in gear, did you?' said Jones mildly, but I could see his colour spiking all around him.

'Do me a favour,' said Jerry in disgust, climbing into the driver's seat in a hurry.

'Handbrake on?'

'Any more from you and you can walk back to Rushford.'

The car jolted again. Quite violently this time and then began to move. The engine was off and I could hear the tyres crunching over loose gravel. A giant force was pulling us backwards.

'Seat belts,' shouted Jones. 'It's going to get rough. Jerry, get us out of here.'

I clipped on my belt again and hung on. Jerry was standing on the brake and Jones was hauling, two handed, on the handbrake and still we were sliding backwards, the tyres skidding in the loose stones on the road. The brakes didn't seem to be working. If anything, we were picking up speed. Slowly, inexorably, we were being pulled back towards Greyston. And whatever awaited us there.

The Year King was screaming with fear, cowering in his corner. 'Don't let them get me. Don't let them get me again'. Jones and Jerry were shouting instructions at each other as the car began to move faster. If we wanted to escape then now would be the time to jump out because in a minute it would be too late.

I clenched my fists and sat quietly, trying to ignore the pictures in my head. Giant stones, black against the sky filled my mind. I tried to concentrate. To focus my mind. To push back. Giant stones ... My world turned blue and purple. I closed my eyes but they were still there. Huge and black and threatening. And injured. What made me think 'injured' instead of 'damaged'?

But they were angry. I could feel it from here. They'd been baulked of their offering. The cycle had been broken – we'd broken the cycle – but there was still time. They wanted him back. They wanted us all back. Their malice flooded my mind.

They were very strong and it hurt my head. In an effort to shut them out, I put my hands over my eyes and groaned.

'Punch it, Jerry,' yelled Jones. 'And don't spare the horses. Everyone hold on tight.'

Jerry pushed the starter. I had a moment's fear the engine wouldn't start, but it did. He gunned it hard. 'When I say now …'

The engine noise rose to a shriek.

'Now.'

We stopped moving. For a moment the two forces, the one pushing us forwards, and the one dragging us backwards, were perfectly balanced. The car trembled with the strain. The engine was racing. Smoke from the tyres and the exhaust drifted past the window. Giant stones loomed over me. I couldn't push them back. The engine roared and roared and then, with a jerk that engaged all our seatbelts, we were away.

In my mind, I saw the stones sway … and then I was free as well.

We fishtailed out of the layby and down the road, with Jerry fighting for control all the way. We took a bend too fast and clipped the hedge. I heard the sound of twigs and small branches rattling off the side of the car. Something white – an owl? – appeared briefly and then was gone. And then Jerry had everything back under control and we were cruising smoothly away.

'Bloody Norah,' said Jones. 'Hell of a way to bring in the New Year, Cage.'

We drove in silence until we reached the outskirts of Rushford. The lights seemed very bright after the darkness of the countryside. I stared out of the window, thinking furiously. The moments at the stones had been scary, but the force that had grabbed our car had been terrifying.

And what had it wanted? The Year King back again? After all, this year's ritual was unfinished. Had barely even started, in fact. What would that mean for the stones? And for the village itself?

Or had it wanted me? To take up my new role as the Mother? Because now Veronica's team was at least one man down. For some reason, I saw Alice Chervil smiling quietly to herself.

Or Jones and Jerry for revenge?

Or had it wanted all of us in one convenient package?

A river of blood would flow tonight if they ever did manage to lay their hands on us. Enough to glut even those stones for months. Enough to repair the damage we'd done. Enough for revenge …

'Hey,' said Jones, softly and took my hand in his own warm paw. The picture blurred and faded away.

I opened my eyes.

'Well,' that brought back memories, didn't it?' he said quietly. 'Are you all right.'

I nodded. Now that I was safe, I was beginning to realise just how unsafe I had been. Only half an hour ago.

'We'll drop off the King of the Fairies. Jerry will go with him, just to make sure, and then I'll take you home. Just hold on a little longer.'

I nodded and closed my eyes again.

We pulled up outside A&E. I felt cheered to see the lights and life. There were people everywhere nursing New Year's Eve related injuries. For everyone else it was just business as usual. Normality is very reassuring.

Jerry helped the Year King out of the car and I wrapped him in a faintly oil-smelling tartan blanket. He was shaken but calm.

And quiet. The posturing man who had strutted his way down the processional way was gone – possibly for ever. I wondered, despite everything Veronica had said, whether they had drugged him after all. Or had it merely been the overconfidence of a young man whose every whim had been indulged for the last twelve months. Whatever it was, the power of Greyston was wearing off. He looked white and cold.

I wrapped the blanket tightly around him. 'I don't even know your name.'

'Dermot.'

'Dermot, it might be a good idea to say as little as possible.'

He said, with an effort at a joke, 'I don't remember a thing. Who are you?'

'That's the ticket, mate,' said Jerry. 'Let's get you inside. You'll be freezing your nadgers off in a minute. See you around, missis.'

'Look after him,' I said and he nodded.

'And thank you, Jerry.'

He nodded again and then he and Dermot disappeared through the doors.

'Well ...' I said to Jones who had moved into the driver's seat. I wasn't sure what to do next and felt strangely awkward, 'Goodnight then.'

He started the engine. 'Get in the front, Cage.'

'Why?'

'It'll make it easier for you to have a go at me.'

'Actually, if it's all the same to you, I think I'll walk.'

'It's not all the same to me at all. I haven't risked life, limb and Jerry's car – look at the state of Jerry's car, Cage – for you to swan off into the night and get yourself involved in something awful. Again. You frighten the living daylights out of me. I don't know what it is with you. I never know what you'll be up

84

to next. And there's no way I'm not delivering you safely to … wherever it is you want to go. So get in.'

We drove the next mile in silence.

'I suppose,' he said, slowing for a group of revellers to make their erratic way across the road, 'there's no point in asking you to trust me'.

I was suddenly angry. 'I did trust you once.'

'And no harm came to you.'

'No harm? No harm? You *kidnapp*ed me!'

'I helped you escape from a secure mental institution where you were being held against your will.'

'I was maced by a homicidal maniac in a haunted castle.'

'Every place you go to is haunted. And I've been maced more times than I can count. Get over it.'

'I don't want to get over it.'

Silence followed this childish remark.

'No,' he said eventually. 'There's more to it than that. Did I do something? Say something?'

'You bugged my house.'

'Well, not me personally. Different department.'

'No – you were the decoy, weren't you? The one paid to lure me away so my house would be empty.'

'I didn't lure you anywhere. You came of your own free will.'

'You know very well I thought you'd invited me because …' I stopped suddenly.

'Because …?'

I took a breath. 'Because all you wanted to do was sleep with me so I wouldn't notice your people fitting my house with cameras and listening devices and God knows what else besides.'

'I didn't sleep with you,' he said indignantly. 'Dear God, when I think of the lengths I went to – separate bedrooms – making sure you didn't drink too much. Really, Cage, your ability to hold your drink is pathetic – and the next minute you're sprawling all over my lap in the most shameless display of immodest behaviour I've ever seen in my life.'

'Relax,' I said. 'It wasn't you I was after but your chocolate brownie.'

'That doesn't make your behaviour any less reprehensible. Now tell me what the real problem is.'

'What? What real problem?'

'The real problem. The real reason you ran.'

'You told me to run.'

'Well, I just thought you'd go next door to Colonel Barton – not disappear off into the night.'

'It was eleven in the morning.'

'Well, whatever. But that wasn't what I meant. You were all ready to flee long before I told you what we'd done to your house. I saw it in your face. Why.'

I said quietly, 'The photo frame.'

'Yes, I know – they broke it when they were installing the equipment. Someone was careless. Is that what this is all about? Because they broke Ted's photo?'

Ted's photo was one of my dearest possessions. A few years before he died, we'd had a weekend in London and the photo was of the two of us, posed against an ancient wall at the Tower of London. We were both smiling. It had been a happy day. The photo lived on a shelf beside the chimney breast, angled so that wherever I was in the room, I could see it and Ted could see me. There were always fresh flowers nearby.

Then I'd returned from my Christmas holiday to find it had been dropped and the frame hastily glued back together again.

For me, this was where reality had torn itself in two. In Jones's reality, it had been damaged during Sorensen's attempt to bug my house. In mine, I'd thrown it at Michael Jones in a last effort to save myself when he attacked me. I knew my reality was wrong because Jones was still alive, but I couldn't forget it ... couldn't let it go.

I said quietly, 'I know how it was really broken.'

'Yes, someone dropped it.'

I gripped my hands together in my lap and said in a low voice, 'There are two realities. In one version, you remember how the photo was broken. In the other ... in the other ... in my version ...'

I stopped.

He waited. He did waiting very well. Quite a lot of time passed and still he didn't move. Didn't speak. Didn't do anything. He just drove in silence and waited.

At last I said, 'You won't like it.'

He sighed heavily. 'No, I probably won't.'

'Or believe it.'

'No, I probably will.'

I turned my head to look at him. 'No, you probably really won't.'

'Well, why don't you tell me anyway.'

I sighed. 'Boxing Day. We went tobogganing. I banged my head.'

'I remember.'

'You asked me if I lost consciousness and I said no.'

'I remember that because just for a second Cage, you looked well and truly out of it.'

'I was out of it. But it wasn't the fall.'

'Did you ... see something?'

'Yes. Yes, you could say that.'

I stopped, really unwilling to go on. Once some things are said you can never go back.

'Just tell me, Cage.'

'All right.' I took a deep breath. 'The sledge hit me. I opened my eyes. I was fine. You said you'd take me back to your place. On the way, your phone rang. You had to leave suddenly because there was a job for you. In the Midlands. We collected my stuff. I went home. That evening … that evening …'

I stopped, living that moment again. The moment his dead girlfriend had come to destroy me.

'That evening, your ex-partner Clare came to me.'

The car swerved. Someone behind us hooted. He pulled over to the side of the road and turned off the engine. 'Clare's still alive?' I saw him remember who he was talking to. 'No, she's not. Is she? She can't be.'

'She's not. She was very dead. I could see the bullet holes.'

I heard him swallow. 'What … what did she want?'

I shut out the picture of Clare and her disfigured face 'Me. She thought I'd taken her place. That I had what she wanted. I tried to fight her off. I was losing. Ted saved me. You telephoned the next morning. You were on your way back to Rushford. You said you had something to say to me. You were excited. You were pleased to see me. I let you in.' I stopped. The next bit would be as hard for him to hear as it would be for me to say.

'Go on.'

I wasn't sure I could do this to him. 'Are you sure?'

He said, harshly, 'Yes. Go on.'

'You attacked me.'

He didn't speak. I didn't give him the chance. He'd wanted to know. I was merciless. 'You hit me. Many times. You threw me around the room. You broke my arm. You broke my ribs. I fell down. You kicked me. You were about to stamp on my face when Colonel Barton came to investigate the noise. He telephoned for help. They took me to the Sorensen Clinic. You were there too. I found you dying in the basement. Clare had used you to hurt me and it had burned you up inside. You … died.'

I couldn't look at him. I turned my head and stared out of the window. 'I was so angry. Everyone – *everyone* had lied to me or hurt me in some way. Everyone I'd trusted.' I struggled again to rein in the anger and tamp it down because I'd once seen what my uncontrolled rage could do and I had no wish to do that ever again.

I continued in the same flat, dead voice. 'And all the time the snow came down. It never stopped. Day after day. We were slowly being buried in it. People were saying it was the end of the world.'

I stopped, remembering the snow. The angry snow. 'I agreed to work with Sorensen. He flew in some people who wanted to see what I could do and, to revenge myself on him – to revenge myself on everyone, I suppose, I brought the clinic down around their heads. I destroyed everything. They died. I died. Everyone died. In the snow. Then I opened my eyes and I was in your reality – the other reality if you like, and I'd only just had the accident and you were taking me to hospital.'

He was silent for a long time, thinking things through. 'So you're saying you broke the photo frame.'

'Yes. I threw it at you and it smashed against the wall. That's how it really got broken.'

He shook his head vehemently. 'No, that's wrong. That's not right. Someone dropped it. I swear to you – that's what happened. It's in the report. The bloke who did it is up on a disciplinary charge. You must have banged your head and dreamed it. There's no other explanation because your … reality … isn't the right one. It didn't happen.'

'It's real to me. My arm still hurts.'

'Because you were knocked over by a runaway sledge. Of course it still hurts.'

'And then you told me you'd bugged my house. Well, not you, but Sorensen had bugged my house and I was still confused and I didn't know which reality was which. I still don't. One is as real to me as the other. And then you said to run … So I ran.'

'I meant for you to just push off for a bit while I dismantled the stuff in your house. I thought you'd be back after an hour or so. When you'd calmed down a little and I'd be able to explain. Not that you'd take off into the wild blue yonder and disappear. I've been worried to death over you.'

'There was no need.'

'No, of course there wasn't. Because you weren't racing around the countryside making yourself ill and getting yourself into more trouble than even you could deal with at all, were you?'

He was becoming angry. 'Cage – I swear to you – none of your reality is real. Sorensen – the clinic – it's all still there. You banged your head, that's all. Jesus, I can't believe that you would think I would hurt you. I thought we … We said … You said … One minute we were going to try to build something together and the next minute you're flying out of the door.'

His colour was boiling around him. The nasty dark patch over his heart was back, spreading its tendrils everywhere. His golden glow was fading. I could see his bewilderment and, deep down, his fear.

I hardened my heart. 'Well it doesn't matter really does it. You still betrayed me. Whichever reality is the right one, you still betrayed me. Either you beat me badly enough to put me in hospital or you colluded with Sorensen to bug my house. To spy on me. Neither is particularly commendable, is it?'

'I don't deny I worked with Sorensen,' he said quietly, which took the wind right out of my sails. 'I let you down badly. But that was in the past. I'm here now. You called. I came.'

'Only so you can report back to Sorensen that you've re-established contact.'

'He doesn't know you're gone.'

I was bewildered. 'But – all the equipment in my house. They must know I'm not there.'

'I dismantled it.'

'But surely someone's noticed I'm not there.'

'Not so far. You're pretty much known to be my responsibility so I'm left to get on with it.'

I was bewildered. 'But what are you telling Sorensen?'

'Well, I only have to report weekly – unless you take it into your head to run off into the night at eleven in the morning again, of course, but according to me you're safe and well at home, leading the blameless and boring life of a suburban housewife.'

'Oh God,' I said with memories of the last few days still bubbling through my brain. 'If only.'

'Yes, I really don't understand you, Cage. You're the original 1950s housewife, aren't you? You sit at home not doing anything in particular, but more happens when you're around than anyone I know.'

'That's odd – I was thinking exactly the same thing about you.'

He looked surprised. 'Me?'

'Is there anyone else here? Really Jones, I sometimes think working for Sorensen is the best thing you could do. You know – free psychiatric care.'

91

He started the engine. 'I'd better get you home before ...' he stopped. We both knew he'd been going to say, before I give you the thump you so richly deserve, and we both knew that suddenly, that wasn't funny any longer.

I heard his clothing rustle as he turned to me.

'It wasn't me,' he said quietly. 'I swear I didn't do that. I think you know, deep down, I would never do that.'

I saw again his cold-eyed emotionless face as he beat me and closed my eyes to shut out the picture.

'I wish you believed me,' he said, not looking at me. 'But honestly, Cage, it wasn't me.'

His colour said he was telling the truth. Or what he believed to be the truth.

I wanted to believe him. I so wanted to believe him. But my reality had happened. I knew it. He could talk about dreams and concussion as much as he liked, but I could taste the cold kiss of snow on my face. I could see his face as he systematically and efficiently broke my bones. It was what he did. It was part of his job. It was part of him. There was another side to him – as there must be to anyone who had a similar occupation – a side he kept hidden from me and I couldn't rid myself of the fear that one day I would see it again.

He went on. 'I did let you down, but if I'd refused to do what he ordered then Sorensen would only have put someone else on the job and I thought you were better off with me. As best I could, I've tried to make things right again. And so long as you don't do anything that brings both of us to his attention, we'll be fine.'

He turned his head away and said quietly, 'I'm taking a chance here. Don't make a liar out of me Cage, or we'll both be in trouble.'

I live in Rushford, up by the castle and we arrived well before dawn. The streets were still full of happy revellers – another world away from Greyston and what had happened there. I'd tentatively mentioned going to the police about Veronica Harlow and Jones had snorted with amusement for the next five minutes.

'But the police should know what's going on up there,' I said, panting beside him as he strode up the hill. 'Or suppose someone from the village reports us.'

'For what?'

'Damage to property?'

'Yes, because that's so much more serious than murdering a young man every New Year's Eve just to ensure the flowers bloom and they don't turn the whole place into a giant motorway service station. They're not going to report you, Cage.'

'But suppose they do. My fingerprints will be all over my room,' I said, years of watching CSI coming to the fore.

'Not a problem unless your prints are on file. Are they on file?'

'I don't know. Are they?'

He shrugged and I didn't push it. Did I want to know? Whether they were or weren't, I couldn't do anything about it, so why bother. It occurred to me that six months ago, the knowledge that the authorities had my prints on file would have frightened me to death. Now I could hardly be bothered to be bothered.

It seemed an age since I'd last been home. So much had happened that I wasn't sure I was the same person I had been when I'd left it on Christmas Eve. Only just over a week ago.

I found my key and opened the front door. He switched on the light. My house was warm and welcomed me as it always did.

Both of us glanced at the empty space where Ted's photo had stood and then looked away again.

He asked, 'Where is it? The photo, I mean.'

I sighed. 'Back at Greyston with the rest of my stuff.'

'You're not to go back there.'

'Don't worry, I won't.' And I wouldn't, but I'd miss my picture of Ted. I had others, but that one was my favourite. The thought of Veronica or, more likely Becky pawing over my things wasn't very nice.

I waited for him to leave, but instead he said, 'I'd better take a look at your wrists before I go.'

I hadn't even noticed. Each wrist was rubbed raw where I'd struggled with Joanne, the flesh red and swollen.

I sat down and he bathed each one in warm water with a drop of disinfectant. 'I'm not going to bandage them because then everyone will think you tried to slash your wrists rather than spend Christmas with me.'

I sat quietly until he finished.

'Thank you. They don't hurt very much at all.'

'They will,' he said. 'Just take things easy for a couple of days.'

I nodded, suddenly very tired.

'I'll call you tomorrow or the day after.'

'You don't have to.'

He looked suddenly tired as well. 'Yes, I do.'

An awkward silence fell.

'Well,' he said eventually. 'I'll be off then.'

I didn't want him to stay but I wasn't sure I wanted him to leave, either.

He stood up. 'I don't know, Cage, it's easier to keep safe half a dozen foreign despots wanted for war crimes the world over than it is to keep you out of trouble. What is it with you? You don't seem to have any friends – you have no social life to speak of – you rarely go out and yet everywhere you go – it's mayhem. What is it with you?'

Since I couldn't answer that question I remained silent.

'Look, I know things aren't very good between us at the moment but I'd feel a lot better if I knew you felt you could contact me if you needed me.'

I nodded again, keeping my eyes lowered so he wouldn't see the tears in my eyes.

He waited a moment and then said again, 'I'll be off then.'

I saw him to the door and locked it behind him.

Chapter Nine

I didn't think I would, but I slept for what was left of the night, deeply and dreamlessly. In fact, it was my throbbing wrists that woke me. Jones had been right. They did sting.

I had a long, hot bath, revelling in the luxury of being in my own home again. I made a resolution that come what may in the future, I would never allow anything – anything at all – to drive me away again. This was my home and this was where I lived.

There was hardly anything to eat in the cupboard because I'd run everything down before Christmas, but I found a frozen loaf and made myself a massive pile of toast. I was just tucking in when the telephone rang. Thinking it was Jones checking up on me I picked it up. It wasn't Jones – it was Jerry.

'He asked me to check you're all right.'

I was to discover he was uncomfortable naming names.

'I'm fine.' I paused. 'Thank you for yesterday. I don't know what I'd got myself into there, but I'm very grateful you were able to get me out of it.'

'You're welcome, missis.'

'What about Dermot?'

'No problems at the hospital. I took him back to my place, found him some old clothes and a pair of trainers and he pushed off. Don't think he could get away quick enough. Anyway, he said to say he'd gone back for your stuff and he'll be round about tennish.'

'Who? Dermot?'

'Course not. Why would he go back for your stuff? Kid's an idiot.'

My heart stopped. 'What? Jerry, say all that again.'

He repeated himself patiently. 'He said to say he'd gone back for your stuff and he'll be round to see you about tennish.'

'Jerry, no, he can't. He mustn't.'

'Too late,' he said simply. 'He set off well over an hour ago. He's probably on his way back by now.'

'But it's New Year's Day,' I said. 'According to them, the first man into the village on New Year's Day is the new Year King. Jerry, we have to go after him.'

'No, we don't,' he said calmly. 'He'll be fine. Have you seen the size of him?'

'They'll drug him or something.'

'Yes, because he's certainly stupid enough to sit down and have a cup of tea with them, isn't he? Listen, missis, he'll walk straight in, demand your stuff, get it, and walk straight back out again. The state we left that place in last night there's nothing they could do to him.'

'The stones,' I said faintly.

'Well, I wasn't in any position to look around me, but I know for certain one of them stones fell down, and for all we know it might have brought the others down with it. And that old lady didn't look none too good neither. Believe me, they'll be running around like headless chickens up there.'

I couldn't make him understand.

'No,' he said, cutting me off short. 'He'll be fine.'

'Trust me,' I said sarcastically.

'No,' he said, seriously, 'trust him. Anyway, gotta go. I just rang to make sure you're all right.'

He put the phone down.

I paced up and down. How could Jones be stupid enough to do such a thing? After everything I'd said, how could he be so stupid? He saw what we were up against last night. How could he possibly be so reckless as to go back there? And on New Year's Day of all days. In my mind, I saw him disappearing under a heaving crowd of vengeful women. I saw revenge running red down the stones, rejuvenating and restoring. And then, illogically, I saw him with Becky, naked in the moonlight, both of them laughing as the crowd urged them on. I saw him turning into the same drink-sodden Year King we'd saved last night, full of befuddlement and a sense of entitlement.

Suddenly, I couldn't stand it any longer. I wrenched open the front door and ran down the steps. I'd go to the top of the hill and wait for him. I'd watch for that familiar figure striding up the hill, his golden-red colour streaming out behind him.

I ran down the path. Castle Close was just beginning to wake up after its New Year's Eve celebrations. I could still faintly smell spent fireworks in the chilly morning air. Curtains were being drawn back. Somewhere a faint electronic beeping denoted someone's alarm clock being ignored after a night of celebration.

The entrance to Castle Close is through an archway between two well-preserved black and white Tudor houses. I stood, panting slightly, staring out down the hill. The streets were deserted. I went to look at my watch and realised I'd forgotten to put it on. And in my haste to get out, I'd forgotten my coat as well and it was a frosty morning. I wrapped my arms around myself and paced up and down, up and down, my breath frosting in the air around me, never taking my eyes off the street. I couldn't miss him. He'd be on foot because the streets up here are too narrow for cars and this was the only way in.

I don't know how long I stood there. Long enough for my feet and hands to grow numb with cold. Long enough to frighten myself to death with my own imaginings. Occasionally there would be the odd flash of common sense and Jerry's prosaic, 'Have you seen the size of him?' would intrude into my worst fears, but mostly I paced to stay warm and worried myself nearly sick.

Time dragged and there was still no sign of him. I'd got to the stage where I was considering summoning Jerry and mounting some sort of rescue – don't ask me how – when Jones appeared at the bottom of the hill, sensibly wrapped against the cold and with my suitcase in his hand.

The wave of relief nearly knocked me over.

He lifted his head, saw me and waved.

I couldn't help myself. I bolted out from under the archway and straight into his arms.

'Well, this is a nice welcome,' he said, dropping my suitcase with a thud and holding me tight.

I hit him on the arm.

'Ow. What was that for?'

'Are you out of your mind? What did you think you were doing? You saw them last night. We barely got away. How could you be so stupid as to even think about going back there? And for something so unimportant as a bloody suitcase. What were you thinking? Why …?'

He caught my flying hands. I was still feebly slapping at his arms and generally causing him slightly less inconvenience than a mayfly terrorising an elephant.

'I don't know, Cage, I turn my back on you for one night and standards plummet. Did you know you split an infinitive back there?'

99

'That's not the only thing I'll split,' I said, struggling to repossess my own hands. 'What were you think …?'

'Let's not discuss it here in public,' he said, taking my suitcase in one hand and me in the other. 'Good God, you're frozen. Where's your coat?'

'I forgot it,' I said in a small voice.

'Yes, that's what every noble rescuer wants to hear. That he's risked life and limb rescuing his princess and the next morning the daft bat goes out without her coat and dies of pneumonia.' He shrugged off his coat and placed it over my shoulders. It was very warm and very heavy.

'Thank you,' I said in an even smaller voice.

It soon became apparent my coat wasn't the only thing I'd forgotten. We stood on the top step. And stood …

'Come on, Cage, unlock the door. It's freezing out here'.

'Um …'

He sighed. 'You forgot your key as well, didn't you?'

'I might have. A little bit.'

He sighed again and pulled out his wallet. 'Close your eyes.'

'Why?'

He took out his credit card. 'So you don't see this next bit.'

'What are you going to do – bribe it to open?'

'I gave you my coat, Cage. Can we dial back on the sarcasm, please?'

'Sorry.'

'So I should think. Just close your eyes will you, before I'm accused of corrupting you even further.'

'What are you going to do?'

There was no answer.

'Jones?'

There was no answer.

Alarmed, I opened my eyes to find myself alone on my doorstep. Michael Jones was inside filling the kettle. No one should have to put up with this sort of thing. I stepped inside, closed the door and laid his coat over the back of the sofa. 'How did you do that?'

'Neatly and with great skill,' he said. 'Can you check your suitcase? I think I got everything, but things were a little confused and they seemed to want me to leave as quickly as possible.'

I unzipped it and rummaged. 'Yes, everything's here.'

'Good, because I really didn't want to have to go back there. I have to say, Cage, I don't know what on earth possessed you to stay there in the first place.'

'Well, it was so pretty and ...'

'*Pretty*?'

'Well, yes. It was like a picture on a chocolate box. All those little cottages, and the thatched roofs, and the gardens were so neat, and the pub was lovely and ... what? Why are you staring at me like that?'

'Cage, it was an awful place. It was dirty, run-down, there was rubbish everywhere, the houses were falling down, and far be it from me to cast aspersions upon our country cousins, but the whole grungy bunch of them looked as if they'd been marrying their own brothers for generations. I kid you not, I saw sheep up there that took more pride in their appearance.'

'No, it wasn't like that at all. It was picture perfect. She said it was part of the covenant. They looked after the stones and the stones looked after them.'

'The stones are damaged,' he said quietly, filling the teapot.

'What? I know you hit one ...'

'We did. The blocky one on the end – but the other two don't look good either. Although I'm not sure that was anything to do

101

with us. Looks as if the whole lot could come down any moment. They must have been very unstable. You could say we did them a favour. They were an accident waiting to happen.'

I was thinking. The covenant had been broken. The stones had not received their payment. Their strength had not been renewed. They'd stood outside of time for so long and now time had rushed back in. The ceremony had failed and now the village was failing too. With luck, never to be restored. I found I wasn't sorry.

'Well, thank you anyway,' I said.' Thank you for going back for my things.'

'That reminds me,' he said, opening his wallet again and passing me my credit card. 'I persuaded the young girl to give me this back. That was good thinking there, Cage. Sometimes I think you're not as away with the fairies as you'd like the world to believe. Good to see you utilising modern skills.'

'Can you teach me that trick with the credit card? When you opened my door.'

'No.'

'But isn't that a modern skill?'

'No.'

He passed me my coffee.

'Well, thank you for rescuing me.'

'I did, didn't I?' he said, looking pleased. 'I'm a real prince.'

'A real prince would teach me the trick with the credit card.'

'How short lived is gratitude,' he said, looking mournful. 'Shall I take your case upstairs?'

'No. I'm going to throw it all away. I don't want it in my house.'

'I risked life and limb for that.'

'You just said they couldn't wait to get it and you out of there.'

'And you were worried enough to stand out in the freezing cold waiting for me so shall we both stop talking?'

He was right. I rummaged until I found Ted's photo and set it up in its old place on the shelf. I never even noticed the cracked frame. That wasn't important any longer. I sat beside him on the sofa with my mug of coffee. 'Well, thank you anyway.'

'You're welcome. Glad to be home?'

I nodded.

He glanced upwards towards the light fitting. 'I meant what I said about the surveillance stuff. That's my problem. You don't have to worry.'

'Again, thank you.'

He turned to look at me. 'I am sorry, Cage.'

We both knew what he was talking about. I blinked back a sudden tear. 'I know. Drink your coffee.'

Chapter Ten

It was wonderful to be home and I was so happy to pick up my quiet life again. I know some people complain of boredom but trust me, boredom is very underrated. I stood in the middle of my little room and inhaled the familiar and well-loved scents of home. It was so good to be back. I decided I would never willingly leave it again. Adventures could happen to someone else somewhere else.

I spent two days cleaning my house from top to bottom, and then sat down with a coffee to enjoy the fresh smells of lavender and lemon. My house isn't large, but it is all mine. I have a long sitting room with a kitchen area at one end, divided by a smart breakfast bar. The walls are a soft cream and the wooden floors a lovely mellow honey colour. There's one bedroom upstairs and a modern bathroom in white and chrome. If I looked out of my windows I could see the castle opposite, dramatic against the sky, with the remains of its old moat fringed by soft willows. My house is a little jewel – the only drawback being the lack of vehicular access. I didn't have a car so this wasn't a problem, but I'd been told delivery men would not love me and refuse collectors would not be my friends, and they weren't. Shopping was a daily occurrence because one bag of food at a time was about all I could carry up the hill. Despite that, I loved my little house. It sheltered me, welcomed me when I'd been away, and kept me warm and dry. I thought it was just perfect.

True, my stairs are only about two feet wide and meander up through the middle of the house and getting anything bigger than a mug of coffee upstairs is almost impossible and anyone larger than me has to turn sideways to get up them, but that's not an obstacle for me so I can safely ignore it.

I made several trips to the shops, restocking the fridge and cupboards. I brought back some fresh flowers to put near Ted's photo. I threw away all the stuff in my suitcase and shoved it back under the bed. Wouldn't it be nice if the nightmare of the last fortnight could be as quickly and neatly put away? Out of sight – out of mind. If only things were that easy. I sighed. Time to get back to life – back to normality – and the best way to achieve that was to behave normally. Ignore the flashbacks. Ignore the dreams. Because, as Jones had said, 'It couldn't possibly have happened, could it?' Time to settle back down again and get on with my life.

I visited the public library, chatted with the staff there, heard all about their Christmases, and came home with an armful of books. Everything was just as it had always been – which was exactly how I liked it. I curled up on the window seat with my books and read away the winter days.

I didn't contact Jones and he didn't contact me. I suspected he was leaving me the initiative and, since I still didn't know how I felt or what I wanted, I was content to leave things as they were for a while.

The weather was cold but sunny and I tried to make sure I went outside every day, either walking around the castle green opposite, feeding the swans and ducks, or walking down into town, across the bridge. I strolled in Archdeacon's Park and admired the early bulbs. I took advantage of the seasonal sales and bought myself some new clothes to replace the ones I'd thrown out. I visited local art galleries and exhibitions. I made sure I kept myself busy and slowly the jangled memories began to fade. I slept better, the bad dreams lessened and I kidded myself I'd put Christmas and its aftermath behind me.

And then, one morning I met my neighbours, Colonel and Mrs Barton who were on their way out. Today must be one of her good days. Her paper-thin colour, a washed-out duck-egg blue, was stronger today and drifted my way when she saw me. The colonel's colour was as dark green and boxy as ever, curled protectively around his wife.

I said good morning and asked if they'd had a nice Christmas.

'Lovely,' said Mrs Barton, her eyes unusually sparkling and focused. 'Apart from all that dreadful weather, of course.'

Her husband turned to her. 'Eh?'

'The snow, dear.'

He laughed. 'What – that little dusting on Boxing Day?'

'No, dear. It came down very heavily – for days – don't you remember?'

I could feel the blood draining from my face. She remembered the snow. No one but me remembered the snow, but Mrs Barton did. I smiled what I hoped was an encouraging smile. 'What snow was that, Mrs Barton?'

She turned to me. '*You* must remember, my dear. All that snow. All that *angry* snow.'

I don't know what the colonel said to that. I know he said something to me and I have no idea what I said to him. I couldn't think at all. Because here was someone who remembered as I did. 'All that angry snow,' she'd said, and she was right. There had been a lot of snow. A lot of angry snow that had suffocated the world in white silence. I hadn't dreamed it after all. Someone else remembered the angry snow.

I remember holding on tight to the iron railings outside my house while I got my breathing back under control. Jones had

106

talked me into believing it was a concussion-induced dream and I'd allowed myself to go along with it. But what if that was the real reality? Was this the dream? Was I, at this very moment, expiring under the weight of all that snow? Were these the last thoughts of my dying brain?

The world whirled around me and for a few moments I experienced pure disorientation. Where was I at this moment? Was it even possible that I was lying in a drug induced coma in the Sorensen Clinic from which I'd never actually managed to escape?

Somehow, I got myself back inside. I shut and bolted the front door and took refuge, as I always did, back in my house. I sat on the sofa and curled into a ball, almost too frightened to move. I was shivering with cold and fear. My thoughts were frightening me and I wondered if I was going insane. Or if I was already insane.

No. *No.* I had to stop this. I had no idea which reality was which and it wasn't something over which I had any control anyway. There wasn't anything I could do except live my life as best I could. Life is valuable and not lightly to be tossed away, as I'd discovered at Greyston. I'd been saved and, in turn, I'd saved someone else. I wasn't going to throw all that away by spending my time crouched in misery at the end of my sofa. Drastic action was called for. Some sort of physical exertion to blast away these dark thoughts.

I couldn't spring clean again. To spring clean a house twice in such a short time was too bizarre even for me. I decided that just for once, the answer lay outside.

The weather was improving. Spring had come early this year. The days were mild and sunny. Early daffodils started to appear in window boxes and the willow trees sprouted soft green shoots. Sap was rising everywhere and mine along with it.

Suddenly, I wanted to be outside. To fill my lungs with fresh air and blow away the winter cobwebs.

I'd seen on the local TV news that the council had opened up the old towpath along the River Rush and it was now possible to walk all the way from Rushford to the coastal port of Rushby. It was eight miles from start to finish, which was too much for me, because that meant it was eight miles back again as well, but I could work up to it slowly. In the meantime, there was a shorter stretch from Rushford to the Whittington Bridge which was three miles there and three miles back. I could walk to the bridge, eat my packed lunch, rest for an hour and then do the three miles back again. I'd probably be exhausted but that wasn't necessarily a bad thing. And it would be good for me to be outside enjoying the spring weather. And a change of scenery would give me something more cheerful to think about. Yes, I'd do the walk to the Whittington bridge.

I picked a Wednesday, because I didn't think there would be too many people around mid-week, packed myself some sandwiches, fruit, crisps, and water, some spare socks, a waterproof and some money for emergencies. Seriously, it looked as if I was setting out for the Arctic. I don't know what I thought was going to happen to me as I strolled along this popular and frequently used footpath, but if anything did then I would be ready for it. I spared a thought for Michael Jones who could probably live on the moon for six months equipped with nothing more than a paperclip and a slab of Kendal Mint Cake.

It was a lovely day. The sun was shining, but it wasn't hot and there was a pleasant breeze to keep me cool. I pulled my door to behind me, waved to Colonel and Mrs Barton as they sat in their window, and set off on what I was calling my Big Adventure.

I picked up the river at the medieval bridge, descended the steps to the path, turned left and set off. The first hundred yards or so were nicely paved. I walked past green-and gold-painted narrow boats with their pots of bulbs blooming away and a ginger cat asleep on the roof in the sun. Their names, picked out in gold and red, glinted in the sunshine. Leon, Lavender, Charlotte, and Valkyrie.

I walked past the old harbour master's cottage, now a small museum, and through the warehouse area. These were big, solid, brick buildings with their names painted in bold black letters across the front. The Victoria Warehouse, the Albert Warehouse, the Bearland Warehouse, and the tiny and still empty Hartland Warehouse at the end. Most of them were now home to trendy coffee shops and inappropriate modern flats.

I walked past the old railway sidings with their rusty rails and derelict engine sheds, also earmarked for development, until finally, around the bend, quite suddenly, there was real countryside.

I'd come about a mile and a half. Time for a break. I stood a while, drinking water, leaning on a gate, and watching lambs bouncing around the fields as if they hadn't a care in the world. The occasional horse and rider passed me. I stepped aside to give them room and they thanked me. Is it being around horses that makes people so polite?

I was really enjoying myself. This was lovely. I made a deal with myself that every Wednesday, weather permitting, I would go out for a walk. A proper one, with sandwiches and walking boots. Rushfordshire is a lovely county and there were plenty of places I could walk to. There was Pen Tor, up on the moors. Or the higher reaches of the Rush valley. That was very lush and pretty with birches and ferns and cascading waterfalls. Now that I was out and about I could see I spent too much time on my own and inside. And I had definitely been spending far too much time in a dark world that was a thousand miles away from this lovely spring day, full of sunshine and prettiness and lambs and nice people and their horses.

I marched along, developing a rhythm, that, while it didn't exactly eat up the miles, at least ate up the yards. My backpack was heavy but that was because I'd brought enough food for four people. It would be considerably lighter on the way home. I was beginning to feel hungry and looked forward to arriving at the Whittington Bridge, which I thought I could see in the hazy distance. I would pass under the bridge and then there was a set of steps cut into the embankment. My plan was to climb up, have a look at the view – they said you could see the sea from there – find a pretty spot and substantially lighten the load of my backpack.

The far side of the river was flat pastureland dotted with cows – the flood plain, but there were woods on this side, ringing with birdsong and the occasional rustle in the undergrowth. Dappled sunshine splashed the path ahead of me. I was enjoying myself so much. This was fun.

The bridge grew larger and closer. It was a Victorian affair, restored when they renovated the towpath, and carried the main railway line from Rushford. The brickwork was a deep purple colour, and it arched beautifully over the river. I could see the reflections of the flickering water on the underside of the roof. The shadows under the bridge looked cool and welcoming. I suddenly realised how hot and tired I was, but I was very nearly at the furthest point of my journey. I heaved my backpack into a more comfortable position and stepped from the warm sunshine into cool shadow.

The world changed.

At first, I thought I'd simply underestimated the contrast between the bright sunshine out there and the sudden darkness here under the bridge. I blinked a couple of times and waited for my eyes to adjust. If they did then it didn't make any noticeable difference. I looked all around me. Nothing but blackness. Thick, heavy blackness.

I remember thinking how remiss of the council not to fit some form of lighting. The tunnel under the bridge was obviously much longer than I expected, so you'd think there would be lights, wouldn't you. If only to stop people like me toppling into the river in the dark.

Blinking had not helped. I wondered if I'd gone blind because to me, darkness is never complete. There are always rich, deep colours within the darkness, swirling and twisting about me. Dark light. But not this time. I wasn't blind but I couldn't see a thing. Except darkness everywhere. The sound of birdsong had died away, along with the gurgling river. I was alone in the silent darkness. My heart began to thump.

I pulled myself together. Really, my nerves were not in a good state at all. Of course I wasn't alone in the dark. I'd walked in – I could walk back out again. All I had to do was turn around and face towards the light. Back from under the bridge and out into the real world of sunshine and birdsong.

I turned around and then I really did start to panic because there was no sunshine. Or birdsong. There was no path back into the real world, just the dark, empty silence all around me. I turned again. And again, spinning around as if I was in some sort of game, and daylight was some mischievous sprite eluding me just for the fun of it.

But there was nothing. I was completely in the dark. And worse – I was lost. Because I'd spun around so many times that I couldn't remember which way I was facing. Where, in all this darkness, was the river? Two steps in the wrong direction could have me falling in and my backpack was heavy and would drag me down. I shrugged it off, hanging it over one shoulder, where I could easily jettison it should I have to, and turned my head this way and that, frantically seeking a lighter patch in this impenetrable darkness.

The sensible part of my mind was telling me that this was ridiculous. I was only underneath a bridge. Just a small bridge carrying a minor railway line over the not hugely wide River Rush. It wasn't exactly the mouth of the Amazon. Fifty feet at the most. There was no way I shouldn't be able to see light at the end of the tunnel. It was impossible. The whole thing was impossible. And ridiculous. And stupid.

And then I had the answer. Of course – for some reason the other end of the tunnel was closed off. That the council hadn't put up barriers was careless in this Health and Safety-burdened world, but these things do happen. There was nothing sinister going on here. All I had to do was calm down and find either the brick wall or the edge of the path – being very careful with that one – and then keep walking until I found the entrance I came in by, which was obviously just around a bend somewhere. Then I could make my way back out. Then I'd have lunch – somewhere in the woods – because once I was out of this place I definitely wasn't coming back in again – and when I was back in the warm, safe sunshine, then I could laugh at myself for being so stupid. I really had to stop thinking bad things all the time. Not everything that happened to me was sinister or evil.

Dragging my feet carefully, keeping all my weight on my back foot and waving my arms around like insect antennae, I inched my way forwards for what seemed like a very long time. Surely, I should have reached my destination – any destination – by now. How big was this bridge?

Suppose it wasn't a bridge at all.

I don't know where that thought came from and I didn't have any time to think about it because away off to my left and ahead of me, I heard a soft sound. The same sound I was making. The sound of someone dragging their feet through loose, dry gravel.

Relief flooded over me. Someone else was in here with me. Someone else was lost too. We'd find our way out together. I opened my mouth to shout, 'Who's there? I'm over here.'

And then every instinct I had said, 'Keep quiet. You don't know what it is yet.'

The smell hit me next. A musty, animal smell. Like the lion house at the zoo, but weaker. And stone. I could smell damp stone. And mould. And stale meat. Like an old butcher's shop. This was not a good smell. Not in any way. And whatever it was that was making that smell was in here with me. In the dark.

I froze, standing rigid, trying to breathe very, very quietly.

That dragging noise came again, followed by another gust of mouldy stone smell.

I turned my head slowly, trying to identify the source of the sound so I could run in the opposite direction. Run as fast as I could. Run away from this place and never come back. Never mind the river – possibly falling into the Rush and letting it carry me away might be the best thing that could happen. At least I'd be out of this place.

From out of the darkness came a long, low grinding sound, like two giant rocks rubbing together. I felt all the short hairs on the back of my neck stand on end and my skin tightening as my body, entirely independently of me, moved into fight or flight mode. Flight would be my preference.

I stood as silently as I could, unmoving, hoping against hope that whatever it was would miss me in this impenetrable blackness and just … go away.

And so, for a moment, it seemed that it would. That long, dragging sound came again, but further off this time. Over to my left and heading away from me. Was it moving away? The temptation to turn and run in the opposite direction was overwhelming, but I swallowed it down and stayed put.

Time passed. Nothing happened. I made up my mind that if the next sound was even further off then I would wheel about and run. Blindly, yes, but arms outstretched and willing to take my chances.

I waited, heart pounding, in the dark. I couldn't believe this was happening. One moment I was out in the sunshine and birdsong and the next moment I was in the dark, lost and terrified. This was another world. Two short steps had taken me from my world to this. And something was in it with me. And even if I managed to evade it – whatever it was – how would I ever get back? Was I trapped in here forever?

I didn't know what to do. Was it safer to move or to stay put?

My mind flew back to my childhood and I remembered being with my dad in his shed at the bottom of our garden. That had been a magical place, full of golden light, where he worked with the wood he loved so much, and I loved to help him. I would hold his pencils and screwdrivers, triumphantly producing each as required, and we would chat – not about anything in particular, but just chat. I heard him now, clear as day. 'If in doubt, lass, do nowt.'

Good advice. I was in trouble. Let's not do anything to make it worse. So I stood in the dark and waited.

For a very long time, nothing happened at all. No sound of movement. Even the smell faded. Or, more likely, my nose was getting used to it. Had whatever it was gone away? I waited, straining my ears for even the slightest sound to indicate that whatever was here with me was still here. I could hear nothing. I could see nothing. Had my immobility worked? Had whatever it was gone away? I had no idea where it could possibly have gone to, nor did I care. Just as long as it had gone. Or was it, like me, just standing in the dark … and waiting …?

If that was indeed the case then I was in trouble because I couldn't stand here forever. I would become hungry, thirsty, tired. I might even just sneeze and then whatever it was would be upon me. I felt the panic welling up inside me. I couldn't breathe properly. The urge to run was becoming unbearable. To run and run. I struggled to remember my dad and his shed. To hear his voice and watch his hands as he measured off a piece of the wood, but like everything else, that golden vision had faded into the dark.

I made up my mind. I would move. I wouldn't run. That would be foolish. I would pick up each foot and place it as carefully and silently as I could and I would keep doing that until … until I found my way to safety.

I lifted my left foot and placed it, flat-footed, about six inches in front of me. Nothing happened, so I transferred my weight and did it again. With my right foot, this time. Again, nothing happened. The silence around me was complete. Whatever it was had gone. It must have. Surely nothing could stand that silently for that long.

I lifted my left foot again and took another step forward and this time my foot encountered an obstacle. Something rolled away with a hollow clatter that sounded horribly loud in this dark space.

I froze again, heart hammering in my chest. If there was something here it couldn't fail to have heard that.

And then …then … I felt a hot breath on my cheek. The smell enveloped me.

It – whatever it was – had moved soundlessly in the dark and was standing right beside me.

I gathered myself to run. Where to was no longer important – I just had to get out of this place before I started to scream and scream – and then something took hold my arm in a grip of stone. I felt claws.

I had a sudden picture of a cold and desolate world. A barren and empty land, lying silently under dark skies and dead stars. A place where long ages of nothing had passed very slowly. A cold and lonely world that yearned for warmth and light and yet, at the same time, harboured a deep and abiding hatred for that same warmth and light. Despair and longing battled for supremacy. A longing for the world of people. And a deep and terrible hunger.

Something snuffled in my hair. It was horrible. I could feel something warm running down my face. But it broke the spell. I could move. I screamed and struggled, hurting my arm quite badly and not noticing at the time, but most importantly, I remembered to shout for help.

'Help. Help. Anyone. Help.'

My voice reverberated, bouncing off distant walls and I could tell from the echoes I was in a huge space.

The thing beside me growled, a low, liquid, bubbling sound and a deep, deep voice, very close to my ear, slowly rumbled, 'Silence.'

Not a chance. I struggled even harder, twisting myself in its grip, shouting, 'Help. Help. For God's sake, someone help me. I'm under the bridge.'

'No. You are in my realm now. You belong to me.'

Something warm, wet and rough, like a giant cat's tongue, licked my face. From my chin, up past my nose, up my forehead and into my hair.

'Taste good ...'

I screamed and struggled some more, battering at something with my fists, kicking out as hard as I could. I had nothing left to lose. The grip on my arm never slackened and I could feel warm wetness running down my arm. I was bleeding which wasn't such a good move as it turned out. There was a massive snuffling noise in the dark and the voice took on a new and frightening note.

'Blood ...'

I kicked out wildly and all that happened was that I hurt my foot, screaming all the time. 'Help. Help me. Someone help me. Please,' and knowing all the time that no one would come. That something had hold of me in the dark and, I was certain, was going to eat me.

I was flailing helplessly with my other arm, hitting out at something that felt like a long-haired, bristly doormat. And smelled like one, too. It held me close, crushing my body against its own, snuffling around my face and neck. It was looking for my throat. I felt teeth. The smell was overwhelming and made my head spin. I kept trying to turn my face away. All the time hitting and kicking and struggling to be free.

'Hunger ...'

I was panting with effort and terror. 'No. Stop it. Let me go.'

It said one last time, 'Hunger ...' and I knew it was about to bite me. To sink its teeth into my throat and drink my blood.

I gathered myself for one last shriek. 'Help me. Someone. Please help me.'

The echoes were still bouncing off the walls when the air changed. Stinging dust blew into my eyes and the whole area erupted in a vast sheet of bright, silver light that blinded me.

I screamed again, convinced that this was the end and squeezed my eyes tight shut. Painful tears ran down my cheeks.

The thing that was holding me bellowed and not only released me, but actually pushed me away. I staggered backwards, caught my heel on a rock, felt the ground disappear beneath my feet and lost my footing. For a moment, I floundered on the edge of nothing, disoriented, blind, and terrified, and then a hand caught mine. A warm, human hand. A voice said, 'Whoops-a-daisy, I've got you,' and suddenly I was standing on firm ground.

A hand clapped my shoulder, not ungently, and a man's voice said, 'I'd just hang on a moment, if I were you. There's a troll to deal with here. Keep your eyes closed if it helps.'

So, of course, I opened them immediately.

Chapter Eleven

I don't know why, but I was clinging onto my backpack for dear life. As if a pile of sandwiches and a couple of bottles of water were my dearest possessions, although at that moment I think they might have been. They represented the safe and the familiar. And believe me, at that moment, I really needed safe and familiar.

I was standing in a vast cavern. Huge stalactites hung from the ceiling and even mightier stalagmites thrust themselves up from the floor. Bright silver light winked off jagged crystals and veins of what looked like gold ran through the rock like shimmering ferns. It was all quite beautiful. Until I looked down.

I was standing on people. Or rather, I was standing on their bones. The rock I thought I had dislodged was someone's skull. I'd kicked someone's skull. Scattered all around were long bones, rib cages, pelvises, and draped across a rock like an ornament, a spinal cord. Most of the floor was covered in dead people's bones – to a depth of several feet in places. It looked as if vague attempts had been made to stack the skulls together or to lay out the long bones in a crude pattern, but not everywhere. As if whoever had started this gruesome work had lost interest and wandered off to do something else instead.

All of the bones had long scoremarks. Or, as something inside me said, teeth marks. I stared, too uncomprehending to take it all in. These people had been eaten. All of the people I

119

was standing on had been eaten. I could feel my mind spiralling down towards hysteria.

A pain-filled bellow filled the cave, hurting my ears. The ... creature ... I still couldn't see it clearly, cowered in a dark corner, enormously long arms wrapped around its head.

'A troll,' he'd said. I'd seen pictures of trolls. Great lumpy misshapen beasts, ugly and stone-like. This one was ginger and hairy with long arms, short legs and what might once have been a great, bulbous belly but now hung shrivelled and empty. It sagged and swung with every movement. I couldn't see its face – it was cowering in the corner, hiding its eyes from the bright, unaccustomed light.

'No light.'

'Yes light,' said a figure I could only see in silhouette, so brilliant was the light emanating from him. I'd thought Jones's colour was bright but this was incandescent. A brilliant, pure silver that penetrated every corner of this cave and cast long indigo-blue shadows across the floor.

He was waving his arms around. 'What are you doing, Þhurs? This was not the agreement. You should die for this.'

The thing moaned. 'Hunger ...'

'Tough. You don't carry people off and eat them. That was the agreement.'

'Did not.'

'Don't lie to me, Þhurs, you snot-laden doormat. I keep telling you – you have to stop carrying off young women. They don't like it. You agreed. You signed the treaty in your own snot.'

'She came to *me*.'

There was a pause. 'Did she now? Stay there, Þhurs. Don't even think about moving or I'll shove lightsticks up your nose until your brain fries.'

The creature groaned again and turned its face to the wall.

The figure stepped out of its own light, turned to me and stared for a very long time.

I stared back, relatively brave as long as he was between me and what was looking increasingly like a giant orangutan with any number of personal hygiene issues.

His colour was so thick it was almost solid. I could barely see through it and he wore it like banner. It streamed behind him, a metallic silver, bright and clear. Unbelievably, like a medieval knight, he carried a sword, although this knight was dressed in army surplus combat trousers, a khaki T-shirt, and a very good pair of boots. I'd never seen a colour like his before. To be honest, I'd never seen a man carrying a sword before, either. Only on a TV or cinema screen, anyway.

'Well?' he said, looking me up and down, 'and what are you calling yourself these days?'

I was suddenly angry. Still grateful, obviously, but angry as well. 'I don't call myself anything. I have a name.'

'Which is?'

I clutched my backpack. If the worst came to the worst, I would throw it at him and run.

'Elizabeth Cage.'

He narrowed his eyes. 'And is that your real name?'

'Of course.'

'Are you sure?'

'Yes. Why?'

He sighed. Suddenly, I don't know why, he reminded me very much of Michael Jones. Perhaps all men have that sigh.

'Has no one ever told you never to tell anyone your real name?'

I blinked. 'Why ever not?'

'It's too dangerous. When you tell someone your real name you give them power over you.'

I considered this. The government, the council, authority in general, Dr Sorensen in particular, yes, they all knew my real name and they all had power over me. He wasn't wrong. 'What's your name then?'

'You can call me Iblis.'

'That's not your real name, is it?'

'Of course not.'

I looked around for the way out. 'I'd like to leave.'

'I don't blame you but why did you come here in the first place?'

'I didn't,' I said indignantly. Was he another of these 'blame the victim' people? 'I was on the towpath. I walked under the bridge. Everything went dark and here I was, with that ...'

'Troll,' he said helpfully. 'One of the Jötnar. His name is Þurs. You pronounce it Thurs. As in Thursday.' He raised his voice. 'And he's broken the treaty.'

There was a muffled moan from the back of the cave. It sounded very much like 'lonely' to me and I suddenly wanted to be out of here and back in the warm sunshine. Or preferably at home, which I was almost certain I would never leave again.

'Give it a rest, Þurs, you broke the treaty. I'll get back to you in a moment.'

He turned back to me. 'Would you like me to show you the way out?'

'Thank you. I really want to be out of here.'

'Yes, most of Þurs's dates feel that way. May I take your arm?'

'Um ... yes. Thank you.'

He shouted over his shoulder, 'I'm coming back, snot-snorter. You'd better make sure you're here when I do. This way, Elizabeth Cage.'

He took my arm. The creature lowed again but we were moving away. The light from his colour showed the way. We crunched over more people.

'Sorry about this,' he said. 'Unavoidable, I'm afraid. He does have a go at clearing up every now and then, but he has the attention span of a flea. In fact, we reckon it's his fleas that do his thinking for him.'

'We?'

He ignored the question. 'Just watch your feet here.'

I watched my feet there, slipping and sliding over bones, shredded clothing, helmets, shields, the occasional weapon. Jewels and golden ornaments winked in his light and I had absolutely no desire to investigate.

'Ready?' he said. 'Close your eyes.'

'Why,' I said suspiciously.

'To protect your eyes because the sunlight will be very bright.'

It was. I put my hand up to shade my eyes and he manoeuvred me against the wall. 'Keep them closed for a moment. Stay here. I'll be right back.'

His footsteps faded away.

I stood as instructed, more grateful for the warm sunshine than I had ever been in my life. The river gurgled past. Birds sang. Occasionally I heard a car in the distance.

I breathed deeply and tried not to think too hard about what had just happened. A troll? He'd said 'troll'. Had he been joking? But I'd seen that giant gingery figure, felt his animal breath, smelled his smell, been enveloped in his mucus. All I knew about trolls was that they lived under bridges. I couldn't

123

help feeling it would have been useful to have remembered that before walking under this one, but I'd walked under bridges before and nothing had happened. And I knew they weren't very bright as a species, habitually being outwitted by small billy goats and hobbits, as well as turning into stone at daybreak.

'All right?' Iblis said suddenly at my elbow and frightening me to death. 'Sorry. Didn't mean to scare you.'

'Where did you go?'

'I just wanted to have a quick word with Mr Congeniality back there and to make sure the doorway was well and truly shut.'

I don't know what made me say it. 'You didn't hurt him, did you?'

'Why would you care?'

'Because, 'I said, 'I don't know if you heard, but the last word he said, as we left the cave, was "lonely".'

Now he really looked at me, up and down, examining my appearance. Since he was doing it to me, I felt it wouldn't be impolite to do the same to him.

He was very tall. As tall as Michael Jones but very much slimmer. In fact, he was built like a whippet. In contrast to his military get up, his long white-blond hair fell to his shoulders. But it was his eyes. You could lose yourself in those deep, grey eyes, and I was willing to bet any number of young women had already done so.

He stood grinning at me, eyebrows raised, waiting for me to lose myself in his eyes.

I grinned back. I'd had an unpleasant experience, but now that I was back in the light – back in the real world – memories of the fear were fading fast. I wondered how much of that was to do with this young man standing before me. If, indeed, he was a man ...

'Are you human?'

He stopped dead and stared, but his eyes were laughing at me. 'Wow. That's rude. What sort of question is that to ask on a first date?'

'So you're not.'

'I didn't say that.'

'Yes, you did, really. The correct answer is "Of course I'm human. What sort of question is that to ask on a first date?"'

'Well, obviously that's what I meant to say. I was just so taken aback by the rudeness of your question. Are you?'

I stepped back. 'Am I what?'

'Are you human?'

'Of course I am. What sort of question is that to ask on a first date?'

'In your case, a perfectly reasonable one. Scores, sometimes hundreds, of people pass safely under that bridge every day but not you. Why not?'

'I don't know,' I said, suddenly tired and taking refuge in tears. 'It was a horrible experience. I just want to go home.'

'Of course you do,' he said, taking my arm again. 'Where do you live?'

I nodded upriver. 'Rushford.'

'Well that's quite a long way off – how about a bit of a sit down and a cup of tea before you set off?'

Suddenly, that seemed a very good idea. My legs were trembling and there was no way I could manage the long walk home. I hadn't even had lunch yet.

'OK,' I said, thinking he'd take me to a café or something up on the Whittington road.

Instead, he plunged off into the woodland. 'This way.'

Michael Jones had once commented severely on my willingness to go off with strange men in uncertain circumstances. Now would be a good time to pay heed to his warnings. So obviously I didn't, following Iblis through the beech trees. We didn't go too far – just into a small clearing, which was apparently where he lived. A small tent was pitched and a string of washing hung between two trees. A small circle of stones held the ashes of a dead fire.

I stared around. 'You live here?'

'Yeah. Why not? It's a nice place.'

It was indeed. A very nice place. The unfurling new leaves gave the light a soft, green quality. Dappled sunlight filtered through the branches. Somewhere a dove cooed. Apart from woodland noises, everything was silent and peaceful.

He was bustling about. 'Sit down. Do you want some tea?'

Since this would involve him making and lighting a fire and fetching water from somewhere before even beginning to make it, I declined politely. 'I only need a moment. Just to pull myself together.'

'Sure. Make yourself at home. That rock over there is particularly comfortable.' In one fluid movement, he crossed his legs and sat down on a carpet of crispy beech leaves.

I made myself comfortable on the appropriate rock. 'Thank you, although now I feel a little guilty at leaving my host sitting on the ground. How long have you lived here?'

He seemed vague. 'I'm not sure. Quite some time. You lose track after a while.'

'I can imagine. Do you live here all year round?'

He nodded. 'It's nice in winter.'

I remembered what Mrs Barton had said and took a chance. 'Even after all the snow last winter?' and watched him very carefully.

Not a flicker. 'Well, there wasn't that much was there? It was all gone the next day.'

Another vote for Jones's reality and I was more confused than ever so I changed the subject.

'How do you eat?'

'Oh, foraging, living off the land, all that sort of thing.'

I suspected these were grand words for petty theft and poaching, but that was his business and nothing to do with me.

'Well, thank you for rescuing me.'

'My pleasure, Elizabeth Cage.'

'How did you know I was there?'

'I heard you screaming. You have a very loud scream, you know. They probably heard you in Rushford.'

I looked around. 'In that case, where are they?'

He laughed. 'It's three miles. Give them time.'

I shook my head. 'You're not going to tell me anything, are you?'

'Fair's fair. You're holding back as well.'

I nodded reluctantly and he grinned at me. He really had a very nice smile. I couldn't help myself. I smiled back.

'That … thing?'

'Yes?'

'Who – what was he?'

'Oh, you don't want to worry too much about him. That's just old Þhurs. He's a bit of a remnant. Left over from the Old Days.'

His assumption I would know what he was talking about was both flattering and unhelpful.

'What was he doing under that bridge? Should we report it to the authorities?'

There was a strange moment. I almost expected him to say, 'Sweetheart, I *am* the authorities,' as Michael Jones had once said to me, but he simply said, 'Where did you expect him to live?'

127

'Well, not under a bridge where everyone walks.'

'Well, that's rather the point of lurking under a bridge, isn't it? There's no point in hanging around a place where no one ever goes.'

'But everyone walks under that bridge. It's a proper footpath.'

'Yes, that's quite interesting, isn't it?' he said. 'Everyone walks there but only you manage to cross over into the realm of the Jötund.'

He stared at me, inviting me to tell him how I'd done it and I would probably have done so if I'd actually known how I'd done it, but I didn't so I changed the subject.

'I ought to go. Thank you.'

He waved that away. 'You've already thanked me.'

'That was for rescuing me. This is thanking you for your hospitality.'

'Ah, again, you're welcome. I'll walk you back to the towpath.'

'What about ...?'

'Old Þhurs? What about him?

I said slowly, 'He's all alone.'

'Yes. He's a troll. They like it that way.'

'No,' I said quietly. 'No, he doesn't.'

'Well, yes, he likes some company, obviously. Young and female if he can get it, but sadly for everyone, his dates never end well. Why? Do you feel sorry for him?'

'Yes, yes, I do, a little. He's old and the world has moved on. He's been left behind.'

'Haven't we all?' he said lightly, and moved on before I could consider his words. 'I don't know how you managed to find your way into his cave. I rather suspect you're ... different.'

128

'Not really,' I said, getting to my feet. 'I'm actually rather ordinary, you know. What will happen to him?'

'Þhurs? I'll have a quick word and tell him to be more careful in future. Although to be fair, if you wandered into his lair, you were fair game.'

'I didn't wander anywhere,' I said indignantly. 'I was on the towpath. All I did was walk under a bridge.'

'And in this country trolls don't live under bridges?'

'What? Every bridge?'

'Well, no, not every bridge obviously. Not any more, anyway, but a few do. They like to live at the water's edge, of course.'

'Why?'

'It's where the land meets the water. Where the boundaries are blurred. Where two worlds connect. That's where you usually find a troll.'

'Really?'

'No, not these days, so don't worry about it.'

'Too late.'

'You'll be fine,' he said airily. 'Although you might want to be a bit more careful in future. Just in case.'

'I will,' I promised, resolving never to walk under a bridge again.

'This way then,' he said, and we set off through the beech wood again. Back the way we'd come. The woods smelled green and moist and his footsteps made no sound.

Back on the towpath, we paused. He held out his hand. 'Nice to meet you today … Elizabeth Cage.'

I took it. 'And you too, Mr Iblis. And please don't be too hard on …our friend. It wasn't his fault I wandered into his lovely home.'

He smiled that smile again. 'Take care,' and before I could say anything else, he disappeared back towards the bridge.

I turned to go and then had a sudden thought. He was living up there in the woods, all alone. That must be tough, even in this good weather, which wouldn't last long, because this was England. I had a picture of him sitting under dripping branches, the sound of rainfall pattering all around him, cold, wet, and hungry. He'd saved me from being eaten. I owed him.

I set off back to his little camp, moving quickly because I wanted to be gone before he came back. I pulled out the sandwiches, fruit, crisps, chocolate and water and laid it all out neatly on his rock. Then, embarrassed at what I'd done, I grabbed my backpack and ran away.

Chapter Twelve

I refused to race back to Rushford in a panic. Besides, I was too tired, so I took my time getting back. Standing on the towpath, I looked down river. The Rush flowed placidly under the bridge. As I watched, two adults, a small boy and a very large, muddy dog passed beneath it with no ill effects whatsoever. I sighed and turned to go home.

The sun was still shining and there were enough people around, sitting on the bank, fishing, or walking their dogs for me to feel quite safe, but I was tired. I stopped frequently to rest, staring out at the silent river flowing past on its way to the sea. People nodded as they walked by because there's something shared about walking for pleasure. People greet each other. It's nice. I walked quietly along the sunny bank and memories of a dark place and its sad and lonely occupant began, slowly, to seem unreal.

The sun was just above the horizon as I made my way back up the hill to Castle Close. Long purple shadows stretched across my path. I crossed under the archway – not without a little trepidation, it should be said, but it seemed to be peril free. Sadly, the same could not be said of my front steps. A figure was sitting there, waiting for me. For one moment, I thought it was Michael Jones and my heart leaped. But only for one moment. It was Iblis. How could he know where I lived?

He stood up as I approached and came down to meet me. He looked so serious that I began to panic all over again. 'What is it? Why are you here? Is it Þhurs?' I remembered the family with the small boy and the big dog. 'Did he eat someone?'

He said heavily, 'You left me an offering.'

I couldn't think what he was talking about. 'I … what?'

'You left me an offering.'

'No, I didn't. I left you my lunch.'

'Same thing. You laid an offering on my altar.'

'No, I laid my lunch on a rock.'

'For me.'

'Of course for you. You're homeless.'

'I said I lived in the woods, not that I was homeless.'

'All right, so you're not homeless and I've offended you. I'm sorry.'

'You don't understand. You left me an offering. I am bound to you.'

'No, you're not,' I said, wishing he wasn't between me and my house.

'The Lore is very clear on this point.'

'What Law?'

'Not Law. Lore.'

'All right – what Lore?'

'The Lore that says offerings must be paid for.'

'You don't have to pay me.'

'I have no choice.'

I thought quickly. 'All right. Fifty pence.'

'What?'

'My lunch. The offering you say I left you. Give me fifty pence and all debts are cancelled.' I held out my hand.

'I don't have fifty pence.'

'Well, give me what you do have.'

'My service. It's all I have.'

'I don't want your service.'

132

'You don't have any choice in the matter. Any more than I have any choice. We're bound to each other.'

I didn't like the sound of that at all. 'For how long?'

'Until the debt is repaid.'

'How long will that be?' My voice began to rise in frustration.

'How should I know?'

I was tired and I just wanted a bath. 'Why don't you know? You're the one standing on my doorstep spouting about debts and Lore.'

'Mrs Cage, is everything all right?'

I'd been so busy trying to get rid of the handsome young man standing outside my house that I hadn't heard Colonel Barton's front door open. He stood on his top step, his face concerned, clutching his phone in case of emergencies.

I made myself relax and smile. 'No, everything's fine, Colonel.'

'Yes,' said Iblis, smiling that smile of his. 'No need for alarm, Venerable One.'

The colonel blinked and I decided I'd had enough for one day.

'Get inside,' I said, pushing Iblis up the steps.

It was only as I was ushering him through the door that I wondered whether he had to be invited inside. Like a vampire. In which case, I'd just done something stupid. I mentioned this to him.

He frowned. 'I'm not a vampire. Why would you think I'm a vampire?'

'I don't know,' I said hastily, since he seemed very offended. 'If you're not a vampire, what are you?'

'I'm Iblis,' he said simply. His silver colour boiled around him, restless and never still. But he meant me no harm – I was sure of it.

'Look, it's been a long day. Why don't you just go home and we'll pretend all this never happened.'

He threw himself onto the sofa and looked around. 'Nice. But small.'

I said pointedly, 'Big enough for one.'

He linked his hands behind his head. 'But where would you live?'

'Look,' I said, politely and reasonably, because that was how I'd been brought up. 'Am I in any danger?'

'Not that I know of.'

'Then you don't need to be here in my home, surely.'

'But I am bound to your service.'

'Then suppose I ask you to leave me. To return to your own home.'

'How can I serve you from there?'

'What exactly does this service entail?'

'Anything you want.'

I waved my arms in exasperation. 'But I don't want anything.'

We were going round in circles.

'Look Mr Iblis, whatever it takes to release you – consider it done. I release you.'

'You can't,' he said.

'I just have.'

'Not that simple.'

'You can't just move in with me.'

'Why not?'

I struggled for words. This day was getting on top of me. I'd met a troll, nearly been eaten, and now a handsome young man

134

was proposing to live with me. I waved my arms in exasperation at his failure to see my point of view.

'Why not? Because I live alone. Because people would talk. Because I don't want you here.'

I'd lost him. He was prowling around the kitchen, his movements sharp and fast. He reminded me of quicksilver. 'Shall I cook for you?'

He lived in the woods. Off the land. I wasn't yet ready for squirrel or hedgehog in my diet. 'Thank you, no. I'm very tired. It's been a long day. I'm going to have a bath and go to bed.'

He was already heading towards the door to the stairs. 'I will prepare a bath fit for a queen. With unguents.'

And then I got it. 'You're winding me up, aren't you?'

'Well … duh … you should have seen your face. When did you twig?'

'The unguents were a step too far.'

He was very close, smiling down at me. 'They needn't be.'

I slapped his arm. 'Pack it in. Why are you here?'

'To serve you.' He held up a hand. 'Before you begin fibrillating again – I can do that from a distance. You have only to call.'

'Thank you,' I said, resolving never to call. I had a very strong impression this young man could be more trouble than he was worth.

'And if I'm to be in Rushford then I need to pay my respects.'

'To whom?'

He didn't answer directly. 'This is not my place. This place belongs to another. I must pay my respects as a courtesy. And you must come with me.'

I said warily, 'Why?'

'She will want to see you.'

135

'Why?'

He smiled that smile. 'Who wouldn't?'

I always thought I wasn't susceptible to flattery but, apparently, I needed to work on that because instead of ushering him firmly to the door, I said, 'When?'

'Now,' he said, seizing my hand.

I tried to pull away. 'But I'm hot and dirty …'

'She won't mind.'

'She – whoever she is – might not, but I do. And it's not very respectful to turn up dripping with troll snot, is it?'

'Good point,' he said, settling back on the sofa and picking up the remote. 'Fifteen minutes.'

I made him wait twenty. I could see he meant me no harm but he was definitely someone I needed to stay on top of. If you see what I mean.

We left the house together. I no longer dripped with troll snot. In fact, as he informed me, I smelled quite nice.

'It's the unguents,' I said, locking the door behind me.

'You don't need to do that,' he said, smiling. 'Your house is warded. No one can get in unless you want them to.'

'Does that include you?'

'You have only to tell me to go.'

'I did tell you to go. Many times.'

He laughed at me. 'Yes, but you have to mean it.'

'I can't believe no one has ever brained you with a brick.'

He laughed again. 'Once or twice … This way.'

There's an area around the back of the castle known as The Prospect. It's a flat tongue of land where, in the old days, the beacon stood, ready to be lit at the first sight of the French, the Scots, the Roundheads, the Yorkists, the Lancastrians, the

Dutch, the Jacobites, the Luddites, the Welsh, the Nazis – I don't know why they didn't keep it permanently lit.

There's still a brazier there, mounted on a high pole and it's occasionally lit for jubilees, coronations or a bit of mischievous arson on a Saturday night. There are also wonderful views out over the Rush as it curls its way through lush meadows on its way to the sea. The council has put half a dozen seats there for everyone to enjoy this pleasant spot.

The last light was streaking the horizon as we approached. Dark clouds raced across a darker sky. Around us the tall trees waved their branches in the rising wind, sighing softly to each other. I could imagine witches swooping low, riding the wind, their hair streaming behind them as they did homage to the moon. On such a night as this, wild things were abroad.

A figure stood at the railings, gazing out into the gathering darkness. I thought it was a man until she turned. She was certainly tall enough. And slim enough. Her hair was knotted tightly at the back of her neck and her face was as hard as iron. I tried not to stare because it was the first time a person's appearance had told me one thing and her colour another. Hard and tight were perfect words to describe her, but I could see her colour – a warm gold, shimmering gently in the gloom. Her colour said soft and gentle, but it was wrapped tightly around her and giving nothing away. There were no swirling shapes to read, no spikes of colour to give me any clues to her thoughts. She was ... encased ... there was no other word for it and completely in control, unlike poor Iblis whose silver colour swirled towards her so far and so fast it nearly left him completely. He loved her. Oh, how he loved her. It was there, plain for me to see. He loved her with everything he had. And it was cruel. His colour rushed towards her, ready to envelop and caress her, as Michael Jones's had once done to me. I pushed that thought away. Her own colour thickened and brightened, strengthening her defences. In vain did the silver mist beat upon it – she would not let him in. After a hopeless minute, it crept back, wounded, and wrapped itself gently around him.

None of this showed in either of their faces and I felt ashamed for having witnessed it.

She stood now with her back to the view, her long coat flapping dramatically in the wind.

'Iblis.'

'Melek.'

They bowed to each other.

'Melek, I recognise and acknowledge your authority in this place.'

'Iblis, I extend to you my welcome and protection.'

They looked at each other for a moment. And very dramatic it was, with the wind in the trees and Iblis's hair streaming around his head.

'So, you have come in from the woods?'

'For a little while.'

'For what purpose?'

'This woman left an offering for me. I am bound to serve her.'

'And you have brought her here?'

'I think you will want to see her.'

'Why?'

'Well, among other things, she entered the realm of the Jötund.'

Some people don't like being discussed as if they're not there but it has never bothered me and I was fascinated by the interaction between them. They were standing close together and where their colours touched, powerful sparks of energy flew off into the wild night. What had I got myself into here?

She turned to me. 'Approach.''

Iblis came and took my arm. He addressed me but his words were for her.

'My apologies, Elizabeth Cage. My colleague was raised by wolves. She would very much like to meet you.'

I stepped forwards. 'Good evening.'

I got nothing from her. Something stirred, but what it was I couldn't have told you. She stared at me, unblinking. I had no clue what she was thinking, but apparently she harboured no ill will towards me because she said, 'Good evening.' There was a pause and then she said softly, 'How are you?'

'Very well, thank you,' I said, briskly. 'And you?'

She smiled. Well, one corner of her mouth turned up. I'd amused her. 'I thank you. I am also well.'

There was a long silence. I could feel Iblis looking from her to me and back again and remembered his interest in me when we first met. If he was expecting some sort of reaction then he was disappointed. Her face and her colour remained unchanged. I could feel the tension between them. And then it was gone.

I offered my hand.

She took it very gently, as if remembering to remember not to wrench my arm out of its socket. 'My name is Melek.'

'I am Elizabeth Cage.'

'Long life and happiness to you, Elizabeth Cage.'

'And to you too.'

She stepped back. That seemed to be it. Meeting over. I was already turning away when she spoke softly. 'You are quite right. He is quicksilver.'

I looked at her, startled.

'But he can be trusted. You will be safe with him.' She raised her voice. 'Iblis – a word.'

139

I wandered a few paces away and pretended to look at the now invisible view. They stood, heads close, talking together and I suddenly thought how alike they were. Like two sides of the same coin. The same stern, sad faces. Yes, as far as I could see she had red hair and his was so blond as to be nearly white, but their build was the same. As was their height. And their eyes were identical – a deep, dramatic grey set beneath thick dark brows shaped like the wings of a bird.

Looking at them together, I suddenly thought: one not as good as she should be and one not as bad as he could be. They were a tragedy waiting to happen. I don't know what put that thought into my head. It had been a long day and I was very tired and more than a little out of my depth. I'd walked miles, been covered in troll snot and met two very strange people. All I wanted was to say goodbye to them, get back to the safety of my house, make a nice mug of cocoa and a sandwich and go to bed.

As if she heard my thought, she turned her head and looked at me. Her colour gave nothing away. Nothing at all. Then she wheeled about, her coat flying, and disappeared into the shadows. I sighed. Very dramatic.

Iblis joined me. 'I am to make you cocoa and put you to bed.'

'You're still winding me up, aren't you?'

'If that is what you would like to believe.'

Chapter Thirteen

Two weeks later and things were calmer.

I'd dismissed Iblis on my doorstep after he'd insisted on accompanying me all the way home. According to him, the apparently respectable town of Rushford was full of peril and fraught with danger as soon as the sun goes down. Once, I would have laughed at him, but over the last year I'd become painfully aware there was a lot more going on around us than most of us are ever aware of. We just live our unknowing lives around it.

I'd had to promise faithfully to call on him should I ever need his assistance. He was mine, he'd said, assuming a dramatically handsome pose on the steps, his eyes laughing at me. In love with another he might be, but quite honestly, I don't think he could help himself. It was part of his charm.

I'd thanked him politely, made up my mind I would never be that desperate, and closed the front door with some relief. Whatever was going on out there, I really didn't want to be a part of any of it. I wanted normality. I wanted ordinary, everyday life. I didn't want the sort of life where a pleasant stroll in the countryside turns into a battle for survival in a troll's cave. And especially, I didn't want the sort of life where the rescuer was only slightly less dodgy than the troll.

It occurred to me that these weird things were happening increasingly frequently. Yes, I'd seen people's colours as a child, and occasionally something had flickered in the corner of my eye which I'd always been careful to ignore, but now things were beginning to happen to me directly. Jones had once asked me if saw dead people and the answer was that yes, sometimes I did, but these days, I seemed to be less of an observer and more of a participant. I often asked myself – were they occurring because I was getting stronger and could see more, or was I becoming weaker and not able to protect myself as well as I used to? Neither option was particularly attractive.

And I was alone again. There'd been no contact with Michael Jones since he'd brought me back from Greyston. I hadn't thought his tactfulness would last this long. It could be because he was off somewhere, working. He led a peripatetic life. He was off somewhere peripateticking. I told myself I wasn't missing him at all.

To keep myself busy, I rejoined the Local History Society. Meetings were held twice monthly in the Reference Library which was part of the castle opposite so it wasn't far to go. My neighbour Colonel Barton was the president and particularly pleased to see me.

'I'm working on a history of Rushford Castle,' he said, 'and I wondered if you'd care to lend a hand.'

'Of course,' I said. 'That sounds exciting.'

He indicated a box full of files, papers and rolled up maps. 'Say that again in thirty minutes.'

Everyone was supposed to have their own little project but I suspected most people came for the company and the very excellent cakes. Except for young Mark who came for even younger Alyson. There were usually about eight of us – sometimes more, sometimes less, but eight seemed to be the regular number.

There was Mrs Painswick, champion knitter and cake-maker. She was a plump, maternal woman, who took very little part in the discussions, seemingly content just to sit, knit and listen. Her main concern seemed to be her daughter, Alyson, whom she watched ceaselessly without seeming to, her orangey colour frequently merging with Alyson's gentle coral.

I worried for the pair of them. It wasn't just that Alyson was here so often on what should be a school day; Mrs Painswick had a clever hand with make-up, but occasionally, when the sun shone through the window and she turned a certain way, you could see the bruises she'd failed to hide. No one ever said anything, but Colonel Barton would be extra assiduous in passing her tea, and everyone chatted gently around her as she knitted furiously. I wondered if the knitting wasn't some kind of displacement activity. I wouldn't be at all surprised if, one day, one of her needles wasn't found rammed into Mr Painswick's left ear.

You didn't need any special gifts, however, to see that most of her attention was for Alyson, a quiet girl with long, pale hair that was almost silver. I was reminded of the description of Elizabeth Woodville, queen to Edward IV, with her infamous silver-gilt hair and all the trouble she caused. Alyson was timid and polite, rarely moved far from her mother's orbit, and spent most of the sessions carefully looking things up in books as young Mark – who invariably sat next to her – took notes on his laptop. I have no idea what their project was – I'm almost certain they didn't either, but I suspected these two hours on a Thursday afternoon, twice a month, were a haven of peace and safety for both mother and daughter.

Moving around the table, there was Mrs Stoppard, the reference librarian who advised us all, and next to her was Mr McClelland, a retired accountant. Her behaviour was never anything other than strictly professional, but it was very obvious to me that they were strongly attracted to each other. Since, however, there was both a Mr Stoppard and a Mrs McClelland, strictly professional behaviour was all they were ever going to get. Her colour was a pinky-fawn and his was a pinky-grey. Occasionally, as one consulted a microfiche file and the other an old newspaper, their colours would reach out and gently touch each other and I would always look away.

Next to Mr McClelland sat one E. Cage, getting stuck into her Rushford Castle project, busy and enjoying herself – and the cake – and on the other side of her was Colonel Barton, himself appreciating a few hours respite from his devoted care of Mrs Barton, whose good days were getting further and further apart.

Our group was completed by Robert Ryder, a sulky young man who so obviously didn't want to be here that I wondered why he bothered. It was only later I discovered he needed to complete a course of study in order to qualify for another course that would get him the qualification he needed.

I would look around us sometimes, wondering what sort of group we were when I was possibly the most normal one there. But they were nice people and I enjoyed it. And yes, I know the whole thing was actually one long tea and cake session, but there was a formal break at half past three when we would ask each other about our week and how our projects were going, and Alyson would smile her pale smile and young Mark would blush and nearly fall off his chair.

Yes, they all had their problems, but on the other hand, no one seemed to be a flesh-eating demon in disguise, and it was so good to do something normal with normal people. Afterwards, I'd help the colonel home with all his paperwork and boxes of materials, wave to Mrs Barton in the window, go home and cook myself egg and chips – the feast of kings – and settle down to watch television for the evening.

I did, more or less, stick to my resolution about getting out of the house on Wednesdays, although I'd learned my lesson about lonely places. I did walk, but I stuck to places where there were always people nearby. I visited local monuments, walked up the river the other way – avoiding all bridges – and enrolled on another Drawing for Beginners course at the library: I hadn't benefited much from the previous one and besides, a lot had happened since then. I even considered a cooking course at the local college. Michael Jones was an excellent cook and it would be nice to be able to meet him on equal terms, and then realised that meant I was considering a future with him in it and I wasn't too sure about that, so I changed my mind.

I read a lot and watched TV in the evenings. I know it doesn't sound exciting but from my point of view no one was trying to eat me or kill me or hold me anywhere against my will, so I was OK with unexciting. Unexciting is good. I don't know why I'm apologising for my lifestyle – it suited me down to the ground. I woke each morning, worked my way through my carefully planned day, and revelled in quiet enjoyment. I had everything I ever wanted. For me, life was good.

And then, I had the dream.

I do dream occasionally and just like everyone else I have the occasional nightmare, but this one was just … weird.

I think everyone always expects strange happenings to take place only in old places. Places with a history. Sinister monks haunting ruined monasteries, or headless ladies drifting sadly through deserted royal palaces, or ghostly battles being fought under empty skies, murders, hauntings, sinister happenings at a crossroads – none of these ever seem to take place in say, bus shelters, or council offices, or housing estates. But that was where I was. In this dream. I was walking down an empty road in a modern housing estate. The street sign was as plain as day – Meadowsweet Road. There was a shiny red post box on the corner. The gleaming black tarmac on the road looked new and the front gardens still had that raw, just planted look about them. I could even see the joins where the lawns had been turfed. There were cars parked in driveways. Basketball hoops hung over garage doors.

There was no one around anywhere. I was surrounded by silence. The sun beat down relentlessly. It was so hot that the new tarmac felt sticky under my feet. The front gardens were too tiny for trees and there was no shade anywhere. I plodded on and on, not knowing where I was going. I was hot and thirsty and alone in this big, modern world. And that was the other thing that was wrong. Everything was just slightly too big. My eyes were level with car door handles. Houses looked enormous. Gates were too big and stiff to open. Mummy and Daddy were always busy. There was no one to play with. I'd left all my friends behind. This new place was boring. I was so hot. And there was no shade.

And then the voice said, 'Hello, little girl.'

I looked up into the sun, shading my eyes. A funny knobbly face, all brown and lumpy, looked down at me.

Mummy says I mustn't be rude but Daddy says I have to tell the truth, so I did.

'Your face is funny.'

'You must be so hot. Why don't you come in here where it's much cooler?'

'Are you stranger danger?'

'No, of course I'm not. That's only for nasty people. I'm not nasty.'

'My mummy says I'm not to speak to strangers.'

'Your mummy didn't mean me. I'm not a stranger. I'm your friend.'

'My friends are a long way away.'

'That is so sad. You poor thing. Never mind. I'll be your friend. Would you like to be mine?'

'I don't know. Maybe.'

'Well, while you think about it why not come in and sit here in the shade. Where it's nice and cool. Look.'

'My mummy …'

'Your mummy will never know. It's my secret place. No one knows it's here. You'll be quite safe and you look so tired.'

'I am sleepy.'

'Of course you are – out in all this hot sunshine. Come into the shade and rest for a moment. Just lie down and sleep … Lie down and sleep …'

The dream shifted. An evil colour was all around me. Strong and hard and malevolent. A thick green, streaked with the brilliant crimson of hate. Something alive and dead at the same time. Something old. I could smell wood – but not good wood, like my dad's old shed. Bad wood. With a rotten heart.

'Where am I? I can't see. Let me out. I don't like it here. I want to go home. I want my mummy …'

A crying child. Cold and terrified. Hurting her hands as she clawed at the walls. In the dark …

I woke in a huge panic, my heart hammering in my chest. My whole body was drenched in sweat and I was all tangled up in the bedclothes as if I'd been struggling. Struggling to get out …

I couldn't bear to be in bed a second longer. I fought my way free of the duvet, wrenched off my unpleasantly damp nightdress and went for a shower, letting the tepid water run down my body, cooling and soothing me.

I dressed slowly, made my rather shaky way downstairs, drew back the curtains to let in the early morning light, boiled the kettle for some tea, and, very unwilling to go back upstairs, switched on the television.

The on the hour news programme had just started and a reporter, his face serious and concerned, was broadcasting from a residential area somewhere.

'The family moved to the Yew Tree Estate just under a week ago, where young Keira Swanson was understood to be settling in well. The estate has plenty of play areas and open spaces and, I understand, police are searching these rigorously. Residents on the estate have been urged to check garages, sheds and outbuildings – anywhere a little girl could have been accidentally locked in. Police and a large group of volunteers from the neighbourhood are out now, combing the area for little Keira who is described as six years old and small for her age.'

They flashed up a photo of a pretty little girl with long dark hair worn in two plaits with pink ribbons.

'Keira was wearing her favourite pink *Frozen* t-shirt and darker pink shorts. Being unfamiliar with the area, it's feared she could have wandered off the housing estate and got lost. Her father raised the alarm last night when she didn't come home for tea. Police began searching the area last night. Now, at sun up, they have been joined by many concerned locals.'

There was TV footage of lines of people spread out across wide meadows, their shadows long before them. Other people were poking in the grass verges, and police dogs with their handlers moved purposefully through the woods. Helicopters swooped overhead.

And then back to the reporter again. They were interviewing a neighbour, a young woman with a little girl, who was saying how shocked they all were. Her husband had joined in the search. 'We moved here because we thought it was safe,' she was saying, shaking her head and clutching her own daughter tightly. The little girl wriggled, but there was no way her mother was letting her go.

I stared at the screen, thinking, as everyone does, poor child. And poor parents. And offering up a prayer for a happy ending.

The reporter was interviewing another neighbour, a middle-aged man this time, who was telling him what a lovely child Keira had been – I noticed they were already speaking of her in the past tense – and how everyone had loved her. Turning to speak to someone else, the reporter moved slightly, revealing the street sign behind him. Meadowsweet Road.

I scrabbled for the remote and turned up the sound some more, listening for all I was worth, my mug of tea cooling in my hand.

The reporter was talking about the housing estate and its occupants.

'Not even completed yet,' he was saying. 'Still several streets and the Community Hall to be built.' Which led him neatly to the community as a whole, which, not unnaturally, was very shocked. There had been many volunteers both from the estate and the surrounding areas.

'Less than one year old, Yew Tree Estate was intended to fulfil the need for affordable local housing. Many families have moved here from neighbouring towns, keen to bring up their families in what was supposed to be a safe, rural environment. There was, initially, some opposition to the houses being sited here – many locals feared for the safety of the old yew tree after which the estate is named ...'

The screen showed an ancient yew, stiff and bristly, its branches sweeping the ground.

'... Environmental officers report that this tree has stood here for at least two hundred years, quite possibly much longer, but planners came up with the novel idea of enclosing the tree – which benefits from a Tree Protection Order – and turning it into a feature. Yesterday it was presiding over a happy area where

149

families would picnic and play together. Today it is a different picture.'

There were more interviews with local people – a farmer, weather beaten and gnarled, two of his sons, not as weather beaten and gnarly as their father, but getting there, the child's headteacher, the vicar – a fine specimen of muscular Christianity with a broken nose, and the elderly, red-faced publican, whose spectacular broken veins were visible, even on TV, and who was providing the refreshments for those involved in the search. The report closed with more shots of people searching a hedgerow and then they moved on to other headlines. I muted the sound, got up for a refill and stared out of the window, thinking hard.

Because now I really was on the horns of a dilemma. I should do something. At whatever the cost to myself, I should tell someone. But who? Who would believe me? If I rang the police and told them I'd had a dream and that I knew where the missing girl was, then their next question would be – so where is she, then? – and when I told them they would just hang up. They might even prosecute me for wasting police time. At the very least they'd assume I was some kind of nutter. They might even send round the men in white coats and I'd had enough of that last year.

But I couldn't get the dream out of my mind. I was right. I knew I was right but how could I convince anyone else of little Keira's location? No one would believe me and I really didn't want to draw attention to myself.

But it's a child, argued the other part of me. You're not important in this. Only you can save her life.

But I don't know anything for certain. It's not as if I've actually seen anything with my own eyes. It's just a dream and when I tell them that, no one will believe me.

Michael Jones would believe me but I didn't know where he was. I hesitated for a moment and then rang his mobile. I rehearsed various greetings and opening sentences and was slightly annoyed to find I didn't need any of them because his mobile was switched off. I fired off a quick email but it came back immediately marked 'message undeliverable'. And I couldn't wait – time was pressing.

I paced again. Jones would have been ideal. He had the authority to see this through. To make people listen. I toyed with the idea of telephoning the police from a local phone box, but then I'd just be another anonymous crank and time was passing. I paced again. There must be something I could do. All I had to do was think of it.

The answer came almost at once. There was someone out there with even more clout than Michael Jones. Someone who would believe me. Someone who could act. Someone who would actually be delighted to hear from me.

Dr Sorensen.

I felt a moment's despair. Would I never be free of this man? I'd only just managed to escape from his influence and if I went ahead with this then I would be voluntarily bringing myself to his notice again. By contacting him now I could be throwing away the freedom I'd gained. I'd worked so hard to hide what I could do. To live a normal life. Every instinct I had said no good would come of this. I would be walking right back into the lion's den, but every human feeling I had said there could be no argument. There was a child's life at stake. The most important thing was to save little Keira. Anything else could be dealt with later. It was my duty to inform the authorities. If they managed to save her then everything would have been worth it. And if I was wrong and she was subsequently discovered safely curled up in a neighbour's garden shed, then all that had happened was that I'd made a colossal fool of myself. With, of course, the bonus of possibly convincing Sorensen that I didn't know what I was talking about after all and was an enormous fake. Looked at like that it was a no-lose situation.

I took a deep breath and picked up the phone and dialled the clinic – a number I knew I'd never forget.

'Sorensen Clinic, good morning.'

I made my voice firm. 'Good morning. Dr Sorensen, please.'

'I'm afraid Dr Sorensen is in a meeting and cannot be disturbed. Can I take a message?'

I'd been expecting this. Dr Sorensen was far too important to take unfiltered telephone calls.

I said, 'Please tell him Elizabeth Cage called,' and replaced the phone, wondering if I'd even have time to put the kettle on.

Only just, as it turned out. He rang back less than three minutes later.

'Mrs Cage? Sorensen here. How are you?'

I didn't waste time with pleasantries. I spoke slowly and clearly, trying to invest my voice with quiet authority.

'Dr Sorensen, please listen very carefully. Time is important. I'm sure you will have seen on the news that a little girl is missing. Please use your authority to direct the searchers to look inside a very large and very old yew tree. It won't be far away. The tree will be enclosed somehow.' No need to tell him of its malevolence. Its spite. Its hatred for all things living. 'The tree is hollow. The little girl is inside the tree. She is trapped and cannot get out. That is all I know. Goodbye.'

'Wait! How do you know …?'

I put down the phone with a trembling hand, trying to convince myself I'd done a good thing, but wondering what on earth would happen next. Would he send someone for me? Would the police turn up? Would he come himself? What was he doing at this moment? Suppose he hadn't believed me. Suppose he didn't act on my information. What if I'd made a mistake? What if it was only a dream after all and I'd done all this for nothing?

I kept the TV on all morning, watching and listening for news. I had no idea what could be happening behind the scenes. I tried to imagine urgent telephone calls being made, decisions being taken at high level, but beyond that I hadn't a clue. Always supposing he'd believed me in the first place.

I paced and paced and wished very much that Michael Jones was here with his casual common sense and matter of fact perspective. The TV chattered on. There were programmes about doing up houses, going to live abroad, discovering hidden treasures in your attic and absolutely nothing about finding the missing Keira.

I couldn't concentrate. I couldn't settle. I switched on my laptop but there was nothing on the news feeds. Surely they must have found her by now. It had been nearly two hours since my telephone call. The tree wasn't that far away. Had I got it all horribly wrong? Had I sent everyone off in the wrong direction? Had I, in fact, distracted them from the real search and just made matters worse?

I was just getting to the stage where I was telling myself I'd done more harm than good and it was a shame I'd ever been born, when the phone rang. I was across the room in a flash. 'Hello?'

'Mrs Cage?'

Well, who did he think it would be?

'Speaking.'

'Philip Sorensen here. I thought you might like to know – they've found her.'

A great wave of relief rushed over me. I had to sit down quite quickly.

'Where?'

His voice was quiet and unemotional. 'Exactly where you said she would be.'

There was a long pause. I was too full of emotion to speak, experiencing a complicated mixture of gratitude and relief that they had found her, and fear for myself and the consequences of what I had done.

'Well done, Mrs Cage, and thank you very much.'

I managed to say, 'Is she all right?'

'Exhausted and dehydrated, but alive.'

I whispered, 'Thank God.'

'Interestingly, she says the tree tried to eat her.' He paused, inviting comment.

I had one last task to perform. I didn't want to. Every word I spoke to him jeopardised the fragile peace I had built for myself, but it had to be done.

I tried to speak calmly but with certainty. 'If you have authority of any kind, Dr Sorensen, have that tree destroyed. That tree *must* come down and make sure they grub out the stump. It is pernicious. The same thing has happened in the past. It will happen again.'

'Mrs Cage, can you tell me how …?'

I hung up, leaned back and closed my eyes, suddenly feeling very cold and very alone.

Chapter Fourteen

The phone rang again about an hour later. I'd been expecting it but it made me jump just the same. I let it ring, still undecided about what to do. I couldn't bring myself to speak to him. It was ungrateful I know, after all he'd done to find Keira Swanson, but I panicked. My instincts still told me to avoid this man.

The phone rang for a long time and then stopped. Ten minutes later it rang again. On and on. I knew I couldn't do this – I had to get out before he came knocking at my door. I grabbed my bag and keys and shot out of the front door. I couldn't run away – I didn't want to do that again – but I could do the next best thing which was to make myself scarce for a while. I'd go shopping. I didn't need anything, but that's not really the purpose of shopping, is it?

I wandered around Rushford, diving into shops as the fancy took me, doubling back on myself, and crossing the road at random intervals, just as I'd done at Christmas when I'd been trying to get away from Sorensen and Jones. I even found myself in that very odd sex shop at the end of Butt's Passage – the one leading down to the river. It was all done out in red and black with some very strange items on display. I backed out, trying not to laugh. For some reason, an image of Michael Jones came to mind. I must remember to ask him if he was on their mailing list and enjoy his reaction.

It had lightened my mood, though, and I went off for a late lunch in a much happier frame of mind. The Copper Kettle was full, so I treated myself to crispy fried beef and two coffees at the Golden Dragon, emerging on a happy monosodium glutamate and caffeine high an hour later.

Rushford, unfortunately, is not a large town, and by late afternoon I'd covered most of it, and that included stopping for an ice cream in the park. I threw the wrapper in the bin and looked around. It would be dark soon. Lights were going on in people's windows and the air was growing chilly. Sooner or later I was going to have to go home, and given my lifestyle these days, anything could be waiting for me on my doorstep.

And it was. There was someone lurking outside my house. The streetlight opposite showed a figure sitting on the top step talking to Colonel Barton over the railings. Not Sorensen – I could tell that from here. Not that he would ever sit on a doorstep anyway. And he certainly wouldn't lurk. He had people to do that for him.

This was a familiar tall, skinny, slightly disreputable but wholly charming young man with a kind heart and dubious morals.

He turned as I approached, his silver colour bouncing all around him. 'You called me.'

'No, I don't think I did.'

'Well, not in so many words, but you called nevertheless.'

That might be true, actually. If agitation can be transmitted then I'd been broadcasting on all channels.

He held up a bottle of wine. 'Tonight, we celebrate!'

I sighed. 'I don't think I'm in the mood.'

He held up the bottle again. 'Tonight, we drown our sorrows!'

'In fact, I think I might be in a lot of trouble.'

He held up the bottle again. 'Tonight, we formulate our battle plan and drink to success!'

I gave up and put my key in the door. 'Actually, I don't have a problem with any of that. Come on in.'

He blew a kiss to Mrs Barton, sitting in her window waving at him. Colonel Barton harrumphed and slammed his front door behind him. Following me inside, Iblis sat at the table while I went to get glasses and a corkscrew. It occurred to me that having him here might be no bad thing if Sorensen did turn up. I'd be interested to see what they made of each other. And it wouldn't do Sorensen any harm at all to know I did have some friends.

He poured two generous glasses. The last time I'd drunk wine had been at Christmas. I'd been warm and safe and very well fed and I'd sat on Jones's lap and negotiated for the last chocolate brownie. The memory of that moment was always enough to send waves of heat washing over me – and not just with embarrassment. I'm not good at drinking alcohol. I don't like to feel control sliding away from me. Sometimes things gather on the very edge of perception, just waiting for a way in … so I don't drink very much. Tonight however, I was prepared to make an enthusiastic exception.

We toasted each other and I sipped. It was very good wine indeed. I should wonder where he'd got it from, but I rather felt I'd fulfilled my ethical duties for the day.

The phone rang.

I said, 'Would you excuse me a moment, please,' got up, and unplugged it.

He looked surprised. 'Do we not want to be disturbed? Will this turn out to be the night I've been dreaming of?'

'No.'

He grinned cockily. 'We'll see.'

I sipped again. One of the few good things about being with people who say the first thing that comes into their head is that they can hardly complain if you do likewise. On an impulse, I said, 'You love Melek with everything you've got. Why are you bothering with me?'

He put down his glass and said nothing. His colour stopped bouncing around like an exuberant puppy and wrapped itself protectively around him instead.

I shook my head. 'I'm sorry. That was rude of me. I've not had a very good day and I shouldn't be taking it out on you. I'm sorry I said it.'

I don't think he was listening. Not to me, anyway. He was staring at me but not seeing me, if you know what I mean.

'I wish that, like you, I didn't remember either.'

I was puzzled. What was he talking about. 'What don't I remember?'

'You don't know, do you?'

I shook my head. 'What don't I know?'

'I forget how long ago it all was.' He flashed me a small, sad, half smile that was even more attractive than ever. 'Time tends to get away from me occasionally. I sometimes think if I ever stopped and thought about it … Time, I mean … It piles up behind us and we don't realise it, and then, one day, we look over our shoulder and all that time is looming over us like a massive cliff, poised to fall at any moment … burying us alive in our memories.'

I shivered suddenly. His image had touched a nerve.

He emptied his glass in one swift movement and topped it up again.

I said softly, 'Who are you?'

He pulled himself together and smiled, blindingly. 'I told you. Iblis is my name.' He waggled his eyebrows. 'Women are my game.'

'Oh, please,' I said, totally unimpressed.

He laughed and his colour slowly began to unfurl.

I said nothing and he stopped laughing and stared at the table again.

'You told me yourself that your name isn't Iblis and women very definitely aren't your game. Just one woman perhaps.'

He changed the subject. 'Good work today, by the way.'

I didn't even bother asking how he knew about that.

'Although you should tell them to destroy that tree.'

'Already done.' And then the implications of his words got through. I sat back. 'You *knew* about the tree?'

'Of course. I know everything.'

'You *knew* that little girl was there.'

He nodded.

'And you did nothing? You would have let her die? Get out of my house.' I scraped back my chair, all ready to escort him to the door in righteous indignation.

'Of course I did something, Elizabeth Cage. I sent you the dream.'

I wasn't sure if that made things better or worse. '*You* did that? How could you do that? Are you messing with my head?'

'Would you rather I had not sent you the dream?'

I thought of that little girl, alone in that tree. Hungry, terrified, thirsty, sitting on the bones of other children, crying for her mummy. 'No. No, of course not.'

'Then don't accuse me of doing nothing.'

'You could have saved her.'

'I don't interfere.'

'She was a child.'

'I don't interfere.'

I blinked. 'Never?'

'Never.'

'But why not? You have … you have power.'

159

'So do you.'

'Not like you.'

He shifted uneasily. 'Let's talk about you instead. Has anyone ever told you how the light plays on your hair ...'

I slapped the table. I think the wine had given me the courage to be angry. And angry I was. 'Stop that. I'm cross with you because you have power and you could help people and yet you do nothing.'

'Just like you.'

The words hung in the air between us. I opened my mouth for an indignant denial, closed it again, opened it again, and finally said, 'I didn't want it. The power, I mean.'

He seemed surprised. 'What has that to do with it?'

I thought about that. 'Nothing, I suppose. But ... every now and then ... I get a ... a warning ... if I use it wrongly and ...'

I tapered off.

'Like a brake.'

I nodded. 'Yes, just like a brake. The warning light comes on in my head, there's a flash of pain and I know not to go any further.'

'And you heed this warning?'

I shivered, suddenly cold and with the taste of angry snow on my lips and lied. 'Yes.'

He nodded and topped up his glass again. 'It's probably best you don't use your power then. Sit in your house and do nothing.'

We sat in silence. I looked at the dark red liquid in my glass and remembered I didn't much like red wine, but this was good stuff.

I don't normally ask people questions about themselves. Usually I don't need to because their colours tell me what I need to know. And often lots of things I don't need to know, as well.

160

And certainly lots of things I don't *want* to know. About Iblis, however, I *did* want to know. I wanted to know about his past. His silver colour, always so vibrant and lively, only told me about him now, in this moment, so I sipped a little more courage and said, 'And what about you?'

He came back from wherever he'd been. 'Me?'

'Yes, you.' I remembered to ask open questions. 'What's your story?'

He smiled a sad smile. 'It's a long one.'

I reached out and topped up both our glasses. 'Off you go then.'

I didn't think he'd tell me anything. Nothing important anyway. I was expecting a few meaningless words that would probably conceal more than they revealed, and then he would find the bottle was empty, or suddenly remember a previous appointment and depart in haste, so I was very surprised when he said, in all seriousness, 'I'm not sure where to begin.'

'At the beginning,' I said helpfully, tipping what must surely be the last dregs into his glass, but it seemed there was a drop still left in the bottle. I held it up to the light and squinted.

'Ah yes,' he said. 'The Bottle of Utgard-Loki.'

'I beg your pardon?'

'The Bottle of Utgard-Loki. Well, it used to be the Horn of Utgard-Loki, of course, but we all have to move with the times, don't we?'

'The bottle of …?'

'Utgard-Loki,' he said helpfully, as if that made everything clear.

I stared at him.

'The unemptyabling … unemptyingly … unemptyable Bottle of Utgard-Loki.'

I stared at him. 'What?'

'It never empties.'

I shook the bottle. It was at least half full and yet I was on my second glass and I'd lost count of his top-ups. I gave up and dragged him back on track. 'The beginning?'

'The beginning,' he said softly, looking at me but seeing something else entirely. 'The beginning is such a long time ago now. When everything was bright and new and the colours were dazzling and we had such hope ...'

He was quiet for so long that I thought that was all I was going to get, but I asked the question anyway.

'Who are you?'

He opened his mouth and I held up my hand. 'And don't say, "Iblis, man of many talents," and so on. Tell me who you really are.'

He opened his mouth to answer and then changed his mind about what he was going to say. He looked at me for a long time and then said, 'I'm a Hunter. We both are. Melek and me. We're Hunters.'

My mouth suddenly dry, I asked, 'What do you hunt?'

'Things that make the world ... unsafe.'

'What sort of things?'

He shifted on his chair. 'In the Old Days – before the first men emerged from their caves, blinking in the light, we had to make a world for them.'

'Make for them?'

'Well, I don't mean manufactured for them, obviously. We had to prepare it for them. They were children. We had to make it safe. Childproof it for them, if you like.'

'You childproofed the world?'

'Exactly. You know. Remove sharp objects. Babyproof the toilet seat. Put a gate across the stairs. That sort of thing.

I leaned across the table. 'How exactly did you make this world safe for them?'

'Read the old stories, Elizabeth Cage. Read of the ice giants, the minotaurs, the trolls, the dragons, the ghouls, the golems, the djinn, the demons, the undead. There was great evil in this world, once upon a time.'

I opened my mouth to say that these were all legends, surely, and then remembered some of the things I'd seen recently. I still wasn't completely sure I believed what he was telling me, but he wasn't lying. He was telling the truth as he saw it. I'm not sure that made things any better. A part of me was still convinced I was drinking with someone who would benefit from a spell of psychiatric assistance.

I said carefully, 'You killed them all?'

'No. Oh no. Some departed quite willingly. Signed the treaty and went … elsewhere. Some fought to the bitter end of course. And their ending was bitter. Very bitter. It was a long, hard struggle. I lost many friends.' He gazed into his wine glass.

He seemed to have forgotten me as he sat, staring into his past, so I said gently, 'What happened?'

It was a non-specific question and I expected a non-specific answer, but I got more than I bargained for.

He sighed heavily. 'I did something bad. Something very, very bad. And everyone suffered for it.'

I didn't know what to say, so I said nothing at all.

He looked up at me and smiled that small, sad smile again. 'You are quiet.'

I said honestly. 'I'm surprised. A little surprised that you would tell me this and very, very surprised that you of all people *could* do anything …' I couldn't think of another word, '…bad.'

He looked surprised. 'You think that of me?'

'Why would I not? You saved me from Þhurs.' I swallowed and said, 'I can see your true nature and you are an honourable man.'

He hung his head. 'No,' he said. 'No, I'm not.'

His colour, usually so bright and lively, hung motionless around him. The edges were darkening. Tarnishing was the word that came to my mind. And something else came into my mind – this was the real Iblis. Not the bouncing, silver Tigger, flirting outrageously with every woman who crossed his path, but this Iblis. This older, darker, sadder ... broken Iblis who, long ago had done something very bad and it had ruined his life. Shadows began to gather in the room and not all of them were because the sun had gone down and the street light was shining through my front window.

He sighed. 'There's a rule. An unbreakable rule. And it was broken.'

'By whom?' And waited to hear him say, 'By me,' because if anyone belonged to the 'See a Rule – Break a Rule Club', it was Iblis.

But he didn't. 'By others. The ones who succumbed. The ones who told themselves there was no harm in it. The ones who fell. That was before my time. Before all our times. We were sent to deal with the consequences. To hunt them down and exterminate them.'

'What consequences?'

He said in a whisper, 'Their offspring.'

I trod very carefully. 'So this unbreakable rule was ...'

'Broken. Many times. By those who should have known better.'

I stopped breathing because I knew what was coming.

'And then by me.'

He hung his head. His colour was writhing with ... what? Anxiety? No, not that. Guilt. Remorse. Self-hatred. Disgust. Loathing. Shame. A dreadful mixture that eddied around him. Suffocating him almost. His colour had darkened almost to black. I caught a faint sense of whirling, disorienting panic. Whatever he had done had affected him so deeply that even now he could barely think about it before tumbling headlong into a vortex of guilt and panic and remorse and a deep, deep, soul-sapping fear. I stared at him. Whatever could he possibly have done that was so bad ... that had changed his life ... that could cause him such horror? Even across the table I could see his distress. Normally, when people are agitated or afraid, their colour wraps itself around them, protecting and soothing, but Iblis's colour was streaming away from him like a banner. Self-hatred, self-reproach, self-loathing. I could hardly believe this was the same noisy, cocky, confident young man who had so effortlessly saved me from the troll and flirted outrageously with everything in a skirt.

I needed to do something, so I picked up the unemptyable bottle, poured him another glassful, and gently told him to drink it up.

It was gone in three or four gulps. He placed the glass carefully on the table in front of him and then pushed it away as if he was afraid of what he might do with it.

I said gently, 'Would it help you to tell me? But not if you don't want to.'

He looked at me. 'You're a good person, Elizabeth Cage, but you wouldn't be so good if you knew what I had done.'

'Have you killed someone?'

'Oh, I've killed lots of things. Some of them people, but usually they deserved to die so my conscience is mostly clear on that point.'

'Did you … hurt a child, perhaps?'

'No, of course not,' he said, so irritably that I was reassured. 'Well, I've thumped a couple around the head once or twice, but that was for their own good. You know – "How many times must I tell you not to play with dragons?" Or – "Stop annoying the leprechauns because they'll turn the milk if you're not careful." That sort of thing.'

'Yes,' I said carefully. 'The usual stuff.'

'Exactly.'

I opened my mouth to say, 'So tell me what you did,' but that seemed a little judgemental, so I changed it to, 'Tell me what happened.'

'I don't want to,' he said heavily. 'I like knowing that you don't know. That you have a good opinion of me. That you're not judging me. Or recoiling in disgust. Or whatever.'

'I'll try not to do any of those things.'

'You won't promise though, will you.'

'No, I can't do that. Promises are serious things and I don't know what you're going to say, do I?'

He reached across the table for my hand. 'Elizabeth …'

'It's up to you. Don't tell me if you don't want to.'

'I don't want to, but I should. You should know what I am. And what I did.'

He seized the bottle and poured himself yet another glassful, said, 'Well, here goes,' and drained his glass.

Chapter Fifteen

'In the beginning,' he said slowly, 'in the Old Days, it was all about the Fiori. You'd call them demons. There are many different types and the Fiori are the worst kind. The sons of the gods lay with the daughters of men and the stories call their offspring giants, but that's because in those days they probably didn't have the words to describe the cruel, vicious, vindictive brutality of them. The Fiori, I mean. They have no redeeming features. There's no kindness in them. No gentleness. And definitely no compassion. There's no redemption for them, either, Elizabeth. Their certain fate awaits them in the deepest, darkest places of the next world, and because they know it, nothing reigns them back in this one. They are the abominations of this world. I can't tell you some of the things they've done over the ages, to other races, even to each other, but if you look back at the worst things that have happened here, in this world – and there are a lot of them – you'll find at least one Fiori in there somewhere.'

He sipped his wine. 'Anyway, it was our job, mine and Melek's, to hunt them down and exterminate them – to make the world safe – and we did. We pursued them from one end of the world to the other and back again. We were a team then and we were unstoppable. They fled at our approach, and yet, no matter how many we slaughtered, or burned, no matter how many of their nests we destroyed, they never seemed to get any less. We pursued them without mercy and without rest. Through the snowy wastes, across vast deserts, in the high places of the world. We were relentless. There was no hiding from us.'

He paused to sip his wine. 'Sometimes we would split up. She would go one way and I would go another and between us we'd drive them into a narrow place and into an ambush. Men were spreading across the face of the earth by this time, and many had suffered at the hands of the Fiori, so there were always those willing to help. Heroes, champions, demi-gods – everyone banded together to bring them down.'

He sipped at his wine again. Putting off the moment, I suspected. 'Anyway, the ages passed, friends and allies came and went, but we – that's Melek and me – stuck at it because, trust me, Elizabeth Cage, the Fiori never grow any less. And then … then we began to hear reports they were gathering in their traditional hunting areas. There were the usual atrocities, but there were also reports of women disappearing – being taken alive. That usually only meant one thing – they were being taken for breeding purposes – and that was something we really needed to do something about. So Melek went off to gather as much support as she could muster and I set off to follow their trail, which wasn't difficult – I just followed the burning villages and dismembered bodies – to attempt to discover their breeding ground. We were to meet in Venice on Midsummer's Eve.'

He stopped again. I sat very still but he made no move to pick up his story.

'In Venice,' I said, hoping to get him talking again.

He nodded. 'Yes. Venice. Depending on what I found, we'd put together four or five small armies, hit the Fiori from different directions and destroy them and their nests before they knew what had hit them.'

He sighed.

'What did they look like?'

He blinked at me. 'Who?'

'The Fiori. Were they as monstrous on the outside as on the inside?'

'That's the sad bit. They look just like ordinary people.'

'But why haven't I heard about them? Why hasn't anyone heard about the Fiori?'

'You have. You hear about them every time you switch on the news.'

I tried not to look horrified. 'Hear? Present tense? They're still with us?'

'I'm afraid so. We're stronger, but there are more of them. It's an age-long stalemate whose beginnings no one can now remember and whose ending seems equally far away.

'Will it end?'

'Yes. Not soon, but one day. Accounts of a final dreadful battle are widespread throughout many belief systems. Armageddon. Ragnarok. It will happen.'

'But not today.'

'No, not today.'

'And not tomorrow.'

'No, not tomorrow, either. But one day.'

'One day you will win.'

'One day someone will win. It might not necessarily be us.'

I resisted the temptation to look behind me. 'So you never actually wiped them out?'

He compressed his lips and shook his head and I resolved to shut up in case he construed that last remark as a criticism. His colour was all dark now, churning about him. I wondered if I should stop him. Confession is supposed to be good for the soul, but not so much for the body, as far as I could see. And, I was asking myself, if it was that bad, did I actually want to know what he had done?

I opened my mouth to say, 'Let's drop the subject and finish off this bottle, shall we?' but he was already speaking.

'It was going well. I reckoned they were only about a day or so ahead of me. The weather was good. I was on their trail and closing every day because I knew the area quite well.'

'You'd been there before?'

He smiled. 'Actually, I don't think there's a square foot on this earth that I haven't trodden many times, but yes, these were their hereditary breeding grounds and I knew them well.'

He sounded so sad. All his cocky irreverence had disappeared. He was just a bowed figure in the increasing dimness of my living room. Night had fallen, but I decided to leave the lights off and give him a little privacy. He was showing me his soul. I didn't need to see his face as well.

'I was making good time – I reckoned they were only about a day ahead of me, and then I emerged from the forest to find a river crossing ahead. There was a bit of a rickety bridge that dumped people in the water as often as it got them safely across, but there was an inn at the meeting of the ways, and I decided I deserved a reasonable meal. I pitched up just before noon. It was a warm day and the landlord had dragged a few tables and benches outside. Men sat around, talking and drinking. A nice peaceful scene and given the lack of blood and screaming, I could assume the Fiori hadn't yet passed this way. I took a table under a tree, ordered an ale and whatever they had to eat, and leaned back to enjoy the scene around me. The landlord was dashing about with beakers and plates. His wife was in the kitchen dishing up the food, not very ably assisted by her young daughter. She was an angel with her long blonde hair and no one really minded that she brought the wrong food to the wrong table. She was probably about eight or nine. There was a boy as well, about ten, I think, feeding the pig around the back. A busy, happy family running a prosperous business in a pleasant spot.'

He sighed. 'I ate a good stew, washed it down with another beaker of really excellent ale, and leaned back in the sunshine. I thought I'd take an hour's rest and then be on my way. I watched the other customers drift away – they had jobs to do, I suppose.

'A hot, afternoon silence fell. I was alone and I should go before I fell asleep. I left some money on the table and reluctantly picked up my pack, all ready to set off.'

He was staring back into the past. 'The landlady appeared at the back door, stretching her back after the afternoon rush and wiping her hands. She asked me where I was headed. I told her to the next town, and she said her husband had business there that afternoon, but he couldn't leave the inn. If I would let her join me than he would allow her to go in his place. The area was safe enough, she said, but he couldn't get away and he'd feel happier if she had someone with her. I didn't really mind. It was only a couple of miles away – it certainly wouldn't hold me up that much, and there just might be Fiori in the area, so I said yes. She appeared with a red cloak and a basket – just like someone in a fairy story – and off we set.

'Well, we introduced ourselves – her name was Allia and she was a pretty girl with a good nature and quick wit. She told me this was the first time she'd been away from the inn for weeks. She was skipping along, interested in everything around her, chattering away, and we had a pleasant journey. We successfully crossed the bridge and set off back into the forest again. The first part was uphill, and it was hot and a bit of a trudge for her, but we got to the top eventually and the trees were thinner and the air slightly cooler up there. She stopped to get her breath back and I took a quick look around to see if there were any signs of the Fiori anywhere.'

He stopped again. For a long time.

I prompted him. 'And were there?'

He sighed. 'There were. I looked back the way we'd come and there was a column of black smoke curling up through the trees. Exactly at the spot where the inn had been. I knew it was the Fiori. Somehow, they'd got behind me.'

He drank deeply. 'I didn't move quickly enough. She screamed, dropped her basket and ran back the way we'd come. It was downhill. I've never seen anyone run so fast. Even I couldn't catch her. She was so breathless as to be nearly fainting when I eventually caught her, struggling for breath, just at the edge of the clearing.

'The bridge had gone. The inn was on fire. What I first thought was the pig had been gutted and burned on a spit and turned out to be her husband. He was unrecognisable as a man. She screamed his name and tried to run past me. I grabbed at her cloak, spun her round and knocked her out cold. I didn't know what else to do. They'd used the little boy for target practice. He was impaled on the barn door with some ten or twelve arrows in him.'

He swallowed hard. 'They'd really enjoyed themselves with the little girl and there was a kitchen maid in the yard with her head gone. I looked at Allia, still unconscious on the ground and went off to see if I could find something to dig a grave. I had them all in the ground before she came around. She screamed at me. I think she hit me a couple of times, but I wasn't going to let her see what had been done to her family.

'Everything was gone – dead, burned, destroyed, trampled – their usual style, and I should get after them because they couldn't be that far away, but I had this woman, Allia, with me and I didn't know what to do with her. There wasn't anyone nearby I could take her to. I certainly couldn't leave her there, so I took her with me. No choice really. I thought I'd take her to the nearest town, drop her off, warn the head man there were Fiori in the area, and get on after them.'

There was very little mirth in his smile.

'Well, none of that worked out as I thought. She wouldn't be dropped off at the nearest town. Not at any price. We argued. She cried. I was becoming increasingly impatient because the longer I wasted my time with her, the further away they were getting, but I don't think she was even listening to me. She was coming with me, she said. She'd hunt the Fiori with me. She'd kill them for what they'd done to her family.

'I tried to change her mind. Everyone tried to change her mind. She wouldn't listen to anyone. I told the head man to lock her up for a couple of days to give me time to get clear, but he refused. Couldn't blame him, I suppose, no one wanted the responsibility of her because we all knew she'd be off after the Fiori soon as they let her out, so in the end, I gave in and took her with me. It seemed the safest thing to do. I honestly thought the first wet night we had would be enough to send her back to civilisation as quickly as she could move. Well, I was wrong. She was small and light and, as I'd already seen, she could really cover the ground, and she certainly didn't slow me down to any great extent. Not enough for me to justify leaving her behind, anyway. Every night when we stopped to camp, she insisted on me teaching her to use a sword. Somehow, she'd acquired one back in the town and now she wanted to learn to use it. She was whirling it around and it was only a matter of time before she accidentally took her own head off. Or mine. I could see she wouldn't last two minutes in a fight, so I gave in. Every night, I taught her a few moves. I taught her how to break free if anyone

173

ever seized her from behind. I taught her how to defend herself in a fight. I tried to teach her how to avoid getting into a fight in the first place, although I don't think she listened very hard to that particular lesson.

'Every night, we'd practice a while, eat our meal, sit around the fire cleaning our swords, and talk a little. She wanted to know everything I knew about the Fiori. She was grim and determined and no, she didn't run home on the first wet night. She was first up every morning and ready to go. She didn't slow me down very much and she could cook. Really, I had nothing to complain about with her at all.'

He poured himself more wine and topped up mine as well. The Bottle of Utgard-Loki was certainly earning its keep tonight.

He was smiling back into his past. 'And it wasn't dull. In those days, I liked to ghost through an area, not drawing attention to myself, picking up what information I could along the way. That was all changed now. We had what she called adventures and I called nightmares. At one point we were set upon by a couple of thieves. Well, that wasn't too serious and I let her deal with that because she needed the practice. She tore into them like a small silver fury. They ran off and word must have got around because we had very little trouble after that. And then I was arrested in one village – a tiny misunderstanding over a goat. Why are you laughing? – and I was locked up in the local gaol. It wasn't a problem, I still had my sword, and come nightfall I would have got myself out easily enough, grabbed Allia, and we'd have been miles away before they even noticed we were gone.'

He sighed and rubbed his eyes. 'I underestimated her ... ingenuity. I was just getting myself comfortable when there was a huge commotion outside the door and then it all went very quiet. The door creaked open – that was a bit of a nasty moment, I can tell you – and there she stood, sword in one hand, our packs in the other, and all ready to go.

'Well, the next day ...'

'Wait,' I said, hardly slurring at all. 'Wait a moment. Go back. I have questions.'

He poured himself more wine. 'Go on.'

'OK. They arrested you but they left you with your sword?'

He said very quietly, 'Can we talk about that later?'

I eyed him suspiciously. 'Had she killed the guard?'

'No. I think she'd tried to stun him with something – there was a broken pot nearby – but that's not as easy as it looks on TV. He was a bit woozy – but mostly she'd tied him up with his own cloak and hidden his boots.'

'Resourceful,' I commented.

He sighed. 'You don't know the half of it. Seriously, there were times when I was convinced I'd created a monster. To say she was a bit punchy was the understatement of the year. Everywhere we went it was all I could do to stop her picking fights with everyone we met. I was always getting her out of trouble, paying people off, apologising for her, or just dragging her away before they threw us both into gaol.'

Survivor guilt, I thought. If she hadn't left the inn that afternoon she'd have been in the ground with the rest of her family. I wondered how often that thought had crossed her mind. Quite often, I should imagine. But he was doing a good job of describing her. I could see her very clearly in my mind – short, sharp, aggressive – and with a massive death wish.

'Anyway, there I was, chasing this particular group of Fiori and never seemingly getting any closer. There was rumour of them everywhere. Walls were guarded, gates were manned, everyone knew they were out there, it was just a case of where they would strike. And when.'

He stopped to drink again.

'And then we came to the biggest town in the area. Their capital, I suppose. It's long gone now, but at that time it was a big place. Big enough to have its own king and he hadn't skimped on effort or expense when fortifying the town. It was built on the slopes of a steep mountain – they'd actually used the cliff as part of the fortifications. The walls were high and the only entrance was through a long, narrow and very easily defended open tunnel. The Fiori would have to be idiots to attack that town. So, of course, they did.

'Somehow, they'd raised an army, supplementing their numbers with all the scum and riff-raff they could find. All lured in with the promise of women and plunderI suppose, which just goes to show what idiots they were because in my experience, as soon as the Fiori achieved their objective, any allies they might have recruited soon found their status altered to that of 'more victims' and were dealt with accordingly. This army marched on the town about a week after we arrived there. I volunteered to fight of course, and the king was glad to have me. Allia volunteered to fight and everyone laughed.' He smiled sadly. 'But not for long.

'True to form, the Fiori took everyone by surprise. Ignoring the gate, they scaled the cliff. The king had deployed the bulk of his forces around the tunnel and was taken completely unawares. Allia had been bundled into a hall in the top part of the city along with all the other women and children. They heard the Fiori coming. There was complete panic, but Allia, apparently, got them all organised. She told them straight. Stop whimpering and fight. Rather than wait and be cornered and taken away by the very army who had slaughtered their husbands, fathers and brothers, they should take the fight to them. Well, obviously they had no weapons, so she organised them into small groups. The youngest children gathered piles of stones, pieces of wood, buckets, roof tiles, bits of masonry, household implements, anything that could be used. The women ranged themselves along the walls. She rallied them. Inspired them to fight. Gave them the courage they needed. They should all have died, of course. I think they expected to. But at least they would die defending themselves and their children. Which, as she told them, was a far better death than cowering in a corner waiting for death to come to you.

'And it worked. They hurled everything they could find over the walls at the Fiori as they climbed the cliff. They couldn't have held for long, of course. Once all the Fiori had made it up the mountain, the city would have been overrun very quickly, but the women and children held them off just long enough for the king to send a detachment of soldiers to the top of the town, and between them and the stone-throwing women, they beat the Fiori back down the mountain. With heavy losses on the Fiori side.'

'Wow,' I said, topping up my own glass and then his. 'A heroine.'

'Yes,' he said to his glass. 'You'd think she would be, wouldn't you?'

'She wasn't?'

He didn't answer directly. I think he was caught up in his narrative. I wondered how much of a relief it was to let go and unburden himself.

'When the fighting was all over, I went looking for her. She'd left the city and was down on the plain with all the other men. Night was falling and it wasn't safe for her to be outside. It wasn't safe for any of us to be outside the city. They'd been burning the Fiori bodies and she was standing, alone, by one of the bonfires, just staring at it. The flames had subsided, but the ashes still glowed bright red and I could feel the heat coming off them. And off her. She was dirty and bloodstained and her lovely hair was coming down.'

He was staring into the distance, talking to himself. I was completely forgotten.

'It was as if I was seeing her for the first time. We looked at each other. The longing for her came right out of the blue. I'd spent weeks with this woman. We'd washed at the same streams together. We'd bound each other's wounds. We'd had each other's backs. She was a companion. And now, suddenly, I realised she was a woman as well.

'I looked at her and she looked at me. There were no words spoken. I was consumed with desire for her. Overwhelmed with it. I *had* to have her. I think I would have died if I couldn't. There was no fighting it. My heart was full of her. And my loins as well. And it was the same for her, too. She couldn't look away. I could see the flames from the pyres reflected in her eyes. I … I bore her to the ground … I … and right there, among the piles of burning Fiori …'

'It's all right,' I said quickly, not wanting to hear the details. 'I understand.'

He shook his head, his colour now a thin, dark, miserable ghost of its former self. 'No. No, I'm afraid you don't. Did you not hear what I said about the Elder Race and the daughters of men?'

I cast my mind back. 'Oh.'

His voice cracked. 'It's *forbidden*, Elizabeth. It's strictly forbidden for any of the Elder Races to sleep with humans. Absolutely forbidden. There is no worse crime.'

I didn't know what to say to him so I said nothing. His colour was writhing around him in a way that worried me deeply. I wasn't going to let him go back to his woodland tent tonight. He would spend the night here in my house, because at that moment, I feared for him.

He swallowed hard and spoke so quietly I had to strain to hear the words. 'Afterwards – a very long time afterwards – we fell asleep together. When I woke up the fires were cold and she was gone. I should have gone after her. I should have talked to her. But somehow, the spell was broken and I realised ... I knew what I'd done. The crime I had committed. I couldn't face myself – let alone her. To my everlasting shame, I avoided her.'

He took a deep shuddering breath and continued. 'The king wanted to reward her for her part in defending his city. He offered her a fine house and a dowry. I was pleased for her. I thought she was all set for the happy ending she deserved.'

He stopped again.

'I'm hearing a but ...'

He sighed. 'It wasn't the men – there was a certain amount of respect for her. And she'd lost her family to the Fiori ...'

'But,' I prompted.

'It was the women. Once word got out she was just an innkeeper's wife – and I've no idea who spread that particular piece of gossip – she was just ... frozen out. It was the type of cruelty only women seem able to manage. They turned their backs. The held their skirts out of the way in case she contaminated them. They wouldn't let their children go near her. Or their husbands. Men who had cheerfully fought shoulder to shoulder with her grew sheepish in her presence and backed away.'

I tried to put myself in her place. The woman who had lost everything. The woman who had given everything. Only to be rejected by those for whom she had fought. I wondered how often she had wished she had fallen in the battle. I said quietly, 'She must have been devastated.'

'She ... was.' He was silent and wouldn't meet my eyes.

I thought, it's been a long time, but we're coming to it now.

He couldn't look at me. 'I could have done something. I *should* have done something, but the Fiori never stop and neither could I. They'd taken a big hit and there would never be a better time to mop up the remnants. I knew Melek must be in Venice by now, waiting for me. I didn't yet know where they were breeding but it ... it was an excuse I seized upon. I started making preparations to move on. I was going to leave her there. If I thought about it at all, I thought she'd be all right. She had a house and a dowry and the king's protection. I told myself that everything would sort itself out and all would be well.

'She came to see me, smart in her new clothes. I remember she wore a green dress – the colour of new beech leaves ...'

I had a sudden picture of the new leaves in the beech wood where he was camping.

'... with long, bright scarlet sleeves. We stood at the door. I didn't invite her in. She looked older and tired and she was very quiet. She didn't throw herself at me. She behaved with great dignity. Far more dignity than all those high-born so-called ladies who had been looking down their long noses at her. I was the one who behaved badly. She had a proposition, she said. She suggested we marry. She knew my purpose, she said. She had a house now and as her husband, I could use it as a base, coming and going as I wished, whenever I wished. Just please, don't leave her there alone.'

He couldn't look at me. 'I refused her offer. And because I was guilty and afraid and full of shame, I wasn't perhaps as gentle as I might have been. In fact, Elizabeth, I was a complete bastard. Every time I looked at her I remembered what I'd done. I just wanted her off my doorstep. I just wanted to forget everything. To try and pretend it had never happened.

'I said no. Even before she'd stopped speaking I was shaking my head. She even offered to give up everything and follow me – to be a companion, as she had been before. Just as long as I didn't leave her.'

He stopped. For a moment, I thought that was the end. That he couldn't or wouldn't go any further, but he struggled for a moment and then continued.

'I left. Right there. Right then. I didn't have my gear with me, but that sort of stuff can be picked up anywhere and I had my sword, which was all I really needed. I told myself I'd done an enormous amount of damage to both of us and the best thing I could do would be to get away as quickly as possible. A clean break would give us both a chance to recover. So, I pushed her away as gently as I could and strode out into the street. I ignored her desperation, the anguish in her voice. I never looked back. Not once. Her cries followed me through the streets. I didn't take my leave of anyone. I didn't pay my respects to the king. I nearly ran through the town in my haste to get away. Down through the narrow passageway where the guards saluted me and out through the city gates.'

He was silent for so long I thought that was the end of the story. I had actually drawn breath to speak when he said, 'I was threading my way around the base of the city, meaning to head west, when, high above me, I heard someone shout. Someone else screamed. I looked up. The sun was in my eyes but I saw what I thought was a bundle of clothing falling down the cliff, bouncing from rock to rock, slowly coming unravelled until, with a noise I can't possibly describe to you, it hit the ground in front of me. Only about fifty feet away. I drew my sword and went to investigate.'

His voice was not very steady. I wondered how long ago this had happened and even now he couldn't easily speak of it.

'I think I knew what it had been. Who it had been, I should say. I couldn't drag my eyes away. After all she'd been through, this was a dreadful death. Violent and cruel. I only knew it was her because of the green dress with the brave scarlet sleeves. I tried to pick her up. I don't know what I was thinking. Every bone in her body was broken and I was responsible. She was a good woman who had lost her family, who had fought alongside me and I had done this to her. This was my fault. All my fault. I'd broken the rule and she'd paid the price. It was my fault. Everything was my fault.

'People were running towards us. There were cries and exclamations of horror. They said she'd fallen, but I knew she'd jumped. And I knew why she'd jumped. Someone touched my shoulder. They'd brought sheets to wrap her in. I got to my feet and moved away to give them room.

'And then ...' He stopped and this time he really was struggling. He put his hands over his face.

'Yes,' I said softly. 'And then?' Because what could be worse than this tragic story?

'And then I realised my sword was gone.'

Chapter Sixteen

I rocked back in my seat. I know I'd been expecting something but it certainly wasn't this. Was that it? He'd lost his sword? I know boys grow attached to their toys, but this? From the little he'd told me I'd become quite fond of this woman, Allia. She'd died because of him and he was upset because he'd lost his sword? So what?

And then, thank heavens, before I could ruin everything by saying something really crass and stupid, something in his colour made me pause. Yes, he'd been sick with remorse before, and his colour had reflected that, but this was different. And even worse. Much worse. I picked up the never-ending Bottle of Utgard-Loki and poured him another glass. 'Tell me.'

'I know what you're thinking,' he said, and yes, I wouldn't have been at all surprised if he had known what I was thinking – it was that sort of an evening – 'but there's something you should know.'

'OK,' I said, pushing his glass back towards him. 'Tell me.'

'You must understand – this is for your ears only. A life other than mine depends on this.'

'Don't tell me if you don't want to,' I said, alarmed. Other people's secrets are a burden.

He looked across the table at me. His eyes were tired and shadowed. I suddenly wondered exactly how old he really was. 'I want to tell you,' he said, 'but I shall understand if you don't want to hear.'

183

It was on the tip of my tongue to say no, I didn't want to hear, and then I had second thoughts. How alone must he be? And for how long? From everything he'd told me and from what I myself had seen, he was always alone. Yes, there was Melek, but she was cold and hard and immovable. And then there was the way his colour alternately surged towards her and then fled from her. No, he needed someone else. Someone who wasn't close and who wouldn't judge. It would do him good to get all this off his chest, and I was a disinterested party. None of it was anything to do with me. Just for once I wasn't involved in any way. And perhaps I could help him somehow.

'No, it's all right. Go on. Tell me. If you want to.'

He was silent a while, considering, I think, how best to tell his story.

'We have swords. Melek and I. *Had* swords. They're our weapons. Each one is made for us alone. One person. One weapon. I'm not explaining it very well, but if I said they were part of us, would you understand?'

I nodded. Yes, I could understand that.

'A Hunter's sword can cleave through steel or kill a demon with a stroke – well, several strokes actually, because they don't usually go down without a fight, but you know what I mean. With it I could split the earth. Bring down a mountain. Light up the darkness. Frighten the living shit out of anything on earth. My sword was me. It was always with me. All the time. I never laid it down. And then, that day, I did.'

I didn't need his words to tell me how important his sword had been to him. His colour was writhing with regret and loss. He'd lost his sword and a large part of him had gone with it. Flecks of red anxiety began to appear, swirling and clumping, threading their way through the tarnished silver of his colour, clouding it with shame. Shadows leaped around the wall.

Darkness loomed. Something trembled on the very edge of my vision. I kept my eyes on him, closed my mind, and said quietly, 'Iblis.'

With a huge effort, he reined himself in and his colour subsided. The shadows faded. My room was normal again.

I needed to pull him back a little, so to distract him, I said. 'I don't remember Melek carrying a sword.'

He shook his head. 'They're not invisible, but others can't see them.' He smiled mirthlessly. 'Not until it's too late, anyway. There must be any number of demons for whom the last thing they saw was my sword taking their heads off. They're weapons of immense power, Elizabeth. They define who we are. They're the source of our strength. They can't be taken from us ...'

He stopped, unable to go on. The shadows gathered again. Patterns of red flickered around the walls.

'But you can lose them,' I said gently, while he gulped at his wine.

He nodded, took several deep breaths and then continued more quietly. 'I drew it because something unknown was falling down the mountain towards me. When I saw what it was – when I picked her up and held her that last time, I laid it down. When I stood up to go, it was gone.'

'What did you do?'

'I panicked. For the first time in my life. Because anything could be standing behind me. With my sword in its hand. We can be wounded, Elizabeth, and we can fall sick but we always heal. I can't remember how many times that's happened, but there are only two things can kill us truly dead and one is a Watcher's sword. For all I knew, something, someone, was about to take advantage of the milling crowd and put an end to me. Because I was utterly defenceless. I didn't even have a knife

185

with me. I kept spinning around, trying to see if I was about to be attacked and when it became apparent that wasn't going to happen, I realised whoever had it must have run off with it. I remember staggering to a rock and sitting with my head in my hands while I tried to think. Someone brought me wine. I suppose they thought I was affected by Allia's death – as I was – but this was much worse. So much worse, because it wasn't just me. After what I had done, I deserved death, but there was Melek as well. She had no idea my sword had been stolen. She could be just standing around one day – any day – unsuspecting, unprepared, and the next moment …'

His voice was beginning to rise.

'Hush,' I said, putting my hands over his. They were ice-cold and clammy. I wondered if I should stop him somehow, but we'd both come too far. I should hear him out and deal with the aftermath.

I said, 'All right. Take a breath. What did you do?'

'I made myself stop and think. I climbed the rocks a little and looked about me. With my back to the mountains, the land before me was all grasslands and flat plains and I could see for miles around. No one was behaving in any way suspiciously. No one was galloping hell for leather as they attempted to get away. My guess was that it had been smuggled back into the city. But by whom? There was a possibility it had only been picked up by a human who had no idea what he had, and I'd track him down sooner or later and get it back. And yes, I could give him a trouser-soiling experience he'd never forget, but there would have been no real harm done. The alternative …' he stopped, and then started again. 'The *probable* alternative was that someone who knew exactly what it was and exactly what it could do, now had possession of it, and was preparing to do the worst. In which case, I needed to warn Melek.

'It only took a moment for me to come to a decision. If a mortal had it then that was the smaller problem. If not ... So I slipped back into the city, found myself a weapon and a good horse and set off. They were just bringing her body in as I galloped out of the gates. I slowed, just for a moment, in her memory. Her death was on me. If I hadn't slept with her ... If I hadn't raised her expectations ... I broke the rules, Elizabeth. Melek always said they were there for a reason and she was right. Just one slip. That's all it takes and more than one life comes crashing down. I did wrong. I thought I could get away with it and I didn't, and catastrophe and tragedy engulfed us all.'

He drained his glass again. I didn't even think about stopping him.

'But you were able to warn Melek?'

He didn't look at me. 'Yes, I was.'

'And what happened?'

'She went off to look for my sword herself,' he said, pretending to misunderstand me and, because I couldn't even begin to imagine the scene they must have had, I let it go.

'But she didn't find it?'

'No. No one has ever found it. The centuries have rolled by and there hasn't been even a whisper of it. I've been telling myself it's part of some long-forgotten king's grave goods somewhere. That it's been buried and forgotten and, with luck, will never come to light until the end of the world. But, most importantly, it seems to have passed from living memory and no one can ever get to it and it's safe.'

'And you?' I said, dismissing the sword because I was more interested in him.

'I'm ... weakened. I do have a sword. You saw it the other day when I was waving it at old Þhurs. It's a good one – it's just not *my* sword, but I have to have something to display. A Hunter without a sword is too suspicious for words, so, as far as the world knows, I still have it.' He reached over his shoulder and suddenly, from nowhere, there was four feet of gleaming steel in his hand.

I leaned back. 'Wow.'

'Yeah. He waved it around, making figure of eights around his head, to the peril of the light fitting.

'I know that's not the real thing but it still looks impressive, though.'

'No one must ever know that. It's not just my life, Elizabeth. It's Melek's as well.'

'The two of you …?' I struggled to frame my question but he understood.

'She says she's forgiven me. But I'm not … not her equal any longer and it shows. We split up. My decision. I said I'd go it alone. And I do. I sally forth every now and then, killing the odd minor demon, frightening a dragon back to sleep again, or inducing a troll to give up his lunch, but it's all bluff, Elizabeth. The big stuff – that's all Melek these days, and it's too much for her alone. The Fiori are increasing all the time and I can't help. In fact, I'm more of a hindrance than a help. I'm a burden. A liability. But she never says anything and I face every day with centuries of remorse and shame and humiliation behind me and centuries more of it to come.'

I said suddenly. 'What's the other way?'

He looked up. 'What?'

'You said there were two ways you could die. By a Hunter's sword is one. What's the other way?'

I could hardly hear his voice. 'By our own hand. We can take our own life.'

I didn't need his colour to tell me this had been – and perhaps still was – a frequently considered option.

I reached out and took his cold hand. 'Iblis, you mustn't think like that. That is not an option for you and you mustn't even consider it. You're not a bad person. I think you're very brave. In fact, I think you're rather wonderful.'

He seemed startled, then shook his head, unable to meet my gaze. Tears ran down his cheeks.

I pulled my chair a little closer to him and said firmly, 'Yes, you are. You said you can die by your own hand, but you haven't, have you? You wake up every day, knowing what you've done – it's your first thought every morning and your last thought at night. And yet you get on with your life. You do what you can. Every day. You saved me. For you, there's no respite, no relief. There's never a moment when you can forget what you've done and yet you're still here, *every day*, doing what you can. I think that's amazing.'

I'm not sure that was as helpful as I intended it to be, because he put his head down on the table and sobbed like a little boy. I moved around to sit beside him and gently stroked his hair.

He cried for a long time and I let him. I think it was doing him some good. His colour was brightening a little. Perhaps his tears were washing him clean – I don't know. I do know that at the end of it, when he eventually lifted his head, he had exhausted himself.

'I'm so sorry,' he said thickly and making a truly heroic effort at his normal careless, insouciant self. 'Really bad form to turn up with wine and then fling snot all over your hostess and her dining table. Not the right thing to do at all.'

'It's not the worst thing that has ever happened in this room,' I said, 'but I don't think you should go back to the woods tonight. Would you like to sleep here? Just for tonight, of course.'

I think it was a measure of his emotional exhaustion that there was no smart reply or invitation for me to join him. He simply nodded. 'I would. Thank you for your kindness, Elizabeth Cage.'

'Come on.' I led him to the sofa. 'Take your boots off and I'll get you some bedding.'

I ran upstairs, returning with a pillow and some blankets and made him up a bed. 'In you get.'

There was no argument. He obeyed me like a small child. I tucked him up, drew the curtains, and he was asleep in a second.

I tidied away the glasses. The bottle still wasn't empty so I put it carefully to one side, checked my guest one more time, and then took myself upstairs to my own bed. It had been a long day.

Glancing at my bedside clock, I was amazed to see we'd been drinking for hours. I know for a fact I'd had at least two full glasses and any number of top-ups and yet I felt fine, which was a bit of a first. I got into bed, curled up under the covers and thought very hard about everything he'd told me.

Because something, somewhere, wasn't right.

Chapter Seventeen

At some point, one of us must have plugged the phone back in again because the ringing woke me. My heart sank. I knew who this would be.

I flailed around until I got an arm free and groped across the bedside table.

'What do you want, Sorensen?'

'Eh?'

Whoever it was, it wasn't Dr Sorensen. I blinked the sleep from my eyes. 'Who's that?'

'Is that …' he paused, '… Mrs Cage?'

I sat up in a hurry. 'Is that you, Jerry? What's wrong? Why are you ringing so early in the morning?'

He sounded slightly reproachful. 'It's twenty past nine, missis.'

Oh God, it was too.

'Sorry,' I said. 'I had a late night and I've only just woken up. What can I do for you?'

'Have you seen him recently?'

I was bewildered and befuddled. 'Who? Sorensen?'

He sighed. 'No. Jones.'

I swung my legs out of bed. 'No,' I said slowly, 'I haven't. And I haven't heard from him either. Have you?'

'No.'

I wasn't sure what to say. I didn't want to give anything away although I suspected old Jerry knew much more about

Michael Jones than I did. 'Is this normal? I mean, I know he goes away a lot. At short notice, sometimes.'

'Yeah, but he usually stays in touch. I haven't heard from him for a while now.'

'Nor me.'

'Listen,' he said. 'I'm not really worried because the bloke has more lives than a sackful of cats, but if he calls, just let me know, will you?'

'Of course.' I looked at the display. 'Can I get you on this number?'

'Yeah. It might transfer a couple of times so ignore all the clicking. You'll get me eventually.'

'OK,' I said, wondering more than ever about Jerry's line of work, and while I was thinking about that, he hung up.

I got up, showered, made the bed, and went downstairs to put the kettle on.

Iblis was up, dressed, and staring out of the window with his back to me. I was slightly surprised to find him still here. I half expected him to have left in the night rather than face me this morning. There was more to this boy than he thought. The blankets were neatly folded with the pillow on top. The room was fresh and clean. He was the perfect house guest.

'It's nice here,' he said, looking out at the view over the castle. 'Have you lived here long?'

I got the message. Still here he might be, but the revelations of last night were not for further discussion.

'About a year now. I was going to ask what you'd like for breakfast. I can do you egg and bacon or nip to the café if you fancy croissants or brioche.'

He shook his head and said lightly, 'You're too kind, but I mustn't outstay my welcome.'

'You saved me from a troll. You have more welcome than a squirrel has nuts.'

He laughed, which was good to hear, but I wasn't convinced. I'd seen this before. People tell you their darkest secrets and then regret it and then all they want to do is get away so they can pretend it never happened. It's not a good thing to do. I had an idea.

'Stay for breakfast,' I said. 'I think I might be needing you later on.'

He shook his head.

'I might be in trouble.'

Finally he turned to face me. 'Howso?'

'Sit down and I'll tell you about it over breakfast.'

We had scrambled eggs on toast and two mugs of coffee each, and I told him all about Sorensen and his efforts to entice me into working for him.

'And now I owe him,' I said, collecting the dishes, 'because of that kid in the tree and he'll make very sure he collects on the debt.'

'Yes,' he said, thoughtfully. 'You have rather placed yourself in his power, haven't you?'

'It was the right thing to do,' I said, defensively.

'I never said it wasn't. Anyway, don't worry. You have me here to protect you.'

I tried to feel good about that, because a volatile weirdo who lived rough in the woods and talked to trolls, and who had lost his killer sword and betrayed everything he stood for, couldn't possibly be a double-edged weapon at all, could he?

We spent a peaceful morning watching daytime TV, which fascinated him. Especially the soaps.

'Well, bugger me,' he said cheerfully, from where he was sprawled on the sofa. 'Nothing changes, does it?'

I looked up from my ironing. 'What doesn't change?'

'Well, look at what we have here. This new soap everyone's raving about. *Olympian Heights*. We've got this grey-haired patriarch, rich and devious, living in a fabulous mansion, shagging everything in sight, with his jealous wife, and his clever daughter, and his rebellious son with the dodgy friends, and his sinister brother from the underworld, to say nothing of the beautiful supermodel married to the ugly man who doesn't trust her. I mean, doesn't any of this ring any bells?'

I shook my head.

'You don't get it?'

I shook my head again.

'Well, thirty centuries ago and more, people worshipped Zeus, the grey-haired patriarch of Olympus – touchy old bugger I always thought - and his very extended and dysfunctional family. You know, Hera, the jealous wife, Athena, goddess of wisdom. And the goddess Aphrodite and her ugly husband, Hephaestus. And before you ask, yes, he really did have a face like a bull's pizzle.'

I stared at him, resisting the temptation to demand clarification on a bull's pizzle because I had a horrible feeling I knew anyway. 'What are you saying?'

'I'm saying it's happening all over again, isn't it? You call yourselves modern and rational and yet you're still worshipping the old gods, following their every move, copying their actions, obsessing over their relationships, sending them presents in the hope they'll notice you – only now you call them celebrities. I bet you good money that old Zeus ...' he made a sign of respect '... wherever he is, is laughing his head off and telling Hera he told her so. Just prior to descending on some unfortunate nymph in a shower of swans, of course.'

'I think you mean either a shower of gold *or* a swan,' I said, folding a T-shirt. 'Not both.'

'I know what I mean. The shower of swans was his practice swing. With unfortunate results. He calmed down a bit after that. Although not by much.'

I wasn't completely convinced he wasn't making all this up, but I never got the chance to discuss it any further because the phone rang again.

I picked it up. 'Jerry? Have you heard anything?'

'Ah, Elizabeth. Philip Sorensen here.'

Damn and blast.

'It's Mrs Cage, Sorensen, and I'm busy at the moment. Can you call back later?'

'I shan't keep you a moment … Mrs Cage.'

'I'm putting you on speakerphone,' I said, 'while I … take something out of the oven. Go ahead.'

His voice filled the room. 'I was wondering if I could prevail upon you to call on me …'

'Sorry, I'm busy at that time.'

'I haven't yet given you the time.'

'Not necessary,'

'Tomorrow.'

'Busy.'

'Shall we say around two?'

'Still busy.'

Out of the corner of my eye, I saw Iblis mute the TV and sit up, swinging his bare feet to the floor.

'I'm quite certain that when you arrive, you will agree the effort was worthwhile.'

'I'm equally certain I won't, Dr Sorensen. I've "visited" your clinic before and if you cast your mind back, you'll remember it didn't end well, did it? Please don't call me again.'

I went to disconnect the call and he said quickly, 'I have Michael Jones.'

My heart began to race. 'I'm sure you do, but you might find that's because he works for the same organisation as you.'

'Not at the moment, Mrs Cage. Mr Jones is, I'm sorry to say, undergoing a period of restricted movement.'

I took refuge in bluster while I pulled myself together. 'Oh God, Sorensen, don't tell me you're indulging in that old cliché, the locked room in the basement.'

'There's nothing wrong with a good cliché, Mrs Cage. Shall I expect you at two pm tomorrow?'

'No.'

'I thought there might be a certain amount of intransigence in your attitude. Allow me to make the decision much easier for you. I have Michael Jones. I have had him for some time now, and unless you present yourself at two o'clock tomorrow afternoon, he will find himself facing criminal charges relating to Miss Clare Woods.'

I started to say, 'I don't know who that is,' but he'd put the phone down and I was talking to the dialling tone.

Slowly, I replaced the handset and sat down.

'The important thing,' said Iblis, 'is not to panic. Now, I shall make a pot of tea while you keep calm and carry on. Because that is what the British do. I've seen posters.'

He bustled off into the kitchen while I tried to pull myself together and think.

He called over his shoulder. 'And you, Elizabeth Cage, will give some thought as to how to address this issue, bearing in mind you have access to Iblis, Man of Action and Infinite

196

Resource.' He filled the kettle. 'You have only to choose between a fire-breathing chimera, the Minotaur ...' He began to rummage for the tea bags, '... a couple of Ice Giants, any number of animal-headed gods of destruction, or Iron Man.' He poured boiling water into the tea pot. 'Oh no, sorry, Iron Man's not real, is he? I get confused.' He placed a perfect cup of tea in front of me. 'Drink.'

I stared at the tea. I could see it sitting in front of me on the coffee table but at that moment it was beyond me to make the connection between cup, hands, and lips. I was paralysed. Nothing was working, including my brain.

I was roused by Iblis gingerly picking up the phone and somewhat clumsily flicking through the menu. 'Ah, here we are. Drink your tea, Elizabeth Cage. We shall need you in a moment.'

We? Who was we?

'Hello? Hello? Can you hear me? I'm not shouting but I'm not sure I'm speaking into the right end. Oh good. Is Mr Jerry there? Of course I will. ... Mr Jerry – we have located Michael Jones and there is a problem. Mrs Cage would very much like to speak to you. Can you call round? As soon as possible, please. Thank you. Goodbye.'

He replaced the handset carefully and stepped back. 'That wasn't bad, was it? I've never been terribly good with those things but I thought I handled that quite well. Drink your tea, Elizabeth Cage.'

I was bewildered. 'Iblis, what are you doing?'

'Repaying my debt. What else would I be doing?'

I was never quite sure how much of the modern world he understood. Far more than he let on, I suspected, but how could I explain that the threat of Sorensen and everything he stood for always left me paralysed with fear, to someone whose first instinct in a crisis would always be to release the Kraken? Obediently, I drank my tea, an action which seemed to meet with his approval.

Ten minutes later, there was a knock at the door.

Iblis got up to answer it and there was a great deal of muttered conversation, after which, he reported back to me.

'He won't come in.'

That jolted me out of my paralysis. 'What? Why not?'

Jerry's voice filtered through the half open door. 'I'll have half your stuff in me pockets before you even noticed and I don't want to do it to a nice lady like you, but I can't help meself.'

I roused myself and went to the door. 'You were in my old house last year. You packed my things for me.'

'Yeah, I remember that. Nice place.'

'While you were there, did you …?'

'Course I did. He made me put it all back again.'

'Jones made you put it all back?'

'That's right.'

'Well, I would very much like you to come in.'

He looked uneasy.

'And then, when you leave, it's up to you whether you give my stuff back or not. Just please don't take my picture of Ted.'

'Wouldn't do that,' he muttered, sidling in through the door.

Iblis had replaced himself on the sofa, sprawling and barefooted. I guessed he was making himself deliberately disreputable.

Jerry turned to me. 'Stone the crows, missis. Every time I see you you've got some weird bloke attached.'

'Cheer up,' I said, brightly. 'At least this one has clothes on.'

He cast another disparaging glance at Iblis. 'Barely.'

I made the introductions. I could see neither was particularly impressed by the other.

'So,' said Jerry, 'where is he this time?' and I realised he was talking about Jones.

'Sorensen has him under lock and key.'

He looked startled. 'What for? I mean, I thought they was on the same team.'

I looked at Iblis who said succinctly, 'Bait.' Which wasn't how I would have put it, but accurate enough.

'It's me Sorensen wants and I can't see any alternative other than to present myself at two pm tomorrow afternoon.'

'Hmmm,' said Jerry, apparently thinking deeply.

'Fancy a beer?' said Iblis, and Jerry brightened up at once. I sensed the onset of a male bonding ritual. I started to say I didn't have any beer but the next moment Iblis was reaching for what looked very much like a bottle of beer on my worktop, knocking the top off in one smooth moment. I suspected the Horn of Utgard-Loki was about to take another bashing.

'Ah,' said Jerry, in satisfaction. 'I've always preferred it from the bottle. Never got on with them cans.'

'Me neither,' said Iblis, and we both watched Jerry drink deeply.

I sighed. 'The only thing I can think of is that we turn things around. I won't go and see Sorensen tomorrow unless he releases Jones first.'

Iblis looked at me pityingly. I felt quite cross. 'It's a good plan.'

'Actually,' said Jerry, carefully putting his bottle down on a coaster – I speculated on the possible presence of a Mrs Jerry – 'It's not bad. But I have a better idea.'

'Which is?'

He grinned at us.

Two hours later we'd thrashed out most of the details. Old Jerry was a bit of a whizz at this sort of thing. 'Gotta go,' he said, setting his still half full bottle on the table. I was no longer surprised at its capacity. 'Things to do.'

'Where will you take him?' I said.

'Abroad,' he said. 'Just for a little while. Out of sight. He's going grey.'

I thought of Jones's head of thick blondish hair and said indignantly, 'No, he's not.'

He sighed patiently. 'No, that's what we call it – going grey. Disappearing from view for a while. Going grey.'

'Oh.'

'Nothing to concern yourself over.'

I picked up my bag. 'We'll need his passport. I'll get that. Do you have a key to his flat?'

'I've already got it.'

I was bewildered. 'His key?'

'His passport.'

'When?'

'When I made it for him.'

'He has a fake passport?'

'Course not.' I breathed a sigh of relief. 'He's got several. One's no good.'

'But … why?'

He regarded me severely. 'Well, he can't go abroad on his real one, can he? Might as well ring them up and tell them where he is.'

Iblis was grinning at me so I said sorry, I hadn't been thinking.

'Right,' said Jerry. 'That's everything sorted. Everyone clear on what they're doing and where and when they're doing it?

We nodded.

I led him to the door, where he paused. Something was obviously required of me. Oh yes. I held out my hand.

Sighing, he rummaged through his pockets, pulling out a silver pen knife belonging to a quite indignant Iblis, an old horse brass that my father had electro-plated for me, and a tea spoon. I thanked him gravely.

'Tomorrow,' he said. 'One thirty down by the bridge. Remember, as soon as you set foot outside your door, act as if they're watching you. 'Cos they probly will be.'

I swallowed and nodded.

'And don't worry. We'll get him back.'

Iblis was going with Jerry. I had no idea what their preparations would consist of and nor did I want to know. I was having enough difficulty with my own role in the proceedings.

I closed and locked the door behind them and turned around to clear up but the beer bottle had disappeared.

Chapter Eighteen

The next day I was ready by twelve o'clock, which was stupid because it left me with nothing to do but worry for an hour and a half. I surveyed myself in the mirror. Jerry's instructions had been explicit. Wear something safe. Old fashioned. Mousy, if you've got it. Non-threatening. Quiet colours. Not trousers.

I'd rummaged away at the back of my wardrobe and found the blue suit I used to wear to work. It was a little dated now, which was perfect, and when I put it with a prissy pink blouse with a pussy cat bow and donned shoes with just the wrong heel height for the length of skirt, I was amazed. And rather horrified, too. I looked a good ten years older than I actually was. I combed my hair behind my ears and applied a really nasty coral coloured lipstick that even your granny wouldn't have looked at and peered at myself in the mirror. I looked dumpy, frumpy and lumpy. It would be only a short walk to the taxi, but I couldn't help hoping I wouldn't see anyone I knew.

The minutes inched by as I ran over everything in my mind for the umpteenth time. I'm really not cut out for this sort of thing and quite honestly, I was terrified. I could only hope Sorensen would put it down to fear of him and what I thought he could to me.

I left the house at twenty past one, carefully locked the door behind me, hoisted my old-fashioned black handbag over my forearm like the queen, and set off. The mid-calf length skirt flapped around my legs. And yes, I was wearing American Tan tights. Michael Jones was going to owe me for the rest of his life. Always supposing any of us survived the events of this afternoon.

The taxi was waiting for me down by the bridge. An old-fashioned saloon model in dark red with a large boot, it had once been a very good car – someone's pride and joy, perhaps – but now that it's walnut dashboard was scratched and dented, and the leather seats worn thin in places, it had come down in the world. On the other hand, if this afternoon went wrong it might be going out in a blaze of glory. I could just see it being Exhibit A at our trial.

The very realistic sign on the door read 'Jerry's Taxis,' with a neat JT logo and a telephone number underneath. I was willing to bet anyone ringing that number would be answered by a bored voice asking where they wanted to go and when. I was beginning to have a lot of faith in old Jerry.

He was leaning against the bonnet with his arms folded, just an old cabbie enjoying the sun while he waited for his fare. He wore an ancient tweed jacket with leather patches at the elbows, baggy trousers and a pair of heavy spectacles. He straightened up when he saw me approach.

'Mrs Cage?'

I remembered what he'd said about assuming we were being watched. 'Yes.'

'Where to, missis?'

'The Sorensen clinic, please. On the Whittington road.'

He held open the rear door for me and I climbed in, the stupid skirt skidding about on the leather seats.

Climbing in himself, he started the engine. 'Seatbelt.'

I looked at his eyes in the rear-view mirror. Not a hint of humour. 'Sorry.'

I clicked my seat belt and sat back clutching my handbag which contained nothing more than a twenty-pound note slipped into the pocket, the awful coral lipstick and a small pack of tissues. Given what we had planned for that afternoon, it hardly seemed adequate.

Mine, however, was the easy part. 'Just play it by ear,' Jerry had said. 'Do just as you would if you were on your own. Don't give us a thought. Your part is to meet this Sorensen bloke and keep him occupied. Just concentrate on that. Leave everything else to us.'

I'd nodded and wondered what I'd got myself into.

I watched the green hedges slip past. Jerry drove well with smooth gear changes and well below the speed limit. I had a sudden crazy picture of him wearing a Ronald Reagan face mask, waiting outside the local bank, gunning the engine, all ready to go the moment the alarms went off … and told myself not to be so silly.

The gates stood open. We pulled in and stopped at the barrier.

Jerry wound down the window and a guard leaned in. 'Yes?'

Jerry jerked his thumb at me. I leaned forwards and said nervously. 'I have an appointment with Dr Sorensen at two o'clock.'

He leaned in further. 'It's Mrs Cage, isn't it?'

'I remember you,' I said, delighted to see a familiar face. 'You were on Ted's team. It's Mr … Goodman.'

'That's right. How are you keeping?'

'Well, thank you. And you?'

'Can't complain,' he said in that voice which says he's going to start any moment now. 'Sign here please driver.'

Jerry scribbled something I was sure would be quite illegible, put the car into gear and we rolled up the drive.

I looked around. Nothing seemed to have changed.

'Nice gardens,' said Jerry, conversationally.

'Yes, very nice.'

They were. Large hanging baskets in lovely shades of yellow and orange lined the immaculate gravel drive interspersed with tubs of red and white. All the hedges were ruler-straight and immaculate and the lawns closely mown. Over there was the bench where I'd sat with Michael Jones plotting our escape. We hadn't got far, had we? Only just over a year later and we were both back here again. I began seriously to doubt whether I'd ever be free of Sorensen.

'Although I prefer a nice veggie patch myself,' said Jerry, dragging me back to the present. 'You can't beat a nice row of cabbages.' I had no idea whether he was pulling my leg. His brown colour was deep and solid and giving nothing away at the moment.

We pulled up at the front doors. He switched off the engine and at once the door opened and one of the security staff came out, saying, 'You can't park here. Round the side please.'

I tried not to panic. Jerry had been most insistent about being able to get into the hall so he could have a good look around. Now, it didn't seem as if he would get the chance.

He didn't seem particularly bothered. 'Give us a minute to get me passenger out, sonny. That's thirty-three pounds fifty, missis.'

'Oh,' I said, flustered and scrabbling for my handbag. Would it be possible for you to wait for me, please? I won't be very long.'

'OK,' he said amiably, settling back in his seat.

'Not here,' said the security guard, firmly.

I left them to it, climbing the shallow steps with a thumping heart and stepped through the open doors.

Very little had changed since my last visit. There were the same deep, comfortable armchairs, although at this time of year, the fireplace around which they were grouped was empty, apart from an expensive looking flower arrangement in shades of red and orange sitting in the grate. Smaller versions of the same arrangement stood on occasional tables. The same artwork was on the walls and the same stairs curved upwards to the private rooms upstairs. Through an open door, I caught a quick glimpse of the library, seemingly deserted on this fine day. The same expensive reception desk stood by the door, manned by an exquisite young man I didn't recognise.

His glance ran over me. Even his delicate lilac colour sneered at me. 'Yes,' he said, dismissively. 'Can I help you?'

I was certain he didn't know who I was or why I was there. He would have a list of visitors on a clipboard but he hadn't associated me with Mrs E Cage. He was someone who judged by appearances and, on the surface, I was definitely not a potential Sorensen Clinic customer. It would seem the frumpy look was working.

'No, I don't think so,' I said, answering his question literally. 'I'm here to see Dr Sorensen.'

He couldn't be bothered to look at me this time. 'I'm afraid Dr Sorensen has an appointment at two.' With someone who didn't look like Margaret Thatcher's grandmother, presumably. I began to remember how much I'd disliked this place.

Knowing he'd never let me go, I said, 'Oh, what a shame. And he was so insistent, too. Never mind. Please tell him Mrs Cage called,' and turned to go, confident I wouldn't get far.

He was out from behind the desk in a flash. 'Mrs Cage, I'm so sorry. My mistake. If you could take a seat, I'll just tell Dr Sorensen you're here.'

Behind me, through the front doors, I could hear Jerry's voice loudly demanding the whereabouts of the bog. The receptionist's head snapped around so I took advantage of his lack of attention to wander away, ostensibly to look at the artwork. I stood behind a pillar, closed my eyes and let my mind wander ... reaching out ... letting it drift ... yes, Jones was here. Somewhere. He was very faint. I wondered if he was unconscious.

I dragged myself back. The receptionist was loudly denying the existence of any facilities for members of the public. Behind him, I nodded at Jerry. Just once. Jones was on the premises.

'Not a problem, mate,' said Jerry, heading for the front door, still open on this nice day, and giving me a heart attack because that wasn't part of the plan at all. 'Any old flower bed will do.'

The whereabouts of an appropriate facility were suddenly remembered. They made him wait while they found him an escort and he used the time to lean on the desk, whistling softly between his teeth and not in any way running his eye down the list of patients and their room numbers, kept on a clipboard by the door in case of fire.

They bundled him off through a door on the left. I watched him go. He was on his own now because at the same moment, Dr Sorensen's office door opened and here he came. He didn't look much different either, except he'd grown a goatee. On some men it looks good. On him it looked ridiculous. Especially as he still favoured slightly too sharply cut pinstripe suits and with a waistcoat, even in this weather. His thin grey hair was swept back from his forehead and his eyes still reminded me of wet pebbles. His manner was quiet and controlled, but his greasy-milk colour swirled towards me briefly before being reined back again.

'Mrs Cage, how nice to see you again.'

I turned my head and nodded. 'Dr Sorensen.'

'Would you like to come into my office?'

'No.'

'Ah,' he said with some sort of grimace I thought might be a smile, 'I had forgotten your penchant for answering questions literally. Please come into my office, Mrs Cage, so we can talk together in private.'

He turned and gestured.

I stood my ground. The receptionist sat at his desk, typing on a smart laptop. Two nurses were crossing the hall towards the library with their arms full of files, and the security guard was standing outside a door presumably waiting for Jerry to reappear. I wondered how long it would be before he went to look for him. Still, as Jerry had said, that was not my problem. My job was simply to deal with Sorensen in any way I thought fit. But I had witnesses, which was all I wanted.

I let my voice carry. 'You should be aware, Dr Sorensen, that my solicitor knows I'm here today, as does my doctor, as do the staff at the local library, as do my neighbours, as do the members of the Local History Group – in fact, everyone I know, up to and including my taxi driver, is aware that I am here this afternoon, and another attempt by you to detain me here, illegally and against my will, is destined to go even more badly for you than the last time. Just a friendly warning. Just so we're all on the same page.'

People were gaping. The receptionist, although staring diligently at his screen was listening with every fibre of his being, his delicate lilac colour deepening with excitement. I was quite sure there were people at the nurses' station upstairs who would have heard as well. Sorensen, however, seemed not the slightest bit discomfited and why would he be? He did possess Michael Jones after all. Although not for very much longer.

He smiled politely and gestured ahead of him.

I took a deep breath, ignored my suddenly pounding heart, and walked quietly past him and into his office.

Chapter Nineteen

Not much had changed in here, either. He had a new, sleek, black laptop open on his desk, but otherwise it was all pretty much as I remembered it.

The same Turkish carpet lay in the centre of the room, surrounded by a gleaming parquet floor. Three or four original pieces of art hung around the walls – fashionable, but not necessarily good. If they were meant to make a statement then that statement was, 'I have more money than taste.' His huge desk sat in front of the French windows. I could just hear Jones now. 'Big desk – small ...' As always, everything was minutely lined up with everything else, right down to the last sharpened pencil in the precisely placed pen pot.

He seated himself, gesturing for me to take one of the two visitor's chairs opposite. I was certain he would expect me to choose the other one, just to be awkward, so I seated myself in the chair of his choice. Just to be even more awkward.

We looked at each other. I waited for him to begin.

He didn't seem in any particular hurry, carefully shutting down his laptop and pushing it to one side.

'Well now, Elizabeth.'

I ignored the provocation, staring over his shoulder at the garden outside, trying not to remember all the previous occasions I'd been here in this office, confronting this man.

He sat back, clasped his hands and said smoothly, 'I know your husband lied to me about you in the past. I know Mr Jones is lying to me about you right now.' He leaned forwards. 'I have to ask myself, what is it about you, Mrs Cage? That's two of our best people you've induced to deceive me. I'm not angry, you understand. I'm more curious than angry.'

I shrugged. 'Isn't it a sign of a serious mental disorder when you think everyone you meet is lying to you? Obviously, I don't want to tell you your business, but I really think you should seriously consider the possibility that the problem might lie with you, rather than the rest of the world.'

His colour swirled about him, darkening slightly at the edges. Opposition could be overcome or ignored, but he was never comfortable with ridicule. There was no indication he had anything in the way of a sense of humour and not taking him seriously always wound him up. Small red tinges began to appear in his colour, like blood in milk.

'Well, shall we leave that for the time being and discuss your success in locating little Keira Swanson without ever setting foot in the area.'

I remembered to keep my body posture loose and neutral. 'I think you overrate my contribution. From what I could see on the news, she was less than one hundred yards from her home. She would have been found very soon, I think.'

'I beg leave to differ. I don't think anyone would ever have thought to look *inside* a tree.'

I shrugged. 'Yew trees make new growth from the outside, frequently resulting in a hollow interior. I'm surprised you didn't know that.'

He remained silent. I was almost certain he was restraining himself from re-aligning the objects on his desk. His office seemed very quiet. Half of me was listening for indications that all was not well on the other side of his door. Shouting, for example, or running footsteps. Or even the alarm bells going off. I made myself stop. That was exactly what Jerry had told me not to do. I must concentrate on what was happening in here, keep Sorensen occupied, and leave everything else to him.

'What do you want, Sorensen?'

He sat forwards, clasping his hands on his desk, every inch the concerned megalomaniac.

'We touched on this subject very briefly last year ...'

'During my last forced incarceration,' I said brightly.

'When you spent some time with us after your husband's funeral,' he corrected. 'I realise that visit didn't go well ...'

'Well, not for you,' I said. 'Didn't your car get stolen? Or something like that?'

He sat back. 'Another instance of your extraordinary powers of persuasion. How on earth did you persuade Michael Jones to steal my car?'

It was on the tip of my tongue to deny my involvement in this, and with some indignation too. As if Michael Jones had needed any encouragement from me. My sole contribution had been to hide on the back seat, trembling with fear at the thought of so comprehensively breaking the law. On the other hand, if Sorensen wanted to think of me as a dangerous and resourceful young woman, with astonishing powers of persuasion, then that was fine by me. Although it was a shame the pussy cat bow and the American Tan tights weren't working. I would be having a word about that with Jerry. Next time, he could wear the tights.

He took advantage of my silence to press on. 'In the matter of providing any information about you, Mrs Cage, Mr Jones has been less cooperative than I would like, but more cooperative than he realises. It's been a struggle but we have begun to make some progress. While I'm gratified to see my training on techniques for resisting interrogation has proved effective, his intransigence is beginning to annoy me. I'm being forced to use methods of which you would not approve. I don't have everything I need just yet, but it won't be long now. I should perhaps take this opportunity to say that the longer these methods are employed, the less chance there is for Mr Jones to make a complete recovery afterwards. In the interests of Mr Jones's welfare, I do recommend you reconsider your position.'

I smiled with my mouth only. 'I rather think the question of Mr Jones's welfare rests with you rather than me. You have only to desist and the problem is solved.'

'I would be happy to do so. Perhaps we could discuss your provision of an appropriate incentive.'

My heart was thumping against my ribs. A trickle of cold sweat ran down my back. I made myself stay calm. Made my voice steady. 'Perhaps *you* could come to the point.'

'Mrs Cage, it was apparent to me – even on our first, brief meeting – that there is something extraordinary about you. Your ability to read and manipulate people is ... remarkable.'

My stomach swooped. Did I do that? Surely not. That was what Sorensen did, not me. I didn't manipulate people. Did I? All my old fears came rushing back. I remembered my dad advising me to keep my 'gift' hidden. Not to advertise the fact I was slightly different from other people. My chest tightened. It was a warm afternoon. I felt my scalp prickle. I would have loved to take off my jacket, but the polyester blouse would have dark patches under the armpits, and apart from that being something of which my mother would not have approved, I didn't want Sorensen to realise I wasn't anything other than completely calm. I wanted so badly to get up and leave but not yet. At least twenty minutes, Jerry had said.

'Wait, wait,' he said, putting out a hand. I suspected that, despite my best efforts, at least some of that had shown on my face. 'Please do not be alarmed, Mrs Cage, I had no intention of upsetting you.'

212

He put a glass of water in front of me. I peered at it. I didn't want to show any weakness, but not fainting was more important.

He seated himself again and clasped his hands in his lap. Neutral and unthreatening. 'I'm sorry,' he said. 'We do seem to have the knack of getting under each other's skin, don't we?'

The cold water was very welcome. He waited while I sipped slowly and then set down the glass. 'What do you want, Sorensen.'

'I want you to work with me, Mrs Cage.'

This was normally the point at which our meetings would take a sudden turn downhill, usually with disastrous results for one or both of us. Bearing in mind what should be happening elsewhere and the need to keep him in here, I took a deep breath and said, slowly, 'In what capacity?'

It was the first time I'd ever responded with anything other than a flat 'no.'

His colour streamed towards me again and I tried not to flinch. We looked at each other for a while.

'Actually,' he said with disarming candour, 'I'm not entirely sure. I suspect you possess remarkable powers of intuition and I would like to begin by working with those.'

'For what purpose?'

'Initially, to attend meetings, negotiations, summits, that sort of thing. To assist with our assessment of various situations and the people involved therein.'

'Are you saying you want me to tell you what people are thinking? I suspect you have over-estimated my abilities, Sorensen.'

His colour roared at me. I shifted slightly to avoid it. 'And I suspect you're doing it right now, Mrs Cage, because I don't think you can help yourself. The only part of the procedure you

213

seem to have some difficulty with is passing your impressions on to the right people. People who can use them to ensure ... favourable outcomes.'

'And who determines which outcome is most favourable?'

He shrugged. 'That is not something with which you would have to concern yourself.'

I shook my head.

He persevered, saying quietly, 'That would only be the beginning, Mrs Cage. The area in which I would really like you to work is ... influencing ... others. Persuading those who may feel a certain reluctance to proceed in a direction we feel would be most favourable. For all concerned.'

'Against their better judgement.'

'I prefer to think of it as for the good of others as a whole.'

My instinct was to stop. To back off. Not to get involved in this. Not even to show any interest, but I couldn't let it go. I still had seven minutes to kill.

'What others?'

He shrugged. 'Many others.'

'The government?'

'On occasions.'

'But not always?'

'No, not always.'

I smiled. 'Ah. You mean the people willing to pay the highest price.'

He ignored that, concentrating on his sales pitch. 'Think about it, Mrs Cage. This is an opportunity for you to do some real good in the world. And to put your mind at rest, it wouldn't just be ... commercial transactions. Think back to Keira Swanson. No child need ever go missing again. Think of all the deaths and disasters you could prevent. Violence that might never happen. Haven't you ever watched the antics of our leaders and thought – I could do better than that. Well, now you can. You can influence negotiations to bring about peace. End the incessant warfare. Bring down corrupt governments and restore prosperity.'

His voice was rising. I shifted in my chair and at once his colour reeled itself back in again.

'I'm sorry – I didn't mean to alarm you. I just wanted you to share my vision.'

Nightmare was more like it. 'And if I don't?'

'Don't what?'

'Share your vision.'

'I am confident that being offered the opportunity to influence the world for good will sway you. Beginning, of course, with Michael Jones. Just think what you can do for him.'

'Ensure he continues to live, for example.'

'Oh, so much more than that. His name cleared. His security clearance restored. All the top jobs could be his for the asking. The two of you might even find yourselves working side by side.'

'And the alternative?'

'Oh, I don't think we want to discuss that right at this moment, do we?'

'Actually, I wouldn't mind at all discussing that right at this moment. What's the alternative, Sorensen?'

He shrugged. 'As you wish. Well, there are a number of questions relating to Michael Jones and past events in his career. He was never completely exonerated over the Clare Woods business, you know. And should evidence come to light that he was guilty of more than ignorance, well ...'

'I believe one bullet to the head and another one to the heart is the accepted solution.'

He didn't bother to deny it.

I was indignant. 'And you know Michael Jones so badly that you think he would take back his job knowing what you're forcing me to do?'

He smiled. 'I don't think we need trouble him with that, do you? No useful purpose would be achieved by apprising him of the *exact* conditions of his reinstatement. And I think it's important for you to know that clearances can be rescinded at any time.'

'So you wouldn't want me to tell him why I'm working for you.'

'I think the fewer people aware of that the better, don't you?'

'So it would be just you and me, then?'

'Exactly.'

I looked around. 'I'm not living here.'

His colour jumped. I'd taken a step towards acceptance. Or so he thought.

'You wouldn't have to. You can continue to live in Rushford where you seem to be happy. You could think of yourself as a consultant, called in only when necessary. There might even be long periods when we don't need you at all. Just three or four small jobs a year and a very generous retainer.'

Under cover of pulling out a tissue from my bag, I looked at my watch. Twenty minutes. That had been the minimum, Jerry had said. Thirty minutes to be on the safe side.

I would give him his thirty minutes. I sighed and slumped in my chair.

'Would you like some tea,' he said, misreading the signs. I hoped.

'Yes, please.' Waiting for tea would kill a little time.

He pressed a button on his telephone and the door opened immediately. His secretary was actually wearing a suit very similar to mine, minus the stupid pussy-cat bow blouse and mid-calf hemline. Her shoes were much nicer than mine as well.

She took a while to pour the tea so that was another few minutes used up. And it was good tea – in that it wasn't drugged, which was a bit of a first for him. I sat back and sipped. His office was very quiet. Everywhere was very quiet. No alarms. No gunfire.

I let the silence drag on, sipping my tea and saying nothing. Eventually, he said, 'You're very quiet, Mrs Cage.'

I told him I was thinking.

'May I hope you are considering my proposition?'

I set down my cup and saucer. 'Be very clear. I am not saying yes.'

'But you're not saying no, either.'

'Because I am not saying no now does not mean I won't be saying no later on.'

'I accept that.'

I doubted that. Especially when he discovered Michael Jones had been spirited out from under his nose by an ancient cabbie and a woman wearing American Tan tights. Iblis was also out there somewhere, but I wasn't sure of his exact role so I ignored him for the time being. I did take a moment to wonder what Sorensen's reaction would be when he discovered I was deceiving him, but on the other hand, he was using Michael Jones as a pawn to get what he wanted.

And what of Jones? If – when – we got him out of this, what would his future hold? If Sorensen was feeling particularly vindictive he might never be able to live in the civilised world again.

Time had ticked by while I was musing. I'd finished my tea. And my thirty minutes was up. It was time for me to go. Staying

217

too long ran the risk of them discovering he was missing before we'd left the premises.

I stood up. 'Give me time.'

'As much as you like,' he said and held out his hand.

I nodded and strode to the door.

The first person I saw was old Jerry, leaning against the reception desk like a man with all the time in the world.

'Sand,' he was saying to the stunned receptionist whose colour was practically climbing the walls in an effort to get away. 'You fill your bucket with sand and plant your seeds. Good drainage, of course, and they love it. Best carrots you'll ever eat.'

The exquisite young man who had probably never given a thought to the origin of carrots in his entire life, was staring helplessly.

Jerry saw me and straightened up. 'There you are missis. Fifty-eight quid on the clock, you know,' thus giving me a perfect reason for leaving quickly.

I shifted my hand bag to my other arm. 'I'm quite ready. Sorry to have kept you waiting.'

'No problem,' he said airily, gesturing around the hall. 'And I got a good look at them nice pictchers, too.' He turned to Sorensen, who must have known people like Jerry existed but never expected to find one of them on his premises. 'You was robbed, mate. Don't know who told you that was an Auerbach but they must have been drunk – or blind – but your Guthrie's genuine. Nice piece.'

I think he would have gone on, but we were interrupted by the strains of Dancing Queen emanating from his pocket. 'Hang on a mo,' he said, fishing out his phone. 'Jerry's Taxis. Yeah. Hang on.'

218

He laid down his phone and fished in his other pocket, pulling out a small greasy notebook and a pencil. Leafing through the pages with great solemnity he said, 'When?' and found the correct date. 'Your address? Where to? Yeah, all right, missis, but they've got the High Street up again, so make it ten minutes earlier just to be on the safe side. Don't want to miss your train, do you?'

Licking his pencil, he slowly wrote Webber, 14 Dunster St, Train Stat. 0950. 'Gotcha missis,' and clicked his phone off.

Turning to me he said, 'Ready?'

I nodded. You had to admire his eye for detail. I'd never seen anything look so greasily genuine as that awful old notebook. And the bonus was that they couldn't wait to get him out of the building. They didn't physically throw him out of the front door, but it was close.

Dr Sorensen said, 'I'll accompany you to your car, Mrs Cage,' and whether this was a courtesy or to ensure Jerry was actually off the premises, I wasn't sure.

We walked around the outside of the building – Jerry rendering Sorensen unable to speak privately to me by loudly casting doubts on the effectiveness of their greenfly treatment. I could see his taxi, parked at a seemingly careless angle near the side door.

As we approached, the security guard emerged from around the corner looking hot and breathless. 'There you are.' He saw Dr Sorensen. 'I'm sorry, sir. I'm not sure how he got away from me.'

'It's not important. At this moment.'

The guard, correctly guessing it would become important the minute our backs were turned, pushed off while the going was good.

To my horror, Jerry whipped the boot open. Right in front of Sorensen. My heart turned over. What did he think he was doing? I made myself look inside. It was vastly and cavernously empty – a completely Michael Jones free zone.

'Suitcase, missis?'

I pulled myself together. 'Um, I don't have one.'

'OK.' He slammed the boot shut and opened the passenger door for me. The inside of the car was also vastly and cavernously empty. Something had gone wrong.

Dr Sorensen said, 'I'll call you, Mrs Cage.'

I didn't want him ringing me every ten minutes. 'No. I'll take a couple of days to think about your offer and then I'll call *you*.'

'As you wish.'

Jerry was still holding the door for me. 'Mind yer head, missis.'

I thanked him gravely.

The last I saw of Sorensen was him walking briskly back towards the front door. He didn't wave but he was looking pretty pleased with himself. Michael Jones was not the only one who might have to go and live abroad.

As per instructions, I said nothing to Jerry as we cruised down the drive. You never knew who might be watching. Or listening. The guard had the barrier up ready for us. I waved as we passed. He waved back and then we turned left and accelerated away.

Chapter Twenty

We bowled back down green country lanes with Jerry humming tunelessly in the front while I fretted silently in the back. Was his saying nothing a good or a bad sign? There was no sign either of Jones or Iblis anywhere. I remembered the empty boot. Had we failed and he couldn't bring himself to tell me?

I couldn't stand it any longer. 'Jerry?'

'Just a minute, missis.'

He pulled over into a layby and fumbled in the glove compartment, pulling out a small device rather like a TV remote, but wider. Switching it on, he waved it around the inside of the car. And all over me. I wanted to ask what he was doing but he frowned and shook his head so I remained silent.

Eventually, he switched it off. 'No, we're fine.'

'Are we? What are we fine about?'

'My main worry was that someone would plant something when I had to go off and leave the old girl unattended.'

'And did they?'

'Dun't look like it.

'So we can talk?'

'Yes, probly and ...'

I interrupted him. 'Jerry, what happened? Where is he? Where's Jones?'

'You're sitting on him.'

I looked down at the back seat in horror. 'What?'

'He's under the back seat.'

I tried to stand up and bumped my head on the roof. 'Ow.'

'Sit still, for Gawd's sake. It's only for a few more minutes away.'

'What's only a few minutes away?'

He started the engine. 'My lock-up.'

I couldn't wait that long. I hung over the front seat demanding, 'What happened? How did it go? Where's Iblis? Give me all the details.'

'Well, the poncey young bugger showed me the bog. Quite smart – all done out in dark blue and white. Very nautical. Mirrors everywhere. Two cubicles, four urinals ...'

'Yes, yes ... not that much detail. You can skip that bit.'

'He wanted to come in with me, but obviously I wasn't having any of that. Gave him my 'Whoa mate, you a poofta?' face and he backed right off.'

'Well,' I said, quite shocked, 'that *was* rather rude of him but I'm not sure we're allowed to say poofta these days.'

'S'alright if you are one,' he said straight faced.

'Oh. OK then. What happened next? How did you get out of the ... bog? Did you climb out of the window?'

'Nah. Too obvious. I went up. False ceiling. Always is in these old places. There's always a mass of pipes and working bits they don't want the posh punters to see. Bit of a struggle 'cos I'm not as young as I was, but I don't weigh a lot and I just crossed over the partition into the next room which was on the other side of the fire doors so he couldn't see me when I nipped out and away down the stairs into the basement. Found the young master easily enough.'

I was astounded. He made it all sound so easy. 'Did you? How?'

He sighed patiently. 'The only locked door.'

I resolved to shut up.

'Lock wasn't a problem. Shifting him was. Whoever knocked him out knew how difficult it would be to lift him.'

'He was knocked out?'

'Drugged. To keep him quiet.'

'So where was Iblis in all this? When did he arrive?'

'Been there since last night. Hiding outside for when he was needed. Which he was. I tell you it was like trying to shift a bloody mountain. I've done me back in right good and proper.'

'Iblis,' I said, getting him back on track.

'Well, I couldn't shift our boy here, could I, so I trotted down the corridor to that side door you told me about.'

'But the keypad?' I said

He made a derisive noise. I gathered the keypad had not presented any sort of a challenge.

'Anyway, that Iblis, he might be built like a long thin streak of wind and piss but he had our boy off the bed and over his shoulder in no time. I went first. Out the delivery door up the steps and round the car park. They really want to get rid of them rhododendrons, you know. Very pretty and the punters probly like them, but they bugger up their lines of sight right good and proper. Don't think a soul saw us. We heaved the young master into the car. Couldn't hang around meself, so I left young Iblis to make things tidy and pushed off back the way I'd come.'

'Wasn't your young man wondering what was taking you so long?'

'Nah,' he said complacently. 'I just wandered out, zipping meself up, told him to stop complaining – it would be his prostate one day – and went out to wind up that snooty sod on reception.' He glanced sideways at me. 'Gotta say, missis, security's gone right downhill since your old man was there. I'd never have got twenty feet if he'd been around. Good bloke, your old man.'

'Thank you,' I said, genuinely touched.

'Well no, actually he was a complete bar steward most of the time, but you know what I mean.'

'I do, and I still thank you, Jerry. And if he was here, Ted would say thank you, too.'

He nodded. 'You're welcome.'

A minute later we were in a small industrial park located on the outskirts of town. We turned into a dilapidated garage block. Jerry's was the big one at the far end. He bleeped the graffiti covered door which rose with a rattle. Inside, however, everything was pristine.

I recognised it immediately. I'd been here before. Jones and I had called in here on our last escape from Sorensen's clinic. I remembered the concrete floor. And the old workbench piled high with what looked like junk. Pieces of cars still lay everywhere. His tools hung neatly from the walls. Four tyres were stacked in the corner. An SUV was parked in the other corner. I recognised it as the one they'd used to rescue me from Greyston. The other vehicle here was a small, anonymous black hatchback. The whole place smelled of oil and grease and the sound of our engine was hollow and echoey.

I was out of the car almost before it had stopped moving. 'Quick. Before he suffocates.'

He sighed and shook his head and I gathered there was no danger of Jones suffocating. He flicked something and the entire back seat folded away and lifted out. I was amazed. 'I didn't know they did that.'

'They don't.'

'Oh.'

'Very useful on a booze cruise.'

'What's a booze cruise?

He just sighed and shook his head again.

He twitched aside a light cover and there was Michael Jones, scrunched up in the tiny space. His eyes were shut and he wasn't moving.

'Oh God, Jerry, is he dead?'

'No. Drugged.'

I couldn't help myself. I made a small sound of distress.

He patted my shoulder briefly. 'Well it makes sense, don't it? He's a big bloke and he knows all the moves. If I wanted to stop someone escaping, and him burning the place down on the way out, then I'd drug him too.'

He bent down to help him out. 'Out you come, sunshine.'

Jones stiffly unfolded himself and gazed about him blearily.

'Can he stand up?'

'Dunno. Let's see.'

We helped him up, got him out and leaned him against the car. His colour, usually a vigorous golden red, flopped around him, vague and insubstantial. He stared at me, then at Jerry, then down at himself and apparently finding it all too much to cope with, he gave up, closing his eyes and sliding slowly down the car. I grabbed him and pushed him upright again, saying loudly, 'Open your eyes.'

To my surprise, he did.

'Yeah, you might want to be a bit careful what you say,' warned Jerry, disappearing around the car. 'He's a bit susceptible.'

'What?'

'It's the drugs. He's already agreed to lend me ten thousand quid.'

'What?'

'Just joking. But watch what you say to him.' He began to rummage in a tool box in the corner.

I turned back to Jones, 'Hey, it's me. How are you feeling?'

He smiled sleepily down at me and I instructed my heart to behave itself.

'Hey, you. I'm OK. How are you?'

'Pleased to see you again.'

'I'm pleased to see you too,' he said. He gazed blearily around the lock-up. 'I know this place.'

'We're in Jerry's lock up.'

He looked around again. 'Is Sorensen here?'

'No. You're quite safe.' Honesty compelled me to add, 'For the moment.'

He seemed to see me for the first time. 'Cage? Hey, nice to see you. How're you doing?'

'Good, I said, struggling to keep up with someone possessing the memory span of a goldfish.

'Good,' he repeated vaguely, staring around him. There was a pause. I shouldn't have done it. It wasn't a nice thing to do. I looked over my shoulder. Jerry was ostentatiously and very noisily rummaging for something on his workbench and not paying us the slightest attention.

I turned back to Jones, stared at the front of his shirt for courage and said, 'Do you …?' my nerve failed me at the last moment. '…like me?'

I knew he did. I knew he more than liked me. I could see it in his colour every time he looked at me, but I wanted to hear him say it.

'Of course I like you,' he said. 'Do you like me?' thus turning the tables so neatly and swiftly that I wondered if he was actually drugged at all.

I took a leaf out of his book. 'Of course I do, but do you lo …?'

'Tell him I've got his passport safe,' said Jerry, materialising beside me.

'Hello, Jerry,' said Jones, amiably.

'Hello, mate. Back in a minute.' He disappeared again.

I tried again. Because I could ask him and get a truthful answer and he'd never remember I'd asked in the first place. 'Do you lo…?'

'Two minutes,' called Jerry from the other end of the garage. Jones waved an acknowledgement that caused him to lose his balance somewhat.

I straightened him up and made sure he was leaning against the car.

'Just tell me, yes or no, do you …?'

'He's gone to sleep,' reported Jerry, passing with a suitcase.

Dammit. And no, I don't swear very often.

'Let's get him in the car. No, the other one.'

I looked around. He was gesturing to the small black car.

'I'll get the doors open. You just hang on to Sunny Jim here.'

He trotted off to the car and I hung on to Sunny Jim here. The lockup was very silent.

A voice over my head said, 'Of course I do.'

I nearly dropped him in shock. 'What? What did you say?'

Too late. Jerry was back. 'We'll get him on the back seat, chuck a blanket over him and hopefully he'll be out like a light for most of the journey.'

'Has he gone back to sleep?'

'Yep. Considering what they pumped into him it's a miracle he even woke for a few minutes.'

'What did they pump into him? Do you know?'

He shrugged. 'Stuff to calm him down. Stuff to make him tell the truth.'

'Where are you taking him?'

227

He looked at me.

'Sorry. Don't tell me if you don't want to.'

'Abroad. But not in this state. At this moment if the border policeman said, "Tell me everything," he probably would. So a week or so to get the drugs out of his system and then somewhere safe when he's a bit less prone to telling the truth.'

We'd reached the car and manhandled him across the back seat. It wasn't easy. I was leaning over him with the blanket and reflecting on the number of young men I'd tucked up recently, when he opened his eyes.

'You look like sex on legs in that outfit.'

'Shut up,' I said, blushing deeply.

'Heavily drugged,' said Jerry, trying to reassure me and not helping at all. He pulled the driver's door open.

Jones managed to get one eye open again. 'Promise me, Cage, that when you eventually get me into bed – and you will one day if you keep trying – you'll wear exactly that outfit.'

'Very heavily drugged,' grinned Jerry.

'You shut up, too.'

I slammed the door on Jones and waited for my face to return to its normal colour and temperature.

Jerry climbed into the driving seat. 'That Iblis'll be here in a minute. He'll take you home and keep you safe.'

'Well, good luck. And again, Jerry. Thank you. A lot of this is my fault and I'm sorry to have got you both into trouble.'

He snorted. 'He was in trouble long before you ever came on the scene and I've never been out of it, so don't beat yourself up, missis.'

'Well, thank you anyway.'

'You're welcome. Now, off you go so I can lock the door behind us.'

'Look after him.'

'I will.'

'And look after yourself too.'

'Always do,' he said simply.

He drove the car slowly out of the garage and I followed him out. The first person I saw was Iblis, leaning against a wall in the sun.

The door came down behind me, Jerry tooted his horn, I waved back, and the little black car sped away. I watched it go until it disappeared around the bend.

Iblis was staring at my get-up in astonishment. I'd forgotten we hadn't seen each other this morning.

'Don't start.'

He spread his hands in innocence. 'I never said a word.'

'You didn't have to. Turn around.'

'Why?'

'Just do it, please.'

He turned around. I kicked off my shoes and hopped around, ripping off the American Tan tights, and losing my balance slightly. I bundled them up and hurled them away from me, where they wrapped themselves around an oil drum and flapped forlornly in the breeze.

'Is this some form of celebration?' said Iblis. 'Should I too remove an article of clothing and throw it over there?'

I slid my feet back into my shoes, suddenly realising I was worn out and just wanted to go home.

'Come on,' he said, quite kindly. 'It's not far. We'll get fish and chips on the way back.'

That sounded good to me and so we set out together and it was a good job he was with me. I'd said I was tired but I was more tired than I thought. Too tired to remember the new one-way system around St Stephens. I looked the wrong way and nearly stepped in front of a van. Iblis yanked me back. The

229

driver hooted, long and loud, and shouted for good measure. I'm obviously not cut out for a life of adventure. My adrenalin was wearing off and I suddenly felt as heavy as lead.

Iblis was all for pursuing the driver down the road to teach him some manners. I managed to dissuade him but that took the last little bit of energy I had left.

The hill was more of a struggle than usual.

'May I take your arm?' he said and I didn't even have the strength to ask where he was taking it to. I nodded and we did the last couple of hundred yards in silence.

I stopped at the foot of my steps and looked at him. 'Are you coming in?'

'Those are my instructions.'

'From whom?'

'From Mr Jerry, of course. He was very insistent you should not be left to face this Sorensen person alone.' He flourished his vinegar-smelling carrier bag. 'And I have the food.'

'In that case, come in.'

I went straight upstairs, wrenched off that wretched suit and blouse and dressed in something more comfortable. When I went back downstairs he had dished up the fish and chips. Salt, vinegar and tomato sauce all stood ready.

'Thank you,' I said, genuinely grateful I didn't have to do anything for myself.

'So,' he said, 'you will want to know how it all went?'

'I do,' I said. 'I've heard some of it from Jerry.'

'He would not have told you much,' he said. 'He is a very close man. It falls to me to amaze you with tales of our courage and ingenuity.'

I forked a chip. 'Go on then, amaze me. Firstly, where were you? I didn't see you when we arrived?'

'I entered the grounds late last night, found myself somewhere snug and quiet and waited. I saw the car arrive and I watched you disappear. Using the skills for which I am legendary, I made my way around to the delivery door, concealed myself behind the wheelie bins and waited. Mr Jerry opened the door – I could have done it myself because my strength is also legendary but he was very insistent on the need for stealth – and we went inside. The man Jones was being kept downstairs in the second room in the first corridor to the left. He was a big man but using the strength ...'

'For which you are legendary ...'

'Oh, you've heard those stories, too ... Well, using the strength for which I am legendary, I heaved him over one shoulder and we took him away.'

I frowned. 'It all seems to have been very easy.'

'Well-planned operations always seem that way. Your desire for violence and bloodshed is understandable – indeed, I share it – but Mr Jerry was adamant. Stealth and silence, he said, so stealth and silence I gave him.'

'But ... wasn't he being monitored? Were there no cameras? No guards? Did no one see what you were doing?'

'Well, I'm not too sure about that because my skills in that area are ... less legendary ... but there was a metal box on the wall – a big one – with the sign of lightning on the front ...'

'A junction box,' I said, from a position of complete ignorance but certain that his ignorance was even more complete than mine.

'I have no idea,' he said calmly, sprinkling more vinegar on his chips, 'and neither do I care. I only know that Mr Jerry attached a small device, informed me we now had only three minutes and twenty-five seconds to complete our task and escape the scene of the crime and to shift my arse.' He smiled disarmingly. 'So I shifted it. And Michael Jones, of course.'

'With the strength for which you are legendary.'

He grinned and shovelled down more chips.

'I took the man Jones to the car. In considerably less than the time allocated, just in case you were wondering. We operated the device that lifts the back seat. I stowed Jones away and, as instructed, drifted silently away, as unseen as the summer breeze itself.'

'How?'

'The river. I rowed up the river, played my part in our glorious adventure and then rowed back down the river.'

Jones himself had told me of this tiny hole in Sorensen's security system. He'd used it, he told me, to enjoy peaceful afternoons fishing – and also to dispose of his empty bottles with all the discretion and care expected of a patient in a high-class mental establishment.

I got up to clear the plates. 'Tea?'

'Yes please.'

I was a little surprised he hadn't brought the Flask of Utgard-Loki again and wondered if perhaps he regretted telling me about Allia. He hadn't mentioned her since that night, so neither would I.

I must have been even more tired than I thought. I dropped a cup. I don't know how I managed that – I'm not usually clumsy. I stared at the fragments on the floor and it just seemed too much trouble to clear them away.

Iblis was behind me. 'Go upstairs, Elizabeth Cage. Rest. I'll see to this.'

'Your legendary cup-clearing skills I assume.'

'How well you know me,' he said, imperturbably. 'Go. And don't worry about anything tonight. I am here.'

Chapter Twenty-One

I thought I would lie awake all night waiting for the knock on the door – if they bothered to knock, of course – but it never came. At least, I assumed it didn't. I fell asleep as soon as my head hit the pillow, and when I went downstairs the next morning, Iblis was watching the morning news and reported a quiet night.

He made us breakfast, saying it was his turn, and we sat down to eat.

'They must have discovered Jones's disappearance by now,' I said. 'Why hasn't Sorensen been in touch?'

Because surely it wouldn't have taken him any time at all to put two and two together. He would know that even though he was my alibi, I was mixed up in it somewhere. As was my taxi driver. They might not know who he was or how he'd done it, but they'd run such CCTV tapes as Jerry had left working and work it out. Jerry would be under investigation at this very moment. I hoped to God he and Jones were well hidden.

We had discussed my going with them but, not to put too fine a point on it, I was the decoy. I was the distraction while Jerry kept Jones safe. I was to remain here, visibly going about my business and seemingly completely uninvolved and unconcerned with events at the Sorensen Clinic. Although, as Jerry had said, if anything happened to me then it would be their job to come and rescue me. Or so I hoped. But I was strongest in my own home. And I had Iblis with me, currently wolfing down scrambled eggs on toast while I made do with a coffee and a piece of toast. I was on edge, constantly waiting for the telephone to ring.

'Or that sinister knock on the door,' he said cheerfully. 'Although I don't know why he should suspect you. You didn't set up the meeting. You appeared at the time and place of his choosing. You remained with him throughout. He never lost sight of you. He walked you to a carefully set up empty car. Your taxi driver was visible and audible throughout almost the entire period. Yes, he disappeared to satisfy a biological need but everyone could see he was a frail old man and completely incapable of lifting the mountain known as Michael Jones. All they know is that the cameras went down for a few minutes and when they came back up again Jones was gone. And they don't know about me at all,' he finished complacently, 'so if anyone turns up you are completely bewildered at this turn of events and none of it is anything to do with you.'

I pondered this. Everything he had said was true.

'But,' he continued, 'I think you're worrying unnecessarily.'

I got up for more coffee. 'How do you work that out?'

'I don't think he'll say anything to you at all.'

'Why ever not?'

'Well, either you were involved and therefore you know Jones has gone and he has no further hold over you so there's no point in him confronting you until he has clear evidence which he doesn't, or ...' he paused for breath '... Or, he doesn't suspect you in any way but he won't want you to know he doesn't have Michael Jones any longer. You may find, should you encounter him in the future, that he behaves as if Jones is still in his custody. You know ... a giant bluff. Only you'll know differently, won't you?'

I thought about this. Again, everything he said was true. And sensible.

'So all I have to do is hold my nerve and continue to act as normal.'

'Just as Jerry instructed you to do, yes. But I am certain you won't hear any more from this Sorensen man.'

The telephone rang. I stared at him accusingly.

He shrugged. 'Or I may be completely wrong.'

I picked it up and said neutrally, 'Hello?'

'It's me,' said Jerry.

I remembered he'd said no names.

'How's it going?'

'Bloody awful. Everything went wrong. Terrible journey. Road works all the way. Traffic jams. Every light against us. Shitty weather. He was sick all over the back seat. Twice.'

'Oh no. How is he?'

'Still not himself. So yeah, everything went wrong. Just one damned thing after another.'

'How can I contact you?'

'You can't. And don't try this number. Throwing the phone away after this call.'

'All right. Good luck. Stay in touch.'

'Yeah.' The line went dead.

I spent the day alongside Iblis on the sofa because I very nearly fell down the cellar steps when I went down to do the washing, and the sofa seemed the safest place to be. We drank tea and criticised other people's interiors, gardens and lifestyles and the day passed very peacefully.

Until someone knocked at the door.

Typical Sorensen – the dawn raid was too uncivilised. He turned up at tea time. Not that he was going to get any.

I had no intention of letting him in. I stood squarely in the doorway. He'd have to knock me down to get past me.

'Mrs Cage, I wonder if I might come in for a moment.'

'Dr Sorensen, I told you, I'll call you when I've made a decision. If you're going to pressure me then the answer is no – I will not work for you,' and went to close the door.

Of course there was no way I was going to get rid of him that easily.

'So I am to tell Michael Jones you've abandoned him to criminal prosecution for his part in the Clare Woods failure? I find it hard to believe you would do that Mrs Cage.'

'And I find it hard to believe you have this reputation for being a clever man.'

He took a moment to think that through, his thin white colour curdling around him. To anyone else he was self-assured and confident, but I could see the faint tinges of red anxiety. He was bluffing. He suspected me but he didn't know for certain. He knew I'd been with him all the time. Not for one moment had I been unsupervised. But his instinct told him I was involved somehow. Was he here to make me give myself away? I let my mind drift a little … did he think I had Jones here? Had he gone to Jones's flat on the other side of the river and found it empty so he'd come here? As if I had Michael Jones hidden in the cellar. Forgetting for a moment that that was the impression I usually tried so hard to give, I felt a certain resentment that he could think I was that stupid.

I swallowed it all down because Sorensen was giving me clues all the time and I didn't want that working both ways. Iblis had been right. He didn't have Jones any longer, but he wanted me to believe he still did.

We'd discussed whether Iblis should hide upstairs. I argued that as far as Sorensen knew, I was alone. If he saw Iblis – if he knew I had friends – or accomplices, as he would think of them – he'd put two and two together and come up with the correct answer. I was banking on him thinking I was the only person in the world who couldn't have stolen Jones out from under his nose. So Iblis stood quietly in the corner, ready to move should he need to, but otherwise sworn to secrecy and silence.

'Might I come in?'

I'm a very polite person. My parents insisted upon it. Always to say please and thank you. Always to be polite. Always to be considerate of others. On the other hand, sometimes it's more important to get the message across than worry about hurting people's feelings.

'No.'

Smoothly, he moved up a gear. 'I should warn you, Mrs Cage, I already have the charges against Michael Jones drawn up. I have only to send them to the appropriate department.'

He didn't. He was lying. I could see it in the way his colour moved.

I put a little panic in my voice, vowing to myself that one day he would suffer for trying to frighten me like this. 'I don't believe you.'

'Believe whatever you wish, Mrs Cage. Perhaps it will help you to reconcile your conscience over Mr Jones's ultimate fate.'

'My conscience is clear.'

'For how long, I wonder.'

'Until you have him murdered, I suppose.'

He hadn't expected me to come straight out with it. His colour was darkening. He was becoming angry. There was disbelief, too. Had he thought this would be easy? I saw him cast a glance over his shoulder. He might have been checking his back-up. There would be some somewhere to handle Michael Jones if they could find him. He took a step closer to me.

People instinctively keep a polite distance. Most people don't like their space invaded. I'm no different. I was determined not to step back but having him almost chest to chest with me was not pleasant. His greasy-milk colour was reaching out to touch me. I felt a moment's genuine panic.

Inside the house a door opened and closed somewhere, and now he knew I wasn't alone.

He stiffened and tried to see over my shoulder. 'So, you do have him here.'

I remembered to say, 'Have who?'

'There's no point in continuing this pretence, Mrs Cage. I have men around the back of your house and two more over there.' He pointed across the green to two men, slightly too smart for their surroundings, watching us from the nearest bench. 'Mr Jones cannot get away.' He raised his voice. 'Come out, Mr Jones.'

Someone put their arms around me from behind and nibbled the back of my neck. I would have jumped a mile but his arms were very strong and warm.

'So,' murmured Iblis. 'Who's this Mr Jones then?'

I leaned back against him, half for effect and half for support, discovering, too late, that for reasons I looked forward to hearing later, he had taken off his T-shirt and jeans and was standing, mostly naked on my doorstep where everyone could see him. A double-edged weapon indeed. Nerves made my voice tremble, but if everyone wanted to misinterpret the reasons for my sudden loss of control then that was fine with me.

'No one you need concern yourself over.'

I should imagine it takes a lot to disconcert Sorensen, but he was disconcerted now. I felt quite insulted that he should be so surprised I had a boyfriend. And not just any old boyfriend, but a ripped young man, barefoot and bare-chested, tossing his blond hair, smiling that smile and, apparently, very eager for me

238

to get rid of my unwelcome caller and join him in a little afternoon delight.

I had to try quite hard not to laugh at the expression on Sorenson's face.

'Are you going to be long?' enquired Iblis innocently.

'No,' I said bluntly, hoping Sorensen would take the hint.

He didn't, still standing on my doorstep.

'Do I gather from this visit that you've lost Mr Jones again?' I smiled. 'He does tend to get away from you, doesn't he?'

'Who is this Mr Jones?' said Iblis again.

'You *have* lost him, haven't you? And you thought he was here. Oh, that's quite funny. Although I wish I'd known that yesterday – I could have saved myself a wasted afternoon. Well, that makes my decision much easier. Thank you for letting me know, but no, Dr Sorensen, I will not be working for you.'

He stood firm, just waiting for me to finish speaking. 'Is he here?'

'Is who here?' said Iblis. 'What is going on and when are you coming back to bed?'

Oh, for heaven's sake. I had a bully on my doorstep, an erratic young man who might be either a help or a hindrance depending on how the mood took him, and Michael Jones, who wasn't actually present, but managing to complicate my life just the same.

I turned to Iblis and took a deep breath. 'Dr Sorensen runs a sinister government establishment just up the road. He detained me against my will last year and a very kind man called Michael Jones helped me escape. I had an enormous row with Mr Jones last Christmas and haven't seen him since. Dr Sorensen told me he is – was – holding Mr Jones in an effort to force me to work for him, only now he's saying he thinks he's here.'

'No,' said Iblis simply – not a man to overcomplicate issues. '*I'm* here. Waiting for you,' he added pointedly.

'An enormous row?' said Dr Sorensen sharply. That was obviously the first he'd heard of it.

'Yes, didn't he tell you? Well, that was rather naughty. I thought, since he was reporting to you, that he had to tell you everything.'

His eyes narrowed with suspicion. 'You didn't tell me either.'

I used the opportunity to climb onto my high horse. 'My private life is none of your concern. Anyway, he's not here so I'll say good afternoon.'

'Mrs Cage, how stupid do you think I am?'

'Are you sure you actually want me to answer that question? Now, I've asked you to go, Sorensen. Don't make me ask my friend here to shift you.'

I don't know why I always seemed able to wind him up. Yes, I gather clues from his colour – for instance, I knew he was bluffing – but I did seem to possess the knack of getting under his skin. And I enjoyed doing it.

'Mrs Cage …'

Iblis opened the door wider and came out from behind me. He was very tall so looming came easily to him. He easily dwarfed the much shorter Sorensen. He was also wearing only a pair of black Calvin Klein underpants, and, I have to say, considerably enhancing my previously quite conventional doorstep. The house on my left contains a small firm of very upmarket solicitors and a good number of them were staring out of their front bay window, mouths slightly open. To my right, Colonel Barton opened his front door and emerged, juggling stick, keys and shopping bags. He stopped dead. I wondered what this was doing to my reputation. He was always civil, however.

'Good afternoon, Mrs Cage.'

And so was I. 'Good afternoon, Colonel. How is Mrs Barton today?'

'Very well, thank you.' He eyed Iblis – two metres of inadequately clothed testosterone standing on my doorstep. 'I'm … um … just off to do a little shopping.'

'Well,' I said, smiling like a madwoman and trying to give the impression that this sort of thing was so normal as not to merit comment of any kind. In fact, to do so would be quite rude. 'That's nice.'

'Good afternoon, Venerable One,' said Iblis politely, because he liked the colonel.

'Oh er …hello,' said the colonel. 'Nice to see you again. How are you?'

'Well, thank you, and waiting for this irritating man to go away.'

Actually, I could have kissed him. Colonel Barton, I mean. That one word 'again' had effortlessly given the impression Iblis and I were in a long-standing relationship. Which might actually be true, given a very broad understanding of the word 'relationship'.

The solicitors' front door opened and a middle-aged woman appeared. She wore a smart suit and had the air of one who never let life throw little difficulties in her path. 'Is everything all right here, Mrs Cage? Do you require any assistance?'

I never before realised what lovely neighbours I had.

'What did you argue about?' said Sorensen, not one to be deflected from his purpose.

241

Well, he did ask. And I wanted to be rid of him. And if he wouldn't go voluntarily then Iblis would make him and then we'd all be in trouble.

I took a deep breath and enunciated clearly. 'We argued about your threats to have him removed from his job unless he colluded in the installation of various listening devices throughout my house.'

'Eh?' said the colonel to my right. 'Isn't that illegal?'

'Yes,' said the solicitor to my left. 'Can you prove it?'

'I don't know,' I said looking at Sorensen. 'Are they still here?'

'I don't know what you're talking about. Of course not,' he said quietly, looking at me in a way I didn't much care for.

'And neither is Michael Jones, so you can get off my doorstep right now.'

Beside me, the Calvin Klein-clad Iblis loomed some more. The solicitor stared from her doorstep. The colonel stared from his. On the green, heads were beginning to turn, although that might have been mostly due to the semi-naked man standing at my side.

Sorensen stood for a long time. Long enough for me to wish I'd handled things better. He'd been angry when he arrived – he was furious now. His colour was swirling around him – like over-boiled milk. I'd made him look foolish, which had been fun, but might also have been a big mistake. Nor had I convinced him I knew nothing about the escaping Michael Jones. And I'd revealed I knew about the listening devices. And he now knew about Iblis. He was coming away with much more information than he had arrived with. Yes, I could probably have handled this better.

I tried for a more conciliatory tone. 'Dr Sorensen, I don't know why you've come here today. I can assure you that whatever has been going on between you and Mr Jones is nothing to do with me. In fact, as you can see, I've rather moved on from Michael Jones. He's very unreliable, you know. Thank you for the kind offer of employment you made yesterday, but I don't wish to work for you – as I think you already know. Now, if you'll excuse me …'

I went to close the door and he put out his hand up to prevent me. Rather than participate in an unseemly struggle – by which I mean Iblis would probably pitch him down the steps and his security men wouldn't like that and we'd all be in trouble, I let him.

He leaned in close and said, with quiet menace, 'You will regret this.'

The colonel pulled out his phone. 'Mrs Cage, would you like me to call the police?'

'That won't be necessary,' said Sorensen, backing off down the steps. 'In fact, I might call them myself.'

'Was that a threat?' said the solicitor sharply, and I loved my neighbours all over again.

Turning away, he said, almost as an afterthought, 'As it happens Mrs Cage, my purpose in calling this afternoon was to inform you my offer of employment is no longer open. In fact, I am strongly of the opinion that not only do I not need you – I don't want you. You no longer have value to me, Mrs Cage, and I shall proceed accordingly.'

At first, I thought it was just an attempt to save face, but I could see he was telling the truth. Turning on his heel, he marched down the steps.

I don't know how it happened – I know I was watching him walk away down the path rather than looking where I was going, but as I turned away, my foot slipped and twisted beneath me. I cried out with pain, because it really hurt, and I would have fallen except that, almost before I knew what was happening, Iblis caught me.

'You should take more water with it, Mrs Cage,' said the colonel, and I wasn't sure he was joking. I was beginning to be really fed up with this day.

'What did you do?' said Iblis, fiercely to Sorensen.

'Nothing,' he said, backing away, his hands held out in front of him.

The pain was jagging around my foot and ankle. I just wanted to get inside.

'It's all right,' I said to Iblis. 'Just stupid carelessness on my part.'

Making a gesture, Sorensen summoned the two men still waiting. One spoke into his lapel so I assumed he was telling the two round the back that they could leave now.

We watched them depart – under the arch and then out of sight.

I became aware I'd been holding my breath and my foot was throbbing fit to burst and I felt sick with the pain. I was certain I'd broken something.

I said something to my neighbours – I can't remember what, and Iblis carried me inside. He kicked the door shut behind him and deposited me on the sofa where we inspected the damage. Big black bruises were already appearing and my ankle bone had disappeared under the swelling.

'Ice,' said Iblis.

'Put some clothes on first,' I said, and he laughed.

I watched him moving around my little kitchen, tipping ice cubes into a tea towel while I lay back and closed my eyes. Sorensen had given in too easily. I had the feeling he'd just been going through the motions. Had he really thought Jones was here? And what had he said at the end? 'I no longer need you.

Not – I no longer need your services, your talents, your skills, whatever, but I no longer need *you*.' And yet, right up until yesterday, he'd been trying everything to get me on board. To the extent of holding and threatening Michael Jones. Something had happened since yesterday.

'Yes,' said Iblis, laying a cold compress on my foot. 'We rescued Michael Jones. He no longer has him to bargain with.'

'And yet, he no longer wants to bargain. What's going on?'

I closed my eyes again. His reactions hadn't been right. Something was … off. I closed my eyes to shut out the pain and tried to think.

The answer came to me suddenly, but with certainty. There was only one reason why he wouldn't need me any longer.

He'd got someone else.

Chapter Twenty-Two

Thinking things over, my first reaction was relief. Sorensen could be out of my life forever. This would take the pressure off both me and Jones who might even be able to come back one day. He could go on to live a normal life. And so could I. I could do as I'd done as a child – just tune everything out in the way that normal people tune out the everyday background noises around them and ignore everything else. Surely Sorensen finding someone else was a good thing. I couldn't understand – why wasn't I happier?

The answer came at once. Because if Sorensen had found someone who could do what I could, then I might be in even more danger than before. Suppose this other person saw me as a rival. Suppose they saw me as a threat. Or, suppose Sorensen wanted to make sure he possessed the only one …

I sat for the rest of the day with my foot up, trying to think through the ramifications. I didn't feel it was something I could discuss with Iblis who, for some reason, was more concerned with how I came to fall down the steps.

'He must have done something,' he insisted. 'No one else was anywhere near you.'

'If he did then I completely missed it.'

'One of his people then.'

'How?' I enquired, bemused. 'They were twenty yards away at least.'

He strode about the room, formulating one daft theory after another. I let it all go over my head until he started talking about anti-gravity rays and hypnotism.

I told him I didn't remember anyone swinging a watch in front of my eyes.

'No, no,' he said excitedly. 'It's all done with trigger words, deeply implanted in your subconscious.'

'And when exactly would these trigger words have been implanted in my subconscious?'

'Yesterday,' he said triumphantly. 'You were alone with him in his office. He implanted the word …'

'What word?'

'Well it could have been anything, couldn't it? What was he saying when you fell?'

I cast my mind back. 'He said, "Well, as it happens, Mrs Cage, my purpose in calling this afternoon was to inform you my offer of employment is no longer open."' And we both waited in case I felt the urge to get to my feet and throw myself down the steps again.

For the record, I didn't. He seemed disappointed.

I sat quietly for the rest of the day and refused to go to the hospital on the grounds that I could wiggle my toes therefore everything was fine. Or would be when the swelling went down. My foot looked as if someone had tried to inflate a rubber glove. Big and circular with little piggy toes on the end.

Iblis, telling me he'd always known I would need him one day, bustled around the kitchen, preparing jacket potatoes, salad and grilled chicken. It was delicious. I sighed. Another man who could cook.

My treacherous mind filled with thoughts of the Christmas lunch I'd had with Michael Jones. There had been delicious food and good wine. And then that moment when we had turned a corner and a new path opened up for both of us. I blinked away the tears, because the very next day my world had been turned upside down and I wasn't sure it was the right way up even now.

Iblis slept on the sofa that night. It was rapidly becoming his second home, he said. I ignored that, but I was glad he was staying and said so.

'I told you you'd need me one day,' he said irritatingly, and asked if I needed to be helped upstairs and even more irritatingly, I did.

The next day was strange. I didn't feel quite right. As if there was a gauze curtain between me and the world. Nothing was quite clear. I couldn't get to grips with anything. It was like trying to grasp fog. I couldn't even think clearly. My thoughts kept sliding away from me. I felt as if I was waiting for something to happen but nothing did. Nor the next day. Nor the next. I should have been happy. I should have been pleased that Sorensen would no longer be interfering in my life. That I could come and go as I pleased. That threats no longer hung over my head. Yes, I should have been happy and I wasn't.

The only feeling I was conscious of was disappointment. I couldn't help asking myself – was that it? Was it all over? Was it all just going to fizzle out leaving me with nothing?

Chapter Twenty-Three

Iblis stayed with me for a few days while my swollen foot subsided and we waited for any possible repercussions from what he referred to as our little excursion to the Sorensen clinic and its aftermath, but nothing happened. Nothing at all. Sorensen made no attempt to contact me. There was no word from Jones or Jerry. I knew no news was good news, but I was anxious all the same. And to have been put through so much and then have it all fade away and come to nothing just didn't seem right somehow.

I mentioned this to Iblis who had taken up his traditional position on the sofa in front of the television, ready to spring into action, he insisted, at a moment's notice. There was no action, however, and there was certainly no springing. I could sense his restlessness and so one morning, I said to him, 'Iblis, your service is discharged and I thank you.'

He opened his mouth to argue and then nodded. 'I understand, but you haven't seen the last of me.'

I smiled at him. 'I certainly hope not.'

He nodded. 'Call me if you need me, but I don't think you will.'

I shook my head. 'I just can't believe it's all over. When I think what the last eighteen months have been like …'

He shrugged. 'We both heard what he said. He doesn't need you any longer.'

'Mm,' I said, still not sure how happy I was about that.

'What are your plans?' he asked.

'I … don't know. After Ted died I just wanted a fresh start in a fresh place.'

'Well,' he said, shouldering his pack. 'Now you have it. Don't just stand there.'

'I know,' I said, 'but …' I trailed away, not really sure what I wanted to say and definitely not sure of what I wanted to do with my life now that I so unexpectedly had it back again.

'I'll call in whenever I'm passing,' he said, opening the front door.

'I'm sure that won't be necessary,' I said gloomily.

'As a friend. And to catch up on episodes of *Olympian Heights*, of course.'

'Of course,' I said gravely. 'Are you going back to the woods?'

He was evasive. 'Not sure.'

'Please give my best wishes to Melek'.

'I shall. See you around, Elizabeth Cage.'

He heaved his pack over his shoulder and strode off jauntily, whistling to himself, and I turned back into my suddenly empty house.

Once it was all I had ever asked for. Just to live quietly, letting the gentle routine of my days lengthen into weeks, then months, with no more excitement, no more peculiar happenings, and especially no more sinister threats from Sorensen. But that meant no more Michael Jones either. And now, no more Iblis. I had everything I thought I'd wanted.

I stared out of the window. It was a beautiful day. The sun flooded in through the window, making patterns of light and shade on the wooden floor. I stood for a long while, looking out at the castle opposite, the willow trees, the children feeding the swans, everyone streaming past on their way to somewhere else. Everyone had something to do. Or somewhere to go. Or someone to be with. Only I stood apart and alone. I'd had no close friends at school – I suspected they referred to me as 'the weirdo'. I'd been pleasant at work – but I'd made no friends there. A few had come to my wedding but I'd never seen them since. I looked around. Was this what the rest of my life was going to be like?

I shook myself. It wasn't like me to have these thoughts. My life didn't have to be like that. I'd been happy enough before – I could be happy enough again. There would be my comforting daily routine. Daily shopping because I couldn't carry more than one bag up the hill. There was the lovely café on the corner to have Sunday croissants and read the papers. I would pursue a ferocious course of reading. There was the Local History Society. The art class at the library. There was an autumn exhibition of local artists at the Guildhall. I could take up yoga. Or do a course in creative writing. I should count my blessings. I had no need to work. I had a lovely house in a lovely part of town. I had my health. I should pull myself together and start to enjoy the life I thought I'd always wanted.

I did my best. I honestly did my best, but my life, far from following the serene and sunlit path I'd mapped out for it, seemed determined to toss me into the nearest bed of nettles. Absolutely everything went wrong. It wasn't disaster piled upon catastrophe or anything like that, but just a continual series of low-grade incidents that depressed my spirits even further. And I missed the company. Well, all right, I missed Michael Jones. He hadn't been around a lot, but until recently I'd always thought he was at the end of the phone, never more than an email away, and now there was silence. I knew it was for his own good – and mine – but I missed him. God help me, I even missed Iblis, glued to my TV with all the enjoyment of a small child.

In those days after Iblis's departure, nothing went right for me and for the first time since just after Ted's death, I was unhappy and I didn't know why. I slept badly, continually roused by dark dreams I could barely remember afterwards and, possibly because of this, I just couldn't throw off this awful feeling of lethargy and disinterest in everything. And then, perhaps because of the weather, which turned blustery and rainy, I suffered a nasty cold and a minor tummy upset that left me drained and exhausted and disinclined even to leave the house. Obviously I had to, otherwise I'd have starved to death, but I found the hill increasingly difficult to cope with especially with a still painful foot, and, one day, pausing to rest just outside the archway, I found myself regretting my choice in coming to live up here. I struggled the rest of the way home, set down my shopping without even bothering to unpack it, sat down on the sofa and cried my eyes out.

I was lonely. Until this moment, I'd never really had the time to mourn Ted. After his death it was just one thing after another, but now I remembered him sitting by the fire reading his paper. Digging his garden. Enjoying a quiet pint in front of the TV. And now he'd gone and I was all alone.

I still wasn't sure that Sorenson's backing off was a good thing. Someone – I couldn't remember who – once said, 'Keep your friends close and your enemies closer still.' I didn't have any friends and now even my enemies didn't seem to want to have anything to do with me. I spent each day wrapped in a lonely bubble of sadness from which I couldn't find the strength to emerge.

Whether this general lethargy led to carelessness or what, I don't know, but nothing went right for me. The microwave blew up and took all my fuses with it. I locked myself out and tried Michael Jones's trick with the credit card, and not only did it not work but I wrecked my card as well and had to order a new one, and there was a problem and I had to limp down to the bank and sign a ton of paperwork. *And* I couldn't find my keys anywhere and had to get new locks which cost me a fortune. The weather continued wet and windy. The bathroom window leaked and I began to fear for my roof. There was no reason to – I'd had the house surveyed when I bought it and the surveyor had assured me the roof was perfectly sound, but once the thought was in my head I couldn't get it out again. I would get up in the night and prowl around the house, listening for the ominous sound of dripping water and searching for damp patches on the ceilings. I wasn't sleeping anyway, so it didn't matter too much, but I did begin to wonder if I was turning into one of those dotty spinsters who would one day be eaten by her own cats. Although I'd have to go out and buy some first.

When I did go outside, the weather was wild. The trees swayed in unseasonal gales. I was convinced their branches were reaching for me. I saw threatening shapes everywhere and was convinced they were out to get me. Whether because Sorensen had dismissed my fears about the yew tree – the one that had swallowed little Keira Swanson – or the Tree Protection Order people had prevailed, I don't know, but no one had taken any action about the malevolent old tree. Without thinking, I'd muttered something to Iblis one day when he was staying with me and, a few days later, the old yew had gone up in flames and been completely destroyed. I'd deliberately not asked a smoke-smelling Iblis about that and, as far as I was concerned, the matter was closed, but in my more unbalanced moments I did wonder if all trees everywhere knew what I'd done and were seeking to avenge themselves.

And as if that wasn't enough, when I eventually dragged myself over to the Local History meeting, it was to discover that things weren't right there either. Neither Mrs Painswick nor young Alyson had been to any recent meetings. As Colonel Barton confided to me over tea and a not very nice shop-bought cake, he was worried. None of them had seen the family for some time and they were all concerned about them.

Of course, there could be a perfectly normal explanation. The family might simply have gone away for a while. I nodded politely and tried to stifle the fear that it was me. That I was spreading bad luck to those around me.

'They might simply have gone to visit relatives,' I said.

'Exactly.' He paused. 'But I wonder…'

'Yes, I think perhaps we should call round. Shall we go after the meeting? Young Alyson should be home from school by then.'

'An excellent idea.'

I looked around the room. There seemed to be fewer of us these days.

'Mark's not here,' he said. 'Now that Alyson has stopped attending, so has he.' His face creased with worry.

'I'm sure it's nothing,' I said. 'They might not have been well. There's a lot going around at the moment and I seem to have gone down with most of it. Perhaps they have as well.'

He nodded, we put down our plates and continued with the history of Rushford Castle.

The Painswicks lived on the other side of the river in a new housing estate built out along the Whittington road. It still wasn't far though. Rushford is not a large town.

We walked slowly and our pace slowed even more as we approached.

They lived in a neat little bungalow. The front garden was immaculate, with a traditional square lawn bordered by flower beds – except that the lawn needed cutting and the plants in the tubs by the front door were wilting through lack of water. The windows were all closed and the curtains part drawn.

'They're not here,' I said, halting on the pavement.

'Doesn't look like it, does it?'

They weren't. We rang the bell several times and the colonel plied the knocker but there wasn't a sound from within.

We hooded our eyes and peered through the windows. Everything was in perfect order. There were no signs of violence and a hasty departure, which was what I'd been looking for and dreading.

The side gate was unlocked and we went around the back. Again, the garden was beginning to show signs of neglect, but the bins had been emptied. The garage was empty. As was the kitchen. The draining board was clear and dry.

I closed my eyes and let my mind drift … there was … something … but … no, I couldn't grasp it. I opened my eyes and let it go.

'They've gone away,' said the colonel. 'A summer holiday.'

I nodded. 'So it would seem.'

'And yet …' he said.

I agreed. If it had been anyone other than Mrs Painswick and little Alyson … I remembered Mrs Painswick's bruises and the way she never let Alyson out of her sight.

The colonel had followed my reasoning. 'What can we do? If we go to the police what would we say? That a family appears to have gone away for the holidays. With no signs of a hasty departure. No signs of violence. Nothing suspicious in any way.'

I nodded.

'And,' he continued, 'if we make a fuss and they return at the weekend to find the police waiting for them … well …' He tailed off and I couldn't help but agree.

'Perhaps,' I said, 'we should give it until the end of the month, which isn't too far off now. The schools will start again soon and if Alyson isn't there then they might know where she's gone. And if they don't ... if they're expecting her back and she hasn't shown up, then, I think, we have a legitimate cause for concern. '

'Agreed,' he said.

'If they've finally plucked up the courage to run away then we shouldn't interfere.'

He looked around. 'And we'd better go before someone reports *us* to the police.'

Life continued, although it didn't seem that way.

The misfortunes continued. Mrs Barton had a nasty fall. They got an ambulance up as far as they could and carried her down to it. The colonel was beside himself with worry and spent most of his time at the hospital.

Our Local History meetings were cancelled for the foreseeable future. It would seem it wasn't just me whose life had taken a turn for the worst. Everyone I knew seemed to be having a rough time.

Ted's pension company rang to say there was a problem. They were very nice about it, but there seemed to be some sort of issue which they were sure would soon be resolved. I put the phone down with a feeling of unease. Financially it wasn't a huge glitch, but if something went wrong with Ted's pension then it soon might be. A week ago, I would have wondered if it was Sorensen, applying financial pressure to make me work for him, but that didn't seem to be an ambition of his any longer so I put it down to just one of my many problems.

I had far too much time on my hands. Too much time to think. I sat on the sofa, too exhausted and dispirited even to put on the TV and I wondered how Iblis was doing without his daily dose of *Olympian Heights*. I wondered if he was still living in the woods and how he was getting on in this weather. I saw his little tent blown to shreds and him shivering, soaking wet, huddled under dripping beech trees.

Which turned my mind to Iblis properly. Because whatever my problems were – and they weren't insurmountable because the electrics had been fixed, I'd nearly killed myself getting a new microwave oven up the hill, my latest cold had cleared up and I could breathe properly again, and the problem with Ted's pension would be resolved, I was sure of it – none of that could hold a candle to the tragedy that was Iblis's life.

I made myself a coffee, closed my mind to the wild weather outside, and settled back to think. I ran through everything he'd told me. It had been the truth, I was sure of it. I'd seen his pain in the way his colour flew around him, comforting and consoling, responding to the torrent of emotions within him. What courage must it take for him to face each day, knowing what he'd done and that the consequences could be deadly, not only to him but to the woman he loved.

I sat back and remembered back to that evening. How he'd looked. What he'd said. Trying to identify that precise moment when I'd felt something wasn't right. I let my mind drift, trying to see events through his eyes. Seeing what he saw – feeling what he felt – because there was something wrong … I just couldn't quite put my finger on it … I closed my eyes and just let my mind float free, putting myself into his mind. I'd never done anything like that before and it was like trying to grasp smoke but I stuck at it, just letting my mind wander, because there was something and if I could just home in…

And then suddenly, shrilly, shattering my concentration – the telephone rang.

Chapter Twenty-Four

I'd been so far away inside my own head that the sudden ringing made me jump and I spilled coffee everywhere. I jolted back into this world, scrubbing at the damp patches and cursing.

'Hello?'

It was Jerry and his first words pushed all thoughts of Iblis straight out of my head.

'There's been an accident.'

A terrible fear shot through me. My head swam and I had to clutch the sofa for support. It took me a while to say, 'Oh God. Was it bad? What happened?'

'Nothing too serious. Someone sideswiped us at a junction. Not much damage to the car.'

I forgot we weren't supposed to be using names. 'What about Jones? Is he badly hurt? Will he die? And you, of course. Are you both all right?'

I thought I heard amusement in his voice. 'Car's fine. I'm fine. Banged my elbow a bit but nothing a strip of Band Aid won't put right.'

'And Jones? How is he?'

'Twisted his leg somehow. He can walk but not very far and not very fast. Otherwise he's fine. Well, still a bit groggy, but that's not a bad thing. Keeps him sitting still, anyway. Listen, I'm ringing 'cos I have to go somewhere – prior appointment that I can't get out of – and I can't take him with me and I can't leave him here alone because he's a bit of a wanderer. He keeps walking into walls. It's the drugs. He's a bit of a cocktail at the minute.'

'He was that before they drugged him,' I said darkly, which seemed to cause him some amusement.

'Anyway, can you come here for a few days? What about that Sorensen bloke?'

'He seems to have lost interest in me so that might not be a problem, but I don't have a passport.'

'Don't need one. We're only just up the road.'

I tried not to sound judgemental. 'Oh. You didn't get very far.'

'Well, no, like I said, we had an accident.'

'When?'

He was deliberately vague. ''Bout a week ago. Something like that.'

I swallowed down the knowledge they hadn't told me.

'So where exactly are you?'

'Just up the coast. Rushby.'

'Oh. OK. Yes, I can get there.'

'Train at two thirty this afternoon from Rushford. Gets in at three fifteen. I'll meet you.'

'Um … OK.'

But he'd gone.

My lethargy had disappeared. I looked at the clock, cursed, and ran upstairs. Grabbing my case from under the bed I rammed in a change of clothes. And then another change of clothes. Nightwear. Toiletries. I pulled a coat from my wardrobe and threw it on the bed. I zipped the case shut and then thought – underwear. And a spare pair of shoes. And my hairbrush. And then reminded myself that I wasn't travelling to the other side of the world and anything forgotten could easily be purchased.

I was running back down the stairs again when I had a thought. I'd be leaving my house unattended. I know Sorensen had backed off but even so … for one moment I even considered whether all this was just an elaborate trap. I really must do something to bring my paranoia back down to an acceptable level.

And then I had an idea. All I had to do was call, he'd said. I sat down on the stairs, emptied my mind, and thought of Iblis. I pictured his long blond hair streaming behind him. I pictured him striding up the hill towards me. And then I thrust the thought outwards, as hard as I could.

And then I felt really silly. It's a very good job I live alone.

I only just had enough time to catch the train so I didn't bother ringing for a taxi, hurrying down the hill into town.

Iblis met me half way up. I was surprised and not surprised, all at the same time. But mostly, I was overwhelmingly grateful.

He eyed my suitcase. 'Are you leaving me, Elizabeth Cage? Is it the mountain Michael Jones again?'

I nodded. 'I must go, Iblis. This is very important.'

'Of course. Where are we going?'

'I'm going to Rushby. There's been an accident. No – no one's badly hurt,' I added as he made to move off. 'Iblis, please, if you can, I need you to watch my house for me.'

'I have told you, your house is warded. Nothing can get in.'

'Does that apply to humans?'

His silence answered that question.

'Look, I have no time to explain. I have a train to catch. Please – just keep my house safe. Just for a few days. You can watch TV. Help yourself to the food. Please.'

'Of course – but would it not be easier if I came too.'

I had a sudden picture of Iblis and Michael Jones in the same house. 'I will call you if I need you. I promise. Now I must go. Here's my key.'

He took it from me with a carelessness that told me he probably wouldn't need it to gain access. 'Take care, Elizabeth Cage.'

It wasn't just the usual phrase tossed out casually in lieu of goodbye. He really was telling me to take care.

'And you too. Goodbye.'

I wheeled about and continued down the hill. When I reached the bottom and looked back, he'd gone.

I remembered to get some cash from the machine so I wouldn't have to do it in Rushby, just in case I was still under surveillance – although I was certain I wasn't – and bought a sandwich for the journey.

I paid cash for the ticket and crossed the footbridge just as they were announcing the train. I jumped in, slammed the door behind me and stared out through the window. No one else got on. No one else was on the footbridge. I peered through the window on the other side. No one was on that platform opposite either. As far as I could see, I was the only person here. And that included the staff.

I was actually rather proud of myself and the precautions I was taking until it occurred to me that if there was anyone following me I'd certainly never know anything about it, so I went and found myself a seat.

The train lurched and then pulled slowly out of the station and I was on my way. I found, to my complete non-surprise, that I was quite looking forward to seeing Jones again. And Jerry, of course.

The distance wasn't far as the crow flew, but the little train – all two carriages of it – stopped at every tiny station along the coast. It was like a bus service. People hopped on and off and no one paid attention to me in any way.

We pulled into the station at Rushby. It was a tiny place with only one platform. An enormous tub of slowly fading flowers welcomed people to the seaside town. No one else got off the train. I lingered, just in case, but no one had their head out of the window watching me. There were only the two carriages and I walked slowly past them, checking no one was on their phone reporting where I'd got off. I handed my ticket to a bored young woman and exited the station.

I hadn't travelled that far but the weather here was completely different. I stepped out into blue skies and bright sunshine. Which made a very nice change. There was a bit of a breeze, but it was warm and pleasant and smelled of the sea. Gulls wheeled overhead, making the appropriate gull noises.

Jerry was waiting for me in the car park. He hadn't been completely truthful about the extent of his injuries. His face was badly bruised down one side.

'Oh my God, Jerry. Are you all right?'

'Yeah,' he said, slinging my case on the back seat. 'Looks worse than it is. Bloody hell missis, what you got in there?' His colour was strong and stable. He was telling the truth.

'And Jones?'

'Stiff, sore, grumpy, and trying to do too much for his own good so not much change there.'

'Jerry – I have to ask – was it deliberate, do you think?'

'Was what deliberate?'

'The accident, of course.'

He shook his head. 'Not unless Sorensen's taken to employing a minister of the church and her sister to do his dirty work. They were on their way to a parish meeting apparently.

Insurance details swapped. No permanent harm done. Not everything is about Sorensen missis. In you get.'

I climbed in and we sped away, down through the pretty little town and out the other side.

'Oh,' I said in excitement, sitting up straight. 'I can see the sea.' And there it was with its ruler straight horizon, glittering in the afternoon sunshine, entrancing me as it had done ever since I was a child. A few dark spots denoted those brave enough to swim in choppy British waters and little boats with white sails scudded back and forth.

I've always loved the sea. My memories were full of holidays at the seaside with my parents, when I spent long days paddling in the shallows with my dad or poking around old rockpools that stank of seaweed. We ate pink candyfloss and walked on the pier. The nights were long and exciting with a funfair and bright lights and strange food and me lying awake, listening to the waves in the dark. We never went abroad – my mum didn't like flying, but I never missed the Costas. Not when I had this. All my memories came rushing back on a wave of childhood excitement.

Although the season was coming to an end, there were still holidaymakers around. Walkers, mostly, from what I could see, bent under their backpacks and picking their way through the cobbled streets. They would be heading down the coast, or up onto the moors, perhaps.

I turned from the window. 'This is lovely, Jerry. Good choice.'

'Well, it's not what I had planned, but it could be worse. It's a holiday place. People coming and going all the time so I reckoned no one would notice us.'

We drove through the narrow twisting streets, around the harbour, empty of boats at the moment, over the bridge spanning the Rush as it decanted itself into the sea, past the long sandy beach, with its donkeys and ice cream kiosks, past the lifeboat slipway, and out on the other side of town. Nestling half way up the cliff sat a row of six or eight whitewashed cottages.

Jerry nodded over. 'We're the pink one on the end.'

'It's lovely. So pretty.'

He peered at it as if seeing it for the first time. I suspected that as long as it had a functioning roof, an indoor toilet and Sky Sports, he wasn't too bothered about picturesque.

We drove along the cliff road, dropping down to a tiny car park. Now that I was closer I could see the cottages were disconcertingly close to the cliff edge.

I climbed out of the car, looked at the – to my eyes – very narrow apron of grass between cliff and cottages and said doubtfully, 'Is it safe?'

'Oh yes, I've been over the place several times. Nothing there. You can talk freely.'

'I meant – is it safe from falling into the sea.'

He shrugged. 'Dunno. I expect so.' Which was probably the best I could hope for. I followed him down the path and in through the back door.

Jones met us in the kitchen. 'There you are.'

I wasn't sure which of us he was talking to, so I said, 'Hello, remember me?'

'I certainly do,' he said, amiably. 'You wore that blue thing and had strange brown legs.'

Of course, he had to remember that, didn't he?

He stared down at the blue and white teapot. 'I'm making some tea.'

There was just the very faintest note of uncertainty in his voice. He wasn't quite sure.

'I'll make the tea,' said Jerry quickly, and I suspected past disasters. Probably something more serious than forgetting to warm the pot, anyway. 'You've got my room, missis. I've cleared me stuff out. Why don't you show Mrs Cage her room and I'll finish this?'

There were two bedrooms, the one upstairs looked out over the sparkling sea and scudding boats. The other was downstairs, had bare boards, was small and dark, and looked out over the car park. Guess which was mine.

Jones dropped my case on the bed, turned around, and I got a better look at him. He looked tired. His colour was still loose and unformed. Not only had he not completely recovered from the drugs Sorensen had given him, but he was shaken from the accident as well. He'd lost weight and his eyes were cloudy. I wondered how long the effects from the drugs would last. It was a fortnight and more since we'd got him away from the clinic. He was a strong man. Not much longer, surely.

'No,' said Jerry, when I mentioned this to him. 'He's better every day. Give him a week and he'll be chasing the girls again.'

I said too casually, 'Does he do that a lot?' and he just laughed at me.

'Right,' he said, putting down his mug, 'I need to be off. Food in the larder. Fridge stocked. You'll be fine for a couple of days and I should be back by then.'

I noticed he didn't say where he was going and I lacked the courage to ask.

We stood at the back door and watched him climb into the car and drive away. Suddenly, I felt very alone.

'Come on,' said Jones. 'I'll show you around if you like.'

The cottage was a typical holiday let, cheaply furnished, but not uncomfortable. All the windows were tiny, built to withstand coastal winds. I noticed there were no trees to break the gales,

265

although a few late-flowering window boxes struggled valiantly on.

A holiday let it might have been, but it had a nice atmosphere and the views from the tiny windows were lovely. We could look out over the sparkling sea and hear the distant boom of breakers crashing onto the shore.

Inside, the sitting room was large and square, and, I suspected, had once been the only room downstairs, because the kitchen and bedroom at the back looked like modern afterthoughts. What had once been an inglenook fireplace had been boxed in and now we had only an electric fire to keep the cold at bay. The stone chimney breast was enormous – this room had once been living room and kitchen combined, I was sure of it.

A modern, grey sofa was pulled up in front of the fire. I suspected it looked more comfortable than it would feel. Shelves ran down an alcove to the right of the fireplace. Most of them were empty. There were very few books. A large and very solid looking red armchair stood in front of the shelves. If there had ever been a corresponding alcove on the other side of the fireplace it had been blocked in at some point, which was a shame because it would have been nice to have one armchair on each side of a roaring fire, and sit, warm and snug, listening to the wind howl outside. Still, this was a holiday let and the owner probably slept much more soundly at night knowing there were no roaring fires on his property.

A small folding dining table and four chairs were pushed against the far wall and an old-fashioned TV stood in the corner.

The kitchen was small and basic, as was the upstairs bathroom. Jones's bedroom was opposite, just big enough for a double bed and chest of drawers. The open windows let in the sea air and the sound of breaking waves below.

'Shall we sit outside?' he said and led the way out through the front door to the little patch of grass outside. I was relieved to see that, this close up, the cliff edge was slightly further away than I had thought. An old wooden bench stood against the wall and we made ourselves comfortable in the sun, staring out at the sea together.

'So,' he said, breaking the silence. 'How's things with you?'

'Do you want the short or the long version?'

'Oh, the long, I think. There's nothing else to do and the TV hasn't got a sports channel.'

'Ah. Now I see why Jerry has run away and abandoned you.'

'He didn't tell you where he was going?'

'No. Did he tell you?'

'I don't always remember things,' he said vaguely, and, I suspected, untruthfully. Still, if he and Jerry wanted to keep their secrets ...

I stared out over the sparkling sea. 'The long version,' he prompted.

'Oh. Yes.'

I gave him the long version. All of it. The Local History Society. The Painswicks – I ignored his offer to go round and sort out 'that git Painswick', although I didn't rule it out completely. Sorensen. All the disasters that had befallen. My credit card crisis. The troll. My plan to walk more. My cold. My tummy upset ...

'Hang on,' he said, turning to face me. 'Hang on. Hang on. Go back a bit. Troll?'

I said defensively, 'I don't expect you to believe me.'

'But I do believe you, Cage, that's the problem. If anyone else had told me then I'd have laughed and accused them of winding me up, but you're Elizabeth Cage and if anyone's going to see a troll it would be you.'

'He wasn't that frightening,' I said, defensively, trying to downplay the incident. 'More like an old doormat, really. He certainly smelled like one too. Anyway, after that, I …'

'And you thought if you just dropped it into the conversation between local activities and your attack of the trots then I wouldn't notice.'

'Of course not,' I said, remembering, too late, that he was an expert in reading an interrogation. 'I just didn't think it was that important.'

'I don't expect you did, but you haven't told me how you escaped, which leads me to believe that that *is* important.'

Oh, well. He asked for it.

'I was rescued by an extremely handsome young man.'

'Not a Billy Goat Gruff, then?'

'Oh, no. He claims to be from an older race and possibly possesses supernatural powers. Although I don't know about that. Anyway, he rescued me.'

'From the troll.'

'Old Þhurs,' I said helpfully.

He faced the sea again. 'How handsome?'

'Not at all. Looked like an orangutan made out of coat hangers.'

'Not the *troll* – the handsome young man.'

'Oh, very handsome. You know the type – lovely long, silky blond hair. Blonder than yours. Very tall. Taller than you. Cooks really well. Better than you. Very good in a fight …'

'Yes, all right, I get the picture.'

'Well, you did ask.'

'And where was this troll?'

'Under the bridge – you know – just outside Whittington..'

'Is it still there – can we go and look?'

'What?'

'Well, I've never seen a troll.'

'Well, I have and you don't want to.'

'What was it like?'

'Mucusy.'

'Cage, you are the epitome of falling standards. Is that even a word?'

'Well, there's hairy and smelly as well, but mucusy pretty much covers it. It certainly covered me. Useful note for the future – it takes hours to get troll snot out of your hair.'

There was a pause and then he said, 'So, what are your plans for the future?'

'I don't know. I don't know what to do.'

There was another pause. 'I've missed you, Cage.'

Now I stared out at the sea. 'I've missed you, too.'

He reached out and we held hands in the sunshine.

'So,' I said briskly, 'What are *your* plans. Because I can't decide if we're safer together or apart.'

'Together,' he said. 'Definitely together.'

We looked at each other and then he cleared his throat and said, 'So what's the deal with this troll-defying blond?'

I sighed. 'It's very complicated.'

'I would have expected nothing less.'

'I … made a mistake.'

He looked away. 'I see. You don't have to tell me if you don't want to. I'll understand.'

'Idiot. I left him my lunch.'

He blinked. 'Well, I'm the first to admit I'm not always up to speed on social etiquette but that doesn't sound too bad to me. Was there not enough mustard in the sandwiches?'

'He construed it as some sort of offering. I thought I was leaving some sandwiches on a rock for him. He thought I left an offering on his altar.'

'Got to admire a bloke with his own altar.'

'You're really not taking this seriously at all are you.'

'Cage, I'm here, free, and with you. As far as I'm concerned, nothing else really matters, does it?'

I thought of Melek and Iblis and how one mistake had blighted both their lives for so long.

'No, nothing else matters.'

He cooked seafood risotto for supper that evening and we tucked in together. It was good to be with him again. We ate and chatted. I noticed there was no wine. 'Not quite back to normal,' he said, although I hadn't said anything.

Afterwards, he cleared away and I made the coffee, taking it through to the sitting room. We sat down on the sofa together.

I wriggled. 'This is not very comfortable. Can we swap seats?'

'Trust me, it's just as bad down this end.'

'Is that old red chair any better?'

'No idea, but there's only one so where would you sit?'

I sighed and gave up.

'So,' he said thoughtfully, stirring his coffee. 'You think Sorensen has found someone else to do his dirty work for him? An upgrade. A Cage Mark II.'

'Very funny.'

'No, what's funny is the expression on your face. You're really not happy about it, are you?'

'No, I'm not. I'm not sure if it's a good or a bad thing.'

He said quietly, 'I don't want to frighten you Cage, but I think it's bad. Very bad. For a start, they – whoever they are – might not have your scruples.'

I tried to lighten things a little. 'You're going to say, "Suppose they use their powers for evil?" aren't you?'

'Well, not now, no. But you're right. And they – whoever they are – aren't going to want you around at all. You're a potential rival. And a threat. And Sorensen isn't going to want anyone else getting their hands on you. In fact, Cage, you could find yourself even worse off than you were before.'

I nodded. 'That thought had occurred to me.'

He stretched out his long legs. 'How do you fancy living abroad?'

I was startled. And not a little afraid. 'Do you think it might come to that?'

'Do you want to hang around and find out?'

I shook my head, feeling tears build up. 'No.'

'Hey,' he said gently. 'Don't cry. I've started again. Several times in fact. It's not all bad. New places. New faces. And let's face it – you wouldn't be leaving a lot behind.'

'No,' I said, wiping my face, 'but it's my home and I hate being driven from it. And I'm making friends. And it's all I've got.'

'But it's not all you'll ever have. And I'll be with you, Cage. I won't let anything happen to you. If that means anything.'

'It means a great deal. Thank you.'

'We'll sort something out,' he said comfortably. 'No need to worry.'

'But where would we go?'

He sighed. 'Doesn't matter really, does it? It's you, Cage. If I take you to a hotel – any hotel anywhere – long-murdered guests are going to start haunting the corridors. If I take you to a remote camping site somewhere, then the skeletons of fallen warriors will start pushing their way up through the soil demanding vengeance. If I take you to a cosy seaside B&B, the apple-cheeked landlady will come after us with a hatchet, intending to bake us into a pie. Face it, Cage, these things happen. To you, mostly. So we'll jab a pin in a map, go there, and just sit down and wait for the next crisis, shall we?'

I didn't know whether to laugh or cry.

'Why don't you have an early night?' he said, taking my mug from me. 'I'll lock up down here and see you in the morning. We'll go to the library, get an atlas, open it at page twenty-nine, stick in our pin, and take things from there.'

I smiled and said goodnight.

Chapter Twenty-Five

Contrary to my expectations, I slept well. I did not dream of cottages sliding into the sea, or dread Cthulhu rising up out of the waves to consume us all, or pirates, or smugglers disguised as Dr Sorensen, or anything, really. I fell asleep to the comforting sound of waves breaking on the shore below, half-waking several times to listen to the far-off booming noise, before finally opening my eyes to another sparkling morning.

There was no sound from Jones's room upstairs, so I nipped into the kitchen to make him a cup of tea. The kitchen door was on the far side of the room and, yawning, rubbing my eyes and not looking where I was going, I walked slap bang into the old red armchair.

I cursed, rubbed my shin, hopped about a bit and cursed some more. I would have given it a good kick but my feet were bare and I was in enough pain.

'What on earth's going on?' said Jones standing in the doorway behind me, wearing a t-shirt and shorts and with his hair on end. 'Why are you trying to attack that chair?'

'I'm not,' I said, with great restraint. 'I've just walked into it.'

'Why?'

'I didn't see it.'

'It's huge, Cage. And red. And in the middle of the room. Should I take you to have your eyes tested?'

'I didn't expect it to be in the middle of the room. Why did you move it?'

'I didn't.'

'Well, I certainly didn't. I can barely lift it.'

We looked at each other.

'Old house,' said Jones. 'There might have been a bit of a tremor in the night and it shifted the chair.' He tried to lift it, grunted and somehow heaved the old chair back into its former position.

'Mind your leg,' I said warningly.

'Never mind my leg, it's my groin I'm worrying about.'

'Poor grasp of priorities,' I said, and went to put the kettle on, leaving him trying to line up the chair using the original deep depressions in the old wooden floor.

'This is interesting,' he called.

I doubted it but played along. 'What is?'

'They don't line up.'

'What doesn't line up?'

'The marks on the floor. Whatever stood here before wasn't this chair.'

'Which chair was it then?'

He looked around. 'Don't know.'

I poured the tea. 'Does it matter?'

'Probably not. Are you doing breakfast while you're in there?'

'You're the cook.'

'I'm the invalid.'

'OK. How about a tasty breakfast of wheatgerm and cod liver oil?'

I was shouldered aside. 'Eggs, bacon and toasted muffins all right?'

I took my tea out to the bench in the front garden and admired the view while breakfast was got for me.

'Any good ideas come to you in the middle of the night?' he asked as we sat down to eat.

I shook my head. 'If they did they were wasting their time. I went out like a light. You?'

'Actually, I had some rather useful thoughts.'

'Yes?'

'Well, if Sorensen doesn't want you then he probably has no use for me. Depends how vindictive he's feeling.'

'He threatened to imprison you over Clare. Or worse.'

'He could try but I'm guessing he won't.'

'Why not?'

'He won't be allowed to. Clare was a horrible mistake. Heads will – no, heads *are* already rolling for that and he was involved. Not hugely but it was Sorensen who did her psychological profile and he missed it. And then he wasted a lot of time pursuing me for it and that turned out to be a dead end, so my guess is that he'll just let me drop. And you too. We're both reminders of two of his rare failures and he won't want to draw attention to that.'

His words were comforting and I so wanted to believe him.

'Anyway, we're not going anywhere at the moment, are we?' said Jones. 'Owing to your lack of foresight in not having a passport. Really, Cage, if you're going to embrace the life of a fugitive then the least you can do is be current with the paperwork.'

He picked up our coffees and we wandered outside to sit in the sun and map out our day.

I remembered what Jerry had said about his passports. Plural. 'Can't you find someone to make me one?'

'Yes, but not in the next day or two, so I've had an idea, Cage. We'll leave the country without leaving the country.'

275

'Of course we will,' I said soothingly, wondering if perhaps he envisaged taking up residence underground.

'Scotland.' He sat back triumphantly.

I was almost certain Scotland was still attached to England and Wales and said so.

He shook his head in exasperation. 'Fishing.'

'Oh my God,' I said in admiration. 'That's brilliant. I'd forgotten.'

'Well, I've been a bit busy recently and I'd forgotten, too.' There was a pause and then he said quietly, 'It wasn't the best Christmas ever, was it?'

I shook my head. Not even close. Mrs Barton's voice came back to me. 'All that angry snow.' I pushed it away, saying as normally as I could. 'So ... fishing.'

'You bought me a fishing holiday. Remember?'

I did, yes. Our Christmas gifts to each other. He'd bought me a beautiful red bowl and I'd bought him a fishing holiday.

'And,' he continued triumphantly, 'you said you'd come too, so I added a guest. You're my plus one. It's all booked, Cage.'

'When for?'

'The end of next week. I was going to ring and cancel it when I arrived here, but that's not necessary now, is it? We'll spend a peaceful few days in Rushby, then shoot up to the Arctic Circle – or Scotland as they refer to it these days – and decimate their fish stocks, while Jerry does the biz with whatever we need to persuade a hitherto friendly country to accept you, and then off we go.'

'But my house ...'

He took my hand. 'It won't be forever, Cage. Just somewhere safe for you. For both of us. While we think about our future. It will only be for a little while. I promise.'

I swallowed and nodded.

276

We spent the rest of the day sitting quietly in the sun. I found a book to read and Jones just leaned back and closed his eyes. Occasionally I raised my eyes from my book to look around me. The colours were very simple, but very satisfying. The sea glittered, gulls were big and white against the blue sky, and the grass was a brilliant green. At that moment, I couldn't think of anywhere else I'd rather be. Sorensen, Iblis, and the strains of the last weeks just faded away in the sea air.

Whether it was the sea air or just general exhaustion, I could hardly keep my eyes open. Jones wasn't much better and, by mutual agreement, we had an early night. He disappeared up the stairs to his very much better appointed bedroom, and I crawled thankfully between my own sheets. I'd brought my book with me, but found my eyes closing half way down the first page, so I tossed it aside, turned out the light and fell heavily asleep.

I don't know what woke me, but something did. I lay for a moment, wondering where I was and what time it was. Dawn couldn't be far away. I could see the grey outlines of the furniture. Turning my head, I found myself nose to nose with a large red armchair. Literally. I was curled on the edge of my bed and it was no more than four inches away from me. A huge dark shadow in my bedroom.

I shrieked. I couldn't help it. I shrieked again and tried to fight myself free of the bedclothes. I was still struggling when the door crashed back against the wall and Jones was there – and he had a gun.

I shrieked a third time and scrambled to the other side of the bed. As far away from the chair as possible.

He was ranging the gun around the room – presumably looking for something a little more threatening than an old armchair. His colour was spiking red with adrenalin. Short, sharp bursts with every heartbeat. Ready for anything. Finding nothing, he shouted, 'What? What's wrong? What's the matter?'

My heart was hammering so hard I could barely speak so I pointed.

'What?' he said, staring round. 'What am I looking at?'

'That,' I said, pointing.

'What?'

'For God's sake, Jones, are you blind? That.'

'The chair?'

'Yes. Obviously the chair.'

'You want me to shoot a chair?'

'Yes. Now.'

He lowered the gun and took a few deep breaths. 'Bloody hell, Cage ...'

I finally got my legs free of the sheet and edged my way around the wall, making sure to keep the bed between me and the armchair, until I fetched up next to him.

'You're afraid of the chair?'

No point in denying it. 'A little.'

There was just the faintest note of exasperation. 'Then why take it to bed with you, Cage?'

'I didn't. It brought itself.'

He sighed. 'The chair moved from the sitting room into your bedroom. All by itself.'

I opened my mouth to say yes and closed it again. 'Well, I didn't do it. Did you?'

'Of course not. What sort of person gets up in the middle of the night and start moving the furniture around? Yes, I'll admit I once had a girlfriend who did that, but she always maintained it was a manifestation of her deep-seated dissatisfaction with my role in our relationship.'

'What? What are you talking about?'

278

'Women who move furniture in the middle of the night. I think her name was Margot.'

'Jones, I swear there is something seriously the matter with you.'

'Whereas heaving an old armchair around and not remembering doing so is the height of normality.'

'I didn't. I've been asleep the whole time.'

'Do you sleepwalk?'

'Of course not'

'How do you know?'

'I slept with Ted for years. He would have mentioned it. Do you?'

'No idea. Trust me, there was always such a barrage of complaint coming from my girlfriends that something as minor as sleepwalking would never even have made it to the long list. Hold this.'

He handed me the gun.

I took it as if it was red hot and pointed it at the floor. 'What are you going to do?'

'Put a stop to this.'

He strode across the room, seized the chair and tried to get it back through the door. I was pleased to notice that he could barely lift it. And he had a real struggle to get it through the door, twisting it this way and that until, finally, with a huge amount of effort and even more bad language, he had it back into the sitting room.

'What are you going to do?' I said, following him in and handing him back his gun.

'Go back to bed.'

'But ... what about ... I mean ...' I trailed away, not knowing what to say.

'Exactly,' he said, 'but if you have any suggestions, now's the time.'

I shook my head. 'Not really.'

'Right then.'

I stood still. I really didn't want to go back to my room. Not knowing there was only a single door between me and … all right, an armchair. But an armchair with possibly hostile intent. And its own power of locomotion.

It was if he read my mind. 'Do you want to sleep with me?'

'Um …'

'In my bed, I mean.'

'Will you be in it?'

'Well, yes, obviously. I'm not sleeping down here with possibly peripatetic furniture.'

I gave it up. 'Yes, please.'

He shut the door firmly on the possibly peripatetic armchair and we trailed back upstairs.

'Which side do you want?'

'The side furthest away from the chair.'

'So you're expecting me to confront whatever comes through the door?'

'Absolutely. You're the one with the gun. Where is it by the way?'

He only grinned.

His bed was still warm. I climbed in and pulled up the covers.

After a while, he said, 'Could you manage to relax a little, Cage? It's like sleeping next to a plank.'

'I can't. I'm scared I'll open my eyes and find it by my bed again.'

'Explain to me how an armchair is supposed to get up the stairs.'

'Explain to me how an armchair got into my bedroom in the first place.'

'You're asking yourself the wrong question.'

'No, I don't think I am.'

'You should be asking yourself *why* was an armchair in your bedroom in the first place.'

'Well, I don't know, do I? For all I know, it wanted to eat me.'

'I think the number of reported cases of people being consumed by their own armchairs is quite low.'

'What about being consumed by someone else's armchair?'

'I think you're more likely to be attacked by your own furniture than someone else's. I mean, you don't often hear of someone being pursued down the road by a neighbour's dining table, do you?'

'I'm so glad you're taking this seriously.'

'Well, you have to admit it's a little hard to believe.'

'And I would be in complete agreement with you if I hadn't woken up and found an armchair four inches from my nose.'

'Good heavens, Cage, what sort of position do you sleep in?'

'I was curled up on the edge of the bed,' I said with dignity.

'As opposed to lying rigid in mine, staring at the door. Seriously, Cage, I'd don't think I've ever been in bed with a woman who's stiffer than me.'

I was just casting around for a suitably scathing reply when there was a dull booming sound from downstairs. And not the sound of waves breaking on the shore, either.

I sat up. 'What was that?'

He was already getting out of bed. 'Stay here, Cage.'

'Not bloody likely.'

'Then stay behind me and don't get in my way.'

There was no fear of that.

He didn't bother creeping about either, clumping his way down the stairs and into the sitting room. I peered anxiously around his bulk.

'Hmmm,' he said

'What?'

'It's moved.'

'Told you.'

'Can I ask that any future contributions from you are slightly more helpful, please?'

'Of course you can. It won't do you any good but you can certainly ask.' I paused. 'So where did you leave it?'

He pointed. 'There. Where it was before.'

I stared at the depressions in the floor. The ones that didn't line up.

'There's been a chair there before, but not this chair.'

He crossed to the chair, knelt down and examined the legs.

'Careful,' I said from the doorway.

'I'm not sure what you think it's going to do to me, Cage.' He peered closely and said again, 'Hmmm …'

I panicked. 'What?'

'Woodworm.'

He moved the chair slightly so one leg fitted neatly in one of the depressions. None of the other legs lined up. The marks were similar, but not quite exact. 'So,' he said, thoughtfully, 'a chair like this one, but not this chair.'

'It was one of a pair,' I said, enlightened.

'A smaller one,' he said. 'His and hers chairs. This is his. Wonder what happened to hers.'

He rocked the chair back and forth on the wooden floor. No booming noise.

I pointed. 'There.'

'Where?'

'Over there. That wall on the other side of the fireplace.'

He squinted. 'What about it?'

'I can see the dents from here. And a scrape on the wallpaper. And there's dust on the floor. And no skirting board and ...'

'Yes, all right.'

'You said you wanted me to be more helpful.'

'I was mistaken.'

He heaved himself up and padded across the room to stare at the wall. 'Yes, I see what you mean.' He thumped on the wall, producing the same dull booming noise we'd heard earlier.

'That's it,' I said. 'That's what I heard last night. I thought it was the waves. Was the chair banging against the wall? Why would it do that? Did it want to get in?'

'Or,' said Jones slowly, 'was something trying to get out?'

I couldn't help it. I backed away. And then brought myself up short. What exactly was I afraid of? An armchair that could apparently materialise wherever and whenever it pleased was the answer to that one. I thrust away thoughts of it devouring me in my sleep because that simply hadn't happened, had it? Yes, I'd been shocked and startled but not terrified. And I'd been no more shocked and startled than anyone would be on encountering an unexpected piece of furniture in their bedroom. I stepped back, closed my eyes and let my mind drift a little ... and then pulled back.

'What,' said Jones.

'I'm not sure. There's grief and loss and ... loneliness.'

'Where?' He looked around. 'Where's it coming from?'

I was reluctant to tell him, but he was waiting. 'From the chair.' And waited for him to laugh.

He didn't and I was almost as irritated as if he had.

'Well, go on – laugh.'

'If it was anyone else, Cage, I'd be rolling about – either that or taking the bottle away from you – but this is you, so I'm not.'

I said nothing, biting my lip.

'What? What's the problem?'

I was reluctant. I had a horrible feeling I knew what I had to do and I really didn't want to do it – but there was so much hurt here. How could I not?

I smoothed my hand over the worn velvet and there it was again. That indefinable something. Calling to me. Trying to attract my attention. Which, let's face it, was what it had been trying to do all along. If ever a chair could shout 'Look at me. Look at me,' that was what this one had been doing, almost since the moment I arrived. Even so …

Jones was watching me. 'You don't have to do it. I can ring for a taxi and you could be back in Rushford by breakfast time.'

'I think I do have to do it. I think that's the whole point. If I don't …'

'Yes?' he said with interest. 'What if you don't?'

'I don't know exactly, but it's like …'

'Yes?'

'Like an unhealed wound. An unscratched itch. An unfulfilled need. I *have* to do it.'

'Why?'

'Because I *can* do it.'

'OK, off you go then. Shout if … '

'Shout if it all goes badly wrong and my brain explodes.'

'Just what I was going to say,' he grinned. 'How well we know each other.' But I noticed he was standing close enough to get to me in a hurry should he have to.

I walked around the chair and gazed at it for a moment and then sat. Resting my head against the back, I closed my eyes …

… The room seemed bigger. Now there were alcoves on both sides of the fireplace. A cheerful fire burned in the grate. The driftwood fire crackled, burning blue and green. Everything was quiet and peaceful. If only it was always like this. I looked up. She was sitting on the other side of the fire, pretending to sew. I watched the needle ply, pulling the red silk through the white fabric. Flowing like blood. She'd rammed pins into the arm of her chair. Her chair. Where she sat every night, thinking her unclean thoughts. Weaving her filthy ideas into the very fabric of our home. Rendering everything unclean just by her very presence. So quiet, so serene, so … innocent. Only I knew better. Only I could see the evil existing inside her. Waiting. Just waiting for the moment when I let down my guard. Waiting for me to look away for just one moment. And then it would unleash itself upon me. Or so it thought.

I watched my hand reach down to take the log from the basket. An old, gnarled hand, scarred and hard. The hand of a man who'd worked all his life. I looked at her hands, white and soft. Watched the red thread pool against the white silk. Like splashes of blood. Felt myself stand up slowly as if to place the log upon the fire. Felt the good, hard wood in my hand. There would never be a better chance. Her blonde head was bent over her work. She was offering herself to me. She wanted me to do it. Did she recognise her own evil? I should set her free.

I swung back, surprised at my own strength. The blow sent a shock wave all the way up my arm.

She fell sideways across the arm of the chair, her sewing slipping from her fingers. I swung again – and this time there was blood. Warm, sweet blood. She shuddered. Not dead yet. I raised the log and brought it down as hard as I could. And again. And again. On and on and on and on. Until my arm ached with the effort. And then there was silence in the room again. Except for the crackling fire. And my own breathing, loud in my head.

Now she was dead.

She'd fallen onto the rug. Neat and tidy, even in death.

No time to lose. I had to act now before the evil inside her was free to find another victim.

I rolled her up in the rug. And then again in the plastic sheeting I'd set aside for another task. I shoved her back in her chair and pushed the both of them into the alcove. They fitted exactly. More than ever I was convinced this was meant to be. A bit of plaster board tomorrow. A coat of paint. Burn the log ... A tale of her visiting relatives and it was done. Now, finally, I could be at peace.

And then ... and then ... the plastic crackled. There was a tiny movement. No. How could she not be dead? I picked up the poker ...

I erupted out of the chair, gasping with terror, straight into Jones's arms.

'It's all right,' he said softly. 'I'm here. I've got you. You're safe. It's all right. You're back. Sit down. Wait.'

He dragged out a dining chair and I sat down with a bump.

'All right?'

I was staring at my hands. My perfectly normal, clean hands with straight fingers and neat fingernails. I remembered again the rage. That red, roaring crescendo of violence in my head.

He fetched me a glass of water. 'OK? How are you feeling?'

I sipped and slowly the terror began to fade. I sipped again and waited for my heart to subside.

'So tell me, Cage. What did you see?'

I closed my eyes and told him what I'd seen. 'She's over there. Behind that wall.'

'So that's why there's no corresponding alcove on this side of the fireplace,' he said thoughtfully, tapping away at the walls. Well, it's definitely plasterboard and every other wall is solid. Back in a minute.'

He disappeared only to reappear a minute later with a small sledgehammer.

I leaped from the chair in alarm. 'Where did you get that?'

'Next door's shed. Don't worry – it wasn't locked. I didn't have to break in.'

That wasn't the point I'd been trying to make.

'But what are you going to do?'

'I'm going to have that wall down. Stand back, Cage. You've had a rough enough night without a wall falling on you as well.'

My heart started up again. 'But it's not our wall. What will the owner say?'

'I should imagine he'll say, "Bloody hell, you bastard, what have you done to my wall? That's going to cost you." Unless he's fleeing to South America to escape justice, of course. Stand back now.'

I didn't move. 'You can't just knock down people's walls willy-nilly. What if there isn't a body there after all. What if I've got it wrong?'

'Then I shall blame you and disappear, leaving you to make whatever feeble explanations you can muster. And reimburse poor old Jerry for his security deposit, of course. Out of the way now.'

Whoever had put in this false wall hadn't made a very good job of it at all. Two or three solid blows from the even more solid Michael Jones made a huge hole in it. I braced myself for an unpleasant smell but apart from a certain amount of mustiness, it wasn't too bad.

He picked up his torch and shone it inside. 'Ah.'

'What? You can't just say "Ah," and leave it at that. Is there a body?'

'Yep. Well, I think it's a body. There's an old red armchair and a plastic clad bundle on the floor. Looks as if it's fallen out of the chair. Want to see?'

I shook my head.

'It's not gruesome, I promise you.'

I sighed. He held the torch and I peered inside. The space was very small and taken up mostly by the chair which looked as good as new. Slightly dusty but otherwise fine. I stood on tiptoe, craning my neck to look around the small space.

'Hang on,' he said. A couple more blows and the wall was almost completely destroyed. The chair and sinister plastic wrapped bundle were exposed. I bent forwards.

'Don't touch it, Cage.'

As if I was going to rip it asunder and pillage the contents.

He went to his jacket, hanging off the back of a dining char and pulled out his phone.

'Wait. Wait.'

Suddenly, something was very important. The thing that had been hammering on the door of my attention finally made itself heard. I looked at the indentations in the floor. I looked at the chair in the alcove. A smaller and lighter twin of the one that had given us all this trouble.

I turned back to the old red armchair. 'You did this.'

'Um, Cage, are you talking to the chair?'

'You did this. That booming noise at night wasn't the waves on the shore, it was you bumping yourself against the wall trying to show us where she was hidden. You've been trying to attract my attention since the moment I got here. All the time you've been trying to tell me where she was, haven't you?'

'OK, Cage, you're frightening me now.'

'Look – one chair is slightly bigger and heavier than the other. The other is more slender. The legs are curvier. You said it. His and hers. Male and female chairs. One for him and one for her. Made goodness knows how long ago when there were real fires to sit beside in the evenings. The master in one chair and the mistress in the other.'

I wondered how long they'd been together. And they hadn't started out in this little cottage, I was sure. A rich merchant's house somewhere. Maybe even in Rushford, and then sold on as they became older and shabbier, but always together. Until …

Until they'd been split up and the remaining chair had … had what? Moved heaven and earth to attract my attention. Done everything in its power to tell us where she was. I had a feeling that the body was incidental. It was the chair that was important.

I looked at the body on the floor. It was too late for her but not too late for …

I heaved at the chair again.

'Cage, what are you doing?'

I puffed. Even the smaller chair was heavy. 'Tampering with the evidence.'

He nudged me out of the way. 'That's my girl, but why?'

'Because this is what it's all been about. Help me.'

He didn't argue.

I shoved the sofa against the wall where it looked perfectly natural. Jones placed the female chair to the left of the fireplace and we heaved the other one to the right. They both looked as if they'd been there since the beginning of time.

'Right,' he said, and picked up his phone again.

'What are you doing?'

'We've found a body, Cage, remember? I'm calling the police.'

I panicked. 'Right. OK. Don't panic. We need to get out of here. Now. No wait. We need to put the plasterboard back. No wait. Fingerprints. We need to clean the house from top to bottom. Our fingerprints will be all over it. And our DNA. And we need to clean out the drains because of hair and things. We'll need bleach. Lots and lots of bleach. I'll go shopping while you try to repair the plasterboard. And pack. And we can't take a taxi because they'll remember us so we'll have to walk. Don't pack – you won't be able to carry your case. Leave everything you don't need. Or better still – burn it. Burn everything. Because of our DNA. But not in here. Burn it out there. Tell people you're having a clear out or something so they're not suspicious. Or a better idea, throw your case into the sea. And then we leave tonight. While it's dark. So no one will see us. We'll catch a train to a big town and disappear. Why are you laughing?'

'Sweetheart, this is nothing to do with us. We're not guilty.'

'But they'll think we are.'

'The body's been here for months. Years.'

'But you're … I paused but couldn't think of another phrase … on the run.'

And your hare-brained scheme will have us *both* on the run. We'll be prime suspects. There'll be a national manhunt and they'll have us before tea time.

'No,' I said. 'You go now and I'll put the plasterboard back and we'll pretend we never saw it. I'll catch you up in a couple of days' time and then we can go abroad.'

He put his hand over mine. 'No.'

'But …'

'No.'

'So … what do we do then?' Trying to reconcile this suddenly law-abiding citizen with the Jones I knew.

He pulled out his phone and dialled. 'Police, please.' There was a pause and then, with a note of panic in his voice, he said, 'Hello, yes. There's a body. In our cupboard. It's horrible. I think it's been dead for ages. Oh yes. David Southey. Number One, Cliffside Cottages. The first one. The pink one. Can you come? My wife is very upset.'

He closed his phone. 'You're very upset.'

'I am now,' I said, grimly. 'Who's David Southey?'

'I am.' He fished for his wallet and showed me his driving licence. David Southey.

'So who am I?'

He smiled. 'Well, one day I hope you'll be Mrs Southey, but I think we both have a long hard road to travel before we get there, don't you?'

To cover my confusion, I went to get dressed.

Chapter Twenty-Six

I watched the two police officers walk slowly across the car park. Their colours were very similar – a gentle blue grey. They liked their job and they liked each other. They were friendly and relaxed and obviously not suffering any of the personal traumas usually conjured for them by over-imaginative screen writers.

We'd left the kitchen door open for them, but they tapped politely anyway. Jones, rightly guessing that my experience in deceiving the forces of law and order wasn't anywhere near as great as his, had sent me outside to sit on the bench in the sun. I could hear the murmur of voices and then the female police officer came to sit beside me. She asked me how I was feeling and was so kind I felt quite ashamed of myself. Moving the chair had not been the action of a responsible citizen. I don't know what my dad would have said.

Beyond verifying my details and asking me to tell her what had happened, she said very little. Apart from the question I'd been dreading.

'What on earth made you knock down the wall?'

Jones's suggestion that we had heard a noise behind the wall and thought a bird or an animal might be trapped was the best we could come up with and I delivered it to the best of my ability.

'But you knocked down the entire wall,' she said.

'Oh no. Not really. Well, not to begin with. My husband only knocked the tiniest hole, shone his torch through, and said, Oh my God … Rachel … there's a body in there.'

'And what did you say?'

'I thought he was joking, so he knocked down the rest of the wall and made me look,' I said, thinking I might try for the sympathy vote.

'And then what did you do?'

'He telephoned the police – that's you – I said, remembering my little woman role. And I came out here. I don't have to go back inside, do I?'

'Not at the moment, no.'

'Oh, thank you,' I said, in genuine gratitude.

I could hear voices inside and a crackling radio. Cars and vans were pulling up the little lane. Soon there wasn't room for me to be inside, even if I'd wanted to. They were getting stuck in and obviously they wanted us out of their crime scene, as soon as possible, so we gave statements, details of where we could be contacted, packed up the few belongings they allowed us to take away and were driven to a small hotel able to take us at short notice. As Jones said afterwards, there was nothing like being chauffeur driven from the crime scene you'd just contaminated. I was nearly speechless with agitation and guilt by now and definitely in no state to argue.

The Linden Hotel was down a street narrow even by Rushby's standards. There was no vehicular access – which seemed to be a recurring theme in my life – and we trundled our suitcases down yet another narrow, cobbled street.

They were waiting for us and our room was ready, for which I was extremely thankful. We were too late for lunch, they said, watching Jones hand over his David Southey credit card. I held my breath, but he was amazingly relaxed about the whole fake credit card thing, reassuring me on our way up in the lift that the card was genuine, the account was genuine, the user slightly less so, but the hotel wouldn't be the loser by the transaction. I tried to feel reassured.

'Right,' he said, unlocking the door to our room, Number Eight. 'You unpack, shower, do whatever is necessary for you to look a little less like an abused spouse, and I'll come and collect you in … say … thirty minutes.'

'I think I'd just like to lie down and rest for a couple of hours,' I said.

'No,' he said with decision. 'A walk in the sunshine and a nice lunch somewhere will leave you feeling much more refreshed than an afternoon nap. And it will help you sleep tonight. Off you go. Don't dawdle.'

I scowled at him but he was parking his own suitcase by the wardrobe. 'See you later.'

He disappeared down the corridor and I turned to survey yet another room that wasn't where I lived. For someone who just wanted to live quietly at home, I was seeing a good number of strange rooms recently.

I appreciated him giving me some privacy but that didn't stop me having a small rebellion and showering *before* unpacking. I must remember to tell him I disobeyed his instructions. And, while I was on the subject, also tell him that he was overbearing, dictatorial and despotic. And anything else I could think of.

Since we appeared to be doing the harmless tourist thing, I changed into a pretty top, light jeans and comfortable sandals, whipping the door open just as he was poised to knock.

His colour looked much stronger today, streaming towards me as usual. 'Pretty,' he said, referring to my top, I assumed. 'Are you in a better mood now?'

'Oh yes,' I said. 'No bodies concealed in the wall, no high-handed spies getting me into even more trouble. Actually, it was quite dull. Although I did enjoy your absence.'

'Shrew,' he said amiably, piloting me towards the lift. 'I wonder if Sorensen realises what a lucky escape he's had.'

Rushby is a pretty place. The sea was bright and calm. The fishing boats were chugging home and there were just enough people around to give the streets a lively atmosphere without too much overcrowding.

We wandered around, exploring the harbour and watching the fishing boats unload their catch. We peered in shop windows, and explored promising looking alleyways, until he asked me if I was hungry and I discovered, to my surprise, that I was.

We walked up the hill until we found a pretty café with a red and white striped awning and matching table cloths.

'Inside or out?' asked Jones.

'Oh, outside, I think. This is so nice.'

And it was. The place was a little suntrap, and all the way up here we had a lovely view down over the town.

Jones took a great deal of care over his choices.

'I'm hungry,' he said simply, and continued to pour over the menu, eventually going for soup and two toasted sandwiches which confused everyone.

'One for you and one for the lady?' said the waitress.

'No, two for me and the lady will choose her own.'

'So you want *two* toasted sandwiches?'

'And the soup.'

'But only one soup?'

'Yes.'

'Do *you* want soup?' she said turning to me.

'No, thank you, I'd like …'

'So, soup and a toastie?'

'No, soup and two toasties. Please.'

'Two separate sandwiches?'

I began to lose the will to live.

'Yes, but you can put them on the same plate?'

'But you want two separate sandwiches?'

'And the soup.'

I tried again. 'And I'd like …'

'Two toasted cheese and ham?'

'No, actually, I think I'll have one toasted cheese and one toasted ham and tomato.'

'So, two separate sandwiches?'

'But on the same plate. But not the soup.'

'You don't want the soup?'

'I do, but not on the same plate as the toasties.'

'I'll have a toasted teacake,' I said firmly. 'Just one. No soup. And a hot chocolate.'

She wrote that down, flashed Jones a look as if to say, 'See, that's how it's done,' and whisked herself and the menus away.

Jones took out his phone, checked the screen and laid it on the table.

'Problem?' I said, the trauma of ordering lunch still fresh in my mind.

'I'm expecting to hear from Jerry,' he said vaguely, and I knew better than to ask.

I sat back in my chair and looked out at the glittering sea, enjoying the warm sun on my face.

'Cage.'

'Mm?' I said, not really paying attention.

'Cage, could you pay attention, please? I have something very important to ask you.'

My heart missed a beat and then thumped painfully. I turned to face him. 'Yes?'

He pulled his chair forwards and leaned across the table. 'Well ...' and stopped.

I waited. 'Yes?'

He sat perfectly still for a moment and then his colour curdled around him, an unpleasant mix of dirty red and gold, before whipping off to one side as if caught in a sudden, violent draught. And then he just got up and walked off. Back up the street. Without a word or a backward glance, he just got up and walked away.

I sat, paralysed. What just happened? Where was he going? Was it something I'd said? Now, too late, I remembered what Jerry had said about his tendency to wander. I sat like an idiot, mouth open, until I suddenly realised he was near the end of the street and if he turned the corner I could easily lose him in the summer crowds.

I jumped to my feet, rummaged frantically in my handbag, left a random amount of money on the table, grabbed his phone and set off after him.

I had no idea where he could be going, or why, but he wasn't difficult to keep in sight. For a start he was a good half a head taller than most people so he was easily visible as I struggled through the dawdling crowds. I honestly expected him to head back to the hotel. Perhaps he'd suddenly felt tired or unwell and wanted to lie down, but he didn't. He headed away from the hotel, climbing up through the town. The houses stopped huddling together in terraces and became larger and more modern. Gardens and garages began to appear. He passed the last building – the very posh Grand Hotel with its wonderful views over the sea to the front and the open country behind – picked his way over a cattle grid, and suddenly we were up on the moors themselves.

I looked around at great rolling sweeps of coarse grass and bracken, just beginning to turn golden. An emptier landscape I'd never seen.

I wasn't dressed for this. I was dressed for wandering around town, poking around interesting looking shops and finding somewhere nice for lunch, not yomping over the moors on my way to heaven knows where. What was he doing? I'd ask him if I could catch him but try as I might, I couldn't get any closer. He was taller than me, fitter than me and wearing more sensible shoes than me. He was still limping slightly from his recent injury, but so was I and although I did my best, even my best speed couldn't close the gap between us. I tried shouting but I was breathless and my feeble cry was whipped away by the wind. It was all I could do to keep him in sight. I was hot, frightened and thirsty. My open sandals were no protection at all against the prickly coarse grass stabbing at my feet. I was never going to catch him. I tried shouting again, but if he could hear me he was paying no heed.

I risked a quick look around. The landscape was empty. There were no trees, no buildings, no paths, not even any sheep. There was complete silence other than the wind and an occasional bird call. I shivered. This was a very lonely place.

I was beginning to worry. This is how people die on the moors. Inadequate clothing and footwear, no maps, no water, and then a mist comes down and they're lost. Then nightfall happens, the temperature drops or it starts to rain, exposure sets in, and then they're dead.

I became aware I was still clutching his phone. Trying at one and the same time to keep him in sight, look where I was going and scroll through his contacts, I eventually found Jerry's number.

It rang for a long time. I didn't hang up. Jerry was my only hope. I remembered what he'd said about letting it ring. There were a series of clicks in my ear and I thought I'd lost him, and then the ringing began again but this time with a different tone. Then another series of clicks. Then silence. This time I did think I'd lost him.

And then a voice said very quietly and very cautiously, 'Hello?'

'Jerry? Jerry is that you?'

'Course it is,' he said, in a reproachful whisper. 'What's the problem?'

I tried not to gabble. 'Jerry, I need you. He just got up and walked off. He was talking to me and he stood up and left. He's up on the moors. I'm not sure he knows what he's doing. I can't stop him. I can't even catch him. I don't know what to do.'

'Slowly, slowly, missis. Tell me again.'

I drew a deep calming breath and, as best I could, explained what had happened. At the end there was a long silence and I thought he'd gone again or I'd lost the signal or something.

'Any idea where you are or where you're headed?'

I squinted into the low afternoon sun. We were heading west. 'We're walking directly into the setting sun. Away from the coast.'

'Not Rushford, then?'

I had a sudden flash of inspiration.

'Jerry – hang on a moment.'

I tried to rummage, one-handed, through my handbag, failed miserably and, in frustration, upended the whole lot onto the grass. Yes – a piece of luck. Just for once. I clean out my handbag as often as most women do and I still had the Woodland Trust leaflet. Creased and crumpled and with one or two dubious stains, but intact. I turned it over to the map and smoothed it out.

The name leaped out at me. I felt sick. How could this be? Carefully, I tried to align the tiny map with the sun, hoping ... but no. I knew. I just knew.

I could hear Jerry's voice. 'You still there, missis?'

I swallowed hard and found my voice. 'Jerry ... Jerry ... I think he's trying to get back to Greyston.'

I was scrabbling my stuff back into my bag as I waited for his scornful comment.

It didn't come. Instead, he said cautiously, 'Because ...?'

I was listening to him, watching Jones and trying to zip up my bag all at the same time. Not looking where I was going, I tripped over a tussock of coarse grass. 'Dammit.'

'You all right?'

I made myself slow down. If I hurt myself up here then both I and Jones were finished.

'Yes, yes, I'm all right.' Ahead of me, Jones was cresting a low rise and slowly disappearing down the other side. I tried a kind of running walk that didn't really cover the ground any more quickly and, at the same time, searched for the right words to convince him.

I closed my eyes and remembered. I wasn't alone on the high moors in the sunshine. I was down in the cold darkness of Greyston, surrounded by baying women, feeling the pull of the stones and their dark powers. My mind filled with the hysteria of that night, the shrieking women, the anticipation of violent death, the sweet taste of the blood. The desire for death ...

I pulled myself back and swallowed hard. I had to concentrate. I had to make him believe me.

'Jerry, two reasons ... One – they still want him as their Year King. The silly sod went back on New Year's Day and they're calling him back somehow.'

I paused to get my breath back and then ploughed on.

'Or, he's the bait and it's me they want. Either to join them, or for punishment. Could be either.'

'Why now?' he said, breathing heavily as if he was exerting himself.

'I don't know,' I said, trying not to panic, because I didn't know. 'Perhaps they couldn't get to him before. Sorensen had him, remember? He was heavily drugged and all over the place. And,' I said, suddenly remembering, 'you told me to keep an eye on him because he kept wandering off. Perhaps it wasn't because of Sorensen's drugs after all.'

I thought again. 'Or perhaps they were somehow ... weakened ...' I saw Miriam's stone fall, '...after what we did to them and they've only now got their strength back. Or there's some other reason I don't know anything about, but I'm more and more certain that's where he's heading. I've got a kind of map here and there's nowhere else around.' I could feel my panic growing. It was a struggle to remain coherent. 'Jerry, I have to stop him and he's moving too fast for me. I can't catch him.'

I was beginning to pant and cry and my foot was throbbing quite badly. Just another of the disasters I'd suffered recently. And then I remembered all the other things that had happened to me. My dreadful run of bad luck. And that of those around me. When everything I touched broke, or crumbled, or fell over, or went wrong ... Ted's pension. My falling down the steps.

Everyone and everything.

Everyone and everything ...

My feet slowed of their own accord.

Everyone and everything ...

Despite the urgency, I stood still and thought. How many people would have a reason to dislike me?

There was Sorensen, of course, always at the top, but he was very quiet these days.

Then there was Thomas Rookwood from last year. As far as I knew he was still miles away up in Northumberland. Besides, he had a lot to lose if his secrets ever came tumbling out. I mentally crossed out his name.

The vengeful spirit of Clare Woods. Jones's ex-partner and girlfriend who had been executed in a grimy basement in Droitwich. I shivered in the sunshine, but again, she wasn't very likely.

And then there was Veronica Harlow. And Becky Harlow. And, if she was still alive, Miriam Harlow. And the Three Sisters themselves. We'd done them irreparable damage. Dealt them a possibly fatal blow. I closed my eyes and saw the stone fall. Saw Granny drop to the ground. We'd wrecked their ceremony. The ceremony that went back who knew how many centuries. The ceremony that ensured their continuing long life and prosperity. We'd destroyed a millennia old tradition in just under thirty minutes.

They might still be powerful. I remembered the moment our car was dragged backwards. The handbrake was on – there was no one in the driving seat and still the car moved. Back towards the place of the stones. For them to take their revenge.

And there had been that moment. I saw, suddenly and with horrifying clarity, that moment at the stones, Veronica crouched over Granny. I saw her slowly stand and face me. I saw her murderous colour. I saw thick blue and purple spikes stabbing towards me. I felt the sudden viciousness of her attack. Felt my

302

heart fail … When the world darkened around me. I needed to think.

'Jerry, give me a moment …'

I didn't need a moment. I knew already. I felt a stone-cold certainty. We'd thought we'd got away, but we hadn't. It had taken them a little while but they'd found us. They were all powerful women. Miriam Harlow was old and sick now – she might even be dead, but what had she been in her youth? Becky was young, undeveloped, but I bet she'd grown up a lot over the last few months. And she'd hated me even before I'd destroyed her way of life. And Veronica, Veronica was a formidable woman who had been baulked of her prey. Twice. Both the Year King and I had escaped her clutches that night. And we'd damaged the stones as well.

But, possibly, we hadn't damaged them enough. Had there been enough power left for her purpose? The answer would seem to be yes.

Veronica Harlow and the Three Sisters. I'd been cursed by Veronica Harlow.

It all made perfect sense.

When looked at individually, my fall, the microwave, my lethargy, the electrics, my keys, Mrs Barton's fall, the problems with Ted's pension, Jerry's car accident, perhaps even the disappearance of the Painswicks, everything had a reasonable explanation, but lump it all together and it was beyond the bounds of coincidence.

I'm not clumsy. I don't fall down. I'm very careful with my keys. My microwave was new. Well, newish, but I take care of it. I take care of all my possessions. I don't microwave teaspoons or tin foil or eggs. I have the electrics and gas serviced annually on one of those schemes. I probably have much more

303

insurance than I need. That's the sort of person I am. That so much could go wrong all at once was … unlikely.

I stood in the lonely silence and let my mind drift a little … just a little … but there was nothing there. I gave myself a little shake – of course there wasn't anything there. People don't get *cursed* – not in this day and age. And if anyone could sense such a thing then surely it would be me.

And yet, I was very bad at reading myself. I can look at other people and their colour and know all about them, but I don't even know what my own colour is. I can't see it. Why I can't see it I don't know but I can't. Perhaps I don't have one although that seemed unlikely. Everything living has a colour. Those of plants and animals are faint and not easy to see and I generally don't bother – except for Old Man Yew, of course, whose malevolence had generated a colour so strong I was surprised no one else could see it. But just because I couldn't detect a curse didn't mean it wasn't there.

But what of Mrs Barton? She wasn't there the night we destroyed the ceremony. Nor were Mrs Painswick and Alyson. Was the curse powerful enough to touch those who touched me? Was I the cause of all this? The epicentre? Was the curse damaging not only me but all those around me?

'You still there, missis?'

I didn't mean to blurt it out – it just happened. 'They've cursed me, Jerry. It's the only explanation.'

He sounded amused. 'Well, no. I can think of plenty more likely explanations that that.'

I brushed that aside. 'How soon could you get to Greyston? You can intercept him.'

'A fair while. I'm a bit busy at the moment.'

'Doing what? What could be more important than this?' I hadn't meant to shout.

'Nothing,' he said soothingly, 'but I'm actually half in and half out of a third-floor window and the gizmo neutralising the security cameras isn't going to last forever.'

I stopped dead. 'Jerry!'

'I'll get to you as soon as I can. Ring that long thin streak of wind and piss. See if he can make himself useful again.'

'Iblis?'

'That's the one.'

Not a bad idea.

'OK.' I rang off.

Ahead of me, Jones was not stopping. Not even slowing down. I couldn't run and talk any longer. One thing at a time. I sat down on a lumpy tussock of rough grass and rang my own number. It rang twice and then a voice uttered dramatically, 'It is I who speaks. Iblis.' I never knew whether he was just winding me up or whether he habitually announced himself in that manner. I did know I was in no mood for theatrics. I could hear my TV in the background. I'd obviously interrupted his afternoon soap session.

'Iblis, I need your help. I'm up on the moors. There's something wrong with Jones and I can't stop him heading for Greyston. I think either the stones want their revenge on us or he's to be their Year King. Neither is good and I need you. How soon could you get there?'

'I am on my way,' he said simply. 'Stay out of sight. You must not let them see you.'

'Why not?'

He hesitated. 'If the man Jones is to be their Year King then he is in no danger. You, on the other hand ....'

He stopped.

I felt my heart grow cold. 'What about me?'

'Have you ever heard of a witch's ladder?'

305

'No,' I said, my heart jumping about all over again. 'What's a witch's ladder?'

'I found one concealed in your porch,' he said, not really answering the question at all. 'It can be used as a focus for ill will.'

I stopped dead. The wind blew suddenly chill and I suddenly realised I was miles from anywhere and I was completely alone.

My throat felt rough and tight. 'Iblis, I knew it. I've been cursed, haven't I?'

'Looks like it,' he said cheerfully. 'No wonder you kept falling over. And dropping things. And breaking things ...'

'Yes, all right,' I said crossly, wiping the sweat off my face. My hair was plastered to my forehead and my top was sticking to my back and now it seemed I was under the influence of some sort of magic talisman. I would have been very happy to have had Iblis dismiss my claim of being cursed but he hadn't. Somehow, that was most chilling of all. Up here, alone, watching Michael Jones slowly disappear from view, it suddenly seemed very real and very frightening.

'Heed my warning Elizabeth Cage and wait for me.'

I looked around at the featureless moorland and Michael Jones, still striding along, showing no signs of the fatigue and thirst I was feeling, and tried not to feel overwhelmed.

'I can't leave him, Iblis. I don't think he knows what he's doing.'

He made no argument which I appreciated. 'Then stay out of sight.'

I looked around me again and, just for one moment, allowed the panic to creep in. 'Iblis, I don't know where I am.'

'That does not matter. I will find you.'

The line went dead.

I slipped Jones's phone in my pocket feeling a little more cheerful now that I knew help was on the way.

It would do no one any good if I passed out from fatigue or dehydration, so I took this moment to rest and get my breath back, which turned out to be a very good move because in the sudden silence, I could hear the cheerful trickle of water just off to my right. I dropped to my knees and ignoring everything I'd ever read about cholera or leptospirosis, I had a good drink. The water was ice cold, tasted slightly peaty and did me the world of good. I splashed some on my face and neck.

Looking around, water still running down my chin, I could see I was quite high up. Almost as high as it was possible to climb on the moors, and on all sides the land sloped downwards. I thought I could see the outline of a rough path. A sheep track perhaps. Whatever it was, I could see it winding its way down the slope, becoming broader and more defined.

Reinvigorated, I set off again. The ground underfoot was firmer as I descended and the going much easier. Now I was out of the grass and rough bracken I found I could pick up more speed. The track became wider and rutted. I could see tyre tracks. Then there was a gate with a cattle grid. Then there was a lane on the other side. The moors slowly turned into green fields. Tall hedges on either side of the lane shut out the light. Now everything was downhill and I picked up the pace.

At the end of the lane was a T-junction. A signpost informed me it was six miles back to Rushby, seventeen miles to Rushford, and three miles to Greyston. My heart sank, but I couldn't help a certain grim satisfaction that I had been right.

I turned towards Greyston and broke into a trot. I couldn't see Jones but I was almost certain he was ahead of me somewhere. There was no reason for him to have gone back to Rushby.

At long last, I was heading back towards civilisation. The green fields were filled with sheep and cattle and their hedges neatly trimmed. I saw an occasional roof amongst the trees. And then I heard a car coming towards me. I considered flagging it down and asking for help, but I wasn't sure I wanted to be seen just yet. Suppose they were from Greyston. Come to meet Jones. And it was going in the wrong direction anyway. I stepped back into the hedge and let it pass me by.

A hundred yards down the lane on the right-hand side of the lane was a brand new shiny metal gate. A notice informed me these woods were private property and trespassing was forbidden. Which made me hesitate. Jones laughs at me sometimes, but I was almost certain the path I could see winding through the trees led in the direction I wanted to go. And I should get off the road. That car had been a warning. I didn't want to be seen, not until I understood what was going on here, so I clambered up over the gate, averted my eyes from the penalties for trespassing, and set off down the broad avenue between the trees.

Chapter Twenty-Seven

After the sun and wind of the moors, being under the trees was actually quite pleasant. I jogged silently along, relieved by the cool shade. The soft ground was much easier on my poor, battered feet. And it was downhill. There was birdsong and dappled light all around me. I breathed in the scents of damp earth and leaves and listened to the tranquil sounds of undisturbed woodland life. This was an old wood, showing signs of careful management. The trees around me were a mixture of evergreen and deciduous. I could see holly and yew, mixed with oak, birch, ash, and others I didn't recognise. I found myself looking for beech trees and thinking of Iblis. Which made me wonder how long it would be before I could expect to see him.

I jogged onwards and downwards, following the path, watching where I put my feet, all my thoughts on what I would do when I arrived at Greyston. And then I stopped. I don't know why I stopped – but I did. I stopped dead. I think I stopped breathing. The hairs on my neck began to rise. Drawing in a long breath, I tried to look around without moving my head. Without moving anything. Because it was very important not to let them know I was here. That thought was in my mind before I knew it. Closely followed by – not let *who* know I was here?

I had run into what I thought was a modern part of the wood. Almost a plantation. Gone was the woodland tangle I'd been seeing for the last mile or so. Here, all the trees stood in neat rows. There was no undergrowth, no ivy scrambling up ancient tree trunks. Young trees stretched away into the dim distance.

Except – they weren't trees.

They weren't trees.

They weren't trees.

My mind was struggling to make sense of what my eyes could see.

They weren't trees.

I stood alone among things that weren't trees. I could hear my own breathing. Feel my skin tighten with dread.

Because they weren't trees. They were men. Or rather – they had been men. Once upon a time, all these had been young men. Men of all different shapes and sizes and colours. All naked. Pale and bloodless. And all with a huge, dark, gaping wound across their throat. Like a bloodless smile. Their eyes glittered. They had no colours for me to read. No expression. No one spoke. They stood and watched me.

I couldn't think of anything better to do than just to stand still. My instinct was to run but where would I run to? They were all around me. All I could hear was my own ragged breathing, very loud in the silence.

I stood stock still and waited. I knew who these men were. Who they had been and how they'd died. What had Veronica told me? She'd said they always buried the remains of the old Year King up in the woods. They'd been doing this for literally ages. These woods must be full of bodies. The bodies of men ritually murdered, their blood flung at the stones and then what was left of them – the bits not required for ceremonial purposes – dumped up here in the woods, without reverence or respect, to wait in the long, dark silence of time for their day of revenge. I was trapped, alone, in a wood full of dead vengeful men.

There were hundreds of them, stretching off into a distance that had nothing to do with measurement. Row upon row. Silent and still. Some were more distinct than others. Some – the older

310

ones I guessed – the ones who had been here for a very long time – were merely a dark shape. How many of them must there be up here? One a year for how many years? How many centuries? There must be hundreds and hundreds of them. Thousands of them. And I was surrounded. By dead men.

The world blurred and whirled away from me and I knew I was lost. If I fell or passed out they would be upon me. I leaned forwards, hands on my knees and tried to breathe. At every moment I expected to be seized by a hundred hands. To feel their ice-cold fingers digging into my warm flesh.

I managed a whisper. 'Please. Don't hurt me.'

The lack of reaction was chilling.

I tried again. 'You must let me go. I have to get to Greyston.'

It was exactly the wrong thing to say. Nothing moved but their glittering eyes. I felt my heart pound. My head swam. I was hyperventilating and it was making me giddy. They were all around me. They weren't letting me out. I didn't want to die here.

'Please – you must let me go.'

Again – nothing.

And then – from somewhere – I found inspiration.

'There is a man down there who needs help. I must help him.'

For a long time, nothing seemed to change. I waited, panting with fear, trying not to cry, or panic, or scream, or anything. I didn't know what to do. Or how to get out of this. And I didn't even want to think about what they could do to me. Or what they *wanted* to do to me. If they thought I was one of the women from Greyston …

'Please … please let me go. I have to save him.'

My eyes filled with useless tears. I was furious with myself. Now was not the time to cry. I rubbed my eyes so hard it hurt and when I looked again, the path was there. I could hardly believe it. There it was, stretching before me, twisting through the trees and out of sight.

I wasted no time, setting off at a jog and very definitely not looking to left or right. I had an impression of movement all around me. I wasn't alone. I was all alone in this wood and yet I wasn't alone. In the worst possible way, I wasn't alone.

I could hear my own feet on the path, but everything around me had fallen silent. Now there was no birdsong, no woodland noises, no wind rustling the leaves. It was worse than silence – it was the complete absence of sound. And worst of all, whatever wasn't making a sound was all around me.

I moved faster. I couldn't help it. Anything to get away from whatever was in this wood. I had no idea how far I still had to go. Not much further, surely. Please don't let it be too far. Please ....

The trees ended abruptly, as did the sense of something around me. Were they unable or unwilling to leave the shelter of the woods? There was no time to think about that now as I found myself on the slope above Greyston and looking down. I hadn't realised before, but the whole village was in a giant basin, surrounded on all sides by green hills which, in turn, were crowned with thick woodland. From here, it was very easy to see how isolated and apart this place was. Just one road in and the same road out.

I had an excellent view. There, clear as day, I could see the pub, the cottages, the green, the Travellers' Rest and the remains of the stones themselves. At the moment, however, it wasn't the stones I was looking at.

Jones had been right about Greyston. It was awful. Gone was the immaculate, perfect English village. The beautifully kept village green had disappeared. Coarse, dead tussocks of brown grass spoiled the smooth lawn I remembered.

The pub roof sagged and not in a picturesque way. The neat wooden tables and chairs outside were gone and replaced by cheap white plastic furniture, all piled up higgledy-piggledy.

There were cars here now. The village was choked with them. The neat verges had been churned up with rows of them parked any old how. Some of them looked as if they'd been there for a long time. One or two were up on bricks.

There was litter everywhere. Dirty plastic bags had been blown into the hedges and flapped forlornly. The hedges themselves were overgrown and straggly.

The windows of Alice Chervil's shop were empty. I wasn't even sure if it was open. The same for the village hall, which had a lost, forlorn look about it. The air of quiet prosperity had completely disappeared. Probably never to return because I couldn't imagine tourists pouring in to see a grubby and unkempt village with a damaged stone.

Two of the stones still stood but Granny's lay on the ground, dark and dead and half hidden in the long grass. The other two looked diminished. I wondered about Miriam. Was she still alive? And if Becky was still the Maiden, how happy would she be about that?

Slowly and carefully I eased back under the trees again, telling myself it would be unwise to make any sort of move until I could see exactly what I was dealing with.

A semi-circle of women stood in front the stones, exactly as they had done before. Again, they'd smeared their faces with thick, white, crumbling clay. Somehow, it looked worse in daylight. Their huge black eyes and mouths made them not of this world. They were drinking. I could hear the clink of bottles. Some of them were very, very drunk. Some were dancing – if

313

that was what you could call their wild cavorting. I could hear a drum beating and some sort of pipe music – harsh and discordant.

This was a very different ceremony from the one I'd seen at the end of last year. Now, long tables of food and drink had been set up and each table was garlanded with summer flowers. Some women wore matching wreaths in their hair. Even the burger stall was here again. I could smell the frying onions. Four bonfires had been lit and their dark smoke rose lazily in the still air.

If I had been anywhere else I would have said this was a wedding. Of course it was. They'd got their Year King back and tonight was his wedding night. I didn't have long to think of some way of getting him out of this. I wished and wished for Jerry. Or Iblis. Or anyone. And then I remembered Jerry's phone. I fished it out. No signal. Yes, now I remembered Becky telling me there was no signal here.

I don't think it was my imagination, but there seemed fewer women than I remembered. Had some of them left the village? Or was it simply because I was looking down on them rather than being among them? Their blue and turquoise colours were swirling around, mixing and merging, and every now and then there would be a huge purple spike of excitement.

A welcome breeze lifted the hair off my sweaty neck and I sat back to think. There might not be as many of them as there had been, but there were still many more of them than of me. And not one of them had any cause to love me. In my mind, I saw Jerry's headlights stabbing through the dark, heard the roar of the car engine, heard the sharp crack as they clipped the stone, saw Miriam fall, her stone broken. The sun was behind me now and I was in deep shadow. I shivered. What could I do? What could one person possibly do?

314

My diversion through those haunted woods must have been some sort of short cut or perhaps the women feared to let him walk through the woods, because only now was Jones arriving. He was walking slowly across the green towards the stones.

I knelt up and peered around the tree trunk. His jeans were plastered with mud below the knees and he limped very slightly, but other than that, he looked completely normal. A huge cheer went up at his appearance. The women began to ululate. An uncanny sound that echoed around the basin and among the trees.

They parted to let him through. I held my breath but no one touched him. If he was to be the replacement for the old Year King then he might have only minutes left, but – and I was almost certain of this – if they were calling him this year's king, then he was safe, because this would be his wedding night.

Whooping and laughing, they closed up behind him.

He came to a halt in front of the stones and waited. The women fell silent. His colour was very muted, visible only as a bright outline. There was no movement and no sound down there.

I moved carefully around the trunk for a better view and waited to see what would happen. My first instinct was to run down and ... I don't know ... save him somehow, but Jerry's words ran through my brain. 'He's in no danger.' Well, he was, but not any immediate danger. I suspected it was induction, rather than execution they had in mind for him, and if I was right then they would all of them die before they let anything happen to him. I, on the other hand, the cause of their failed ceremony at the end of last year, would probably not receive a warm welcome.

I lowered myself to the ground and using my forearms, inched forwards through the long grass. I could see Veronica and Becky, both clothed in black. Becky stood before her usual stone, the slender Maiden. She'd grown taller since I'd seen her last. Her face was expressionless but her colour said plenty, shot through with acid orange resentment. Far more so than on the last time we had met.

Veronica had obviously been demoted. She was standing in front of the fallen stone. Miriam's old stone. The Crone. She too stood, silent and still, her hands clasped submissively before her. Her colour was as still as she was and much harder to read. I left it for the moment because she wasn't the important one here.

The dominant position in front of the central stone, the Mother, was now occupied by Alice Chervil, her colour blazing in a triumph of purple with only a very little blue and turquoise around the edges. This was not good news. The reasons for her aggressive hostility towards me were now very obvious. I had been Veronica's choice, brought in from the outside. With me and her daughter Becky, Veronica would have retained control over the … I wasn't sure the word coven applied here, but I couldn't think of any other word. Whatever I called it, though, Veronica would have remained in charge. Becky was her daughter and I would have been no more than a puppet, easily controlled and manipulated.

Veronica must have been delighted when I turned up, bedraggled and lost, but instead, her plans had backfired spectacularly. She'd bitten off a lot more than she could chew with me, and now she was paying the price. Miriam, I suspected, was dead, Veronica's prestige had plummeted and Alice had seized her opportunity. I have to say though, if I was Alice Chervil, quiet though she was, I would not have turned my back on Veronica even for a moment. For now, though, she and Becky were standing silently by their stones as Alice ran the show.

The three of them must have collaborated to bring Jones back here all the way from Rushby. That surely had taken a great deal of power and cooperation. Much more than only one person could manage alone. And then there was this witch's ladder thing that Iblis had found. They would have had to work together on that as well. I wondered vaguely which of them had hidden it in my porch and how long it had been there. A movement below brought me back to what was happening.

In contrast to Veronica's and Becky's quiet black gowns, Alice had chosen to mark the occasion with long, theatrical robes in silver and gold. They flowed around her, dragging on the grass. I was pleased to see they were already extremely dirty around the hem. On anyone else they would have looked ridiculous, but such was the power emanating from her at this moment, they actually enhanced her appearance. I half expected to see them embroidered with mystic runes and had to remind myself that getting off on a power trip and wearing silly clothes didn't make anyone less dangerous.

Three women stepped forward. They wore white. I was reminded of the ones who had escorted the old Year King to what should have been his death. This time, one was scattering flowers, one was carrying lengths of red ribbons, and the other was carrying a robe. *The* robe. The golden robe of the Year King.

I remembered from before, the flowers and the ribbons carefully laid at the foot of the stones. Ready for the sacrifice. The red ribbons had flowed like blood. I wondered whether, after the ceremony, they would carefully gather them all up to present them again at the end of the year.

Alice Chervil walked slowly across the grass until she stood before Michael Jones. This was it. If I was going to do anything it should be now. I clenched my fists. I was only one person. What could I do?

Jones stood quietly as they slipped the robe over his shoulders. He stared blankly at the ground. Was he even aware of what was going on around him?

Becky and Veronica continued to stand motionless – not participating at all. And then I had it. They were holding the spell in place, freeing up Alice to …

To conduct the ceremony.

The singing rose to a tuneless crescendo. Looking at the state of them, most were mightily drunk. They began to stamp their feet. Faster and faster. The drum picked up the rhythm. The pipes joined in. The emotional temperature was sky high. Their faces were ugly with anticipation. Yes, there had been a hiccup, but here was the new Year King; the age-old ceremony would proceed and everything would be as it should be. The singing died away and now they began to shout. Urging her on.

She was loving it. She turned in a slow circle, arms held above her head as they whooped and cheered.

She slipped off her robe and now I knew if I was to do anything it would have to be now, because underneath she was stark naked. Because this was their wedding night. The night when the new Year King impregnated the Mother, confirming her power and setting his feet on the path to his own death. I suddenly thought – this would have been me. The woman standing there would have been me. Naked and exposed to whichever man the stones had selected to be king for that year. It would have been me …

There had been no need to drug Alice Chervil. Her colour boiled with her eagerness to begin. To confirm her position in the eyes of the village. To offer herself up to the stones. To put one over on Veronica and her daughter. To succeed where her predecessor had failed. Her purple colour was nearly incandescent with anticipation. She couldn't wait.

She held out her left arm. Two women grabbed Jones's left arm, holding it against Alice's. Another began to twist the long red ribbons around them. Binding them together ...

Somewhere, a new drum began to beat, dark and dangerous. The women began to sway. I could hear their soft, low chant with that familiar rhythm. Their colours mixed and blended together, forming an opaque semi-circle that surrounded Jones and Alice and the stones. I don't think it was my imagination – the stones leaned towards them, anticipating the ceremony. They were still alive. And they were very hungry.

I had only a moment to wonder about that before the crowd parted again. Someone dragged out a small, skinny mongrel on a piece of string. He was displaying a considerable reluctance to participate, digging in his paws and practically sitting down as he did everything he could to resist. They were literally dragging him along on his hindquarters. He was twisting his bristly head from side to side, trying, unsuccessfully, to bite at the string knotted tightly around his neck.

It would appear there was to be blood after all. A life would be taken in lieu of the last sacrifice. The one I'd ruined. I wondered if dog blood was as potent as human blood, but I wouldn't have been surprised to learn that to these monstrous women – and their even more monstrous stones – blood was blood. In these leaner days, they would take what they could get.

Every hair on his little body was bristling with fear and his lips were drawn back off his teeth in a snarl of terror. At the sight of the stones, he flung himself to the ground and howled. The poor thing might not know exactly what was about to happen, but he did know he didn't want to be a part of it. Which made two of us.

A woman – I think it was Joanna from her bulk – picked him up by the scruff of his neck, contemptuously tossed him onto the table and picked up the bronze sickle I remembered from before. His terrified yelps were pitiful to hear. The chanting quickened. The women swayed. The setting sun cast long, long shadows over them all.

Joanna raised the knife high and at the same time, Alice began to sway, slowly, in front of Jones. The noise intensified. We were approaching the climax of the ceremony.

She stood before him, naked, the two of them handfast, her robe pooled silver at her feet. Her colour softened and streamed out around him, enveloping him in gentle purple, stroking and caressing him. Slowly, very slowly, Jones reached out and touched her breast. He didn't look drugged or hypnotised. His eyes were open – he looked aware of what he was doing.

I was completely unprepared for the huge, hot, murderous jag of rage that coursed through me. If I had a colour of my own it would have lit up the landscape. I saw myself striding down amongst them, sowing the storm, reaping the whirlwind, dealing death and destruction to them all. I saw the ground gape. I saw the stones tumble, crushing screaming women beneath their weight. I saw myself tearing down their world in a blizzard of blood and terror. Dealing it out to those who had previously dealt it out to others.

Behind me, something stirred ...

The air cooled and now, far from being a summer's evening, the familiar scent of snow was in the air. Angry snow. A lone snowflake danced before me. And then another. The world around me turned to shades of grey.

My vision blurred and suddenly I was somewhere else. I was back at the Sorensen clinic. Back in my reality. The reality that had never gone away. It was real. I knew it was real. I'd always known it was real. Jones and the rest of the world could say what they liked about concussion and suchlike, but, at that moment, I knew I'd never accepted their comforting words. I'd never accepted the easy explanation.

Memories and emotions came rushing back and I remembered how I'd been betrayed, manipulated, lied to. I remembered the moment I'd realised I wasn't as powerless as I had thought. I'd conjured up a whirlwind of angry snow and pulled the world down around me. I had done that. Me. Elizabeth Cage. Discounted. Overlooked. Deceived. Used. I remembered how I'd felt. How I'd revelled in an orgy of ruin and revenge and destruction. I'd done it once. I could do it again. A familiar warning pain throbbed and the thing that lived in my head opened its eyes ...

... and Veronica turned her head slowly and looked directly at the place where I was hiding.

Chapter Twenty-Eight

I felt her shock. And her surprise. But most importantly of all, I felt her concentration falter. The spell snapped like the pressure change in an aircraft and, as it did so, Jones's colour burst out around him; the familiar golden-red engulfing the purple that was Alice Chervil. I knew, from bitter experience, that, when he had to be, he was an expert in violence and pain. His size and strength gave him a natural advantage, anyway, but now I saw how good he really was.

He didn't waste a single moment staring around in bemusement or demanding to know what was going on, or why he was wearing this silly gold dress, or why that woman didn't have any clothes on. His first act was to protect himself and secure his position. To give himself a safe platform from which to operate.

He reached out in one smooth movement, grabbed Alice Chervil and twisted her round until he had her pinned tightly against him while he took in the situation and gained control. He wrapped one arm around her neck. The other forced her head to one side. Almost to the point where her neck could snap. They were still tied together with the red ribbons and the way they wrapped themselves around her neck made it look as if she'd already had her throat cut.

She drew a breath – to scream, I think, or possibly to curse him, and he tightened his grip even further, saying, 'You'll never know anything about it.'

He was speaking for everyone's benefit, not just Alice Chervil, but the words drifted up to me quite clearly. I wondered if this little basin was an acoustic trap in the same way ancient Greek theatres could effortlessly capture every word. Whatever the reason, I could hear almost as clearly as if I was down there.

He was a big man and he was strong and there was no doubt he knew exactly what he was doing. She was forced up onto tiptoe, crushed against him, her face darkening as she fought for breath.

The women had fallen silent. Shock and surprise and fear written across their faces and then someone – I think it was Joanna. Big, strong Joanna – took a cautious step towards him. The little dog seized his moment, twisted and nipped her hard. She shrieked and jumped back. Obviously her enthusiasm for blood didn't include seeing her own. He jumped down and fled. No one tried to stop him.

Jones forced Alice's head around even further. 'Stay where you are. If just one of you moves – I will break her neck.'

Veronica laughed. She actually laughed. Joanna took another tiny step forwards. Veronica held up her hand to her and laughed again. She looked contemptuously at Alice Chervil and then at Jones. 'Go ahead. Kill her. Please. Blood – any blood – is always acceptable.'

Becky smirked, the orange of resentment rippling through her colour.

Intentionally or otherwise, with those words Veronica had wiped out any advantage Jones might have had. It's hard to control a situation when no one cares whether the hostage lives or dies. Especially if the hostage dying is the preferred option.

She hadn't finished. Turning to where I was hidden, she called, 'I can see you, Mrs Page. Come down, please.'

There was no point in hiding. I had a sudden picture of what would happen if I tried to run away. I saw wild-haired women, their faces caked in thick white chalk hunting me through these ancient woods, hounding me down ... I saw what they would do to me when they caught me ... A word flashed through my head. Maenads ... in all their frenzied fury ... naked and bloodstained ... screaming as they hunted me through the wild woods.

I stood up and at the same moment, Jones shouted, 'Cage. Get out of here. Now.'

I couldn't. I didn't have it in me. I hadn't been well. I had half walked and half run all the way from Rushby. And there was no way I was going back into those woods and whatever waited there. I really had no choice.

I began to walk down the slope towards the stones. I took it very slowly, concentrating on keeping my feet and trying to ignore my thumping heart. My legs felt leaden.

I pushed away all thoughts of Jerry and Iblis and any rescue. I was alone. I had no weapons. There was just me and I had no idea what to do next.

The women were all gathered in a tight cluster around the stones, arms raised, intoning something under their breath. I couldn't make out any words. I suspected they were invoking the protection of the stones.

I took my time getting there. The sun was very low now and this place was full of shadows. A pale moon was emerging, thin and insubstantial, lying on its back like a pair of horns. I looked up at the woods and the tops of the trees still tipped with gold and thought, just for a very brief moment, that I saw something move. The chanting faltered and stopped as I entered the circle. In the silence, Veronica and I stared at each other. Her colour had transformed, stabbing towards me, shot through with red and black. Shot through with hatred and murder. And, licking around the edges, uncertainty and fear. I saw her eyes narrow. Her colour gathered itself. And then she had herself back under control, looking over my shoulder. She was checking to make sure I was alone.

I moved to the centre of the circle, staying well clear of Michael Jones. That was always his instruction. 'Stay behind me, Cage, and don't get in my way.'

I stayed well clear of everyone and addressed the other women, all standing uncertainly. Their colours were wavering. I was certain they would remember me and the catastrophic events of New Year's Eve. Would this be the second ceremony I'd ruined?

I should speak before they realised I was only one person.

Remembering how good the acoustics were, I spoke in normal tones.

'I can see you all remember me. Veronica Harlow made a grave mistake in trying to keep me here against my will, but Alice Chervil made an even greater one when she brought this man here today. You could not have chosen a worse Year King. This man is a stone-cold killer. He is brutal, misogynistic and cares for no one. He has killed before. Many times. And he will again. I beg you, for your own good, to stand very still and do as exactly as he says.'

Veronica said wonderingly, 'Who *are* you?'

A very good question and one I wished I was able to answer. I channelled Michael Jones and bluffed. 'You know who I am.'

Her face twisted with bitterness. 'I should have killed you the second I laid eyes on you.'

I nodded. 'Yes, you should.'

'What do you want here?'

I nodded towards Jones, still holding Alice Chervil in a death grip. 'I want what is mine.'

325

She looked around at the crowd of silent women. No children, I noticed. This was obviously the sort of place where it was perfectly all right for them to witness a man having his throat cut and his blood thrown over a couple of old rocks, but sex was considered unsuitable. Family values at their finest.

The silence dragged on as we all looked at each other. I held her gaze, not daring to look away even for a second. I could hear the crackling bonfires and smell the smoke. Her colour had slowed and calmed. She was assessing the situation, working out how to twist things to her advantage. It wouldn't take her long. She held all the cards. Yes, Jones had a hostage, but that hostage had no value. In fact, Alice's death would not only feed the stones and make them stronger but rid her of a hated rival at the same time. She had numbers on her side. Jones and I could easily be overpowered. She would have both a new Year King and me at the same time. I couldn't help a stab of admiration. Not liking. Never liking. Not for any of them, but I couldn't help admire her strategic planning.

I said, as quietly as I could. 'Jones. Stop. You mustn't kill anyone. That's what the stones want.'

'Well, I'm not hanging around while they kill me Cage, so think of something.'

Veronica smiled, although there was no mirth there. I suspected her thoughts had mirrored mine. I could see it in her colour. A way to bring down Alice Chervil and reinstate herself. We – Jones and I – might only have a few seconds left before we became victims of their nasty little power struggle. And the stones wouldn't care. As long as they had their worship and their blood, they didn't care who stood in front of them. Or for what reason.

I called to her. 'There are other forces at work here besides your stones.' I paused to let that sink in. 'Forces that only I can control. Forces not even your silly stones can withstand.'

I gestured at the stones, dark and looming in the failing light. 'Why don't you call on them? Go on. Call them.' I drew a deep breath and chose my words carefully. 'Go on. I *challeng*e you.'

I half expected my words to ring dramatically through the air, but there was a soft, distorted, almost muffled quality to them. My imagination saw the stones, not so much listening, as absorbing every word. Absorbing everything going on around them.

I turned to face the stones and closed my eyes. There *was* power here – and not necessarily from the stones. There was power in the earth. Power in the air around me. But mostly, there was power up in those woods. I took a deep breath and the thing that lives inside my head spoke with my voice, filling it with authority. I felt no fear. It was as if I was someone else. Opening my eyes, I addressed the spirits of the stones themselves.

'Depart. You have outlived your time. Depart while you still can. I am not afraid of you and you know who I am.'

Silence. The stones brooded. The horned moon hung silently in the darkening sky. Shadows grew, reaching out towards me.

Unable to move her head, Alice rolled her eyes at Veronica, venomous and spiteful, somehow managing to hiss, 'This is all your fault. You brought her here.'

'Yes,' I agreed. 'You should have let me go when I told you to. You have brought this upon yourselves'.

Now she rolled her eyes back to me. I don't know if the physical strain of having her head pulled back was affecting her voice, or whether the malice of the stones spoke through her, but I felt the hair on my neck rise. 'He belongs to *me*. He is the Year King. Ancient custom and tradition confirm my right.'

I took a few deep breaths. Partly to make her wait, but mostly to calm myself and then I shook my head and spoke so everyone could hear me. 'The line has been broken and cannot be restored. There was no blood for the stones this year and now they are old and weak. Their time is over.'

I turned to the stones. 'I speak to the things that live within you. You are finished. Your time is ended. Depart while you still can. You have never shown mercy and none will be shown to you. Depart.'

There was no response. Not from the stones. Not from Veronica. Or Alice. Or the women gathered around. Or from the woods above. I didn't dare look at Jones. Only I could do this. But how?

I considered. One thing hadn't changed. Becky was still the weak link. From her colour, I could see she was even more resentful and aggrieved than ever. Her sparkling orange bitterness far outweighed her feeble blue. It just remained to be seen whether her resentment could overcome her fear of reprisals.

I turned to her and said quietly, 'Listen to me, Becky. Do you really want to live here forever? Do you really want to spend the rest of your life always being the youngest? You'll never have a future if you do this.' I sought for something that would matter to her. 'You'll never have a boyfriend. Ever. You'll never get away from here. You'll spend your whole life serving the stones and they'll suck the life from you. No matter how long you live you will never leave this place. With Alice Chervil as the Mother your time will never come. She's not that much older than you. By the time she's too old to be the Mother, so will you be. You'll be passed over. You'll be the perpetual Maiden. Until one day you'll wake up and find you're the perpetual Crone. And by then it will be too late for you. Far, far too late.'

I gestured at the stones. 'They are weak. Their power is diminished.' I pointed at Alice Chervil. 'And *she* is not yet the Mother. You still have a chance at a normal life. I will destroy them. Stand aside, Becky. Please.'

They stared at me. Black eyes in long white faces. Nobody moved. No one made a sound. Even Alice was silent.

We all looked at each other. I could feel my heart pounding in my chest, but the longer they stood without moving, the less likely they were to be hostile and the more likely they would see sense and let us go. It wasn't too late for them. So I told myself and still the silence dragged on. Their colours were flat. Almost motionless.

I stood, waiting, willing them to disperse. They would, I was sure of it. There might be some muttering but the crowd would break up. They would make their way back across the green to the safety of their own homes. I had Michael Jones watching my back. I had Jerry – any time now. I had Iblis – possibly. And I had the dead, waiting silently in the woods for me to deliver their revenge. This could be nearly over.

And then Veronica laughed and my feeble optimism fled. 'What can you do against the power of the stones?'

I moved slowly sideways until we were face to face, about twenty feet apart.

'I can bring them down.'

Her colour flickered. Just for a moment, and then reasserted itself. She was confident. She was on her home ground. She had the power of the stones behind her while I had …

Something small and white floated gently through the air and fell softly to the ground in front of me. At first I thought it was ash from the bonfires but it wasn't. It was a tiny, tiny snowflake. And then another. And another.

This was a warning sign which I should heed because nothing good ever happens in the snow.

A few more flakes drifted silently to the ground. I heard someone say, 'Is it snowing?'

I should stop. I should stop right now before I lost control again and more people died. Pain slashed behind my eyes. I ignored it. I could do this. I had to do this. As long as I was careful ... There is a balance to maintain. There must always be a balance. Last time I'd lost the balance and everything had ended in death and darkness. This time I would be more careful. This time it would be different. This time I would control it. I tried to fill my mind with strength. There was great evil here and driving it from the world was more important than my life. And Jones's life as well.

I walked slowly to Becky's stone. The Maiden. It watched me approach. I could feel its eyes on me.

I said to Becky, 'Stand aside,' and reached out and touched the stone.

I heard Jones shout, 'Cage, what are you ...' and then his voice was cut off suddenly as if someone had slammed shut a door and he was on the other side.

The world flickered. Black. White. Black White. Black. White.

And then, suddenly, everything was different.

Chapter Twenty-Nine

The shock of the cold made me gasp. The air was biting and I was only in summer clothes. The world was flickering. Black. White. Black. White. Like a broken film. A wave of sickness rolled over me and I closed my eyes, fighting nausea and vertigo. A few deep breaths of cold air cleared my head a little until I felt well enough to open my eyes and look around.

I was standing up to my ankles in snow. Everything here was either black or white. Black trees caked in white snow. A black sky dense with white stars. A lost, lonely, black and white world in which nothing moved. Thick with silence, except for the desolate song of the wind.

I knew at once that I hadn't gone anywhere. I still stood in the same hollow. The same woods were still up there. Thicker and wilder and much closer, but the same woods. The same two-horned moon hung in the sky.

I turned. And wished I hadn't.

This world wasn't just black and white. There wasn't just the white silence of the snow. Or the dark light of the night. There was red as well. Lots of it. There was red blood everywhere, wet and glistening and soaking into the snow.

About twenty feet away stood a small … I shall say hut, although that really was too grand a name for it. Four rough posts had been rammed into the ground at odd angles. The walls were made of stones, turf and scrub, all jammed together and held with mud. The low, flat roof was covered with thick snow through which tufts of frozen dead turf showed. A low doorway led down into darkness and the unknown. There was a small fire burning at the entrance. I assumed it served the dual purpose of heating the hut and keeping out anything stupid enough to think this looked like a desirable dwelling. The smell of animal fat, blood, excrement, damp stone and sour earth was overwhelming.

And that was the whole world. Just white, and black, and red.

I became aware of them at exactly the same moment as they became aware of me.

There were three of them, crouching over something that had once been a man. He lay, sprawled on his back in the scarlet snow, his long hair and beard tangled in blood. His face was turned towards me, contorted in the terror that must have been the last thing he ever knew in this world. There was the familiar gaping wound across his throat. Like a bloodless smile. He had been ripped from his crotch to the bottom of his rib-cage and his innards spilled, red and purple, across the snow.

I would have known they were from Greyston. Here were the familiar long, white faces and the unnervingly pale eyes, ringed with dark ash from the fire. The three of them were wrapped in foul-smelling skins and furs that can have done very little to keep out the cold. Their thick, greasy hair hung in elf locks, braided with twigs and feathers and all held in place with blood. Their feet, blue with cold, were cut and bruised.

That they must have been starving there could be no doubt. They were little more than skin and bone. Their empty breasts dangled pendulously, splattered with fresh blood. Their mouths were red with it. Their arms were bloodied to the elbows as they rummaged inside for the soft bits. They pulled and snatched and gobbled and went back for more and any thoughts I might ever have had of dealing them mercy or compassion disappeared as if they had never existed. This was an evil from the beginning of

332

the world and it must be destroyed. I had a sudden picture of Iblis, hair flying, sword in hand. Well, he wasn't here, but I was.

I was certain this sorry excuse for a shelter occupied the exact spot where the stones would stand. This was where it had all begun. This must be *when* it had all begun as well. I remembered the story. The three women. The passing man who had saved them. He had cared for them and they had killed him. Their first victim. The first of so, so many.

And here they were. Right in front of me. The first ones. The Mother, the Maiden and the Crone, who would survive, in one form or another, from this moment right down to the present day. These were, I was convinced of it, the living personification of the stones. Renewed from year to year. Only not this year. This year there had been no blood and they were weak.

Weak or not, they were stronger than me. And there were three of them.

They looked up at me, jaws still working. We all regarded each other for a long time. I could see what they were thinking. Very slowly, they stood up. The youngest reached for a knife. A sickle-shaped affair that looked very familiar.

All right, I wasn't a man, but this was a long, hard winter and I was still food.

They stood in front of me in their traditional formation. The Crone to one side, the Maiden to the other, and the Mother in the middle. She was pregnant. The man had fulfilled his function and could now be discarded. The long story of blood and death had begun here. It could end here as well.

The world still flickered around me. Black. White. Black. White. Like a broken film. Their evil faces came and went. White – they were twenty feet away. Black – I could see nothing. White – they were ten feet away, red mouths gaping. Black – I could see nothing. White – they were gone. Black – I could see nothing. White – three stones gazed down at me. I could see their faces within them. These were living stones.

And then, without warning, I was back in the right world – dazed and sick. Again, I staggered. For a moment, dark light still filled my vision and I could see nothing.

Veronica's voice was gloating. 'You see now why we have nothing to fear. They live on in the stones. They are indestructible. They are our protection. The man is ours. You will die tonight. There will be blood and everything will be as it was before.'

My voice was hoarse. 'I *will* stop you.'

'You are only one.'

'Excuse me,' said Jones and the dark light fled. His voice brought back light and sunshine and warmth. And he was right. I wasn't alone.

She smiled but there was no amusement. 'Well, since you insist upon it – two.'

And at that very moment, almost as if he'd been awaiting the perfect moment to make his entrance, Iblis himself appeared from behind the Mother stone. He walked slowly into the circle and when he was certain every eye was upon him, flung wide his arms and smiled that smile. 'Well hello, ladies.'

I couldn't take it in. I stood there like an idiot wondering where on earth he could have come from. My only consolation was that I wasn't the only one. Everyone stood frozen, staring at Iblis, dressed as usual in combat trousers, T-shirt and boots. His white-blond hair blew around his face, even though there was no wind. He stood – no, he didn't – he *posed* in front of the stones, hands on hips, tossing his hair, fully aware of the sensation he was causing and thoroughly enjoying every minute of it.

Only one person wasn't too stunned to move.

'Just a wild guess,' said Jones to me, 'but I'm thinking this must be your Billy Goat Gruff.'

Iblis looked him up and down then turned to me. 'Why is he holding a naked woman? Can I have one?'

'Get your own,' said Jones.

'All right,' said Iblis. He turned to smile that smile at me.

'*Not her.*'

Iblis turned to me. 'He's not as exciting as you would have me believe.'

'Cage, who is this person?'

'I am Iblis,' he said, 'Smiter of Foes, Man of Steel, Man of Infinite Resource, Terror of the Old World, Bringer of Strength. And you, I believe, are …?'

'Jones.'

'Just Jones?'

'Just Jones.'

I was feeling better with every second. With Iblis here, we had a fighting chance. A more than fighting chance.

Alice Chervil's face was congested with fury and lack of oxygen. Heedless of Jones she swung her head to Veronica. 'This is all your fault.' She was nearly crying with rage and frustration.

Veronica ignored her. Drawing herself up she made a gesture towards the other women. 'What are you waiting for? There are only three of them.'

For a second nothing happened and then they began to close in. Not a mad frenzied rush but an altogether much more sinister one step at a time. They were tightening the circle one step at a time.

Not fast enough for Veronica. 'What are you waiting for? They're unarmed.'

'Well, actually,' said Iblis, and reached over his shoulder. I didn't see it happen but the next moment he had four feet of glittering steel in his hand. He did one of those complicated figure-of-eight things so beloved of the makers of sword and sandal films.

The women halted uncertainly.

'For Heaven's sake,' shouted Veronica, which I thought rather inappropriate, 'it's just a sword.' Apparently willing to sacrifice any number of her followers, she shouted again. 'It's just a sword. It's not as if he has a gun.'

'Yes,' said Jones. 'You're right. It's just a sword.' He looked over to Iblis and said complacently, 'But *I* have a gun.'

Iblis shrugged. 'Where is it then?'

'Well, I have my hands full at the moment.'

'Yes, I don't understand. Why would you waste your time on this one …' he gestured at Alice, 'when you could have this one.' He grinned at me.

I could only be grateful for the gathering dusk which hid my burning face.

'Good point,' said Jones and pushed Alice away from him as hard as he could. She stumbled and nearly fell over her robe, still lying on the ground.

'Cage, come and stand by me.'

I skirted Alice, hastily pulling her robe around her, careful to give her a very wide berth but as it turned out, it wasn't me she was interested in. It was Veronica who was her target. Without even bothering to fasten her robe, she threw herself at her, shrieking incomprehensibly. Veronica held her ground, standing calmly and, as she came within range, fetched Alice a backhander that knocked her to the ground.

I winced. There had been a great deal of pent-up dislike behind that blow.

Alice lay, crying and beating her hands against the ground in fury and frustration. Veronica flung her one last contemptuous look and reached out and touched the Mother stone for power. It was working. I could see her colour strengthening and brightening. Pointing at me, she began to intone words I didn't understand. Nothing seemed to happen, but I felt my heart slow and flutter. The world darkened around me.

I heard Iblis say to Jones, 'Would you excuse me for a moment.'

'Be my guest.'

Iblis began to run. One, two, three steps. He leaped high into the air. For a moment, he was silhouetted against the horned moon and then, raising his sword high, two-handed and with the full force of his body, he smote – there really is no other word for it – he smote the stone a massive blow.

Sparks flew, brilliant against the night sky and his sword shattered into a hundred glittering pieces. But it had served its purpose.

The stone screamed. Loud and long. A dreadful cry of malice and hatred that hurt my head, my heart, hurt everything. The sound echoed around the village, up the hill – and into the woods. A great gout of blood spurted high into the air, black and stinking, falling back again to drench both Alice and Veronica. They screamed too, but their cries were swallowed by the death cry of the stone.

Slowly, ponderously, with the sound of ancient roots being torn from the earth itself, the stone tipped, hung for a long moment, defying gravity, and then toppled. I had a brief glimpse of a familiar face, struggling to emerge. Old beyond belief. Hair still braided with the blood of the first man. Malevolent. Evil. Its mouth gaping in an impotent, ear-splitting scream of death.

Everything happened in slow motion. Veronica stood, literally petrified. Alice sprawled at her feet. They both looked up as the massive stone toppled forwards. Its shadow fell across them. They screamed – the last thing they would ever do – and then the whole enormous monolith crashed to the ground, crushing them both into the earth. One arm, Alice's I think, was all that could be seen. Her fingers curled into her palm like a child's.

The impact made the ground jump beneath my feet and as it did so, the smaller stone, the Maiden, lurched sideways. I grabbed the still screaming Becky and dragged her out of the way as that too, crashed to the ground.

For a very long time, nothing moved. No one moved. And then Joanne stepped up. I was reminded of that Hydra thing where you cut off one head and another takes its place. Or two heads. I couldn't remember and at that moment I didn't think it was that important. Shock and hatred and fear were written across her face.

'You will die for this.'

Jones stepped forwards. 'I have a gun. I will use it.'

Joanna smiled an unpleasant smile. 'And I have a small army. You cannot kill us all.'

Now. Now was the moment. I felt it. From the woods they called to me.

'You may have a small army, I said, softly. 'But I have them.'

I pointed up the hill to the woods.

The dead were clearly visible now, standing under the trees. Even Jones could see them.

Iblis grinned. It wasn't a nice smile. 'There is a power here which will destroy you utterly. Let these people go and you may live a little longer.'

338

'You are making idle threats.' But her colour was shot through with fear. She could see them. Row upon row of dead men. Their numbers far outweighing those of the living.

He shook his head. 'Last warning. Let these people go. Now.'

Still she would not give in. 'Why should we? We are protected.'

'Your protection has gone forever and they are waiting. Look.'

We all looked. The dead were emerging from the woods to stand in an unbroken ring around the village, as immovable and silent as the stones themselves had been. Some were more shadowy than others. Some of the old ones were very shadowy indeed, but none-the-less dangerous for all that.

Jones caught my arm and pulled me behind him. 'Are they who I think they are?'

'Yes. You'd better stick with me.'

'It's all right, Cage. I won't let them hurt you.'

'That wasn't quite what I meant.'

Becky was still screaming. Many of them were still screaming. One turned and ran. Another followed her. Hysteria was everywhere.

'Don't run,' I shouted. 'Don't try and leave. You can't get out.'

'Oh, I don't know, said Iblis, casually. 'Let them run. Who cares?'

That focused their attention far better than anything I could have said.

Voices bombarded him. 'Why? Why not? Who are they? What do they want? Why can't we get out?'

Joanna pulled herself together.

'Shut up everyone. We're safe. They can't get in. If they could, they'd be here by now. We're safe. They can't get in.'

'And you can't get out,' said Iblis, and paused to let that sink in. 'Well, you can try, of course, but your chances of making your way safely through their ranks are … Well, it's not going to happen.'

She persisted. 'But they can't get in?'

He smiled and it wasn't pleasant. 'They don't need to. They have only to wait.'

'For what?'

He raised his voice so they could all hear. 'For you to die. As you all surely will. This year … next year … sometime … whenever. And when you do – they'll be waiting for you. And they've waited a very long time.'

Joanna scrabbled at me. 'Save us. You have to do something. You called them. I know you did. You did this.'

I shook my head. 'I did nothing. They were here. They've always been here. All I did was open the door.'

'No. You can't leave us like this. You have to save us. Send them away.'

I spoke so they could all hear. 'You have woven your own fate. No matter how far you run, they will always be with you. Watching and waiting. Death will not release you. Nothing can save you from what you have done over the years. One by one, you will die. And then you will belong to them.'

They stood, lost and bewildered among their dead stones and dying bonfires. Many were crying. I found I didn't feel sorry for any of them.

'I can't help feeling,' said Jones quietly, 'that it would be rather an anti-climax if we stay any longer.' He indicated with his head. Jerry's car was pulling up outside the pub. 'Shall we go?'

Chapter Thirty

I was never more glad to see anyone. Jerry got out of the car and wandered across the green, taking it all in. Finally, he put his hands on his hips and surveyed the scene around him, saying with massive understatement, 'Well, bugger me.'

'Yes,' said Jones, 'although I can't help feeling you're not seeing it at its best right now.'

I was staring at Alice's arm, unable to drag my eyes away. He gently turned me around. 'Don't look, Cage.'

I looked up at him. 'What are we going to do? Should we call the police?'

He sighed. 'Cage, even you can't be involved in two separate investigations on the same day.'

The events at Rushby seemed another world away. This time yesterday we'd been sitting in our cottage eating supper. Now ...

'But surely we should tell someone,' I persisted.

'Tell who? And tell them what? No, we'll just get into the car and drive quietly away and leave someone else to sort all this out. I should imagine the women will say they were having some sort of folk-lorey, rusticky traditional ceremony thingy and there was an unfortunate accident. How they'll explain that woman ...'

'...Alice Chervil ...'

'Alice Chervil being starkers is not our problem. To the car, Cage, and don't spare the horses.'

'A moment please,' said Iblis. 'We've forgotten something.'

'What?'

341

'Unfinished business.'

'Oh yes?' said Jones, suspiciously. 'And what's that, then?'

For an answer, Iblis groped around inside one of his many pockets and tossed something down on the grass. 'That.'

'What on earth is that?' said Jones.

I thought at first it was some sort of snake. It certainly looked like one, coiled on the grass, black and wicked. Then I saw it was comprised of black cords, all carefully plaited together with black feathers. Complicated knots had been woven in every few inches.

'That,' said Iblis, 'is a witches' ladder. Every knot represents a curse.'

There were a lot of knots. The thing lay at my feet and though it wasn't alive and had no colour, I could see the dark light with which it surrounded itself.

'Is that what you found in my house?'

'In your porch, yes. I just want to be absolutely sure these ladies aren't going to give it another go.'

Despite everything, Joanna had craned to look. Even Becky had stopped crying. Joanna shook her head. 'Nothing to do with us.' She stared harder. 'Not our style.'

By which I suspected she meant 'not enough blood', but her colour said she wasn't lying. Nor Becky.

'They're telling the truth,' I said. 'It's not theirs.'

'Interesting,' said Iblis, 'but it doesn't matter now.' He picked it up, grasped the ends and tugged. Massive muscles stood out on his arms and chest. He really was immensely strong.

'Show off,' said Jones in my ear.

The witches' ladder came apart in his hands and he tossed the pieces into one of the bonfires. It flared briefly – a small fire within a larger one – and then it was gone. Completely destroyed. A weight I hadn't known I was carrying lifted from my shoulders.

'Yes, very impressive,' said Jones, unimpressed. 'But unless there's something else you want to astonish Cage with, we'll be off.'

'Just one more small thing,' said Iblis, and disappeared back into the dark.

Jones turned to me. 'Cage you really do know the strangest people.'

I looked him up and down. 'I do, don't I?'

Iblis reappeared almost immediately, casually tossing his long hair back over his shoulders, his face attractively smudged with dirt, and with a grubby mongrel tucked securely under one arm. It only needed a throaty female voice in the background singing, 'I need a hero ...'

'Oh, please,' muttered Jones. 'Not only does he save the day but he gets to rescue the little dog as well.'

Jerry scowled and muttered something about not wanting scruffy mongrels in his car.

'Or the dog either,' said Jones. 'Can we go?'

'The less dog-like scruffy mongrel got you out of Sorensen's clinic,' I said quietly.

'Did he? I thought he seemed familiar.'

'Well, you don't think either Jerry or I could lift you, do you? But by all means be as ungracious and ungrateful as you can. Which, I should imagine is quite a lot. In fact, now I stop to think about it, at one time or another, you've been rescued by everyone here. I'd pipe down if I were you.'

He smiled down at me. 'Feeling better now?'

I smiled back. 'Yes, thank you.'

'Good to see you're as much of a shrew as ever,' he said amiably. 'But I'm still feeling the urge to be well away from this place.'

No one disagreed. We climbed into the car. And opened the windows.

'Dear God,' said Jones. 'How can one small dog have such a giant smell?'

'Are you going to keep him?' I said to Iblis.

He scratched the little dog's ears and we laughed as his hind leg came up and jerked in time to the scratching. It felt good to laugh. Not one of us was quite as calm and collected as we were pretending.

'What are you going to call him?'

Iblis considered. 'He's brave and resourceful. What is the name of your greatest warrior?'

'Nigel is the name of our greatest warrior,' said Jones from the front seat.

'Nigel, it is,' said Iblis, who knew perfectly well that it wasn't. 'Nigel the Ninja.'

'Property of Iblis the Idiot,' said Jones, pouring oil on dying flames because we all needed to see something other than falling stones crushing the life out of people. Or hear their dying screams.

'Will they rebuild, do you think?' I asked anxiously.

'Doubt it,' said Jerry, starting the car. 'Oh, someone will have to come along and have a look, but I'm pretty sure they'll say the stones are obviously unsafe. I expect the *Daily Mail* will claim they've been demolished to make way for a mosque. Although they'll have to get them two buggers out from underneath, of course. Can't leave them just lying there.' His tone indicated this would be his preferred option.

344

We reversed into the pub car park and then pulled away. Everyone fell silent. The question none of us were asking. Would we be allowed to leave?

Jones reached over the seat and took my hand. I squeezed it hard. We passed the pub, then the bus stop, then the last cottages, and there he was, The First Man. Right in the middle of the road. Pale in the pale moonlight, his hair and beard matted with blood. Dark wounds on his throat, his abdomen gaping. I couldn't help it – I drew in my breath with a hiss.

'What do I do?' said Jerry, slowing.

'Drive slowly,' said Iblis. 'They know who we are.' He looked at me as he said it.

I gripped Jones's hand. Who were we? Who were we actually? There was Jones, the spy. There was Jerry, the thief. There was Iblis, the … I still wasn't sure what Iblis was. And me – and I didn't have a clue about me, either.

We had slowed down nearly to a halt. No one said a word. Nigel whimpered a little, though.

I closed my eyes. What would our life be like here if they wouldn't let us through? But no sooner had that thought formed than the man stepped aside, out of the headlights. The road was open. I thought he bowed his head as we pulled past him.

'Go, Jerry,' said Jones and Jerry needed no encouragement. We were already going. And with more speed than dignity, but, as Jones said afterwards – it was the going that was the important bit.

Chapter Thirty-One

I leaned back and tried to relax, watching the tall hedges flashing past. I saw the eyes of some animal briefly gleaming in the headlights and then, with no effort at all on my part, I knew exactly what was wrong with Iblis's story.

I sat up sharply. 'Jerry, please stop the car.'

Jones twisted in his seat. 'What's the matter, Cage? Are you hurt?'

'No. Stop the car.'

Jerry muttered something under his breath and pulled over.

I opened the car door. 'I need to talk to Iblis. It's very important.'

Jones twisted in his seat. 'Now?'

'Yes.'

He sighed. 'Don't go far away, Cage. Stay where I can see you.'

I nodded, not really listening.

Iblis climbed out after me, still clutching Nigel, and we walked a little way from the car, out of the headlights, and stood in the dark. Inside my head, all the pieces gathered together to make a complete picture. And I had to tell him now – right now – so I didn't give him a chance to speak.

'Iblis, I'm sorry, I know you don't want to talk about it, but this is important.'

He narrowed his eyes, his colour beginning to wrap itself around him. 'All right. What is it?'

I took a breath for courage. 'Do you remember when we ... when we spoke of Allia?'

He nodded and pretended to be interested in stroking Nigel.

I persevered anyway. 'You told me that after the battle, down on the plain outside the city, when they were burning the Fiori, you saw the flames reflected in her eyes.'

He stood very still for a moment, then looked back over his shoulder at the car. 'We should ...'

'Just tell me. Did you see the flames reflected in her eyes?'

'Yes, I did.'

I caught his arm. 'No, you didn't.'

Angrily, he pulled it away. 'I don't want to ...'

I had a feeling I wouldn't like him when he was angry, and Nigel was baring his horrible yellow teeth at me, but I pushed on anyway, because this was important. 'No. You didn't. Think about what you said. You said the flames had died down. That only the ashes remained. How could you have seen leaping flames reflected in her eyes?'

'But I did. It's not something I am ever likely to forget.'

'No. I mean, yes, you're right. You did see the flames in her eyes but they weren't a reflection from the bonfires.' I took another deep breath, aware that my heart was pounding, and made myself speak slowly and calmly. 'That was her true nature asserting itself, Iblis. She was on the brink of success and she just couldn't contain herself.'

He stared at me.

I forged on, still clutching his arm. 'No, don't pull away. You must listen to me. Allia was a Fiori. She always was. She tricked you.'

He couldn't take it in. His colour had screeched to a standstill. I think he had stopped breathing. He just stared at me. I don't know where his mind had gone.

347

I took another deep breath and watched all the pieces fall gently into place, forming a path to the truth. All I had to do was follow it.

I shook his arm. 'Iblis, *listen* to me.'

He refocused. 'All right. Go on.'

'She wasn't the innkeeper's wife. She was never the innkeeper's wife. You never saw the innkeeper's wife. The innkeeper's wife was probably already dead in the kitchen when you arrived. Or shortly afterwards. The body you found there – the one you assumed was the kitchen maid – the one conveniently without a head so she couldn't be identified – *that* was the innkeeper's wife. You saw Allia in the doorway and you just assumed ... Tell me, did you ever see Allia and her husband together? At any time? Did you see her interact with her children? No, you didn't. Allia took her place and got you out of the way while the other Fiori attacked the inn.'

He was bewildered. 'But why? It wasn't important in any way.'

'She was setting the scene. She was becoming the poor woman who so tragically lost her family. You felt sorry for her. She persuaded you to keep her with you and off the two of you went. In pursuit of the Fiori. But you never caught them, did you? You said yourself – you couldn't catch them. They were always just ahead of you. Well, who do you think made that happen?'

He shook his head. I think he'd been without hope for so long he couldn't allow himself. 'No. This can't be true.'

I caught his arm again and shook him slightly. Beneath the sleeve of his T-shirt his arm was rock hard. 'It is, Iblis. Think about it. She was always picking fights. Getting you into trouble. That wasn't survivor guilt. That was her true nature asserting itself.'

'But the attack on the city … Hundreds of Fiori died.'

'The city was never the object. She sacrificed her own people.'

'So what *was* the object?'

'*You*, Iblis. Well, not you as such – it was your sword she wanted. She seduced you.'

He flinched and Nigel growled at me.

I tried to ignore him. 'Yes, I'm sorry, but she did. I'm not sure whether that's better or worse than sleeping with a mortal.'

'It's not good,' he said faintly, 'but it nowhere near as bad as …'

I pushed on. 'She seduced you. She knew how you'd react afterwards. She knew you'd avoid her. Everything she did was designed to pile on the guilt. She staged that final scene and just as you were leaving the city she – or more probably an accomplice – threw some poor woman off the walls. She was probably already dead,' I said quickly, seeing his face. 'Allia dressed the body in her own clothes and they threw her down the mountainside, knowing she'd be unrecognisable by the time you saw her.'

He turned and took a few steps away from me. Trying to think, I guessed. I wondered if he was too dazed for most of this to go in. Perhaps I could have chosen a better time and place but time was short. I had to tell him. He had suffered for so long.

He turned back to me. 'But why? This is a long game for a Fiori. They don't think like that. What was the point?'

'Your sword, Iblis. That's what she was after all along. I'm guessing she followed you down through the town, watched your reaction to what you thought was her body tumbling down the mountainside and quietly took your sword the moment you laid it down.'

349

Slowly, he lowered Nigel to the ground. He was shaking his head. His colour was motionless, which for him was remarkable. The phrase, frozen with shock, sprang to my mind. He couldn't take it in. He couldn't believe what I was telling him. At that moment, I don't think he wanted to let himself believe it. I would have to be careful. Sometimes good news is as devastating as bad.

'No, I can't … Why didn't she just kill me there and then?'

'Well, firstly she knew Melek would never rest until she'd avenged your death. She'd follow Allia to the ends of the earth and beyond to revenge herself upon her. You know that.'

He nodded, staring at the ground.

'And secondly, what would happen if you died? Would you … I don't know … be replaced?'

'Probably,' he said hoarsely, and I could see his colour slowly swirling around him. He was beginning to function again.

'So she'd be no better off. In fact, your replacement might even be bigger and faster and stronger …' and waited for him to say he was Iblis and no one was bigger or faster or stronger and I think it was a measure of his distraction that he didn't.

'But this way you're weakened. In fact, both of you are. You said yourself – you took yourself out of the game and Melek tried to carry on without you and it's too much for one person and the Fiori have been getting away from you ever since. I'm right, Iblis. I know I'm right. Yes, you made a mistake but not the mistake you thought. You were tricked into taking her with you. She seduced you. You weren't responsible for her being rejected by the women of the city because she was only the wife of an innkeeper. In fact, she probably spread that rumour herself. Iblis, you never slept with a mortal. You weren't responsible for her death. She didn't die because of you. She didn't die at all.'

He was still looking dazed. Now was not the time to discuss the details. I had to ram home the message.

I seized his hands and held them tightly. They were ice cold. 'Iblis, you're innocent.'

His face showed nothing but bewilderment. 'I *didn't* sleep with a human?'

I shook my head.

'All this time I've been thinking ...'

I shook my head again.

'I didn't sleep with a human.'

'No, you idiot. You slept with a foul, hideous, bloodthirsty, murdering demon.'

His smile was enormous. 'I did, didn't I?'

'Everything all right here?' said Jones, appearing beside me.

'Yes,' I said. 'Believe it or not, yes.'

'We can't hang around, Cage.'

'Yes, I know. I won't be a moment.'

He nodded and turned away. 'One minute, Cage. Then we're going. Ready or not.'

'Iblis, listen. Time is short and we have to get out of here. Go and see Melek. Tell her what I told you.'

'Melek,' he said uncertainly. 'I can't ... no ...'

'Listen, you went to her before and it was the right thing to do. She held you together. When it really mattered she was there for you. She's been there for you ever since. Go and talk to her. Talk to each other. Please.'

Tears were rolling down my face, and when he turned back to me, I could see they were rolling down his face as well.

'Elizabeth ...'

'I know,' I said softly. 'I understand. Just go and talk to her. I know it won't be easy but you have to do it. Promise me you will.'

'I will,' he said hoarsely, cleared his throat and said, 'I will,' again, more strongly this time. He ran his hand through his hair. 'I don't know what to say.'

'You'll think of something. You're Iblis. Your woman-handling skills are legendary.'

'I mean, I don't know what to say to you.'

'Nothing', I said quietly. 'Between friends, there's never any need to say anything.'

'I can't believe … All this time …'

'I know,' I said, 'but it's not as if time is a problem for you and the important thing is that you now know the truth.'

'The truth,' he echoed, and I could see him putting the pieces together, going back in his mind, seeing past events in a new light. A clearer light. One not distorted by guilt or shame.

Jones stuck his head out of the window. 'Cage …'

'Coming,' I called. 'Go and see her, Iblis. Talk.'

He nodded. 'I will.'

'Come on then. We have to go.'

'No. No. If you don't mind, I'll walk. I need to think. To clear my mind. To think about what to say to her.' He looked at me, his silver colour as fresh and new as a rain-washed cobweb through which the sun's brilliance reflected every colour of the rainbow. It roared out towards me and, just for once, I didn't mind. His grey eyes were blazing. He was dazzling. Perhaps, once, he had looked like this all the time. The playboy was gone. I assumed it was a persona he had manufactured in which to hide his disgrace. In its place stood a mature young man.

'I didn't do it, Elizabeth. I didn't do it.'

'No, you didn't. Now go and tell her.' I took a step backwards towards the car. 'Good luck.'

We looked at each other and then he took my hand. His hand was very strong and cool and mine lay in it lightly, as if he was afraid of hurting me.

'Thank you,' he said. 'With all my heart – thank you.'

'You are very welcome,' I said. 'It was my pleasure. There is no need to speak of it again.'

He bowed.

'I have to go,' I said, edging back towards the car.

'You've always been a good friend to me. Stay safe.'

'Um … OK …You too.'

'I will,' he said, drawing himself up and beginning to look like his old self again. 'My staying-safe skills are legendary. Now you must go before the man-mountain becomes over-anxious.'

'That looked serious,' said Jones as I climbed back into the car.

'Yes,' I said.

'Thought so. Hang on a minute, Jerry.'

He jumped out of the car and Jerry cursed again. Catching up with Iblis, the two of them talked together for a moment.

'What's going on?' I said to Jerry, suddenly anxious.

'He's just making sure the long thin streak of wind and piss is OK. Dunno what you said to him, but it certainly knocked him sideways.'

I sighed. 'They don't like each other, do they?'

He looked surprised. 'No, they like each other very much. I'm amazed you missed that.'

I sighed again. 'Men are very mysterious.'

He put the car in gear. 'You want to try understanding women.'

353

Chapter Thirty-Two

Jones climbed back into Jerry's car and we drove slowly away. Jones and Jerry were in the front. I was a little hurt Jones wasn't in the back with me. I could really have done with a large and comforting presence nearby. Perhaps I should be less self-reliant in the future. It was hard to believe that only last night we'd shared a bed together – even if for only about ten minutes.

To break the silence, I asked Jerry what he'd been up to when I telephoned him.

'Oh, I was up at yon posh pillock's place.'

I was baffled. 'What posh pillock's place?'

Jones twisted in his seat and grinned at me. 'He means Sorensen's clinic.'

I gripped the front seat in alarm. Why? What were you doing?'

'*He* wasn't doing anything,' said Jerry, changing gear to negotiate a bend.

'All right, what were *you* doing?'

'I was pinching his Auerbach.'

'Ah, you got it, did you?' said Jones, casually.

I gripped even more tightly, even though I knew the answer. 'What Auerbach?'

'You know – the one in his hall.'

'The one you told him was a fake.'

'And now it is.'

'You *stole* it?'

'I swapped it,' he said reproachfully. 'Not the same thing at all.'

'I think you'll find it is,' said Jones, mildly.

I closed my eyes to shut out the dizzying sense of reality skidding away from me again. What had happened to my safe and well-ordered world?

'Got someone lined up for it?' Enquired Jones.

Jerry nodded. 'I'll just drop you two off and then be on me way.'

I was gouging great lumps out of the front seat. 'It's here? Now? In this car?'

'You're sitting on it.'

I resisted the urge to stand up and bang my head on the roof again.

'But he'll know it was you.'

'Why would he think that? I'm the one who told him it was a fake.'

'Was it?'

'It is now.'

I closed my eyes again.

'Don't get your knickers in a twist, missis. If he remembers me at all – which I bet he doesn't, because people like him don't even think about people like me – but if he does then he'll think, wow – that cabbie had a good eye. But he won't. It could be years before it's discovered. If ever.'

'But when he calls the police ...'

'She has this thing about calling the police,' said Jones in explanatory tones. 'Just work through it and she'll be fine.'

'He's not going to do that,' said Jerry, in the slow and careful tones of one addressing a person of restricted intelligence. 'Tell the world he's not as clever as he thinks he is? I don't think so, missis. My guess is that when he finds out – if he ever finds out – it'll get shoved in a cupboard somewhere and forgotten.'

It struck me that in his own way, Jerry was as good at psychological games as Sorensen himself.

We reached the place where, last time, the car had been pulled back towards Greyston. I didn't realise I was holding my breath until I wasn't. We passed without incident.

'Where shall I drop you?' said Jerry.

'I want to go home,' I said, suddenly realising I very much wanted to go home. I was cold, dirty, starving hungry, exhausted, and my feet hurt. I kept thinking longingly of a long, hot bath and the glass of wine I really deserved.

'And I would very much like to go home with you, as well,' said Jones, 'but I think we need to spend the night at the hotel first and pay our bill in the morning like normal people would do. And I still have something important to say to you, Cage.'

I was seized with a sudden panic. 'I'm too hungry to concentrate.'

'Well, no restaurant's going to let us in looking like this,' he said cheerfully. 'Pull up at the first chippie, will you, Jerry.'

The lights of Rushby were all around us. I heard the 'tink-tink' of the indicator and Jerry pulled over.

'I'll go,' he said, switching off the engine and undoing his seat belt. 'You two stay here and sort out the rest of your lives.' He slammed the door behind him.

Jones turned to me. 'Back there – when you were shouting about me being a stone-cold killer – you were just talking me up to those women – right?'

I hesitated. Yes, I'd been trying to get my message across. Trying to make them understand they had a tiger by the tail. But I didn't have to try very hard to see his face as it had been last Christmas. Detached. Dispassionate. Efficient. Brutal.

I'd hesitated for too long. He took his hand away. 'This is about last Christmas, isn't it? You just can't get past it.'

I was about to refute this with indignation, but it was true. I hadn't got past it. The more time passed, the more I was convinced I was right and the rest of the world was wrong. I remembered Mrs Barton saying, 'All that angry snow.'

'It wasn't your fault,' I said. 'You weren't yourself.'

'That's not quite answering the question, Cage.'

I didn't know what to say. I didn't even know what to think. On the surface he was a perfectly pleasant, charming man. People liked him. I liked him. But I'd seen the darkness that ran underneath. Well, of course I had. He'd be no good at his job without it. I probably hadn't even seen the worst of him. He was no Ted. But on the other hand, Ted had married me on instructions from Sorensen. Was that better or worse than being Michael Jones? Who, at least, had never lied to me. And how fair was it to compare the two? And – the bottom line – if I had done what I was becoming increasingly convinced I had – for how many deaths was I myself responsible?

I'd been silent too long.

'Look,' he said softly, 'it didn't happen, Cage. I promise you it didn't. I told you once I'd never do anything to hurt Ted's wife and I meant it. I still mean it. But if you can't get past it … if it's all too much for you …'

He did mean it. I could see it in his colour. He was telling the truth. Well, the truth as he saw it. And now the time had come for me to make a decision. Whatever he'd done to me physically hadn't been his fault. And his subsequent actions – bugging my house and so on, had been the result of Sorensen's manipulations. But if I let it go … if I opened myself up to him … what would I get?

And should I let it go? Should I forget it and move on? Close the door and accept the official version – the one that said it had never happened – and get on with my life? And should that life include Michael Jones? For all his talk of flocks of dissatisfied girlfriends and failed relationships, I suspected he'd had few attachments and even fewer of those had been close. Apart from Clare, and Clare had died. As had Ted.

I suddenly remembered. 'What was your question?'

'What?'

I sighed patiently. 'What was your question? The one you were going to ask me at the café?'

'Well, I know it's a little early to be talking about it, but I thought I'd get in ahead of the crowd, so to speak.'

He stopped.

'Yes,' I said impatiently.

'I was going to ask you - what do you want to do for Christmas this year?'

This supposedly simple question stopped me dead in my tracks. Because that wasn't what he was asking. He was really asking about us. Him and me. Whether we had any future together. And this would be the only time he would ask. There would be no do-overs. I had just this one chance to get it right. The answer to this one question would decide my future. And his.

I didn't rush to answer and he didn't press me. I sat looking at the bright lights of the fish and chip shop. And the off-licence next door. I looked at Jones, his golden-red colour muted and shot through with far more anxiety than showed in his face. It occurred to me that neither of us was making a success of our lives and this might be the last chance for both of us.

I smiled and took his hand. 'Well, I think it's my turn this year. Don't you?'